CLOAK OF WOLVES

JONATHAN MOELLER

DESCRIPTION

My name's Nadia, and I do favors for the High Queen Tarlia of the Elves.

Tarlia is not the kind of woman who accepts no for an answer.

So when the High Queen orders me to help a top investigator solve a murder, I have to do it. Even though I've spent most of my life on the run from the law.

I don't like the investigator, and he doesn't like me.

But that doesn't matter, because if we don't work together, the creatures we're hunting will kill us both...

Cloak of Wolves

Copyright 2019 by Jonathan Moeller.

Published by Azure Flame Media.

Cover design by Clarissa Yeo.

Ebook edition published November 2019.

All Rights Reserved.

This novel is a work of fiction. Names, characters, places and incidents are either the product of the author's imagination, or, if real, used fictitiously. No part of this book may be reproduced or transmitted in any form or by any electronic or mechanical means, including photocopying, recording, or by any information storage and retrieval system, without the express written permission of the author or publisher, except where permitted by law.

❦ Created with Vellum

1
IT'S JUST THE COST OF DOING BUSINESS

I kicked off the holiday season by threatening the former governor of a US state.

On the surface, this seemed like a bad idea.

Still, I don't think I had any better choice at the time. And in hindsight, it was the beginning of the entire mess when I met Colonel Owen Quell of the Department of Homeland Security.

Yeah, I should probably back up and explain.

It was November 4th, Conquest Year 316 (or 2329 AD according to the old calendar), and I had lots to do. My husband and I had just moved into our new house in Brookfield. It had been a present from a grateful dragon (long story), and we were in the process of getting it set up and a good security system installed. That by itself was quite a lot of work, though the house had already been furnished and we weren't particularly fussy about our living space. I didn't mind. It distracted me while my husband was out of town on "business," which was what we called his jobs for the Family of the Shadow Hunters.

The rest of my time was going to my brother's company.

My brother Russell Moran had managed to convince the High Queen to give him the sole license to import fruit from the Elven homeworld of Kalvarion through the Great Gate. At the time, I had thought it just a curiosity. Russell, though, realized the huge potential market. Humans liked to imitate their Elven overlords, and fruit from Kalvarion was a new and exciting curiosity. And that didn't even consider the Elven free cities, where Elven commoners lived on Earth away from humans. Many of them had been born on Kalvarion, and they hadn't eaten the produce of their homeworld in centuries.

Moran Imports grew, and quickly. The Milwaukee metropolitan area had three main grocery chains, and we had orders from all of them before Thanksgiving. We had received a massive shipment of fruit from Kalvarion through the Great Gate in October, and all of it had sold while I had been busy in New York helping out that grateful dragon. Now Moran Imports had orders to fill for every grocery store in Milwaukee and starting next year, we would be shipping fruit to a dozen different Elven cities in the United States.

The growth was astonishing. I hate to say it, but it helped that the Archons had enslaved Kalvarion for centuries. So when the Mage Fall destroyed the Archons, there was already an infrastructure of Elven farmers who needed to sell their crops. Turns out free farmers work a lot harder than slaves (funny how that works), and so the amount we paid for the fruit was more money than any of them had seen in their lifetimes.

It also helped that Russell and Robert Ross did most of the work. I mean, I did a lot of the work, but Russell did three times as much. He interviewed people, he made phone calls, he secured arrangements with trucking companies, and more. All this while he still wasn't technically a legal adult – I held his share in the company in trust, and I had to approve everything he did.

My old friend Robert Ross joining the company was a stroke of luck. He was a former man-at-arms who had served for Duke Carothrace of Madison, and I had met him a few years ago during that business with the Nihlus Stone and Rosalyn Madero, and again during the Sky Hammer battle in New York. He had a baby who had needed a great deal of medical care, and his wife Alexandra was pregnant with another child. Robert wanted to make more money in the civilian sector to pay for all those kids. He retired from the Duke's service, and Russell had hired him as our business manager, luring him in with a share of the profits.

Assuming Moran Imports turned a profit next year, of course. Russell had spent all of the two and a half million dollars he had gotten after Nicholas Connor's death, and I had added a million dollars of my own money. That wasn't enough to cover our costs, so the company had borrowed nine and a half million more dollars. I didn't think the bank would lend us that much, but it turns out that if your business is based on an exclusive license from the High Queen, the loan officer suddenly gets way more friendly. Obsequious, even.

So, we borrowed a lot of money.

God. Nine and a half million dollars. My head spins to think about it.

Except if everything went according to plan, by the end of next year, we would pay it all back, meet our payroll and equipment costs, and turn a small profit. The year after that, we would make a much, much bigger profit. Especially if the company kept expanding to new markets.

If nothing went wrong for us, of course.

But on November 4th, Conquest Year 316, things started to go wrong.

Or to put it more accurately, Arnold Brauner, former governor of the state of Wisconsin, made sure things started to go wrong for us.

It was a Tuesday, and I was in Moran Imports' main warehouse in Waukesha. It had once been a distribution center for a retail chain that had gone out of business about ten years ago, and Russell and I had gotten the place cheap. It wasn't in the greatest repair, and it was more space than we currently needed, but it hadn't taken much work to get the refrigerators running. And we would use the space for our expansion next year.

I was working in my office. Well, I say "my" office, but Russell, Robert, and I all shared the same one. It was a concrete-floored room with a single window offering a scenic view of the parking lot. My desk was a folding table with a computer and a lot of paperwork. I was going over a bill of lading we had gotten for the latest shipment through the Great Gate, making sure that a pallet or two of Elven strawberries hadn't "accidentally" fallen off the back of the truck. I was wearing a tank top, black jeans, and running shoes, because I had just finished helping load a truck since we were short on workers.

"Hey, Nadia?"

"Yeah?" Robert Ross leaned into the office, frowning. He was a ridiculously handsome Hispanic man, and when I had met him for the first time, I had thought that he and his pretty blond wife Alexandra would have cute babies. Turns out I was right. I wasn't the sort of woman to get gooey over babies, but their son Felix was indeed very cute. Right now, Robert wore a sweat-stained polo shirt tucked into cargo pants, and he looked concerned.

"There's a guy here, says he's a lawyer," said Robert. "He wants to talk to one of the owners of the company."

"That means me," I said, getting to my feet. Russell was at school, going through an accelerated program so he could graduate early from high school. After our experiences with the Rebels and the Sky Hammer, he had lost all interest in school, but he needed to finish before he could devote his full attention to the company. "I'll talk to him."

I followed Robert from the office, through the warehouse floor, and to the front lobby. Six trucks were in the process of getting loaded, and I cast a hard look over the process. Everything was going well, but I would double-check later. Hiring reliable unskilled workers is damned challenging.

We entered the front lobby of the warehouse, a small area with a linoleum floor and an empty receptionist's desk since we couldn't afford a receptionist yet. I reminded myself for the thousandth time to have the lobby repainted, or just do it myself.

A man in a suit awaited us. He was about forty, not fat but with the plump build of a man who had never done physical labor and whose doctor hadn't forced him to exercise. His brown hair had been combed in a neat part, and he had glasses over cold eyes. Right away, my instincts buzzed a warning.

"Mrs. MacCormac?" said the man.

"Yeah, that's me," I said.

"My name is Thomas Hawley," he said. We shook hands. Soft hand, but firm grip. "I represent Governor Arnold Brauner, and I wondered if I could have a moment of your time."

I grinned my mirthless grin at him. "Former Governor Arnold Brauner."

Hawley answered with an equally humorless smile. "A courtesy title, of course. But Governor Brauner remains engaged in both the political and business life of the state of Wisconsin."

"He sure does," I said.

Which made sense, once you realized that Brauner was basically a racketeer. It had paid off for him. At the age of twenty, he had inherited a dairy farm on the verge of bankruptcy. Forty years later, he was the richest man in Wisconsin. He had served three terms as state governor, a post now occupied by his eldest son Martin. His second son Luke was a US Senator, and his youngest son William was currently the mayor of Milwaukee. Everybody knew that.

What most people didn't know was that Brauner controlled most of the organized crime in Wisconsin, with the imprimatur of Duke Tamirlas of Milwaukee and Duke Carothrace of Madison. I knew that because back in the bad old days, Lord Morvilind had sent me to steal from Brauner's organization a few times, and I had sold stolen goods to Brauner's people (while Masked, of course) since Morvilind never bothered to pay me and I needed the cash.

I had wondered when some of his people would start sniffing around.

"Let's head to the conference room," I said. "I bet we have lots to talk about."

Robert went to supervise the loading of the trucks, and I led Hawley to the conference room, such as it was. Right now, it mostly held collapsed cardboard boxes, a pair of pallet jacks that needed repair, and two dead printers. It also had a pair of folding tables and a coffee maker. I poured two cups of coffee, took one, set the other in front of Hawley, and sat down across from him.

"So," I said. "What did you want to talk about?"

"Merely to extend Governor Arnold's congratulations and best wishes on your business," said Hawley. Since there had been two Governor Brauners, people tended to refer to them as Governor Arnold and Governor Martin. "It is quite impressive what you and your brother have built in a very short time, and the potential for growth is nothing short of amazing."

I shrugged and took a sip of coffee. "The world's changing. The Great Gate's open, and there are no more Archons. There's a lot of opportunity for people who want to help the High Queen rebuild Kalvarion."

Which was why the High Queen had given Russell the exclusive license to import fruit from Kalvarion and sell it on Earth. I think she wanted to use human companies to rebuild Kalvarion, which would prevent the Elven nobles from amassing too much power, provide an economic stimulus for Earth, and repair the damage to the Elven homeworld. It would also create a group of powerful human businessmen dependent on the High Queen for their power and wealth. And it gave the High Queen another means of keeping me under control.

I hadn't been Tarlia's shadow agent all that long, but more than long enough to realize she never did anything for just one reason, and that her plans had layers upon layers.

"It's an exciting time for both the state of Wisconsin and the city of Milwaukee," said Hawley. "With the Great Gate to Kalvarion open just outside of the city, it means both big changes and big opportunities are coming to Wisconsin, the United States, and the entire world."

"Yep," I said, wondering when Hawley would get to the point.

"But change can be disastrous if it's mismanaged," said Hawley. "Governor Arnold is concerned about the impact these changes will have on the working families of Wisconsin."

"We're going to add a lot of jobs," I said. "And not just Moran

Imports. I think in another ten years Milwaukee's going to be twice the size it is now."

"That's the reason for my visit," said Hawley. "First, to see if you and your brother would consider making a donation or an ongoing contribution to the Brauner Foundation. The Foundation's charitable work will be of great value in these unsettled times. Second, Governor Arnold has friends in a lot of the state's major businesses. Construction, trucking, commercial HVAC – all things your business is going to need as it grows. The governor would be happy to help you network with his friends in the businesses you will need."

Ah. This was a shakedown.

The Brauner Foundation did a lot of charitable work, that was true. It was also a slush fund for the Brauner family and its political ambitions. The charitable donations tended to get delivered to the constituencies of people who did favors for the Brauners or who could deliver votes when one of Governor Arnold's sons was up for reelection. As for the companies, the Brauners had shares or controlling interests in a lot of construction and utility companies in Wisconsin.

It wasn't hard to see why Hawley was here. The Great Gate had shaken things up, and new companies were starting to trade with and do business on Kalvarion, companies that Brauner didn't control. If he wanted to preserve his power and pass it on to his sons, he needed to get his fingers into some of the new pies.

"That's an interesting offer," I said. "I'll have to discuss it with my brother before we come to any final decisions."

Hawley nodded, calm and reasonable. "Of course. But, Mrs. MacCormac, it would be better to come to a decision sooner rather than later. Moran Imports is a young and growing business, and new businesses have all kinds of growing pains. Governor Arnold has a lot of experience with that, and he might be able to help you through them."

I smiled, and a pulse of pure fury went through my head.

That had been a threat. I had no doubt that if Russell and I refused to play ball, Brauner's "friends" would start inflicting growing pains on Moran Imports until we knuckled under.

In that instant, I thought about killing Thomas Hawley then and there.

Most people have violent thoughts but don't act on them. For those who do act on them, if they have an iota of self-control, they plan them out. People with violent impulses and no self-control tend to end up on Punishment Day videos.

But for me...

I could kill Hawley in five seconds, and I would never get caught.

It would be easy. A sphere of fire to drill a tunnel through Hawley's skull. Then I would open a rift way to the Shadowlands and dump his corpse through it. Some wandering anthrophage or wraithwolf would devour his body, and that would be that. No one would ever know what happened. We didn't have working security cameras in most of the building. Hawley's car was in the parking lot, true, but I could dispose of that as well. The High Queen wouldn't approve of casual murder, but so long as it didn't cause problems for her, I doubt she would stop me.

Because it would have been so easy, I didn't do it. I didn't want to be a monster. Maybe I was already a little bit of a monster. I had helped Morvilind kill millions of Archons, though none of those Archons had been innocent. I was pretty sure that a lawyer working for a racketeer like Arnold Brauner didn't exactly have clean hands, either.

But...I had gained immense personal power, and I had the responsibility to use it well. The price of power was responsibility. And could I look at Riordan and Russell and tell them that I had murdered a man for making veiled threats? No.

Instead, I took a deep breath.

Hawley shifted a little on his folding chair. I suppose he had been around enough violent people that he recognized the signs of someone calming down.

"That's a very kind of Governor Arnold," I said. "I appreciate that, but I can't make a decision right now. I need to talk it over with my brother first. This is his company."

"You have shares in it, I understand," said Hawley.

"Yeah, but I'm just running things until he comes of age," I said. "I can't make a unilateral decision of this significance. I'll have to talk to him and get back to you."

Hawley nodded. "I can understand that. Governor Arnold believes family is the most important thing. That was a centerpiece of his campaigns for governor." He reached into his jacket and drew out a business card. "My number's there. When you and Mr. Moran are ready to talk things over, you can reach me here day or night."

"All right," I said. We stood and shook hands. I squeezed a little harder, just to show that I could. "Thanks for coming down. I think we'll talk soon, probably before Thanksgiving. Let me walk you out."

I did, and I scowled at his car as he drove away.

Okay. So that had been the first offer.

Brauner wasn't the kind of guy who took no for an answer, and I don't mean that in a complimentary way. Granted, I hadn't exactly said no, but I hadn't given an enthusiastic yes either. And I had been telling the truth, I did want to talk to Russell first. Because the hard truth was that we were going to have to come to an accommodation with the Brauner family. They were powerful enough that a business of our size (and our potential size) was going to have to deal with them sooner or later.

Unless, of course, I Cloaked, walked up behind Brauner, and shot him in the head...

Nope. Wasn't doing that. Not unless he crossed some lines first.

Well, I would talk to Russell, and we would figure something out.

I expected trouble from Brauner if we waited too long.

I did not expect trouble the very next day.

Riordan was in the UK again, dealing with a problem for the Shadow Hunters. I had driven home, slept well, exercised hard, showered, and come back to the Moran Imports warehouse. Until the High Queen had a job for me, I was going to work full-time at the company, and she hadn't given me a task since that business with the dragons and the cyborg. Which surprised me – I thought she would use me a lot more. Not that I minded. Maybe she kept me in reserve for serious problems. Which meant that when she did have jobs for me, they would be serious – like that business with the dragons and the cyborg.

Cheery thought.

It was about 9 AM, and I was on my second mug of coffee and working my way through a stack of paperwork when Robert burst into the office. He was only breathing a little hard, and he was in good enough shape that meant he had sprinted to get here.

"What's wrong?" I said.

"Homeland Security's in the parking lot," he said. "They're arresting Jacob."

"What?" I said. "All his documents are correct, they're…"

Then I remembered my conversation with Hawley yesterday.

"Shit," I said, surging to my feet. "Shit, shit, shit." I grabbed my black navy pea coat and threw it on. "We have to deal with this right now." I reached to the table, grabbed a camera, clipped it to my lapel. "Actually, I better deal with it." I synced the camera to my phone and selected network storage. "Come with me but let me do the talking."

"What?" said Robert.

"Because I need a witness, and I don't want you to get arrested," I said.

I hit the RECORD button on my phone and dropped it into my pocket. I opened the file cabinet we used for employee records, grabbed the file for Jacob Boyer, and headed out the door, Robert following.

I rushed into the parking lot. It was an icy November day, and the chill sliced into me, all the more since I was holding my magic ready in case this went ugly. On the west side of the parking lot was a concrete slab with some picnic tables, and the warehouse workers tended to have cigarette breaks there. Right now, a crowd of a dozen workers stared in alarm at two Homeland Security officers, who were in the process of cuffing an alarmed Jacob Boyer.

Jacob was…how do I say this? Jake was a bit of a weasel. He

finished his six-year enlistment as a man-at-arms of Duke Tamirlas with an honorable discharge, but he never got promoted because of his habit of starting fights with people who annoyed him. Most men-at-arms picked up useful skills while serving, but Jake had been too busy screwing around and drinking. When he had been discharged, the drinking had gotten worse, right up until he drove into a tree. Nobody had been hurt, so he avoided a more severe punishment, but the fine had bankrupted him, and he had gotten ten lashes on a Punishment Day video.

Because of that, it was hard for him to get a job. But he was a good worker when he was sober if someone kept an eye on him. You might wonder why we hired a guy with a drinking problem (even if it was under control), but it's really hard to find reliable people for warehouse jobs. The thing about warehouse work is that it's difficult, exhausting, and doesn't pay very well, so the minute that someone can make better money doing something easier, they do. Russell and I couldn't be too picky about our warehouse workers. Half of them had criminal records of some degree or another, a few of them severe enough that they had suffered terms of enslavement to Elven nobles for a few years.

"But I didn't do nothing!" Jake said as I approached. "Boss, tell them, I didn't do nothing."

The two Homeland Security officers glared at me, and I took a dislike to them at once. One was in his later twenties, young and buff. A former man-at-arms and new recruit, one who probably spent a lot of time in the gym. His nameplate read KIRBY, and he watched me with hard eyes. The second man was older, in his middle forties, and a bit thicker about the middle, but he had the stone face of a veteran law enforcement officer. His nameplate read HOPKINS.

"Ma'am," said Hopkins in that flat voice Homeland Security officers used. "You're going to want to step back."

"Why are you arresting him?" I said.

"I didn't do nothing!" Jake protested.

"Why are you arresting him?" I said again.

"You heard him," said Kirby, his flat stare turning into a glare.

This wasn't a man used to being questioned. "Step back immediately."

"This is my building, and you're going to tell me why you're arresting one of my employees," I said, shifting so the camera on my lapel was pointing at him.

Anger flashed through Kirby's eyes. I think he wanted to take a swing at me, which made me dislike him more. I could have killed everyone around me with a few spells in about two seconds, but he didn't know that. What he knew was that I was a foot shorter than him and less than half his weight, and he was going to intimidate me.

Ha. When you've had a wraithwolf rip out your guts a few thousand times, your threshold for intimidation gets just a bit higher.

I had a sudden vivid image of blasting off the top of Kirby's skull, but Hopkins cleared his throat. Kirby stopped and glanced at the older officer.

"Mr. Boyer has failed the terms of his probation," said Hopkins.

"Has he?" I said. I suspected this was the first of Brauner's attempts to intimidate us, and I was right. If Boyer had robbed a gas station or started drinking again and passed out on somebody's porch, that was one thing. But the terms of his probation included going to regular alcoholic counseling sessions, and I knew beyond all doubt that he went. The administrative assistant of the addiction counselor emailed us the attendance records every week, and Boyer was up to date.

And that meant Brauner or one of his goons had told Homeland Security to make trouble for us, and they had latched on to the easiest target.

Anger flashed over Kirby's expression, and if there hadn't been so many witnesses nearby, I think he would have punched me, and then arrested me for using my face to assault an officer's fist. But Hopkins cleared his throat again. I think he was smarter than Kirby, or at least he had spotted the camera clipped to my lapel.

"Arrest order came through this morning," said Hopkins. "Mr. Boyer failed to attend his last mandatory addiction counseling session, and…"

"But I didn't!" said Boyer. "I went for the whole goddamned ninety minutes! I even missed the first half of the football game."

"Guys, there's been a mix-up," I said, opening the folder and pulling out the counselor's report. I turned it so the camera on my coat would pick it up and then showed the document to Hopkins. "Boyer here went to all his counseling sessions."

"He still violated his parole," said Kirby with a snarl.

"No, he didn't," I said. "Here's the proof."

"Let me see that," said Hopkins, holding out his hand.

I handed over the report. I half-expected him to wad it up and throw it into my face. Good luck with that – I still had electronic copies. Hopkins produced his phone, scanned the report, and then handed it to me.

"Stay here for a second," said Hopkins to Kirby, and he walked a dozen yards away and made a phone call.

We waited. Boyer kept twitching. Kirby alternated between glaring at him, glaring at me, and glaring at the other warehouse workers. Then he saw the camera on my lapel, and his eyes went wide. Seriously, he hadn't noticed it before? Then he started to get angry again. He really didn't like being recorded.

Hopkins finished his call, returned the phone to its holster on its belt, rejoined us, and unlocked Boyer's cuffs.

"You're free to go," he said.

Boyer scuttled several steps away from the two officers.

Kirby started to protest, but Hopkins spoke first.

"You had better be careful, Mrs. MacCormac," he said. "A new business like this...there are a lot of violations that might cause you trouble. Better take care of them."

I got the message just fine. I had better deal with Brauner, or else his friends in Homeland Security and the state government were going to find ways to make trouble for me. I was getting really pissed off, but I wanted to calm down before I did anything, and I wanted to talk to Russell first. It was mostly his business. I was just keeping an eye on it for him until he could turn his full attention to it.

Hopkins and Kirby turned, got into their waiting blue Homeland Security SUV, and departed.

They did not bother to use the turn signal when turning out of the parking lot.

"Jesus, boss," said Boyer. He was trying to smile but there was a tremor in his voice. "I thought I was screwed. I mean, I went to the stupid counseling session and listened to that prick of a counselor for an hour and a half, but they wouldn't have believed me."

I let out a long breath. "Let's go back inside."

With that, we returned to the warehouse, and work resumed.

∾

THE NEXT MORNING, I arrived at the warehouse to find more trouble.

We had to use refrigerated trucks to ship some of the fruit, for obvious reasons, and so far we had used refrigerated trailers. That way a standard truck cab could simply connect to the trailer, which cut down on costs a little. When I had left the night before, there had been three trailers parked in our docks.

During the night, all three of the trailers had their tires slashed.

"Goddamn it," I said, glaring at the trailers.

"We have to get those fixed right now," said Robert. We both stood outside the truck dock, the cold November wind whipping past us. "We've got deliveries due out in three hours. By the time we call Homeland Security and get a report filed for the insurance, it's going to be late."

"No," I said. "We're not calling Homeland Security for a report." I wagered that some off-duty Homeland Security officers or some of Brauner's other friends had slashed the tires. "Call the tire place and have them deliver some tires out there. I can replace them myself if you help me."

Robert blinked. "You know how to replace trailer tires?"

"Yeah." I didn't tell him that I had spent a few decades in the Eternity Crucible driving the same semi truck over and over again. Sometimes the tires had burst, and I had taught myself how to replace them. "But they're too heavy to move by myself, so I'll need your help. Get a couple of the warehouse guys to give us a hand. And once we're done…I'm going to deal with this."

Robert frowned. "Deal with it?"

"Yeah," I said. "Let's start getting those tires off."

Changing trailer tires in November weather was not the most enjoyable thing I had ever done, but it definitely wasn't the worst, either. The truck arrived from the tire place just after we removed the last ruined tire, and Robert and I wrestled the new ones into place and inflated them.

We finished with about five minutes to spare.

"You know," said Robert, "when you and Russell hired me, I didn't think I'd spend the day changing truck tires."

I grinned at him as we watched a truck cab connect with the trailer. "Still beats getting chased through Venomhold by wraith-wolves, yeah?"

"Can't argue with that," said Robert. He gave me a serious look. "What are we going to do about this? If a guy like Arnold Brauner is putting pressure on us, it's only going to get worse."

"I know," I said, reaching for my phone. "I'm going to make a call."

I pulled out Hawley's card, punched in the number, and waited.

Hawley picked up on the third ring. "Hello?"

"This is Nadia MacCormac," I said. "My brother and I are going to meet with Governor Arnold tomorrow."

"One moment, please," said Hawley.

I waited, and then Hawley returned.

"Mrs. MacCormac, Governor Arnold would be pleased to meet with you and Mr. Moran tomorrow at 10 AM," said Hawley. "He'll be at Brauner Farms. You know the location?"

"I do," I said. "Thanks."

I terminated the call and slid the phone into my pocket.

"Are we getting in bed with a guy like Brauner?" said Robert. "Everyone knows he's crooked."

"He is," I said. "We're not getting in bed with him. We're both married, for God's sake." Robert snorted out a laugh. "But we have to deal with him. He's too powerful to ignore. Can you take charge here for the rest of the day?"

"Sure," said Robert. "Where are you going?"

I grinned at him. "I'm going to make sure Moran Imports has a favorable bargaining position."

∽

IF BRAUNER WANTED to play hardball, I would do it right back.

I did a little research on a burner phone, got what I needed, and set off across Milwaukee.

Arnold Brauner had three main residences in Wisconsin. He had an apartment in downtown Madison when he went to the State Capitol on business. He had a condo in the fanciest building in Milwaukee. But his main residence was in the suburb of Shorewood, and I arrived there a little before 5 PM.

It wasn't all that far from my old master Lord Morvilind's mansion, which had passed to the High Queen after he died. Brauner's house was a mansion set in an acre of lawn. Probably six bedrooms, and a four-car garage. With all the leaves falling, it looked autumnal and picturesque. There was even a festive display of pumpkins on the front porch.

I parked my car six blocks away, and I donned a hair net and a ball cap, a mask over my nose and mouth, and leather gloves over my hands. It was only a small risk, but I didn't want to leave any hair or usable DNA behind in Brauner's house. I got out of the car, used the Mask spell to disguise myself as an elderly woman in a tracksuit, and walked to Brauner's mansion. I strolled around the block, noting the security features. There was a black metal fence around the property, and a motion detector over the gate to the driveway, along with a security camera. I spotted more motion detectors, floodlights, and cameras on the house. But there weren't cameras along the entire fence. I did see a pair of security guards in dark suits sitting in a booth by the garage, but that wouldn't be a problem.

After one walk around the block, I had what I needed. Brauner's security was good, and it would stop most conventional thieves and seriously slow down any armed attackers. Likely he had designed it to stop any business rivals who were annoyed that he was playing rough with them.

But it wasn't sufficient to stop someone like me.

I levitated over the fence, landed on the other side, and cast the Cloak spell. Invisible, I walked across the lawn and to the base of the house behind the garage. I dropped the Cloak spell and levitated up to an upper-story window. As I had suspected, the windows on the first floor had alarms, but the ones on the second floor didn't. I used a telekinesis spell to undo the lock, slid open the window, and climbed inside.

I found myself in a guest bedroom. It had a double bed, a chair, a table with some prepackaged toiletries, and a small bathroom off to the left. I slid the window shut behind me, cast the Cloak spell again, and took a quick stroll around the house.

It was a nice place. A big formal living room, with stairs leading up to a balcony and the bedroom. The themes of the formal living room, I suspected, were patriotism and the political power of the Brauner family. There was an enormous portrait of the High Queen, looking stern. The picture didn't really capture the icy weight of her eyes. There were pictures of Brauner and all his sons in the uniforms of men-at-arms. A large picture showed Arnold Brauner getting sworn in as governor, his wife beaming at his side. I saw a dozen pictures of Brauner with Duke Tamirlas, who always looked mildly constipated in pictures.

I walked into a large dining room with a fancy table, probably for when the full Brauner clan and all the grandkids came. Off that was a TV room that looked far more relaxed than the formal living room. Various sports memorabilia adorned the walls, along with pictures of Brauner grandkids, and two recliners faced a big TV. The end tables on either side of the recliners had the sort of lived-in clutter that the living room and dining room lacked. I suspected that Brauner and his wife spent most of their time here when they were home.

I sat against the wall in the corner by the TV, crossed my legs, and held the Cloak spell. I can only hold the Cloak spell for eleven or twelve minutes while walking around, but when I'm motionless, I can maintain it indefinitely, and it's not even that much of an effort.

I only had to wait about an hour.

At 6:30 PM, Arnold Brauner and his wife Tansy walked into the room.

Former Governor Arnold Brauner looked like a dairy farmer, which made sense as that was how he had gotten his start. He was a big, red-faced man of about sixty, with thick arms, a big chest and a big gut. Right now, he wore a flannel shirt tucked into old jeans and carried an open can of beer in his right hand.

Tansy looked like a former beauty queen who had kept in shape as she aged. In fact, I think she had been Miss Dairy or Miss Butter Wisconsin or something thirty years ago, which was how she and Brauner had met. They sat down, turned on the TV, and talked about inconsequential things – what one of their grandkids was doing, or how much of the family was coming for Thanksgiving, or whether they should have Christmas at Martin's house or Luke's. Looking at Brauner and listening to his conversation, he sounded like a prosperous farmer and businessman, not a ruthless racketeer.

But I suppose I don't look like what I really am at first sight, either.

Tansy held the remote control and flipped through the channels, while Brauner read a paperback novel, something by a guy named Louis L'Amour with a picture of an Old West cowboy on the cover.

I waited.

At about seven, Tansy stood up.

"I've got to run to church quick," she said.

Brauner grunted. "What for?"

"The potluck on Sunday," said Tansy. "We want to set up the tables tonight."

"You want help?" said Brauner.

"Nah, it's a girls' night," said Tansy. "We're going out for dessert after."

"Well, don't stay out too late," said Brauner.

"I won't," said Tansy.

"Be sure to check in with Bart and Jim on the way out," said Brauner. I assumed they were security guards.

"I will," said Tansy. "And don't you spend too much time in the study. The boys can look after their own careers."

"I'll stop if you get home at a decent hour," said Brauner.

"Deal," said Tansy. She leaned down, kissed him, and walked out of the den. I wondered how much she knew about her husband's business. Probably most of it. They had been married for thirty years, and whatever else could be said about Arnold Brauner, he wasn't the sort of man to take a mistress. (Unlike some of his sons.)

I waited some more.

Brauner finished off his beer, grunted, slid a bookmark into his cowboy book, and got to his feet. Probably he had to take a piss and then would head to his study. I stood, still holding my Cloak spell, and followed him in silence. As I did, I picked up his Louis L'Amour book and stuck it into the interior pocket of my coat. I trailed him upstairs, into the master bedroom, and he vanished into the bathroom.

I didn't follow him in. That would be weird.

A minute later, I heard him washing his hands, and he walked out and headed down the upstairs hallway to his office. I stepped into the bathroom and took a quick look around. It was big and luxurious, with a massive shower and a wide counter. I assumed Tansy and Brauner had separate sinks since the sink on the left was surrounded by various female cosmetics. Brauner's side was more utilitarian, with cologne, shampoo, sunscreen, shaving cream, and so forth.

I took his toothbrush, put it in a coat pocket, and left the bathroom. I escaped from the house the same way I had entered, retreated across the lawn, levitated over the fence, Masked myself as a Homeland Security officer, and walked to my car.

I drove home, made sure that I wasn't followed, and went to bed.

The next morning, I slept late, had a vigorous workout at our home gym, and then drove to Moran Imports.

Russell and Robert met me in the office.

My brother was looking healthier than he had before the battle in New York. He had taken up weightlifting, so he was considerably more muscular than he had been a year past. He was also a foot taller than me, which just wasn't fair. But his hair and eyebrows were still snow-white. The High Queen had cured his frostfever in exchange for my service, so Russell was no longer in danger from the disease. But it had left his mark on him. Even with the weightlifting, his stamina was limited, so he would never be a man-at-arms. He would probably live a normal lifespan, but he would need medication to keep his blood pressure and digestion under control.

Despite all that, he seemed to have boundless energy, and threw himself into both finishing high school and starting Moran Imports. It was, in the end, his company, despite my shares. I was just managing it for him until he became a legal adult next year.

Russell was wearing jeans and a heavy hooded sweatshirt. I wore my usual outfit of a gray sweater, black jeans, running shoes, and heavy black pea coat. I also made sure to wear black leather gloves, since I was pretty sure I wouldn't want to leave any fingerprints on certain items later this morning.

"Any more trouble?" I said, dropping into the last free chair.

Robert shook his head. "No vandalism, no trouble with Homeland Security. Patrol cars have driven past us more than usual, but nothing major. I think Brauner's not going to make any more trouble for us until he sees how your meeting goes." He scowled. "But I am installing those security cameras today."

"Just as well," I said. "We'd need that anyway."

"Nadia," said Russell. "Should we talk about our meeting with…"

"Nope," I said. "Not in front of Robert."

Russell frowned. "Isn't that kind of rude?"

"If I don't hear about the conversation," said Robert in a quiet voice, "I can't testify about it later."

Russell considered this.

"That's a good point," said Russell.

"Ready?" I said. "I'll drive."

We left Robert in charge and walked out to my old Duluth Motors sedan. I started the engine and pulled into traffic, heading south to Brauner Farms.

"All right," I said. "I think this is what we're going need to do. We have to make an accommodation with Brauner."

"Why?" said Russell. "He's trying to extort us."

"Yup," I said. "But he's powerful enough that we have to play ball with him. We can't just make him magically disappear." I could, but I didn't want to commit murder. "I'm going to show him that pushing us around is a really bad idea and he doesn't want to do it anymore. Then we need to offer him at least some carrot after the stick. Like, um, a percentage of our profit donated to the Brauner Foundation. A small percentage. Just enough to make the gesture." Assuming Moran Imports did indeed turn a profit. "Maybe we'll use one of his construction companies for the warehouse expansion, or we'll work with his trucking business."

Russell thought about this for a few miles as we drove into the Wisconsin countryside. It was a bleak November day with gusty winds. All the corn had been harvested, and from time to time, the wind blew dancing clouds of dried husks across the road.

"All right," said Russell. "If you think that's best. But should we really be getting involved with organized criminals like Brauner?"

"We're not getting involved," I said. "We're going to scare Brauner a little, show him what happens if he keeps pushing, and then give him a carrot, so he's mollified." I snorted. "Half the businesses in the state donate to the Brauner Foundation. We'll be in good company, at least." I hesitated. "When it comes time for the carrot, I think you had better do the talking. I can get a little…"

"Forceful?" said Russell.

"I was going to say terrifying, but yeah, forceful is a nicer way of saying that," I said. "And you're…well, you're nicer than I am. Better at talking to people. You'll have a good chance of making Brauner see reason after I scare him."

"What are you going to do to him?" said Russell.

I shrugged. I didn't really want to confess burglary to my brother. "I borrowed a book."

About fifteen minutes later, we arrived at Brauner Farms.

Arnold Brauner had gotten his start as a dairy farmer, and I think he was still a dairy farmer at heart. Now he owned the biggest dairy farm in Wisconsin, with something like eighteen thousand cows at any one time. We turned off a county highway and drove through a red-painted wooden arch with BRAUNER FARMS in golden letters. I saw dozens of long metal barns, and hundreds of cows wandering through pastures. There were big tanker trucks that I think hauled milk, but what did I know? I don't know anything about dairy farming.

I drove to a building that looked like a one-story farmhouse, but a sign out front said OFFICE. A man in an overcoat stood on the porch, watching us approach, and I recognized Thomas Hawley. I parked the car in front of the house, and we got out. Hawley strode over to greet us.

"Mrs. MacCormac, welcome," said Hawley. We shook hands, and he turned to face Russell. "Mr. Moran, good to meet you. Governor Arnold is out back. He's looking forward to your discussion."

We circled around the farmhouse. It was cold enough that the ground had frozen, and the grass crunched beneath our shoes. I noticed three farmhands in tan jackets following us at a distance. Brauner's people, no doubt making sure we didn't freak out and attack their boss.

I hoped Brauner didn't freak out on us.

Arnold Brauner stood behind the farmhouse, gazing at his barns. He wore a tan work jacket similar to the farmhands/bodyguards, jeans, and old work boots. A green hat with the golden logo of a tractor company rested on his head. He turned in our direction and smiled a brilliant politician's smile at us, but his eyes remained shrewd and as cold as the November day.

"Governor," said Hawley. "Russell Moran and Nadia MacCormac to see you."

"Hello, Mrs. MacCormac. Mr. Moran, good to meet you," said Brauner. They shook hands. "Thanks for coming on down to talk."

"What can we say, Governor?" said Russell with an easy smile. "You're a hard man to say no to."

"If you talk to my wife, she'll disagree," said Brauner, and he and Russell laughed. I didn't. "You guys mind if we walk while we talk business? I've spent too much time sitting behind a desk today."

"Sure," said Russell. "Nadia?"

I inclined my head.

"I'll be in the office if you need me, boss," said Hawley. Translation: once Brauner had bullied us into accepting his terms, Hawley would have the documents ready to sign.

"That's great, Tom," said Brauner.

Hawley nodded and walked back into the house, and Brauner set off at a sedate pace deeper into the farm. The farmhands/bodyguards followed us at a discreet distance.

"Hell," said Brauner, "I'd enjoy it if we had time for a proper tour. You know, of all the things I've done, this is my pride and joy, right here. When I inherited the place from my dad, we had a thousand acres and maybe three hundred cows, and half of them were sick."

"What do you have now, Governor?" said Russell, picking up on the cue.

"Nineteen thousand four hundred thirty-two," said Brauner with obvious pride. Given how hard it was to turn a profit farming, I wondered how much of the money from his illicit businesses he had funneled into this place. Maybe Brauner Farms was a giant money washing machine. "Milk, cheese, and other dairy products from Brauner Farms are sold and eaten in every state in the country. We have our own buttery and creamery and make our own cheese."

"Cheese curds?" I said. "Seems like an efficient way to get atherosclerosis."

Brauner ignored the insult. "Oh, yes, those too. Especially around State Fair time. People love deep-fried cheese curds." We stopped about halfway between the office and the nearest barn, and even in the chill air, I smelled the earthy odor of cow manure. "Of course, you two are in the agriculture business as well. Importing Elven fruit to compete with homegrown American produce."

"Technically we're wholesalers," I said.

"It almost happened by accident," said Russell.

"Did it?" said Brauner.

"It was at my sister's wedding," said Russell. "The High Queen was a guest, which was a huge honor. One of her handmaidens brought a basket of Elven fruit as a gift. I sort of ate half of it, and when I was talking to the High Queen, I mentioned that it would be a good idea to sell the fruit stuff on Earth. She gave me a license to important Elven fruit and sell it here, and I decided to make the most of it." Russell shrugged. "I'm never going to be a man-at-arms," he gestured at his white hair, "so I'm always going to be an outsider. I'll have to make my own way with my own business."

"I admire that, I really do," said Brauner. "Seems like you were dealt a bad hand, but you're making the most of it. And, hey, maybe our businesses complement each other. Both Elves and humans like fruit and cheese, yeah? But I know hard it is to turn a profit in agriculture."

"I don't know," I said. "The agriculture's not a problem." I met his gaze and offered a chilly smile. "The people are the challenging part."

"Believe me, I know," said Brauner. "I've had problems with strikes, sabotage, employee theft, eco-nuts…I even had these vegetarian protestors turn up and claim that eating cheese is a violation of the cows' fundamental rights. Whackos." He shook his head. "But I know how hard it is to start a business of any kind, especially an agricultural business. I thought I could help you out."

"That's really generous, Governor," said Russell. He looked so earnest. "What kind of help did you have in mind?"

"Oh, all sorts of ways," said Brauner. "You're going to have to expand, and I have construction companies that can help with that. You need to ship your fruit quickly to market, and my trucking company has experience with it. And there are so many regulatory and compliance problems with a new business. My lawyers could write up some documents for you. If you're having employee problems, or maybe money problems, I could help with that, too."

"That is very generous," said Russell, glancing at me.

I took a deep breath. It was time to put aside the carrot and bring out the stick.

"Before we get into all that," I said, "I'm going to have to ask you for a favor, Governor."

"What's that?" said Brauner.

"Don't screw with us."

Brauner smiled an easy, confident smile. "We're just talking."

"Yup. We're just talking. I'm just showing you some stuff. Tell your guys not to shoot me when I reach into my coat," I said.

Brauner's smile widened. "We're only talking, Mrs. MacCormac." But he made a small gesture with his right hand.

"Sure," I said, and I reached into my coat, drew out the Louis L'Amour book I had taken from his table, and held it out. "Do you want to know the ending?"

Brauner's smile vanished, and his gray brows knitted in confusion. "I know the ending. It's one of my favorite books. I read it every year. How…"

"You might have lost this, too," I said, and I held out his toothbrush in my other hand.

Brauner took the book and the toothbrush, confused…and I saw him get it.

Rage and alarm flickered over his face. He knew that I had been in his house. What was more, he knew that I had been in his house while he had been at home and that none of his security had detected me. Hell, he probably hadn't even realized that anything was wrong. He had likely assumed that he had misplaced his book and his toothbrush, that he had set them down somewhere and gotten distracted.

Before he could get to the end of his train of thought, I kept talking.

"Please don't screw with us," I said. "I am begging you, from the bottom of my heart, not to screw with us. Because I don't know how that will end. No, I do know how that will end, but I don't want that on my conscience. God knows it's already pretty crowded in there."

Brauner looked at the book, at the toothbrush, at Russell, and then at me.

"There are rumors about you, you know, Mrs. MacCormac," he said. His voice was calm, but his face was redder than it had been a minute ago. His bodyguards had picked up on it and were drifting closer, hands in their pockets.

"Yeah, I can imagine."

"That video of you in New York, when you were supposed to have stopped that nuclear bomb," said Brauner. "I thought it was just propaganda."

"Governor, I was there," said Russell. "That definitely happened, and that video was just a thirty second clip. A lot of other stuff happened before that, too. But we didn't come here to make threats or anything. You've done a lot of great stuff for the state of Wisconsin, and we respect that."

"If you didn't come here to make threats, are you going to issue demands?" said Brauner.

"Not at all," said Russell. "We'd like to donate a percentage of our profits to the Brauner Foundation."

That caught Brauner off-guard. "Would you, now?"

"We would," said Russell.

"Assuming there are any profits next year," I said, though there seemed a good chance of that.

"If there are profits, we'll commit to one percent per fiscal year," said Russell. "Net, not gross." A smile flickered over Brauner's face. That was a common trap for the unwary – I had even heard Riordan mention it a few times when discussing the evils of publishers.

"That's very generous, Mr. Moran," said Brauner. "The foundation does good work for deserving people." People from whom Brauner wanted to collect favors, I thought, but I kept my mouth shut. The book and the toothbrush had made my point for me. "And a young company like yours, it might benefit with help from an older, more experienced business."

Russell glanced at me. "We have been planning some warehouse expansions in the next two years. Maybe you could recommend someone?"

"Warehouses take a lot of concrete," said Brauner. "My friends at Doyle Concrete & Construction might be able to help you out."

"Not Doyle Concrete & Construction," I said at once. "They have a terrible reputation. They built that building that fell down and killed some people. I'm surprised the company hasn't been sued to oblivion."

"That's still under investigation," said Brauner. "But I can understand that. Maybe we can find someone else to help you."

We haggled for a bit and then settled on another of Brauner's companies to help with the warehouse expansion.

"All right," said Brauner. "I think this has been a productive meeting, don't you? Why don't you stay for lunch?"

"Yeah, why not?" said Russell. I repressed a grimace.

"I can have Thomas Hawley draw up some contracts before you go," said Brauner.

"We're not signing anything until our own lawyer looks at it," I said.

Brauner smiled at Russell. "You're fortunate to have such a loyal sister. Family is everything, you know."

"I always thought so," said Russell.

∼

AN HOUR AND A HALF LATER, we left Brauner Farms with a folder full of contracts to review. I didn't think Brauner would play games with the contracts, but best to be careful. I was pretty sure Governor Arnold and I understood each other at this point. Russell and I had been willing to play ball with him, and he knew not to screw with us.

The mutual messages had been delivered.

"Those cheese curds," said Russell from the passenger seat, "really were amazing."

"Yeah," I said. I hadn't eaten all that much. Too much cheese upsets my stomach, and my digestion isn't great at the best of times.

Too much tension, I guess. I'm probably a high-risk candidate for ulcers.

"Nadia," said Russell. "Can I ask you something?"

He had gone serious. Uh oh.

"Yeah, sure," I said.

He took a deep breath and looked at me. "Why didn't you kill Brauner?"

A bunch of emotions went through me.

Anger, first, that he thought I would do that. Then hurt, that my own brother thought I was some sort of ravening psycho. Then logic kicked in and pointed out that it was a reasonable question. Russell had seen me kill a lot of people. Granted, it had all been in self-defense, but still.

"Did...you want me to?" I said, my voice tentative.

"No!" said Russell. "I'm really glad we got out of this without anyone getting hurt. I was afraid it was going to end up in a fight. But...you know..."

"Yeah, I understand," I said. "Look. Brauner's an enormous asshole...but he's not as bad of an asshole as someone like him could be. He's got rules. He was screwing with us, yeah...but nobody got hurt or killed. We were out a few thousand dollars in truck tires, and that's basically it. Which sucks, but it won't hurt us in the long term. Hell, Boyer didn't even get arrested. Those Homeland Security officers could have made a lot more trouble for Boyer. If we were in China or Russia, the negotiations with someone like Brauner would have started with him sending us somebody's head."

"Better the devil you know," said Russell.

"That's basically it," I said. "Also, Brauner is Duke Tamirlas's shadow councilor, so we'd have trouble with the Duke if we killed him."

"Shadow councilor?" said Russell, frowning. "Is...that like you do? Like a shadow agent?"

"No," I said. "Remember our trip to Las Vegas when Nicholas had us rob that casino?"

Russell snorted. "That's not the kind of experience you ever forget." He grinned. "I don't think Riordan will ever forget it, either, not the way he was staring at you in that cocktail waitress outfit..."

"For God's sake, don't be gross," I said, but I laughed as I said it. Most people who knew who I was were afraid of me, and there were very few people who could tease me. "But remember how Nicholas said that Duke Orothor let the Las Vegas syndicate run the casinos in exchange for a cut of the profits?" Russel nodded. "It's a formal arrangement. A Duke can pick someone to run the organized crime in his territory, a shadow councilor. The Elves are more interested in order than in anything else, and Brauner keeps things orderly and civilized."

Russell almost said that was elfophobic, automatically. I all but saw the thought appear, then he stopped himself. The indoctrination of the public school system was a powerful thing, though I wouldn't know. I hadn't been to an actual school since kindergarten.

"Killing him would make a mess," said Russell at last.

I shrugged. "If Brauner dies, maybe someone worse will take his place. His sons aren't as smart as he is."

"I didn't know that," said Russell. "About the shadow councilors. Suppose I should have figured it out."

"It's all right," I said. We were drawing closer to the Milwaukee metro area, and I stopped talking long enough to concentrate on merging into the freeway. "But you and I already know all kinds of things we're not supposed to know. What's one more? And..."

I paused. Russell let me work out my thoughts.

"I've never just flat-out killed someone in cold blood," I said. "I've been in a lot of fights, and I've killed people, but I never just killed anyone because they were in my way or because it was convenient." I shuddered, remembering how I had almost killed Robert's wife Alexandra for just that reason. That experience, and the nightmares and guilt I had felt after had been a turning point in my life, though I hadn't realized it at the time. I hadn't even been able to kill Lord Arvalaeon in cold blood, though God knows the asshole deserved it. "I've got too much power, Russell. I don't want to abuse it. I mean, if Brauner comes after us, I'll make him regret it, but if he's willing to see reason and play ball…no. I'm not gonna kill someone over some money."

"I know," said Russell. "I'm sorry you had to deal with this."

I shrugged. "Eh. Stuff happens. And there are some benefits. If another shadow councilor comes sniffing around the company, we'll be able to get Brauner and his goons to run them off. Or if we have actual problems with actual criminals, we can get Brauner to deal with it. No one would dare to steal from him."

Russell snorted. "You did. Though why'd you steal his toothbrush?"

"Seemed like a good choice. Showed I could get in and out of his house whenever I wanted, and it wouldn't really hurt him."

Russell laughed.

"What?" I said.

"I don't know," said Russell. "It's kind of absurd when you think about it…Nadia MacCormac, master thief and shadow agent to the High Queen, steals a toothbrush."

"Yeah, maybe gum disease will get Brauner," I said, and it was so absurd that I did laugh.

"I am sorry about this," said Russell when I calmed down. "That you had to deal with it. It's just so…egregious."

"What do you mean?" I said.

"That Brauner can get away with stuff like this," said Russell. "It isn't right. I mean, I know he's not as bad as he could be like you said…but still. It bugs me."

I shrugged. "The world's a shitty place full of shitty people. Isn't that what they say at your church every week?"

"The pastor doesn't phrase it quite like that," said Russell. We came to our freeway exit, and I took the offramp and came to the stoplight. A lot of traffic – with the Great Gate nearby, Milwaukee would need some more freeways soon. "It's too bad we can't just call Homeland Security and have him arrested for racketeering."

"What?" I said, incredulous. "Homeland Security?"

Why on earth would he think that?

Oh, right, public school. Russell had probably seen videos of friendly Homeland Security officers standing on corners and helping little old ladies cross the street. Or for adults, there were all those TV dramas and novels about intrepid Homeland Security officers hunting down serial killers or Rebel terrorists or drug dealers or whatever, usually with moody atmospheric lighting, dramatic music, and tempestuous romances.

The United States' national police force wasn't anything like that in reality.

"They're useless," I said. "I know their motto is to protect and serve, but none of them are like that. There are only two kinds of Homeland Security officers. The thugs who get off on bullying people." My encounter with Officer Kirby came to mind. "Or the timeservers who want to sit in their chairs, do nothing, and keep their heads down until they can collect their pension."

We drove in silence for a while. Our warehouse came into sight, and I turned into the parking lot.

"There must be at least some good Homeland Security officers," said Russell.

"I concede it's possible," I said. "But if there are, I've never met one."

2

THE DETECTIVE

Colonel Owen Quell got dressed for an execution.

Owen didn't like going to executions. No one in Homeland Security did. In fact, showing too much interest or enjoyment in attending executions put a red flag for a psych evaluation in an officer's record. But it had been Quell's murder case, he had gathered the evidence, the prosecutor had presented it to the jury, and the sentence had been given.

And Owen was entirely certain of the man's guilt. The legal standard for conviction was "beyond reasonable doubt" but thanks to Owen's unique gifts, he had absolutely no doubt whatsoever. Dean Osmond was guilty of three murders.

Still, Owen didn't want to attend the execution, but it was necessary. The families of the victims would be there, and the literature claimed it would give them closure and help them move on with their lives. Owen supposed that was true enough.

But as the High Queen had told him, more than once, justice was covered in blood and tears.

Owen donned his dress uniform in his office and checked his reflection in the mirror on the back of his door. He was slightly annoyed that he had grown a small gut that he seemed unable to lose. Still, he was forty-six, so he supposed it could be worse. At least he had all his hair, though it was more gray than brown now.

And the dress uniform...

In his opinion, the Homeland Security dress uniform was overdone. Navy blue trousers, with a gold stripe up the sides, and shiny shoes. His uniform jacket had too much metal on it – the badge, the various service ribbons, the colonel's eagles, the thunderbolt emblem that marked him as a former member of the Wizard's Legion. The face beneath the uniform cap with its badge didn't look like a colonel's face. It looked like the face of a bar brawler, with an oft-broken nose, dark eyes, and a scar down the right side of his jaw that looked like a knife strike but had come from an anthrophage that had tried to rip his head off.

Still, he had to concede that the jacket and the broad belt did an excellent job of concealing his gut.

On his left hand was his wedding band.

On his right...

Only Owen could see the golden ring with the blood-colored stone on his right hand. Well, only Owen, the High Queen, and her other shadow agents.

He had worn that ring for sixteen years. Almost seventeen now, come to think of it. The twins' birthday was coming up in December. Seventeen years and Owen could still remember the day of the twins' birth, the day he had gotten the ring.

"Anything you want," Owen said in his memory.

"That's right," said the High Queen. "You will."

Owen pushed aside the thoughts and stepped out of his office, closing and locking the door behind him. His office overlooked the homicide bullpen of Milwaukee's Central Office. The bullpen held a dozen desks separated by low cubicle walls, the working space of the detectives. Owen's rank rated him an office of his own. His title was technically Head of Special Investigations. In practice, that meant he often helped the other departments within the Central Office with their overflow. Homicide tended to get overloaded during the hot summer months and right before the holidays. It also meant that

Owen received the high profile cases, the hard ones, and sometimes Homeland Security flew him around the country as a troubleshooter.

Given his specific talents, it made sense.

Most of the detectives were at their desks, doing paperwork. It had been a quiet week with no murders. But it would pick up. Thanksgiving was coming, and people could only stand their relatives for so long.

Owen exchanged greetings with a few of the detectives, then crossed the room to the elevator. Another man in a blue Homeland Security dress uniform waited there, a major's insignia on his collar. He had dark skin and dark eyes and the thin, gaunt build of a distance runner.

"You're coming to this?" said Owen, hitting the button for the elevator.

"Yeah," said Major Jacob Giles. "Head of Homicide. Have to put in an appearance."

The elevator door opened, and they stepped inside. Owen had known Giles for almost thirty years, ever since they had both been men-at-arms for Duke Tamirlas. In boot camp and training they had been bitter rivals. Then during their first battle in the Shadowlands, Owen had almost gotten his head ripped off by an anthrophage, but he had saved Giles's life in the process, and they had been friends ever since.

Giles was one of the few officers in the Milwaukee branch of Homeland Security who knew the full extent of Owen's abilities.

"Surprised you got that case," said Giles as the elevator doors slid closed. "Seemed pretty open and shut."

"It was," said Owen. "Osmond was a vicious dumbass with a drug problem. But one of the victims' brothers was a Rebel, died in New York back in July. The branch commander thought the killer might be a surviving Rebel, wanted to jump on it right away. It took us all of one afternoon to find Osmond, and he still had the money and the murder weapon on him."

"You get all the easy ones," said Giles.

Owen grunted. "Oh, yeah. I'm taking naps in my office."

"Well, next time you get an easy one, pass it on to one of my guys," said Giles.

Owen grunted again. "You mean Lieutenant Warren. Isn't he busy with the Doyle murders?"

"Yeah," said Giles. "That's some weird shit. Warren hasn't made a report yet, but he thinks something from the Shadowlands did the killings."

"Hell," said Owen. That was always messy.

"We're probably going to have to talk to the Elven nobles about this one, or they'll have to call in the Inquisition or the Wizard's Legion," said Giles. He grinned, his teeth white in his dark face. "Or they'll have Special Investigations look at it."

"Right," said Owen. "Then I'll get to call the Inquisition."

"Hey, they gave you those colonel's birds for a reason," said Giles. "What's the point of having rank if your subordinates can't hand you problems?"

"You're always an optimist."

The elevator dinged, and the doors slid open. Owen and Giles walked down a short corridor and into the punishment yard.

It was a square courtyard at the rear of the Central Office and behind the parking ramp. The concrete walls were twelve feet high and topped with barbed wire. This wasn't so much to keep prisoners in as it was to prevent people from taking unauthorized recordings of judicial punishment. Homeland Security reserved the exclusive right to post videos of judicial sentences on Punishment Day. The courtyard was empty, save for a wooden post about ten feet high with a long wooden arm extending from it.

The ground sloped at a gentle grade to a drain in the center of the courtyard.

There was a crowd of about forty people already. The officers in charge of operating the camera had set up, their equipment and microphones pointed at the wooden post. The families of Osmond's victims stood against the wall. Some of them spoke in quiet voices, a few others wept in a mixture of grief and anger, but most watched in stony silence. One of Duke Tamirlas's executioners, an Elven noble named Sir Caulomyth, stood near the door, smoking a cigarette. Caulomyth was tall and pale, with the sharp ears and alien features of the Elves, his eyes a vivid shade of green. The eerie eyes seemed all the starker against the black clothes he wore. The Elf saw Owen and Giles approaching and put out his cigarette and tossed the butt to the ground.

"Lord Elf," said Owen.

"Colonel," said Caulomyth, and they shook hands. "Osmond one of yours?"

"That's right," said Owen. Caulomyth's title was technically Executioner to the Duke of Milwaukee, but Owen knew another law enforcement officer when he met one. The Elves were alien, but Caulomyth talked like a law enforcement officer, with the same black sense of humor.

"I thought they gave you the hard ones," said Caulomyth. "Osmond, he's a little shit. Dumb as a dog and mean as a starved rat."

Owen shrugged. "Homicide was busy that month. They needed the help."

"I did him a favor and gave him an easy one," said Giles. "Figured he could use the break. The colonel's getting up there."

"I'm three weeks older than you," said Owen.

"And don't you forget it," said Giles.

Caulomyth laughed once and then sobered. "Well, it's time. We'd better get started. Keep an eye on the families, will you? Wouldn't want Osmond to die two minutes earlier than planned."

The executioner walked to the door leading to the holding cells, and Owen took a few moments to speak with the families of Osmond's three victims. Their gratitude was almost painful, and he didn't like it. He knew watching the execution would not make them feel better, would not ease the grief. Still, it would bring at least some closure. And justice was better than no justice.

Owen understood. He had been there, in their shoes, before he had been a Homeland Security officer or a soldier of the Wizard's Legion.

"Remember," reminded Giles, "stay behind that line." He pointed at a yellow line spray-painted across the concrete. "That will keep you out of the camera feed. We won't arrest you if you cross it. But we will have to restrain you."

"We're going to start," said the officer operating the camera.

The door to the holding area opened, and Caulomyth returned, holding a leather whip. Two Homeland Security officers followed, dragging a man wearing a paper jumpsuit, his hands shackled before him.

Executions had rules and procedures, and Caulomyth started speaking, detailing Dean Osmond's crimes for the camera. Five months earlier, Osmond, high on a variety of illegal stimulants, had robbed a convenience store. The clerk hadn't resisted, but Osmond had shot him to death anyway and emptied the register. Two elderly women had come into the store as he escaped, and Osmond shot them both.

All of it had been caught on camera. It had taken Owen only two hours to find someone who knew Osmond, and another hour to find his address. Three hours after the murder, he had found Osmond sleeping off his drug binge in his apartment, the murder weapon next to his stained mattress. It had been a simple, straightforward arrest, and one of the easiest cases that Owen had worked.

And he knew, beyond all doubt, that Osmond was guilty.

That was both the gift and the curse of the mindtouch spell.

Some law enforcement officers – the honest ones, at least – worried about arresting and convicting an innocent man. Owen had known a detective who had arrested a man for murder, got a conviction, and then an execution. About two years later, evidence had emerged proving the executed man innocent. The detective had gone home, put his children to bed, kissed his wife, and then went out to the garage and blew his head off with a shotgun. Since he had been a homicide detective, he had known just where to put the shotgun to kill instead of accidentally maiming himself.

That, at least, was something Owen didn't need to fear. He had used the mindtouch spell to peer into Osmond's thoughts, and he knew the man was guilty. Osmond didn't think it was his fault, of course. If the clerk had cooperated faster and gotten the money out, then Osmond wouldn't have gotten annoyed enough to shoot him. And if those two old women hadn't come into the store when they did, well, Osmond had to protect himself, didn't he? It was their fault for interrupting him. Nothing was his fault. His friends had gotten him started on drugs in high school. His local Elven noble had refused to take him as a man-at-arms, so he hadn't been able to find a decent job. It was their fault, all their fault, and everyone was conspiring to screw him over.

The human mind was a sewer, but Osmond's had been worse than most.

Tradition demanded that Osmond be given a chance for last words, and Caulomyth gestured for him to speak. Osmond had been gaunt when Owen had arrested him, but several months without illegal stimulants had filled him out a bit. His eyes still had their manic, sullen gleam, and Owen wasn't surprised when Osmond launched into a torrent of abuse, shouting curses at the families. Not only was he glad that he had killed all three of his victims, he wished he had killed their children and molested the old women first.

One of the sons of the dead women started to step forward, hands balled into fists. Owen had been expecting that, and he caught the man's shoulder, looked into his anguished face.

"Don't worry," said Owen. "It's going to be over soon."

"All right," said Caulomyth. "You're done."

He gestured to the officers assisting him, and they ripped off Osmond's paper jumpsuit, leaving him naked. They wrestled him to the wooden post, punching him in the gut a few times to ensure cooperation, and shackled his arms over his head and his ankles to the bottom of the post, so his face was pressed into the wood.

"Dean Osmond," said Caulomyth, uncoiling the whip from his belt. "You have been sentenced to flogging and execution by a jury of your peers and handed to the officers of Duke Tamirlas for the carrying out of your sentence. The sentence will be delivered now. May God have mercy on your soul."

With that, Caulomyth began flogging Osmond. For the first five strokes or so, Osmond kept screaming curses and threats. By the tenth stroke, he was just screaming. By the twentieth, it was a mixture of howls and sobs. After that, it was just a constant keening sob. When Owen's daughter Sabrina had been four, she had fallen down the stairs and broken her left arm so badly that the bone had torn through the skin. Her cry had sounded like that.

Owen forced the memory aside. He didn't want to think about his family during this.

After the fifty strokes had been delivered, Osmond's back was a bloody ruin of torn skin and muscle. If he didn't die of blood loss in the next hour, infection would probably finish him off, but Osmond didn't have much time left to worry about it. Caulomyth's assistants unshackled Osmond from the post and bound his hands behind his back, ignoring his cries of pain. Another man tied the noose to the wooden arm, and Osmond saw it and started weeping and trying to get away, but the flogging had left him with no strength, and the officers made him stand on a wooden box. With precise, efficient movements, Caulomyth tied the noose around the sobbing Osmond's neck and shoved a black hood over his head.

Then he kicked the box aside, and Osmond was hanged by the neck until dead.

Owen watched the man die. These were always horrible to watch. But what else could have been done? Would it have been better to lock Osmond in a concrete cell for the rest of his life? Owen had done research into judicial punishments for his master's in criminology, and he knew that the pre-Conquest United States had maintained a vast prison system, one that had been rife with abuses and corruption. Would that have been better? Or would it have been more humane to simply shoot Osmond in the head? But Dean Osmond had murdered three innocent people in cold blood without remorse. How much mercy did he deserve?

Owen didn't know, but he was glad when the execution was over.

One of the assistants cut down Osmond's body, and another

produced a hose and began washing the blood and urine down the drain.

Later, once the families had been escorted out, Owen retreated to his office to finish up his paperwork before he went home.

But Lieutenant Kyle Warren was waiting for him.

Warren was the Homicide division's rising star, the most competent detective under Giles's command. He looked like a movie star, with the sort of commanding jaw and strong build that would have gotten him a movie role as a maverick Homeland Security investigator on the trail of Rebel terrorists. Despite that, Warren was well-liked within the Milwaukee branch. Homeland Security, Owen had sourly noted more than once, had "tall poppy" syndrome in spades. Exceptional performers tended to get frozen out lest they make the mediocre lifers look bad. Warren, though, had the rare knack of sharing credit with his partners and subordinates, making sure that everyone involved looked good when he closed a case.

Warren was probably going to go far in politics one day, Owen thought. Maybe he would become governor once old Arnold Brauner finally went to the big dairy farm in the sky. Or maybe sooner – having both of Wisconsin's senators be Brauner's sons would just look bad.

"How'd the execution go, Colonel?" said Warren, straightening up.

"About like you'd expect," said Owen, unlocking his office door. He gestured for Warren to take one of the visitors' chairs and then sat behind his desk. "You here about the Doyle case?"

"Yeah," said Warren. He sighed. "I've got no choice but to pass this one onto the Inquisition."

Owen frowned. "It's that bad?"

Warren nodded. "Ronald Doyle, his wife, and his three children all murdered inside their locked apartment? And not just murdered, but ripped to pieces? Had to be a Shadowlands creature. That means magic, which means I have to pass the case to the Inquisition."

Owen shrugged. "That's what the Inquisition is here to do." Well, that, and keep an eye on the Elven nobles, so they didn't betray the

High Queen. He sighed and tapped a pen against his desk. "I hope they get someone to look into it quick. This kind of thing always starts bad and gets worse."

"The problem is that there are too many people with too many reasons to kill Ronald Doyle," said Warren. He glanced at the office door to the bullpen. "Doyle was one of Governor Arnold's guys, yeah? Brauner doesn't usually kill people who piss him off, but maybe he's branching out. There are a dozen different lawsuits ongoing against Doyle Construction because of defective concrete, and the company is losing money. I'm pretty sure that Doyle himself was having an affair, and not for the first time." He spread his hands. "And that doesn't include the possibility that Doyle was randomly targeted by a leftover Rebel, or this is the start of some sort of incursion from the Shadowlands."

"Let's hope it's not an incursion," said Owen, remembering the Archon attack several years ago. Not that the Archons were a problem any longer, but the High Queen and Elves still had numerous enemies beyond the Shadowlands, which meant that humanity shared those enemies by default. "Until you hear from the Inquisition one way or another, keep working the case. Check out the people who had the strongest motive to see Brauner dead, see if they had any links to someone who could summon Shadowlands creatures."

"That's what I was going to do anyway," said Warren, and he grinned. "But it helps to have permission from someone higher in rank."

"That's what the department is," said Owen. "A mechanism for spreading the blame."

They talked for a few moments longer about the details, and then Warren left to work on his case. Once he passed it to the Inquisition, that would be that. The case was out of their hands, and unless the Inquisition wanted local help, there wasn't anything they could do about it. But perhaps it was just as well. Homeland Security was equipped for a lot of things but fighting things from the Shadowlands wasn't one of them.

Owen spent the rest of the day finishing his recent paperwork, which meant a lot of time typing into the UNICORN database. The Unified National Intelligence Crime Online Reporting Network (the acronym, Owen thought, was proof that government agencies should never name their own projects) was the Homeland Security database, containing case notes and records. It also held records of every United States citizen, holding a wealth of information about their finances, criminal histories, employment histories, and so on. As a colonel, Owen could access most of it, but UNICORN was hosted in the Inquisition's data centers in Utah, which meant certain sections of the database were blocked out to everyone but the Inquisition.

As a shadow agent of the High Queen, Quell had more access than he would have otherwise.

Definitely more than he might have wished.

He finished up his shift and headed home. There had been times in his career when he had put in a lot of eighteen-hour days, but today wasn't one of them. That was just as well. Marriage to a Homeland Security officer was sometimes a challenge, and it had put a lot of strain on Anna, who had done more than her share of the work with the kids and the house. Well, Christmas was coming. Perhaps he would take some time off, and they would go to her sister's house in Cincinnati. He didn't particularly enjoy sleeping in the guest bed, but Anna and the kids always seemed to enjoy the trips. And another year and a half, the twins would be old enough for college, and Owen would see a lot less of them.

He shook off thoughts of work as he fought the rush hour traffic to get home. The downside of finishing his shift at the normal hour – the traffic in downtown Milwaukee was heavy. But it only took him about thirty minutes to get out of downtown and to his house in northern Wauwatosa.

It had started as a four-bedroom house, but Owen and Anna had learned from their experience with the twins that teenage girls got along a lot better when they had their own rooms, so they had added another bedroom. Owen pulled up the driveway and into the two-car garage behind the house. Anna's car was in its place. The old Duluth Motors sedan they had gotten for the twins to use was in the gravel parking spot next to the driveway. More than once, both Sabrina and Katrina had complained about having to clear snow off their car in the morning last winter, but Owen had responded that it built character (which was true), and he also didn't want to chisel ice off his windshield in the morning (which was also true).

He closed the garage behind him and started to walk up the driveway to the kitchen door.

"Colonel Quell? Colonel Quell?"

Owen bit back a sigh. He'd been expecting this.

He turned towards the fence next to the driveway. It wasn't much of a fence – wooden, about five feet tall, designed more for privacy than actual security. Mrs. Cornelia Fischer was just tall enough to look over the fence. Behind Cornelia rose her immaculate house with its white siding and well-trimmed yard. Her husband had been rich, and he had died before Cornelia could get pregnant. That had been thirty years ago, and now Cornelia Fischer had nothing better to do than interfere in other people's business. When a Homeland Security captain had moved in next door, she had been delighted to have an authority figure to whom she could bring all her grievances about the neighbors. Ten years and Owen's promotion to colonel had not changed her.

"Good evening, Mrs. Fischer," said Owen.

She peered at him from behind the fence, a tiny old woman in a housedress and a sweater. "There were four suspicious cars on the street today, Colonel. Four!" She passed him a slip of paper. "I wrote down the license plates."

"I'll look into that," said Owen, tucking the paper into his jacket pocket.

"Also, the Whartons three houses down – you know the Whartons – still haven't raked their leaves. Their house is becoming an eyesore, Colonel, an eyesore. People will think bad things about our neighborhood, think we're elfophobic and support Rebel terrorists."

"Because the leaves haven't been raked," said Owen.

Sarcasm, as ever, bounced off the invincible fortress of Cornelia Fischer's grievances.

"Exactly," said Cornelia, bobbing her head. "You understand."

"Both the Whartons work full-time," said Owen. "Hard jobs, too, utility repair and a nurse. They'll get to it. They always have, haven't they?"

Cornelia gave him a suspicious look, but she nodded. "That's true. I suppose I can be patient." Owen was relieved. Cornelia was an endless source of nuisance calls to Homeland Security. She saw a burglar in every parked car and a potential Rebel terrorist in every stranger who happened to walk his dog past her house. "But you'll check on those license plates, won't you?"

"Of course," said Owen. "But I have to go. I promised Anna I'd be home by 6:30, and I've got only two minutes left."

"Well, then you had better go," said Cornelia, her lips pursed.

Owen bade her a good evening and walked to the back door of his house.

And as he did, he cast a spell.

He felt a little bad about using his aurasight before coming home every night, but not that bad. After the twins hit adolescence, they had started having furious mood swings that sometimes led to bitter fights with each other or their mother. Trying to understand the moods of adolescent girls was difficult enough, and Owen figured he could use every advantage to help maintain familial harmony.

A shiver of pain went through his head as the spell activated, and he swept the aurasight over the house. At once, he saw the emotional auras of his wife and four daughters. Anna was in the kitchen. The twins were in their bedrooms. Antonia and June were in the living room, with Antonia likely helping June with her homework. He didn't see any upheavals in their emotional auras. Anna was concentrating on something. To judge from the intent concentration in their emotional auras, Sabrina and Katrina were texting their friends, or possibly each other. For some reason they liked to communicate through text messages even though their bedrooms were right next to each other. Owen had relented and let the twins get their own cell phones when they turned fourteen, but he had also installed a hidden monitor app that let him read all their messages and monitor their call activity. He felt no guilt about that whatsoever. The girls were impulsive, and a lot of psychos viewed teenage girls as prey.

He had seen that firsthand again and again, often on steel tables at the medical examiner's office.

And somehow, despite that knowledge, he had wound up with four daughters. How had that happened?

Owen unlocked the back door, stepped into the kitchen, and saw the reason he had ended up with four daughters.

Anna was standing at the kitchen counter, humming to herself as she chopped vegetables. Owen's mind flashed to eighteen years ago when they had first met. It had been a murder case, naturally. Anna liked to say that they met on his first case, but that was artistic license. It had actually been his fifth one. The case itself had been open-and-shut. One of the partners at Anna's accounting firm had been having an affair with his secretary, and the secretary had murdered the partner's wife and then the partner. The physical evidence had been overwhelming, and the woman had cracked under interrogation in about five minutes.

But while interviewing witnesses, Owen had met Anna, and his first immediate impression was that she had a nice ass. Once the case was closed, he had set out to seduce her, and somehow, he had been the one who had gotten caught. Not that he minded.

Though it had set his life on what was a dangerous path at times.

Unconsciously, his thumb rubbed the blood ring on his right hand.

"Oh, good, you're home," said Anna. Owen stepped over and gave her a quick kiss. "Listen, do you mind cleaning up after dinner? I've got to finish the paperwork for one client, and I'm chaperoning Antonia's class's trip to the museum tomorrow, so I won't have time in the morning."

"Yeah, no problem," said Owen. "Kids getting along today?"

"Everyone's cheerful," said Anna. "Helps when school tires them all out." She glanced towards the dining room, made sure the girls were out of earshot. "How did the execution go?"

"Messy," admitted Owen. She stopped chopping vegetables to

squeeze his hand. She knew he hated going to the execution. "Nothing went wrong. Osmond, well...he didn't beg. Just screamed a lot."

"He got what he deserved," said Anna. "If someone shot you or shot my mother while she was shopping, I'd watch him die."

His aurasight was still active, and he saw the dark surge that went through her emotions.

"I know," said Owen. "But it's done. Until the next time, anyway."

"Dad?"

He turned his head as his youngest daughter June came into the kitchen. She had changed out of her school uniform and wore a blue T-shirt and jeans. She carried an art project that he was reasonably sure was supposed to represent the house and her family.

"Hi, kiddo," he said, and picked her up and kissed the top of the head.

"Look what I made!" said June, holding out the art project.

"Is that our house?" said Owen.

"It is," said June. She pointed out the various members of the family and repeated the praise her first-grade teacher had given her. He listened to her, nodding gravely, though he couldn't see the resemblance to the stick figures on the page and reality. But she was six, so that didn't matter.

A flicker of old fear went through him. Osmond's victims had simply been going about their day, and they had been killed. It could happen to anyone. Even his family.

It was a reminder that no matter how solidly Owen built the locks on the doors and windows, no matter how secure the panic room in the basement, no matter how carefully he trained his daughters in self-defense and the use of firearms, the world was a dangerous place. Owen had been careful to keep the darkness of his career from touching his family, but he couldn't always protect them.

"Dad?" said June. "You're not listening!"

"I am so listening," said Owen, and he turned his head and cupped a hand to his ear. "See?" The girl giggled.

"You weren't listening when I told you how to do your math

homework," said Antonia, coming into the kitchen with a scowl. Unlike June, she still wore her school uniform – blazer, white dress shirt, a tie, and slacks. Girls had a choice between slacks and skirt for school uniforms, at least in the US, and Antonia always went for slacks. So did Sabrina, though Katrina wore skirts whenever possible and as high as she could get away with, which was concerning.

"I was so listening," said June.

"Well," said Owen, putting her down, "you both can do math homework after you help me set the table."

"Dad," they protested in unison, but they headed to the cabinets and started collecting plates.

With that, Owen tried to put aside the bloody day and focus on his family. You had to appreciate things while they lasted. And not just because of the dangers that lurked beyond his home. Even if everything went well and no misfortunes befell them, someday all four girls would be grown up and out of the house, married with children of their own. In another five or six years, Owen might have a grandchild.

Grandchildren. Now there was a strange thought.

But he hoped, for their sake, that any grandchildren he had did not inherit his magical ability.

Dinner went smoothly enough. Everyone was in good spirits, and nobody fought. There had been times in early adolescence when Sabrina and Katrina couldn't get through five minutes of civil conversation. Though it helped that both girls were tired out from volleyball practice. Sabrina was talking about college applications, which made Katrina glassy-eyed.

After dinner, Anna went to the study to get some work done. She was still an accountant, though usually, she worked from home, getting chunks of work done in bursts between the various obligations of an involved parent. Owen cleaned up the kitchen and washed the dishes (four kids meant that leftovers were a rarity), changed into exercise clothes, and descended into the basement to lift weights. The aging state of his knees meant he didn't run as often as he used to, so he had been replacing it with more strength training, which was probably better for him anyway.

Owen had just finished his second set of bench presses when the blood ring on his right hand shivered, and the High Queen's voice filled his head.

"Owen Quell," said Tarlia. "Tomorrow, you will take over the investigation of the murder of Ronald Doyle and his family. Additionally, unknown forces may be at work behind the murders. I am therefore sending you assistance. Tomorrow morning you will meet another of my agents, a woman named Nadia MacCormac. She will be at your office at 10 AM." That familiar dry note entered her voice. "Likely you will not get along. I suggest, for your sake, you put aside your differences and work together. Find who killed Ronald Doyle and report the details to me."

With that, the contact ended.

Owen sat on the end of the weight bench, breathing hard from the exercise and sudden fear, sweat pouring down his face.

"Shit," he said at last.

He rubbed the blood ring and remembered the day the High Queen Tarlia had given it to him.

∾

OWEN HAD FOUND life in the Wizard's Legion amenable if challenging and would have signed up for a second six-year term of service, but he had instead accepted an honorable discharge after his mandatory tour was complete.

It seemed safer that way.

His growing talent for mind magic had become harder to hide.

The soldiers of the Legion learned to use magic, but the magic of the elements – fire and lightning and ice and earth. In the Shadowlands campaigns, they often acted as artillery, raining destruction on the Elves' foes and supporting the human men-at-arms. Owen had been good with spells of lightning and fire.

But he had been better with spells of the mind.

That was a problem. Humans were absolutely forbidden to learn any spells of mind-alteration or illusion. Owen had wanted to follow that law, but he couldn't help it. The ability just came to him naturally. Some fluke of nature had meant that he was born with magical talent, and his talent tended towards spells of mental magic. He had done his best to suppress it, but towards the end of his term in the Wizard's Legion, he had seen more and more Elven nobles giving him sharp, puzzled looks as if there was something that disturbed them, something about Owen that caught their attention.

It was better to go before they figured out what it was.

He had finished his term in the Wizard's Legion and used his veteran's preferment to join Homeland Security, becoming a detective. After what had happened to his brother Christopher, Owen had wanted to work for law enforcement in some capacity anyway. He had settled into his new role, and then he had met Anna. A year after that, they were married, and a year after that, Anna was pregnant with twins.

The twins had come on time, but they hadn't been healthy.

A problem with their livers. The organs hadn't formed correctly in the womb. A rare, fluke occurrence, but it did happen. Owen had been sitting at Anna's bedside when the doctor explained that the condition only had a twenty percent survivability rate, and they needed to prepare themselves for the worst in the next three days.

Anna broke. Owen had not seen her cry like that before or since, racking, shuddering sobs that sounded like a wounded animal rather than anything human. Owen held her hand and murmured useless words until she had at last fallen into an exhausted sleep. Dazed, he got up and walked to the patient lounge to get a cup of coffee. His mind couldn't process it. They'd bought a house. They'd bought two cribs. Owen had spent every weekend for the last six months getting ready for the babies. Murder cases during the workday, baby prep on his days off.

Maybe he should have been getting ready for the death of his children instead.

He was so distracted that he didn't notice the shocked silence at the nurse's station as he walked past.

"Lieutenant Owen Quell?"

Owen blinked, came to a stop, and finally noticed the Royal Guard standing in front of the nurse's desk.

The Elf was tall and gaunt, with vivid purple eyes, pointed ears, and a shock of gleaming golden hair. The Elven man wore silver armor made of overlapping metal plates that covered his body, and a sword and a pistol hung on the leather belt around his waist. Owen recognized the Royal Guards at once. He had fought alongside them in the Shadowlands campaigns since the High Queen often took direct command of the Wizard's Legion.

"Lord Elf?" said Owen.

The analytical part of his mind, the part of his mind trained by Homeland Security and not currently paralyzed by grief, wondered what the hell a Royal Guard was doing at a hospital in Milwaukee.

"Come with me," said the Royal Guard.

There was no question of disobedience. Owen followed the Guard through the hospital's corridors.

"My wife, Lord Elf," said Owen. "She is very sick. I should be with her when she wakes..."

"She is well-cared for here," said the Guard, "and this will not take very long."

They entered the hospital's administrative wing, the floor carpeted, the walls painted in neutral shades of sea green. The Elf stopped before the door to the office of the Chief of Medicine, knocked twice, and swung it open. Why would the hospital's chief of medicine want to talk to him?

Probably to give him more bad news in person.

Owen followed the Royal Guard into the office and froze.

The office was large, its furniture screaming of sober medical authority, and there were four other people inside. Two were Elven Royal Guards, standing on either side of the massive desk. The third, somewhat incongruously, was a middle-aged human man wearing jeans, work boots, and a denim button-down shirt. He looked like a shop teacher, and there was a nervous expression on his lean face.

Tarlia, High Queen of the Elves, sat behind the desk, watching Owen.

His brain froze up in shock for a moment. He'd seen the High Queen in portraits and news clips all his life and in person several times during the Legion's campaigns in the Shadowlands. Standing up, she would have been seven feet tall, with flame-colored hair and ghostly blue eyes like fire licking the bottom of a copper pan. She wore the armor of a Royal Guard, a crimson cloak, and a simple gold circlet upon her red hair.

For a moment, Owen gaped at her. His reflexes were good in a crisis, but his brain had absorbed one too many shocks today.

"Mr. Quell," murmured Tarlia, her voice soft and musical. "Do close your mouth. This is a hospital."

"Your Majesty," said Owen, and he went to one knee, his brain trying to work through his surprise and grief. The High Queen was sitting in front of him. She had summoned him, personally.

That couldn't be good.

"Have a seat, Mr. Quell," said Tarlia, flicking her hand at one of the guest chairs. She wore rings of gold and silver and steel, each one set with a stone of different color. "It is time for us to have a conversation."

Quell rose and seated himself. The Royal Guards watched him, impassive. The shop teacher tried to give him a reassuring smile and failed abjectly.

"I was disappointed when you left the Wizard's Legion, Mr. Quell," said Tarlia. She opened a folder on the desk and Quell realized it was a personnel file. His, most likely. "You had considerable talent. Why did you leave?"

Owen forced moisture into his mouth. "I wanted to settle down and get married, Your Majesty." He had just lied to the High Queen, to her face. "I wanted to have kids and..." He felt his voice start to break and forced down the emotion. "I wanted to start a family."

"Mr. Quell," said Tarlia, a faint note of disappointment in her voice. "That's a lie, and we both know it. You left because you could no longer suppress your talent for mind magic and it was becoming impossible to hide."

Quell stared at her, the certainty of utter ruination closing around his mind like a fist. In a single day, he was going to lose his daughters and leave his wife a widow.

To his astonishment and mild alarm, he felt himself laughing.

Tarlia raised an eyebrow. "Is something amusing?"

"No, not at all," said Quell, wiping at his eyes and forcing himself back into control. "Well, yes. The doctor just told my wife and me that our babies are going to die in the next three days. Now the High Queen has come here to execute me, personally. Your Majesty…when the shit hits the fan, it just sprays everywhere."

One of the Royal Guards snickered, once. Tarlia shot him a look, and the Elven man's expression returned to impassivity.

"Fortune, alas, is a fickle bitch," said Tarlia. "I believe Job in the Bible had something to say on the topic. But you misunderstand, Mr. Quell. I am a bitch, but I am not a fickle one. I came to Milwaukee to make you a," she paused to think about her words, "a job offer, let us say, but your daughters' illness expedites matters." She gestured at the shop teacher. "This is Mr. Vander. He has a particularly rare magical talent called bloodcasting. I won't waste time with the technical details, but he can heal nearly anything. Including the particular sort of liver deformity afflicting your daughters."

Owen blinked several times. Hope, which had been crushed, flared to new life in his chest.

"He can?" said Owen.

"Yes," said Tarlia. "But Mr. Vander is my liegeman. If I allow him to help you, I'll be doing you a favor. If he heals your daughters, what kind of favor will you do me in turn? You see, you have a set of useful talents, and I need those talents. Ruling both Elves and mankind presents me with endless challenges, and I need capable people to handle those problems. So, to come to the main point, Mr. Quell…if I have your daughters healed, what will you do for me?"

There was a long, long pause.

Owen had heard about this kind of thing, about Elven nobles binding humans to their services through favors. He knew it did not often end well for the humans involved.

But he thought about Anna's broken sobs, about the small, dying bodies shifting in the incubators in the nursery.

There was only one possible answer to that question.

"Anything you want," Owen said.

"That's right," said the High Queen. "You will."

～

But it hadn't been as bad as he feared.

Owen had thought the High Queen would use him as an assassin, or a spy, or for something that would forever scar his conscience. But it wasn't anything like that. She wanted him to do what he was already doing for Homeland Security.

She wanted him to investigate.

Just more thoroughly.

That very day, Mr. Vander healed Sabrina and Katrina. The High Queen also took a sample of Owen's blood, transformed it into a crystal, and set it in a golden ring. That ring, the ring of a shadow agent, let the High Queen communicate with him from any distance. It also allowed him to project an image of her seal, giving him the authority of a Royal Herald, but she emphasized that he was to avoid using it.

Tarlia taught him several spells of mind magic. Aurasight, which let him view the emotional state of those around him. The mind-touch spell, which permitted him to look into the mind of another, though there was always a measure of risk to it. The High Queen arranged his transfer to Special Investigations, and both Tarlia and the Department of Homeland Security used him on the hard cases, the ones that baffled the normal investigators. Owen's abilities with mental magic gave him a powerful advantage. He could look into the mind of a suspect or a witness and know at once whether or not they had committed the crime in question. Then it was a matter of collecting the physical evidence that would gain a conviction before a jury.

Several times Tarlia's staff had Owen flown across the country simply to question someone and find out if they were telling the truth.

Owen kept an uneasy balance between the three sides of his life – his family, his job with Homeland Security, and his role as the High Queen's shadow agent. He had done it for nearly seventeen years, though his jobs for Tarlia had nearly gotten him killed several times, and he had seen more horrors than he cared to recall. The Rebel cell that had nearly bombed a kindergarten in Seattle, for example, or the cult of Dark Ones that had been kidnapping children and sacrificing them to the horrors from beyond the Void.

And the High Queen never gave him easy jobs.

∼

OWEN WAS SITTING on the end of the bench, lost in the dark memories, when Sabrina came downstairs and headed for the washing machine, a basket of laundry on her hip. He suddenly remembered the way she had looked in that incubator as a newborn, hours from death.

"Dad?" said Sabrina, blinking at him. "Is everything all right?"

"Yeah," said Owen. "Do me a favor. Ask your mother to come down here for a second. I have to talk to her."

Sabrina nodded and went upstairs at once. Owen realized that he had been speaking to her in his interrogator's voice, what his kids called his Scary Dad voice. He had only shouted at his children maybe half a dozen times in the last seventeen years. But when he got really angry, or when something was seriously wrong, his voice got deeper, quieter, harder.

Anna came downstairs a moment later.

"What's wrong?" she said, worry in her eyes. "You didn't hurt yourself, did you?"

"No," said Owen. "The High Queen contacted me. She's got a job."

Anna took a deep breath. "When do you leave?"

"I'm not going anywhere," said Owen. "It's the Ronald Doyle case."

Her brows creased. "Ronald Doyle? I know that name, don't I? It's the concrete guy, yeah? The one who's getting sued because his buildings kept falling down."

"Something like that." Owen rubbed his face. "Warren had the case."

"Warren?"

"Oh. Kyle Warren. Giles's star investigator. New kid. I don't think you've met him," said Owen. "Warren thinks Shadowlands creatures killed Doyle and his family. He was about to recommend the Inquisition take the case."

"But the High Queen wants you to take it," said Anna, folding her arms across her stomach. He didn't need to use his aurasight to know that she was frightened.

"Looks like it," said Owen. He had seen lies destroy a lot of marriages during his career, so he hadn't kept anything from Anna during the years they had been married. Owen had told her about his deal with the High Queen, about the blood ring (even though she couldn't see it), and whatever else she wanted to know. And he always told her when he had a case. Though he hadn't volunteered details unless she asked. Like the reeking cellar where the Dark Ones cultists had buried their sacrificial victims. Or the recording of the Rebels giggling about how many kindergartners their bombs would kill, how that would shock the complacent sheep who supported the Elves.

She didn't need to know that. Owen would tell her if she asked, but he wouldn't inflict that on her.

"Okay," said Anna. "I'll tell the girls to be extra cautious. I'll make sure that the security system is working, and that all our guns are ready."

"Thank you," said Owen. "I don't think I'll be alone this time. The High Queen said she was sending someone to help me."

"Oh." Anna smiled, some of the fear lifting from her face. "Someone to watch your back, that's good. Did she say who?"

"Some woman named Nadia MacCormac," said Owen. That sounded familiar, come to think of it. Though he feared she might be one of the High Queen's more dangerous minions. Rulers, Tarlia had told him, had to get their hands dirty. Which meant they needed people of limited conscience to do what needed to be done when the time came.

"And who keeps those people from going over the line?" Owen had said. Even now, seventeen years later, he remained shocked that Tarlia let him speak so frankly to her. But the High Queen grew angry when her retainers prevaricated or told her anything but the truth or their honest opinions.

Tarlia had smiled. "Why, Colonel, you do."

"The Worldburner?" said Anna. "She was the one from New York, wasn't she?"

The memory clicked. Nadia MacCormac, formerly Nadia Moran. She had been the one to stop the Rebels' nuclear bomb during the battle of New York. At the time, there had been speculation that she had been an Inquisition agent, though that had been drowned out a few weeks later with the destruction of the Archons and the announcement of the Day of Return. Now, if Owen remembered correctly, MacCormac owned a fruit company.

A fruit company? Damned odd.

"Guess she's one of the High Queen's agents, then," said Owen.

"Like you," said Anna.

"Yes, like me," he said. Owen had the uneasy feeling that this MacCormac woman was one of the people Tarlia used to do her dirty work. "She's supposed to meet me at my office at 10 tomorrow, and then we'll get started."

He started to stand, but Anna sat next to him on the bench and hugged him. It made him feel better. Owen gripped her hand and squeezed.

"You're going to get your clothes sweaty," said Owen.

"I have to do laundry this week anyway," said Anna.

Owen smiled. "Okay. I had better get started."

Anna didn't stand up. "What are you going to do?"

"Kiss you," said Owen, and he did. "Then I'm going to finish my workout and take a shower. And then I'm going to start reading the case file for Ronald Doyle."

Because the sooner he figured out who had killed Doyle and his family, the better.

He knew from bitter experience that the longer these jobs from Tarlia lasted, the worse they would be.

3
THE BASIC PRINCIPLES OF INVESTIGATION

I was worried that Russell would brood over our deal with Arnold Brauner, but my brother was more resilient than that. Our lawyer reviewed the draft document, said it had no hidden traps or poison provisions, and so we agreed to donate one percent of Moran Imports' profits (net, not gross) to the Brauner Foundation, assuming there were any profits.

At least it would be tax-deductible.

The funny thing was that Russell didn't worry over it at all. He accepted it as one of the costs of doing business and went right back to finishing up his schoolwork and turning the rest of his attention to the company. I focused my attention on Moran Imports, working with Robert to get our shipments out on schedule, and the rest of the time I spent upgrading the security systems at my new house.

But I started to brood over the deal.

I don't know why.

I think part of it was that Riordan was in the UK for Shadow Hunter business. Riordan said that I was one of the few people who could make him laugh, which was nice, but he also did a very good job of keeping my brain on the rails. My brain liked to go off the rails a lot because that locomotive was towing a freight train full of bad memories from the Eternity Crucible, and...

Man, that metaphor sucks.

But I started to get pissed off. Or a sort of black mood chewed at my ever-troublesome brain. I had done some crazy things in my life, faced down some powerful enemies, and I had survived them all. To have to deal with a toad like Brauner began to gnaw at me. Hell, I could have killed him and wiped out his security guards in about five seconds. I didn't want to, but I could have.

Two nights after we signed the deal with Brauner, I had a vicious nightmare about the Eternity Crucible. In it, I fled through the streets of the ghostly small town inside the Crucible, killing wraithwolf after wraithwolf. Finally, they cornered me on the main street and ripped me apart, tearing chunks of flesh from my legs and stomach as I screamed and thrashed and fought.

The nightmare was vivid because I had lived through that exact scenario thousands of times. Well, I say I lived through it, but I died over and over again.

I woke up shaking and covered in sweat and ready to start killing everything in sight. I groped for Riordan's side of the bed, but it was empty. That was right, he was in the UK. He was good at calming me down after a nightmare in a couple different ways, including (I'm a little embarrassed to admit this), using his Shadowmorph to inspire lust in me so I fell asleep after we had worn each other out.

Hey, it worked. And it was really enjoyable besides.

But he was thousands of miles away, and I was alone in our house.

I needed to calm down, so I went to the basement and worked out. We had gotten a home gym and set it up in the basement, and I powered through a set of weights, deadlifts and bench presses and pullups. It was probably stupid to do bench presses without a spotter, but I was in too bad of a mood to care. After I finished the weights, I was drenched with sweat, and my arms and hips felt a little shaky, but I ran six miles on the treadmill anyway, until I was so tired and dehydrated that I started to see spots.

After that, I showered, drank a gallon of water, and managed to sleep for four hours until it was time to go to the warehouse.

I must have looked rough because Robert frowned when I walked into the office.

"You okay?" he said.

"What, do I look like I saw a ghost or something?" I said, dropping into the chair behind my computer.

"You kind of look sick," said Robert.

I did. My little nightmare episodes often left me looking paler than usual, with dark circles under my eyes. I sort of looked like I had the flu.

"I'm fine," I said, unlocking my computer. I left my coat on, which probably didn't help my argument, but I was usually cold and heating this huge drafty warehouse was damned expensive.

Robert gave me a doubtful look but turned his attention back to his computer.

The morning was busy but uneventful. Six trucks arrived at the warehouse, carrying more fruit from Kalvarion, and our crews went to work sorting it and packing it for distribution to our various customers. We were building up a big client list. There was more demand for the fruit than our supply could meet, especially since a big part of it was getting shipped to the cities of the Elven commoners. We didn't have enough warehouse workers to handle the shipments we did have, so Robert and I helped load two of the trucks. My shoulders and hips still ached from my early-morning workout, but I didn't mind. It helped distract me.

Just before noon, Russell called me on my cell phone.

"Central Milwaukee Printer Repair," I said. "You jam it, we'll fix it."

There was a pause.

"That stopped being funny like, five years ago," said Russell.

I laughed. "Then why do I keep doing it?"

"I'm not going to speculate about that," said Russell. "Hey, why don't you come over for dinner tonight? James is grilling steaks."

"Grilling?" I said. "For God's sake. It's November 12th."

"You know James," said Russell. "He'll keep grilling until the snowflakes are literally falling on the grill. I think we're inviting Robert and Alexandra over as well. You're coming?"

I hesitated. I could see what Russell was doing. Robert must have called or texted him to check on me. Russell had then called James and Lucy Marney and probably convinced them to invite Robert and Alexandra. I started to say no, that I had work I wanted to do on the house, but I stopped myself. The house felt too big and empty without Riordan, and I didn't feel like being by myself.

"Yeah," I said. "Sure. Why not? I'll see you at five."

The day passed without incident, and at five PM, I left the warehouse and headed to the Marneys' house.

I took my motorcycle, a black Royal Motors NX-9 sportsbike with orange highlights. It was getting a bit chilly to ride motorcycles, but it hadn't snowed yet, and I intended to use the motorcycle to the last possible moment. Sort of like James and his grill, I suppose. I had taken the bike to the warehouse because I thought it would cheer me up, and by God, it did. I loved motorcycles – the feeling of speed, of power, of freedom. I suppose the feeling was illusory. Then again, I had lot more power, freedom, and money than I had back when I had been stealing things for Lord Morvilind. The downside was that I had to use that power responsibly, which meant not murdering a jackass like Brauner when it was convenient.

Thinking about Brauner pissed me off, so I gunned the throttle and shot through a yellow light before it changed to red, which cheered me right up.

I came to the Marneys' street. It was lined with three-bedroom houses on either side, most of them with small garages and little privacy fences screening the backyard. In summer, the trees growing over the curb tended to create the illusion of driving down a leafy green tunnel. But all the leaves were down, and the barren tree branches were stark against the darkening sky.

I pulled into the Marneys' driveway and shut the bike's engine off. The Marneys' house was like all the others on the street, though I thought the front door and maybe one of the front windows looked crooked. That always bothered me, since I had helped rebuild the front wall after the Archon attack on Milwaukee. Russell's car was in the street, as was Robert's shiny black SUV. (He had explained to me, in copious detail, how he thought an SUV would be safer for his kids in the event of an accident.) I tugged off my helmet, dropped my gloves into it, and let myself inside.

"Nadia!" said Russell from the kitchen.

I grinned and looked around. The Marneys' living room had a pair of large, comfortable couches, one facing the big TV mounted on the wall and the other at a right angle to it. There was a stack of historical adventure novels on the end table next to Russell's preferred spot. Alexandra Ross sat on the couch, holding her year-old son Felix. She was blond and pretty and ridiculously photogenic, and she and Robert had produced an equally photogenic son. Good thing they were both nice people or I would have to hate them for it. Robert sat next to her, one hand resting on her knee.

"Hi, guys," I said, shrugging out of my heavy jacket and putting it and my helmet in the front closet.

"Hey, boss," said Robert. "Want to talk about work for the next three hours?"

"If you want," I said, and then realized that he was joking. "Oh, wait, that would be rude. Sorry, I don't do many parties."

"It's not a party, dear, it's a friendly barbecue," said Lucy Marney, emerging from the kitchen. She was a fit woman in later middle age, with that sort of birdlike quality some women have. Lucy gave me a hug, and then passed me a large travel mug of coffee. "Thought you might like this."

"You're a saint," I said, taking a sip.

"Sorry it's in a travel mug, but we just had the carpet cleaned, and James is paranoid about spills," said Lucy.

"You're a saint," I said again, grinning. "But if you're worried about spills, why did you invite a couple with a one-year-old?" Both Robert and Alexandra laughed at that.

"James and I both work at the hospital," said Lucy, and she patted

Felix's head. "We've both seen much worse than this little champ. Sit down, sit down."

"I'm going to go say hi to James quick," I said.

I walked through the small dining room, which had a portrait of the High Queen and an American flag on the wall. The cold blue eyes of Tarlia seemed to watch me from the picture as I crossed the room, which I'm mostly sure was my imagination. I passed through the kitchen, where I saw a couple of dinner courses in progress, and I reminded myself to return and help Lucy finish preparing dinner. A glass door opened onto the little concrete deck behind the house, and I stepped through it and joined James and Russell.

James Marney, MD, stood before his propane grill, a spatula in hand. I had seen pictures of him as a young man-at-arms, and not to put too fine a point on it, he had been tall, strong, and handsome. Thirty years later, he was still tall and quite strong, but his cane was propped against the side of the house, and he was a bit on the gaunt side. At the moment, he was wearing slacks, a button-down shirt, and a hideous orange apron with the phrase LORD OF THE GRILL in black letters across the front.

Russell stood next to him. They usually grilled together. I'm not sure why it took two of them. Maybe it was a male bonding thing or something.

"Hey," I said, and I gave James a side hug since he was holding a spatula and watching some sizzling steaks. "Thanks for inviting me."

"Figured you'd be bored since Riordan is out of town on business," said James.

I laughed. "I'm never bored."

"You'd sit in the dark and practice spells," said Russell. "Or spend all your time working on renovating your house. There's bored, and then there's bored."

He said it lightly, but I could tell that he was worried. I was touched. After all the things I had done, I didn't deserve people who cared enough to look after me. But I did have them, and they had gone to all the trouble of having a barbecue in November to cheer me up. Even if they did get one of James's delicious steaks out of the deal.

I resolved not to think about Brauner for the rest of the night. Besides, I just had to follow my own damned logic. It was like I had told Russell – our little tussle with Governor Arnold could have been much worse.

It wasn't like anyone had gotten killed or hurt or anything.

I helped Lucy set the table and make salads and rolls, and by then, the steaks had been grilled to satisfaction. We sat down around the table, and James led us in prayer. I was pretty sure Robert and Alexandra were Catholic, but then the dinner prayer didn't say anything positive or negative about the pope, so that was all right. My own relationship with God was a mixture of belligerence and wary gratitude. If God was good, then why was the world so screwed up? Then again, a couple of times in very dark places I had prayed out of desperation, and things had gotten better after. And I had been going to church with Riordan because he liked going to church and it seemed odd to make him go alone, so maybe some of it was wearing off on me.

Russell and Robert did most of the talking, describing Moran Imports in glowing terms. I contributed comments when necessary. Halfway through dinner, Alexandra got up to feed and change Felix. I wondered if it was weird for Lucy to host a pregnant woman with a small child for dinner, since she couldn't have kids herself. Then again, she was an ER nurse, so she had probably seen like a billion pregnant women in various stages of distress. Given all the myriad ways a pregnancy could go wrong, maybe she was grateful to be spared the experience. I didn't particularly want kids, and given that Riordan was a Shadow Hunter and how the regeneration spell had messed with me, we probably weren't going to have them. I mean, I'd do the best I could if it did happen, but I wasn't disappointed by the lack of kids.

Robert and Alexandra would have been, though. And I think Russell would be, too. Maybe in a few years, he would get married and have some kids of his own.

I could be crazy Aunt Nadia.

Now there was a disturbing thought.

After dinner, we had dessert – apple crumble and ice cream. I was in a good mood, so I ate more than I usually did, and I didn't have any nausea, and dinner stayed down. That was a nice surprise. Because of the frequent bouts of nausea, I sometimes skipped eating until I got light-headed. Riordan had told me, as tactfully as he could manage, that low blood sugar did not improve my overall temperament.

Once we were finished, Lucy, Russell, and I washed up the dishes and put the leftovers away (not that there were many) and James, Robert, and Alexandra retreated to the living room. I didn't think the Rosses would stay late since no doubt Felix had an early bedtime.

We had just finished in the kitchen. Russell sat in his usual spot next to his stack of paperback books, and I was going to sit next to Alexandra, who was holding Felix. Hopefully, the kid wouldn't throw up on my lap or anything. I'd saved his life, so it would be really ungrateful of him to puke on me, but babies have no sense of gratitude.

I was about three steps from the couch when the blood ring on my right hand went cold, and the voice of the High Queen filled my head.

"Nadia MacCormac," said Tarlia inside my skull. "Tomorrow you will go to Homeland Security's Central Milwaukee Office and meet Colonel Owen Quell. Be there by 10 AM. You will work with him to find the killer of Ronald Doyle and his family. He is another of my agents, and together you will find Doyle's killer." A note of amusement entered her voice. "Do try to get along with him." The amusement faded. "Be wary. There is something unusual about Doyle's death. If there is a threat to my rule behind his murder, I wish it stopped sooner rather than later."

The mental contact ended.

"Nadia?" said Russell.

I blinked and realized that I had stopped in the middle of the living room.

"You okay?" said James.

I was standing in front of the TV and had blocked the football game.

"I'm good," I said, which wasn't true. "I'm just going to step outside and text Riordan. Get some fresh air."

With that, I snagged my coat from the front closet, shrugged into it, and walked through the kitchen and onto the patio. It had gotten cold out, well below freezing, and the chill hit me like a slap. That was good. It helped me focus, helped me concentrate on the problem at hand.

Because I did have a problem. The High Queen wanted me to solve another murder? Damn it. The last time I had solved a murder for her, I had wound up riding a dragon over New York as we chased an enslaved cyborg and his traitorous controller.

But she wanted me to work with a Homeland Security colonel? I didn't like that thought.

Wait. Owen Quell. I had heard that name somewhere before, hadn't I? I fished out my phone since I was supposed to be texting Riordan anyway, and I did a search for Owen Quell. There were a bunch of hits. The top one was his directory page on Homeland Security's Milwaukee branch website. Wasn't much information there – Colonel Owen Quell, head of Special Investigations, office number and phone number, which was just the main desk number for the Central Office. But some of the other hits were for bookstores, and I pulled them up.

Then I remembered where I had heard of Quell. When I had been a teenager, spending half my time learning from Morvilind's retainers and the other half stealing things, Quell had written a book called *The Basic Principles Of Investigation*. It had become the standard manual for Homeland Security detectives and was used in some other countries. Morvilind's retainers had insisted I read it to learn about Homeland Security procedures so I could evade the law, and I had. I had learned so much about Homeland Security procedure and technique that I probably knew more than most low-level officers.

I'll say this for Morvilind. When he made me his shadow agent, he trained me thoroughly. He wanted a return on his investment.

I pushed aside the memory as another thought occurred to me. Ronald Doyle? That was the concrete guy, wasn't he? The one Arnold

Brauner wanted us to use for the warehouse expansion? I searched the news sites and found a story from two days ago. Ronald Doyle, local construction magnate, his wife, and his three children had all been found dead under suspicious circumstances. Homeland Security was investigating…

The door slid open, and Russell stepped onto the patio with me.

"Hey," he said, closing the door. "You okay? You had a really weird look on your face."

"What, like this?" I said, and I closed one eye and stuck out my tongue at him.

Russell laughed. "Not like that." He sobered. "Like something was wrong."

"I don't know yet," I said. "The High Queen has a job for me." After the battle of New York, I had decided that I would be completely honest with two people in my life. Russell, because I hadn't told him the entire truth and he had nearly gotten killed searching for me. And Riordan, because we had gotten married and he had gone to insane lengths to save my life.

"Uh oh," said Russell. "What is it?"

"Tomorrow I'm supposed to go to Homeland Security and work with another shadow agent to solve the murder of a guy named Ronald Doyle."

Russell frowned. "Doyle? Isn't that the construction guy? The one Brauner wanted us to use?"

"Yeah," I said. I turned my phone towards Russell so he could see the news story. "Says he died in 'suspicious circumstances' two days ago, Homeland Security is investigating, no details released to the public at this time, blah blah blah. That could mean anything from a murder-suicide to a gas leak in their house."

"The High Queen wouldn't send you to investigate a gas leak," said Russell.

"She would if someone deliberately caused the gas leak," I said. Russell nodded to concede the point. "Still. I wonder why she cares."

"Yeah," said Russell. "I mean, she's got two worlds to rule, right? Earth and now Kalvarion. People get murdered every day, which is sad, but that's just the way it is. Why does she care about one murder in Milwaukee?"

"Well," I said, thinking it over. "Milwaukee's the city right next to the Great Gate to Kalvarion." I waved my hand to the west.

"West is actually that way," said Russell, pointing.

"You know what I mean," I said. "Maybe it's significant. Maybe Doyle was a Dark Ones cultist. Maybe he was a leftover Rebel, I've run into a few of those." I shrugged. "Suppose I'll have to find out tomorrow."

Russell hesitated. "You'll be okay?"

"Don't see why not," I said.

"You don't really like Homeland Security," said Russell.

"No one likes Homeland Security," I said. "They're a collection of thugs, incompetents, and timeservers. But I can pretend to be civil... don't give me that look. I can totally pretend to be civil."

Russell thought about that.

"Well...yes," he said at last.

He was a terrible liar.

I made a face. "See, you're not very good at pretending to be civil."

"Do you need any help?" said Russell.

"I don't think so," I said. "I mean, it doesn't sound that complicated. I'm supposed to go meet Quell and help him figure out who killed Doyle and why."

Except there were always, always, always hidden depths to the High Queen's missions. Two months ago, in New York, she had told me to find the murderer of an art dealer, which had seemed a pretty trivial problem for her to worry about. Except the art dealer had actually been a disguised dragon. And he had been murdered by a cyborg created by the mad science of the Catalyst Corporation, which was apparently being used by a terrorist organization or individual called the Singularity.

Yeah. There would be more here than met the eye.

"Well, Robert and I can look after the company," said Russell. "I'm almost done with all my exams anyway. Just have to study for a few more, and I'll officially be a high school graduate."

"Great," I said. "Besides, it's your company. I just own some shares, and I'm helping manage it until you're done with school. And Riordan should be back from the UK soon." Just thinking about that cheered me up. "If I run into trouble, I'll ask him for help."

"He's probably better at providing help for this sort of thing than I am," said Russell.

"I don't know," I said. "You did pretty well against the Rebels." But I was being nice. Russell kept his head in a crisis, but Riordan had been a Shadow Hunter for decades.

"Hey, are you cold?" said Russell.

"Freezing. Want to go back inside?"

"Very much so," said Russell.

"Hey," I said. "Thanks for worrying."

Russell grinned. "You're a worrying sort of person."

I rolled my eyes. "Yeah, thanks so much."

He wasn't wrong, though.

We went back inside and sat on the couches. James, Robert, and Russell turned their attention to the football game. Alexandra was also a major football fan. To my complete lack of surprise, she had been a football cheerleader in high school and college and retained enjoyment of the game into adulthood. Lucy read the news or maybe a novel on her tablet, and I produced my phone and started researching.

I looked at Ronald Doyle first, picking up what I could from the news reports. Usually, the news was about as reliable as a stuck clock, but there was a lot about Doyle. His company specialized in construction and concrete, and he was in the middle of a bunch of lawsuits because one of his crappy buildings fell down and killed some people. There was even speculation he would be liable for criminal prosecution, though I bet Brauner shielded him from that.

Had Brauner ordered Doyle killed? I really doubted it. That wasn't Brauner's style. If he'd wanted to get rid of Doyle, he'd withdraw his protection and let Doyle's various problems eat him alive.

I switched gears and started looking up Owen Quell. He appeared in a lot of stories – usually as the investigating officer in various criminal cases. Quell seemed to get a lot of high profile investigations. Which made sense. If he was a shadow agent of the High Queen, then Tarlia wouldn't give him the easy jobs.

Pity she hadn't sent him to investigate Max Sarkany's murder. I might have avoided a lot of trouble. Then again, I had gotten a new house out of it.

I logged into UNICORN and did a search for cases related to Quell. I had gotten high-level UNICORN access when Tarlia had sent me to find Malthraxivorn's killer. That had proven useful. In the old days, working for Morvilind, I had to gather information surreptitiously and carefully. Now I had official access to enormous amounts of government data. There were advantages to working for the High Queen.

After I entered the query, I thought my phone had frozen up, but there were so many results the phone had locked for a few moments while Quell's list of cases loaded. The man had worked a lot of different investigations, and he had an amazingly high closure and a conviction rate. I wondered how he had managed that. Maybe he was the sort of Homeland Security officer who manufactured evidence and railroaded innocent suspects. Tarlia didn't care much how the sausage got made.

I didn't like Quell already.

Regardless, I was going to have to work with him.

I sighed. Tomorrow promised to be an interesting day.

4

THE DEPARTMENT

I slept in a bit late the next morning since I didn't need to be at the Central Office until ten and I had been putting in a lot of early mornings and late nights at Moran Imports while Riordan was gone.

After I had solved her uncle's murder, Della Sarkany had given me a house to express her gratitude. Which was a bit much, I thought, but Riordan and I had needed a place to live in Milwaukee, and anyway it's churlish to refuse a gift. It was a big place, four bedrooms with a two-car garage and a long driveway since the lot was an acre and a half. It had come with a decent security system, which I had been steadily upgrading since. All the windows had wire frames running through them, making them much harder to break. The doors had steel cores with reinforced frames and multiple deadbolts. Motion-triggered security cameras covered the driveway and all the approaches to the house, along with floodlights. I could access the camera feeds from anywhere in the house so long as I had a device on the local network. In case someone tried to cut the power, there was a backup generator in a locked shed behind the garage.

Naturally, we also had a lot of guns secured in a pair of safes in the basement, and I kept handguns hidden in our bedroom and in the living room.

All this might seem excessive, but I had pissed off a lot of powerful people during my career as a shadow agent for Morvilind and Tarlia. Granted, a lot of those powerful people had gotten killed during the Sky Hammer battle and the Mage Fall, but still. And the security would be useful against non-magical threats, like Arnold Brauner and his goons if he decided to blame me for Doyle's death.

Or from someone like Colonel Owen Quell, if he turned out to be an asshole.

Because I was pretty sure he was going to be an asshole. You didn't get high rank in Homeland Security without that particular quality.

After I woke up, I exercised. We'd set up our gym in the basement, so I powered through some weight sets and then did a run. I showered off and got dressed – black jeans, gray sweater, black work boots with steel toes, and my black navy pea coat that had enough room to conceal a shoulder holster. I didn't don a holster, though. The Central Office had weapons detectors at the door. That didn't mean I couldn't get a weapon into the building, but if I had to work with this Quell guy, best to start things off without antagonism.

The weather forecast showed a chance of snow, and I didn't want to attempt that in my motorcycle. I suppose it was time to concede defeat and stow the bike for the winter, and I decided to do that after I finished dealing with this Doyle thing. Instead, I took my old, reliable Duluth Motors sedan, after I loaded some guns and other supplies into the trunk. Just in case.

I had taken this car to the meeting with Brauner.

Was Doyle's murder involved with Arnold Brauner somehow? It was possible. The Brauner family had a lot of enemies, and Doyle had been one of Governor Arnold's most loyal supporters. Then again, Doyle had been his own man, and a couple of people had been killed in the building collapse that had been traced back to his crappy concrete. Maybe one of the families had taken vengeance.

But the High Queen wouldn't send me to investigate a normal

murder. She definitely wouldn't send two shadow agents. No, I was sure that something weird was going on. But I couldn't make any assumptions until I had seen things with my own eyes.

My mouth twisted.

That was an entire chapter in Quell's book, I remembered – the danger of an investigator making assumptions before reviewing the evidence and the facts. Good advice for a Homeland Security investigator, I supposed. And, as it turns out, excellent advice for a thief.

I left Brookfield and drove downtown. It was past rush hour, so I missed the worst of the traffic, but there were still a lot of cars on the road, and progress was slow. To my annoyance, I felt a growing sense of unease. All my life, I had avoided Homeland Security, fearful of what would happen to me if I got caught – and terrified that Morvilind would stop the cure spells and let Russell die of frostfever. Now Russell was cured, and I probably had more authority to act as I saw fit than any Homeland Security officer or investigator. There was no rational reason for me to be uneasy and tense.

But, that's the thing about emotions. Sometimes they just don't make sense.

I was already in a bad mood by the time I reached the Central Office.

I arrived a half-hour early and drove around the block. The Central Office of the Milwaukee branch of Homeland Security was a massive ugly cube of a concrete building perched on the eastern side of I-43. It had been built of the site of the pre-Conquest Milwaukee County Courthouse (a historical nugget the website cheerfully informed you of, as if it mattered), and the building had all the charm of a cinder block. Probably by design, I supposed. I didn't see anything amiss, though this was the least likely place in Milwaukee for someone to make trouble.

There was a parking ramp a block away, so I pulled into it, paid too damn much for parking, and stashed my car on the second-highest level. That way, if it did wind up snowing, I wouldn't have to brush off the windshield. I got out of the car and hesitated, staring at the trunk. The need to bring a gun with me was so intense that it almost felt like an itch. But I didn't want to start trouble, not unless Quell started it first, and carrying a firearm into a Homeland Security office was asking for a mountain of trouble.

Besides, if there was trouble, my magic would make a better weapon than a pistol.

I took a deep breath, telling myself to suck it up, and left the parking ramp. A cold wind lashed at me as I headed down the sidewalk, and I tugged my coat tighter around myself and thrust my hands into my pockets, even though I was wearing gloves. I had problems with cold. My subconscious defaulted to holding my magical power ready, which had the annoying side effect of draining off my body heat. When I was calm and relaxed, I could make my subconscious release my power, but right now, both my conscious and subconscious mind expected big trouble.

I walked up the front steps to the Central Office. Out of habit, I double-checked that I was wearing gloves. I didn't want to leave any fingerprints in the building, even if I was here legitimately. Old habit – and I could thank Homeland Security for that.

The lobby was a rectangular space with a polished floor and harsh fluorescent lights overhead. On the wall were portraits of the High Queen and Duke Tamirlas of Milwaukee, looking solemn. On another wall were long rows of polished brass plaques holding names – Milwaukee branch Homeland Security officers who had fallen in the line of duty. On the far wall, over the elevators and the doors to the stairs, was a giant painting of the Homeland Security shield with the words PROTECT AND SERVE beneath it.

Protect and serve. Yeah. Sure.

Four metal detectors and weapons scanners blocked the front of the lobby, manned by a pair of officers in blue uniforms. Visitors would have to sign in and get a special badge before they went further. I walked towards the scanners, and one of the two officers did a double-take and stepped towards me. A big guy, young and fit, with close-cropped hair and hard eyes, and the nameplate on his uniform below his badge read KIRBY...

Ah, shit. He was one of the two officers who had been hassling Jake Boyer.

"Ma'am, I'm going to need you to stop right there," said Kirby.

I stopped and waited. Kirby remembered me. I could see the malice in his eyes.

"What is the purpose of your visit to the Central Office today?" said Kirby.

"I have an appointment with Colonel Owen Quell at 10 AM," I said. A flicker of distaste went over Kirby's face. Guess he knew Quell.

"And what is the purpose of your visit, Mrs. MacCormac?" said Kirby.

"I don't know," I said. "Quell didn't tell me. You want to call up and ask him?"

His expression went stone cold. "You've been flagged as a suspicious person. Come with me now to submit to an enhanced search."

A tide of rage rose up in my throat. I remembered all the times I had lied to Homeland Security officers, knowing that if I screwed up, I would end up on a Punishment Day video and Russell would die of frostfever. These stupid time-serving thugs with badges had given me trouble for all my life, and now this idiot was hassling me just out of spite.

Except I didn't have to put up with it.

I badly, badly wanted to use my blood ring to summon Tarlia's seal, but the High Queen would not like that. Instead, I grinned my humorless rictus of a grin.

"Changed my mind," I said. "Bye."

I turned and walked back out the doors.

If he came after me, I decided, I would hurt him. Wait until he grabbed me on the stairs, then I would use a gauntlet of telekinetic force to break his arm or leg. To the camera mounted over the doors, it would look like he had slipped and fallen on the stone steps. After all, a woman my size couldn't physically threaten a guy as big as Kirby.

But he didn't follow me, and the second I was out of sight of the cameras, I cast the Cloak spell.

Invisible, I turned and ran back up the stairs and caught the heavy door before it closed. I slipped inside and saw Kirby arguing with the other officer manning the checkpoint. Evidently, the second officer wondered why Kirby had been giving me a hard time. I ignored them both and walked through the weapons scanner. It should have picked up the steel toes in my boots, but the Cloak spell protected me. I crossed the lobby, came to the elevators, and scrutinized the directory mounted on the wall. Quell was head of Special Investigations, and his office was off the Homicide department on the second-highest floor of the building.

I took the stairs, keeping my Cloak spell in place. I passed perhaps a dozen Homeland Security officers and civilian workers, no doubt on their way to plant evidence, harass suspects, and frame innocent people for Punishment Day videos. Okay, that probably wasn't fair, but I wasn't in a good mood. I did pass several women, both uniformed officers and civilian workers. In the old days after the Conquest, Homeland Security had been entirely male. The High Queen's view was that human women in general ought to be focused on producing and raising the next generation of her soldiers and workers, not spending their fertile years on careers. Except there had been a massive scandal when it turned out that some officers had been systematically abusing female prisoners before Punishment Day videos, so Homeland Security had been reformed to include female officers in various roles.

The recollection of this fact did not improve my mood.

I reached the Homicide department, which was a large room filled with low cubicles and desks. The door was locked, and I didn't want to lower my Cloak spell to unlock it, so I waited until someone went inside and I followed them. The room smelled of disinfectant and bad coffee. Detectives in either uniform or plainclothes sat at their desks, doing paperwork or talking on their phones. Working for Homeland Security involved a lot of paperwork, and I saw the

UNICORN interface open on every computer screen. Doors lined the room since higher-ranking officers got their own workspace.

I followed the wall until I came to the office of Colonel Owen Quell.

The door was partly open, and Quell sat at his desk, a UNICORN file open on his screen and a printed case file spread next to his keyboard. I'd seen his official picture on the Homeland Security website, and he looked...rougher in person. I could tell that his nose had been broken a few times, and there was an old, vicious-looking scar on the right side of his face. Quell was a big guy who looked like he had just started running to fat, but he was probably in good shape, especially for his age. He had deep, heavy-lidded dark eyes and black hair that was well on its way to gray.

There was a wedding ring on his left hand and the blood ring of a shadow agent of the High Queen on his right.

I felt a faint magical aura around him. He was a wizard. I hadn't expected that since none of the information I'd found about him had mentioned that he had been part of the Wizard's Legion. But former members of the Wizard's Legion tended not to advertise the fact on the Internet.

I wasn't sure what to make of him, at least not yet. My initial impression was that he was another dumb thug, Office Kirby in another twenty years, who had played the internal politics of Homeland Security well enough to reach the rank of colonel. He probably watched Punishment Day videos for entertainment. Then again, he could use magic, and I could not see Tarlia recruiting an incompetent shadow agent. If she wanted a dumb thug, they were as common as dirt among both humans and Elves.

Well, I could stand here speculating all day, and it wouldn't accomplish a damn thing.

First impressions are important, and I decide to make a lasting one on Colonel Owen Quell.

His office door was half-open, and I eased through it. Then I settled into one of the guest chairs in front of his desk. The office was small enough that I could reach the door handle. I gave it a sharp jerk, and the door slammed shut.

Quell's eyes snapped up from his computer in surprise, and I dropped my Cloak spell, resting my head against my right hand so he could see the blood ring.

"So," I said. "Seems like our boss wants us to work together."

5

SHADOW AGENTS

The office door slammed, and Owen Quell looked up in annoyance. If someone wanted to talk to him, they should have knocked first...

Then he saw the woman sitting in his guest chair.

Owen had been absorbed in the Doyle case file, reading the grisly details, but he had been in Homeland Security for a long time, and his guard never went down completely. There was no way the woman could have gotten into his office without him hearing it, especially since she was wearing heavy steel-toed boots. For that matter, she was a civilian, and she didn't have a guest pass. If she had come through the front door, they would have questioned her, given her a pass, and called up to let him know he had a visitor.

His hand had started to slide towards his holstered pistol when he saw the ring on her right hand. It was a heavy gold band set with a red gemstone that looked like a ruby but wasn't, and Owen recognized it at once. It was the ring of a shadow agent of the High Queen of the Elves.

Which, now that he thought about it, explained how she had gotten into his office without anyone seeing her.

"So," said Owen. "I assume you must be Nadia MacCormac?"

"Yep," said Nadia, watching him.

Owen looked at her, years of experience in detective work noting details.

She was short, slim, and pretty. Fit, too, to judge from the veins Owen saw on the back of her hands. Probably lifted a lot of weights. Had he been unmarried and twenty years younger (okay, ten years) he probably would have tried to get her into bed. She wore a heavy pea coat and black jeans, the coat loose enough to conceal a weapon, though the jeans definitely were not. Her brown hair had been pulled in a loose tail, and her gray eyes were flat and hostile as they watched him.

They were a killer's eyes.

The idea that you could judge someone's character by looking into their eyes was, of course, total bullshit. Owen had interrogated killers and con men who radiated sincerity. Yet there was a kernel of truth to it. The subconscious mind, the instincts, often knew when someone was dangerous, and the conscious mind chose to interpret that as someone having "dangerous eyes" or a "killer's eyes" or something.

And all of Owen's instincts and experience screamed that this woman was dangerous.

With an effort of will, he worked the aurasight spell.

At once, he saw that his instincts were correct. Nadia's emotional aura did not look at all like that of a normal, healthy human woman. For one thing, it was charged with power. She had more raw magical strength that any human Owen had ever met and quite a few Elven nobles. Nadia clearly found Owen suspicious as well. Her aura seethed with dislike and wariness and something like old hatred. There was something more, though, a distortion in her aura that he associated with long-term persistent trauma.

He realized that Nadia was probably one of the High Queen's pet killers. As much as Owen believed in the value of his work, he didn't look at the High Queen with rose-colored glasses. Ruling two worlds was a nasty, dangerous business, and sometimes Tarlia got her hands dirty. Or she sent someone to do it for her. Likely Nadia MacCormac was such a woman, a woman who had left a trail of broken and ruined lives behind her, people who had wept the way the families of Dean Osmond's victims had wept.

Maybe she was someone like Peter Walsh.

She had stopped the Rebels in New York, he knew. But he suspected that she had worked with the Rebels and likely helped them locate the Sky Hammer weapon. Which meant that Nadia MacCormac was a Rebel terrorist who had managed to secure a pardon for herself by betraying the other Rebels. He wondered how many of Nadia's victims would never know justice.

"What are you doing?" said Nadia with a frown.

She sensed the aurasight? She shouldn't have been able to do that. But if she was as powerful as he suspected, she might have been able to sense the spell. Nadia gestured with her left hand, and there was a pulse of gray light around her fingers. The spell to sense the presence of magic, he thought.

"Ah," she said, settling back in the chair. "Some sort of emotional sensing spell, isn't it? Bet you're picking up all sort of interesting things from me. That kind of thing is illegal for humans, but I think that's why the High Queen recruited you. Someone realized you could use mind magic, and instead of executing you, she made you a job offer."

"Something like that," said Owen. She was very quick on the uptake.

"Bet it's real useful in Homeland Security," said Nadia. The dislike in her aura strengthened. "Can't solve a crime, so hey, just grab someone off the street, use the mindtouch spell to magically compel him into confessing, and then you're hitting your Punishment Day video quota for the month. Then it's time to kick back and have some coffee and doughnuts."

"We don't have quotas," said Owen. She was deliberately trying to irritate him, seeing how he would react. If he had to guess, he would say she could use mental magic or illusion magic, which explained how she had gotten into his office without anyone seeing her. If she hadn't been a Rebel, then she was probably a former thief the High Queen had recruited, maybe a shadow agent she had poached from another noble. That would explain why Nadia hated Homeland Security so much. Those who had spent their lives running from the law tended not to enjoy the company of law enforcement officers.

He wondered how many crimes Nadia had committed, how many people she had murdered before Tarlia had recruited her. Owen had tried to do some research on Nadia, but her UNICORN entries were suspiciously empty or under heavy lock. Only the highest levels of the Inquisition would have the clearance to view her information.

Then the horrors in the Doyle case file had absorbed his attention, preventing him from doing more than cursory research on Nadia MacCormac.

"Sure you don't," said Nadia. "Just a word of warning. If you do have the mindtouch spell, don't look into my thoughts. Seriously, don't." The emotion drained out of her face, but the sense of trauma in her aura intensified. "It won't be good for you." She smirked. "But I bet you won't be able to stop yourself. If there's one thing a Homeland Security officer can't resist, it's planting evidence and breaking the law."

To his annoyance, he felt a pulse of irritation. Nadia was trying to get under his skin, and it was starting to work. Well, two could play at that game. He had spent nearly twenty years listening to Anna complain about her coworkers (especially the other women in her office), and he remembered one of her pet peeves.

"We're going to have to work together, so we might as well get started," said Owen. He nodded at the coffee maker on top of his file cabinet. "Why don't you make us some coffee? Then you can take notes."

She grinned at him. It wasn't really a smile, though, more of a rictus that showed a lot of teeth, almost a snarl. "Why don't you get off your ass and get your own coffee?" She paused. "You could probably use the exercise."

Ouch. He'd lost that one, hadn't he?

Owen snorted in amusement, got to his feet, and walked around the desk. Nadia watched as if expecting him to attack. "All right. We don't like each other, that's obvious." He took a mug and poured coffee into it, steam rising from the black liquid. "But we're going to have to work together. I don't think our boss will like it if we screw this up because we were too busy insulting each other."

"She would not," said Nadia, still watching him. She looked relaxed, but he could tell she was wound tight.

"No," said Owen, and he passed her the cup of coffee.

Nadia looked at the coffee, and him, and then back at the coffee as if she expected it to explode.

"It's coffee," said Owen. "You do drink coffee, right?"

She seemed to come to a decision, and some of the tension in her emotional aura receded, though didn't vanish entirely.

"Yes," said Nadia, and she took the cup. "Thank you."

"You are welcome," said Owen, and he poured himself a cup. He would have to remember to make more before they left. He thought about leaning on his desk, but then realized he would tower over her, so he walked around and sat back at his chair. "Did the High Queen tell you what she wants us to do?"

"Yeah," said Nadia. She sipped at the coffee. "She wants us to find who killed Ronald Doyle."

"You know who he is?" said Owen.

"Property developer," said Nadia. "Construction guy. Owns a company that made a bunch of defective concrete, and he's getting sued for it. Or he was, anyway. He's in tight with Governor Arnold and the Brauners, and they've been covering for him." Her mouth twisted. "Suppose that won't be a problem for the Brauner family anymore."

"No," said Owen. She knew that the Brauners were crooked, which would save time. Then again, if she was a shadow agent and had lived in Wisconsin for any length of time, it was easy to realize that the virtuous patriotic image the Brauner clan presented to the world wasn't entirely accurate. "Did she tell you any details?"

"No," said Nadia. "She just told me to show up here, so I did. Early, I might add." Her mouth twisted. "I figured there was no point in digging up details since you people were going to do that all anyway."

"All right," said Owen. "So, here are the details. Three days ago, Ronald Doyle, his wife, and their three children were all found dead in their condo in downtown Milwaukee."

"How did they die?" said Nadia.

"They were torn apart," said Owen. "Which is how the bodies were discovered, incidentally. Some of the blood began leaking out beneath the door and into the hallway. One of the neighbors called it in. The responding officers had probable cause to enter the residence, so they did, and they found the bodies. See what you think for yourself."

He reached into the printed file and drew out the crime scene photos and autopsy reports.

"I should warn you," said Owen, "these will be disturbing."

"Yup," said Nadia indifferently. She stood, dragged his guest chair closer to the desk, and then sat back down, setting her coffee mug next to his business cards.

Owen passed her the photos, and Nadia flicked through them. He had seen a lot of violent death over the years, but what had happened to the Doyles had been particularly bad. Especially since the oldest of their children had only been twelve. One of the responding officers, a veteran of fifteen years, had gone outside and thrown up. People responded to violent death in many different ways, and he was curious to see how this arrogant, unstable woman would react.

Nadia's expression did not change as she looked at the mortal remains of Ronald and Josephine Doyle. She even took another sip of coffee. Her expression remained unchanged as she looked at the pictures of Doyle's kids, but her emotional aura altered, began to roil with anger.

To put it more bluntly, she was pissed off.

"Wraithwolves," said Nadia, arranging the photos back into an orderly stack.

"You think so?" said Owen.

"I know so," said Nadia. She started to hand the photos back to him, thought better of it, and flipped through them again. "Look. Here and here. You see this wound on Josephine Doyle's leg? That's a wraithwolf bite mark. And the cuts across Ronald Doyle's chest? Wraithwolf claws. It was trying to disembowel him. Looks like it succeeded on the third try or so."

"Bad way to die," said Owen.

For an instant, her emotional aura turned entirely black.

"Yes," said Nadia. She set the photos back on his desk, and Owen returned them to the file.

"As it happens, the medical examiner agrees with you," said Owen. "So did Kyle Warren, the chief investigator on the case. Which meant the case would get passed over to the Inquisition…"

"And then Tarlia started talking inside your head," said Nadia.

"Yeah," said Owen. He dismissed his aurasight. Using it too long drained his strength and gave him a headache, and watching the roiling mixture of rage and dislike in Nadia MacCormac's aura was disturbing. "This is already an unusual case, but if Tarlia is giving it to people like us, that means something exceptionally unusual is going on."

"Okay," said Nadia. She took another drink of coffee and rubbed her forehead. "As far as I can tell, there are four possibilities."

"Go on," said Owen, curious on what she had deduced.

"One, the Doyles were killed by a stray pack of wraithwolves that slipped in from the Shadowlands. Rare, but it happens. Two, someone in the Doyle family tried to summon wraithwolves, screwed it up, and got everyone killed. Three, someone else summoned the wraithwolves and sent them after the Doyle family. Four, something strange we don't know is going on. Can't make any assumptions." Her mouth twisted halfway between a smirk and a grimace. "Isn't that what like half of your book is about?"

"You read my book," said Owen. Ever since it had become the textbook for Homeland Security's investigative training course, he received no end of complaints and ribbing about it from other officers. Still, the royalties were nice, especially after Anna had gotten unexpectedly pregnant with June.

"Yeah, I was forced to," said Nadia. "It helps with insomnia." He snorted. "Still, I remember some of it. But four possibilities. Random wraithwolf pack, one of the Doyles was a summoner, someone else summoned the wraithwolves, or something weird is going on."

"It's possible the wraithwolves slipped through from the Shadowlands," said Owen. "Incursions from Shadowlands creatures have been happening more frequently in the last few months."

"I'd heard that."

"But the Doyles' condo was on one of the upper floors of their building in downtown Milwaukee," said Owen. "If wraithwolves were going to attack random victims, there were easier targets closer at hand."

"What time were they killed?"

Owen checked the file, even though he already knew the details. "Sometime between 6 PM and 9 PM. The neighbor saw the blood leaking beneath the door at around 9:30. His emergency call came through at 9:33."

"Okay," said Nadia. "6 PM. Downtown Milwaukee on a weeknight. Tail end of rush hour. If the wraithwolves just wanted to grab a bite to eat, there were lots of easier targets around. That means someone either sent the wraithwolves after the Doyles or someone in the family summoned them up and it went bad."

"There is absolutely no evidence that Doyle or anyone in his family was involved with the Rebels or the Dark Ones cults," said Owen.

Nadia grunted. "You know about the Dark Ones cults, then?"

"I've been a shadow agent of the High Queen of seventeen years now," said Owen. "It's hard not to have run into the Dark Ones cults during that time."

"Seventeen? God," said Nadia. For the first time, an emotion other than anger or disdain went over her face. It might have been sympathy if he had squinted and looked at it in the right light. "It's amazing that you still have all your hair."

"We may be grateful for small miracles," said Owen. "But my working assumption is that someone summoned the wraithwolves from the Shadowlands and sent them after Doyle. There are a few other pieces of evidence to support that view." He paged through the file and handed a few more pages to Nadia. "For one, both Ronald Doyle's and Josephine Doyle's phones were missing. We couldn't find them anywhere in the condo. Their oldest had a phone, but the parents' phones were missing. Second, Ronald's wallet and Josephine's purse are missing."

"Hell of a messy way to commit robbery," said Nadia She read over the pages and handed them back. "I might have an idea on how to proceed."

"Please," said Owen. He already had his investigation underway. As the head of Special Investigations, he could commandeer detectives from other departments, and Giles had given him some of his best, though Lieutenant Warren had already been assigned to another case. Owen had men digging through Doyle's sketchy finances and the finances of his company. He had also assigned an investigator to sort through the backgrounds of the people currently suing Doyle for his defective concrete. Anyone who had a motive for revenge on Doyle was a suspect. Summoning wraithwolves to kill Doyle's family seemed like an excessive response...but then so was taking an M-99 carbine and shooting up your workplace the day after you got fired.

Both happened.

"We need to narrow this down," said Nadia. "I assume you've got guys going over Doyle's money and everyone who's suing him, right?" Owen nodded, impressed despite himself. "Okay. That's a good start. But I might be able to determine whether or not the wraithwolves were summoned in the condo building."

Owen frowned. "How?" She had been able to sense the aurasight spell but detecting the traces of a summoning spell three days after the fact would be a lot harder.

"Aetherometer," said Nadia.

"You have an aetherometer?" said Owen. "I thought only Elven nobles had those."

"It was a wedding gift," said Nadia.

Owen thought about that. He wondered what kind of man would voluntarily marry someone like Nadia MacCormac. Her husband either had to be a rich but soft man she dominated entirely or some sort of exceptionally dangerous killer.

"You can use it to check for the traces of a summoning spell?" said Owen.

"I think so," said Nadia. "I want to have a look at the Doyles' condo and the building. If there's anything odd there, magically speaking, my aetherometer should pick it up." She shrugged. "Maybe we'll find that Doyle had a secret shrine to the Dark Ones hidden in the furnace room and accidentally conjured up wraithwolves that ate him."

"That would make things simpler," said Owen. He stood. "Shall we go now?"

"Yeah, let's get on with it," said Nadia. She threw back the rest of her coffee in a single gulp and stood. "We're past the first seventy-two hours now. A lot harder to catch a murder suspect then."

"You did read my book," said Owen, picking up his uniform jacket and shrugging into it.

She smirked. "But the High Queen gave us this job, Colonel. We can't just arrest some random guy off the street, pin the murder on him, kill him on a Punishment Day video, and then take a break for coffee and doughnuts. No, we actually have to get it right. Novel idea for Homeland Security, but here we are."

Something about her contempt for Homeland Security grated on him. Owen was used to hatred and fear, but icy contempt and disdain were unusual. He remembered the images he had seen in Dean Osmond's mind, remembered his victims lying in their blood in that convenience store. A welter of other memories welled through his mind, of lives ended or broken by murder and assault. He was surprised by the urge to throw them into Nadia's face, to wipe that smirk off her pretty face, to tell her that a woman who had no doubt been a career criminal had no right to judge the officers of the law.

Owen forced aside the urge. For one, he doubted it would work. No doubt Nadia would just laugh in his face. More importantly, he had a job to do. Owen had worked with plenty of people he had disliked during his career. Nadia MacCormac would just be one more.

"Let's go," he said, and opened the office door.

6

BLOODSHED

Owen offered to drive to the Doyles' condo building, and I agreed. I told him to meet me at the entrance to the parking ramp after I had gotten my aetherometer out of my trunk. Before I did, Owen gave me a consultant's ID card, which I clipped to the lapel of my coat. I strolled out of the lobby of the Central Office, enjoyed the surprised scowl from Kirby, and stepped into the November chill. It hit me like a slap, and I tugged my coat closed and took deep breaths, sucking the cold into my lungs.

That was good. It would help clear my head.

I had to stop provoking Owen Quell.

A lot of things had changed about me during my century and a half in the Eternity Crucible, but my smart mouth definitely had stayed the same. When I was scared or angry, my mouth tended to run away with itself. I had gotten better about controlling it (maturity, yay!) but the tendency was still there. I hadn't been frightened in the Central Office building or while talking to Owen. I knew enough about interrogation techniques to realize that opening crack about getting coffee had been a test to see how I would react. I hadn't told him to shove his coffee cup sideways up his backside, so I decided to chalk that up as a win for self-control.

But I was angry. Not furious, but low-level angry. It had started when Officer Kirby had tried to bully me at the security checkpoint. And that low-level anger seethed during my entire meeting with Owen. The bald fact was that I hated and distrusted both Homeland Security and its officers. That anger had kept bubbling out during the conversation in the form of snide remarks. I needed to work with Owen until we had figured out who had killed the Doyles. Deliberately provoking him was not a good way to do it.

Damn it all, why had the High Queen told us to work together? Owen was a freaking Homeland Security Colonel. He had more resources and (official) authority than I did. Owen didn't need my help. If Tarlia had wanted it resolved quietly, then why hadn't she sent me alone?

The answer suggested itself to me as I walked into the parking garage. Owen might have both magical skill and the resources of Homeland Security, but he wouldn't be able to fight an entire pack of wraithwolves and their summoner. I could, though, and I had done that kind of thing in the past with great effectiveness. I wished she had sent the Inquisition to deal with it, but maybe the Inquisition was busy.

Or maybe there was something weird going on.

Like the business with Della Sarkany.

"Shit," I muttered as I walked back to my car and opened the trunk.

The best way to deal with all of this was to solve the Doyles' murders and report success to Tarlia. Then I could go back to ignoring Homeland Security and Colonel Owen Quell.

So, suck it up, Nadia, and get on with it.

I drew out a laptop bag and slung the strap diagonally across my chest. Inside was my aetherometer and a variety of other items that made a good toolkit for a high-end thief, but now that I was legitimate, I supposed they were my shadow agent's toolkit.

I walked back to the curb, and a minute later, a blue Homeland Security SUV pulled up. The passenger door opened, and I saw Owen sitting in the driver's seat. I took a deep breath, climbed into the SUV, and closed the door. The locks slamming shut as Owen put the SUV back into drive sounded like deadbolts being thrown. I consoled myself with the thought that I could blast my way out of the SUV with ease, if necessary.

The interior of the SUV looked like a typical Homeland Security vehicle. A wire mesh cage sealed off the back seat and the cargo area, preventing "guests" from making trouble. A ruggedized laptop had been clipped to the dashboard, along with a radio communication and dispatch system. A holographic heads-up display showed notifications and messages on the dashboard since staring at a laptop was a great way to drive into a tree. I watched the HUD for a moment. Those weren't available on the general market, and it was always a shock to see symbols and letters flashing across a windshield.

Owen saw me staring. "Suppose you're used to sitting in the back."

"I'm used to seeing Homeland Security SUVs in my rearview mirror, getting smaller," I said. I started to add that it probably wasn't necessary to outrun Homeland Security SUVs since the officers within were busy using the HUD to watch movies on the taxpayer's dollar, but I remembered my resolution to get along with Owen Quell and stopped myself.

Owen only grunted at that.

We drove in silence to the building that had housed Ronald Doyle's condo. It wasn't far, only about three-quarters of a mile, but the numerous stoplights and heavy traffic slowed us down. At last, we came to a building of about thirty stories, with shops on the first floor, offices on the next nine, and condos on the rest. Doyle, if I remembered the file right, had lived on the twenty-fifth floor.

I started to ask where we were going to park, but Owen simply pulled into the loading zone in front of the building and turned on the SUV's flashers. Right. Homeland Security could park wherever they wanted.

"Let's go," said Owen.

"Hang on a minute," I said, reaching into my bag. I pulled out my aetherometer. "I want a quick look at the building with this."

Owen peered at my aetherometer with frank curiosity. It looked like a big compass about the size of my palm, except there were a dozen different dials beneath the crystalline lens. I concentrated on the instrument, and I felt my telepathic link with it.

"What do those dials mean?" said Owen.

"It changes based on context," I said. The dials spun and twitched as the aetherometer measured the local magical fields. "The interface is telepathic, so it tells me what the symbols mean. Don't try to look into my head with the mindtouch spell. I know Homeland Security likes to break into places without a warrant, but it'd have bad effects on you."

I regretted saying that. Hadn't I just promised myself I'd try to stop provoking him? But Owen's attention was on the aetherometer, and he didn't respond.

"Can you tell me what the dials mean?" said Owen.

"No. Well. Not yet," I said, watching the aetherometer. "Like I said, it's telepathically linked to me, so it will tell me what the dials mean in context. It changes depending on the strength of the local magical auras. Give it a minute or…wait, here we go."

I scrutinized the dials, the knowledge of what they meant appearing in my head through the telepathic link. The aetherometer was picking up my magical aura, and it was also registering Owen's. It detected a cluster of magical auras across the street. I wondered why, and then remembered Duke Tamirlas had offices in the building across the street. I was picking up some minor Elven nobles and their retainers. I didn't feel anything at all from Doyle's condo building.

Except…

"Okay," I said. "Doyle's condo was on the twenty-fifth floor, right?"

"Yeah."

"There's a…" I frowned, trying to describe what I sensed. "There's a weird magical echo on the twenty-fifth floor. Like a resonance."

"Echo of what?" said Owen.

"A summoning spell, I think," I said.

"Well." He stared at the smooth glass and steel sides of the condo building. "If you're right, that narrows it down a bit."

"But it doesn't look right," I said. "The echo of a summoning spell is obvious. This is..." I frowned, and the answer came to me. "This is like the echo of a magical device."

Owen's brows furrowed. "Like someone used an enspelled object to summon the wraithwolves?"

"Reads like it."

"Well, that's just great," said Owen. "That's the last thing the city needs. Someone running around with a magical relic capable of summoning wraithwolves."

"I want to do a walkthrough of the building," I said, tapping the aetherometer's crystal face. "This thing is better at close range. We might pick something up."

Owen nodded. "Every floor?"

"Nah, every fifth floor ought to do it," I said. "Then we'll need to do a walkthrough of the Doyles' condo. I want to see it for myself."

"So do I," said Owen. "I just took over the case from Warren, and haven't seen the condo yet."

"Warren?" I said, slipping the aetherometer back into my bag as Owen opened the door.

"Lieutenant Kyle Warren," said Owen as we got out of the SUV. "Star of the homicide division."

I started to make a joke about faking evidence, stopped myself.

"He did all the preliminaries?" I said, thinking of the copious amount of notes in the case file.

"Yeah," said Owen. "Did a good job of it, too." The condo's doorman saw Owen's Homeland Security uniform and let us in. He also helpfully provided a key that would let us into the basement and the hallways, but not the individual condos. The lobby beyond the front doors had a lot of polished marble and steel. I was reasonably sure that none of Ronald Doyle's concrete had gone into the construction of this building.

"All right," I said, watching the dials on the aetherometer. "Let's go for a walk."

It took about ten minutes. We started in the basement and then climbed up the stairs in five-story intervals. I walked the hallways, keeping an eye on the aetherometer. In the corridors of the office floors, we drew odd looks, but since I was walking with a Homeland Security colonel, no one gave us a hard time. I didn't detect any new anomalous readings, but my fix on the odd echo on the twenty-fifth floor grew sharper. It did indeed look like the echo of a summoning spell, though unlike one I had ever encountered before.

"I'm not picking up anything but that summoning echo," I said. "Let's head up to Doyle's condo and take a look."

Owen nodded. "You know the rules for visiting a crime scene?"

I repressed the urge to sigh. "Don't touch anything," I was wearing gloves, so that would be fine, "don't move anything, don't leave anything, and note it in the case file in UNICORN."

"Good," said Owen as we headed for the stairs.

"But it's been three days," I said. "Your lab people have already gotten everything they're going to get from the scene."

He gave me a sidelong glance as he opened the stairwell door.

"Told you I read your book," I said.

"That you did," said Owen.

"Question," I said, noting the security camera in the stairwell. "You've got people reviewing the camera footage?"

"Yeah, Warren did that on the first day," said Owen as we started up. "I've got people reviewing, but it looks like the only people in and out of the building during the time of death were residents and a few pizza deliverymen. All the entrances into the building are monitored."

I said nothing as we climbed to the twenty-fifth floor. That reinforced the idea that Doyle had been playing with summoning spells and gotten himself killed. Then again, it was still too early to say.

We reached the twenty-fifth floor and started down a carpeted hallway towards Doyle's corner. I went around the corner and froze in surprise for a half-second.

Another Homeland Security officer stood before the door to the condo. He was somewhere in his thirties, and strikingly handsome – strong jaw, clear skin, well-built beneath the uniform. Owen Quell looked like an aging bar brawler. This guy looked like he ought to have been playing the lead in a TV drama about Homeland Security, the sort of show where our heroic investigator realizes that the Rebel conspiracy goes All The Way To The Top or something while, of course, having a different girl every week.

He smiled, and I immediately didn't like him.

"Sir," said the lieutenant. I slipped my aetherometer back into my bag. "I heard you have taken over the case." His eyes flicked to me again.

"Yeah," said Owen. "Sorry about that, Warren. Orders came from way up." That was true. "Didn't mean to step on your case, but orders are orders."

The lieutenant, presumably named Warren, shrugged. Then I realized who he was. He was the Lieutenant Kyle Warren who had started investigating the case. He'd taken good, detailed notes and documented everything he had done thoroughly, so at least he was competent.

"Can't do anything, so no sense in being sore over it," said Warren. "And I knew in the first hour that someone else was going to get the case." His expression hardened. "The bodies...it was pretty clear something from the Shadowlands had done it. Not the sort of thing you forget."

"No, this is the kind of case that stays with you," said Owen.

Warren looked at me. "Who's your new friend?"

"I'm a consultant," I said. I tapped the badge clipped to the lapel of my coat. "See? It says so right there."

Warren smiled. I think he meant it to be charming. He did look very handsome, but his sudden shift from solemnity to smiling was grating. "What's your field of expertise?"

"Printer toner," I said. "You'd be surprised how often it turns up at crime scenes." A smart remark, I know, but I was really trying to dial it back.

"I see," said Warren, nonplussed.

Owen sighed. "This is Nadia MacCormac. She's a consultant, and she's going to help Special Investigations with the case." I resisted the urge to grimace. I didn't want Warren to know my name.

"Pleased to meet you," said Warren, holding out his hand.

I had no choice but to shake it. Warren held my hand a little too long.

"Yeah," I said. I looked at Owen. "Look, we've got work to do. Can we get on with it?"

Warren grinned, though something flashed in his eyes. "I can tell when I'm not wanted."

"I might have something for you to check on later," said Owen. "Thanks for all the work on the case. It's going to make closing it a lot easier – I'll make sure your name is on it when we do."

"Thanks, Colonel," said Warren. "If you need anything, I'll be at the Central Office."

With that, he disappeared into an elevator further down the hall.

"There was no reason to be rude," said Owen. "Professional courtesy..."

"Yeah, yeah, Homeland Security officers are all brothers in arms, and you all cover each others' asses when you break the law and frame people," I said. I reminded myself to be civil. "Look, our boss said I had to work with you, so I'm going to work with you, personally. But she didn't say anything about every random idiot in a blue uniform. And if we do run into a pack of wraithwolves before this is over, a guy like Warren has no defense against them. They'll rip him apart. There will be even more blood on this nice carpet."

I pointed at the bottom of the door to the Doyles' condo. The carpet had been stained with dried blood.

"Let's get on with it," said Owen. He pulled on a pair of gloves from his jacket pocket. I tied back my hair into a ponytail and donned a ball cap. It had been three days, so the crime lab technicians had already gotten everything useful they were going to get. Still, no sense in messing it up more than necessary.

Owen undid the Homeland Security seal and opened the door.

An unpleasant mixture of odors assailed my nose. There was the scent of the various chemicals crime lab techs used – fingerprint powder and blood detector and the like. Overlaid with that was the unpleasant odor of old blood and a hint of bowels. Whoever owned this place was going to face spending a fortune to clean the condo.

I followed Owen through a small entry hall and into the living room. The place had been luxurious, with a large living room opening into a dining room with a polished wooden floor. Past the kitchen was a hallway leading to bedrooms and an office. Massive dark stains marked the floor, and the furniture had been destroyed by slashing claws. My eyes flicked over the living room, noting details and comparing them with things I had seen in the file. Doyle's body, most of it, had been found there. His wife on the ruined, bloodstained sofa. The oldest two kids on the floor. The youngest had been found halfway in the living room closet. The boy had been trying to hide from the monsters killing his family, who had then dragged him out of the closet and torn him apart anyway.

My lips thinned into a hard line. I didn't like Owen, and I didn't trust Homeland Security. But I was going to find whoever was responsible for this and make them regret it.

I glanced at Owen, saw him looking at me.

"Yeah," he said, voice quiet. "Bad, isn't it?"

"Yep," I said, pulling out my aetherometer again. "Let's track down whoever did it and make them sorry."

Owen didn't say anything as I turned in a circle, frowning as I watched the aetherometer's dials spin. I was still picking up the odd echo the instrument had detected earlier, but I still had no idea what it was.

"Anything?" said Owen.

"Give me a minute," I said, scowling at the aetherometer.

He waited, no trace of impatience on his face. I suppose Homeland Security officers had to be good at waiting.

"Okay," I said at last, lowering the aetherometer. "There was definitely a summoned creature in this condo. I'm not sure if the creature was summoned in here or if it was summoned outside the building. But I'm entirely sure the wraithwolf was summoned by a magical device of some kind."

"Something the Elves built?" said Owen. "Something like your aetherometer?"

"Maybe," I said, tucking the device away in my bag. "I don't know. I've seen machines that can summon wraithwolves." I remembered the automated summoning circles I had found in Last Judge Mountain, machines that the pre-Conquest US government had developed in the final decades before the Conquest. "It's possible human technology could do it."

"The device isn't still in the apartment, is it?" said Owen.

"No," I said. "Beyond all doubt. It would radiate magic. You'd be able to detect it. You know the spell to sense magic, right?" As if to demonstrate, he cast it and promptly found nothing. "Yeah. It's not in here. Either someone brought it in here, or Doyle was playing with it and got himself killed, and someone took it, or…"

I scowled at the door to the hall, an idea coming to me.

"The camera footage didn't show anyone coming and going in the hallway during the probable time of death?" I said.

"No," said Owen. He consulted his phone. "Some pizza deliverymen arrived during that time, but we can account for their movements. They didn't go higher than the fourteenth floor."

"All the corpses were found in the living room," I said. "None of the other rooms were really disturbed, were they?"

"No," said Owen. He picked up on my line of thought. "You think they came through that window?" He pointed at the big dining room window. "The techs didn't find any fingerprints but the family's on the window."

"Might not matter," I said. "Wraithwolves can become mist, right?" Owen nodded at that. "They could have flowed right through the window. Help me get this open, will you?"

We unlatched the big window and slid it open. A gust of cold November air hit me in the face. The screen rattled, and I noticed that it was torn in the corner like someone had shoved a knife through it.

Or a claw.

"Look at that," said Owen.

"Like a claw, right?" I said.

Owen scowled. "How the hell did we miss that?"

I shrugged. "Twenty-fifth floor, you don't expect someone to come through the window, yeah? Let me get this screen out, I have an idea."

I pulled the screen out, propped it against the wall, and leaned out the window. The street was a long, long way below. I was suddenly very aware of Owen standing behind me. I had a brief vision of him giving me a quick shove out the window. Of course, if he did that, he was screwed. One levitation spell later, I would come back up the window and blast his head off...

I pushed aside the paranoid thoughts and looked at the metal and glass below the window. From the street, the building had looked entirely built of glass and steel, but that wasn't right. There were bands of ornamental white stone between each of the floors and windows.

I saw the bright streaks of claw marks working their way up to the Doyles' living room window.

"Holy shit," I said.

"What?" said Owen.

I pulled my head and shoulders back through the window. "Look down and to the left. Don't worry, I won't push you out."

He gave me a dubious look but leaned out the window. Owen stared at the side of the building for about thirty seconds and then straightened up with a grunt.

"It climbed in through the window," he said.

"Yeah," I said. "Wraithwolves don't usually do that. They can turn into mist. So why bother climbing? Give me a hand with the screen."

We put the window back together, both of us looking at the buildings across the street. It was a mixture of businesses, smaller condo buildings, and a parking ramp. I could tell our thoughts were running in the same direction.

"You know," I said. "I bet at least one of those buildings had a security camera pointed at the sidewalk and the side of this building."

"I think you're right," said Owen. "Let's go knock on some doors and request help from the citizenry."

"Bet they'll be delighted," I said.

~

As it turned out, people were cooperative. The various managers and administrators of the buildings across the street, once Owen explained things, were more than happy to let us look through their security footage.

And at the seventh business, we found something.

It was a pizza place, and the owner had installed a pair of expensive cameras over his front door. Not because he had been robbed (he explained this at some length), but because his employees had been giving away free pizzas to their friends and he wanted to put a stop to it. The cameras had a good view of the sidewalk outside the restaurant, and also a good angle on the street and the side of the Doyles' condo building. Even better, his server kept camera footage for the last two months, so it was easy to go back to November 10th and watch the footage from 6 PM to 9 PM.

Owen sat at the owner's desk, which occupied a cluttered little office at the back of the restaurant that smelled of garlic and pepperoni grease. I stood behind him, watching the monitor, and the owner alternated between hovering near the door and barking orders to his employees. He didn't sound like a real pleasant guy to have as a boss. No wonder his workers had been stealing pizzas.

The blue-toned video flickered and blurred on the screen as Owen fast-forwarded, and then the image froze as he paused it.

"There," he said. "What the hell is that?"

The creature appeared on the video for less than fifteen seconds.

It ran along the base of the wall, moving faster than a human could. Then it scrambled up the side of the building's wall, keeping between the windows. I wondered how no one had seen it, but it had been dark, there weren't that many streetlights on that section of the sidewalk, and all the passing cars would have been unable to see past their lights.

"Pause it seven seconds back," I said. "I think we'll get the clearest image there."

Owen complied, and we gazed at the screen in silence for a moment.

I had never seen a wraithwolf quite like that.

It had the head of a wraithwolf and bony armor plates that covered its body. It also had a scorpion-like tail tipped with a barbed stinger. Unlike most other wraithwolves that I had encountered, the thing was walking on its hind legs. It would have stood seven or eight feet tall, and it was a solid pillar of muscle. The image was clear enough that I saw that the creature had hands, actual hands with thumbs, though the fingers were tipped with big claws.

"What the hell is that?" said Owen.

"Good question," I said. "It looks like a wraithwolf, but I've never seen one that walks on two legs."

"Neither have I," said Owen.

"Hey," I said, another thought occurring to me. "Run that forward a couple of seconds. When it starts climbing up the wall."

Owen complied and froze the image again. The wraithwolf-thing had started scaling the sheer wall as easily as if it had been a ladder. In the still image, on the wraithwolf's back, I saw a metal plate among the bony armor. Based on its position, it would have been at the base of the creature's spine, and I thought that it was about the size of my hand.

"That looks like..." Owen frowned. "I can't make it out. But it looks like a metal plate grafted to the creature's back. We're going to need a copy of this recording. Maybe some of the lab techs can clean up the image a bit."

"Well, go wave your badge at the owner," I said. "He seems happy enough to help. Maybe you can bully some free pizza out of him, too."

Owen only grunted, and then summoned the owner, who as it turned out, was more than happy to allow us access to the video recording. I watched as Owen cautioned the owner against sharing the file with anyone, since it might put his life in danger, and then copied the video clip to his phone and then uploaded it to the case file in UNICORN. I took a copy for myself and stashed it on my phone since I suspected I was going to need it soon.

"You really want to put the video into the case file?" I said.

Owen looked surprised. "It's vital evidence. Vital evidence goes into the case file, along with notes explaining how it was obtained and under what circumstances."

I snorted. "What, you're going to put the wraithwolf on trial when we catch it? Tarlia gave us this job to do it quietly, not to run it through the court system."

"And I suppose you're going to go around murdering people without accountability?" said Owen.

"Like the wraithwolf?" I said. "See, this isn't like your usual cases, where you fake enough evidence to get someone on a Punishment Day video. No, we actually have to get results, and if half of Homeland Security sees the footage of the wraithwolf, whoever summoned it might go into hiding."

"You think someone in Homeland Security summoned the creature?" said Owen.

I shrugged. "A lot of former members of the Wizard's Legion in Homeland Security, aren't there?"

"It's more likely the work of a renegade wizard," said Owen. "Someone who knows illegal spells that she shouldn't."

We stared at each other. It wasn't quite a glare, but it was getting there. I rebuked myself for provoking him. I didn't like Owen Quell, but we had to work together until this was done.

"Okay," I said. "Maybe I'm jumping to conclusions. Your book says we shouldn't do that, right?" Owen inclined his head. "But I think it's fair to conclude that somebody summoned up the wraithwolf and sent it after the Doyle family. Ronald Doyle didn't do it himself."

Owen let out a breath. "You're probably right. It must have been a targeted killing. He pissed someone off, they summoned up that wraithwolf and sent it after him. If the wraithwolf was going to kill at random, it wouldn't climb up the side of a building to do it. It would have gone on a killing spree until it was stopped."

"I know people who might be able to help," I said, thinking of my husband and the Shadow Hunters. "People who might have encountered a two-legged wraithwolf before."

"More illegal wizards?" said Owen, half-seriously.

"No, they're perfectly legal," I said. "Royal charter and everything."

"Warren's got a good run-down on Doyle's finances in the file," said Owen. "He has some discrepancies flagged. I'll start following up on them, see if we can find someone who has an obvious motive." He glanced at the clock on the office wall. "It's getting late. Let's meet back at Central at, say, nine AM tomorrow? We can continue then."

"All right," I said.

We thanked the owner, exited the restaurant, and stopped on the sidewalk. It had gotten dark, and rush hour was in full swing.

"You want a ride back to the parking ramp?" said Owen.

"Nah," I said. "It's only a half-mile. The walk will do me some good. Hell, traffic's so backed-up I'll probably get there before you do. See you tomorrow."

He nodded, and I headed down the street. I waited until I had turned the corner, and I pulled out my phone. It was, what, a seven-hour time difference between the UK and Wisconsin? Riordan might be asleep or busy. Then again, he might not, and I needed some information.

A two-legged wraithwolf. I'd never seen anything like that. But if anyone knew about the creatures of the Shadowlands, it was the Family of the Shadow Hunters. If there was a dangerous Shadowlands creature loose in Milwaukee, help from the Shadow Hunters might catch the creature before anyone else got killed.

And it had been an unpleasant day, and I really wanted to talk to my husband.

I'd start with Riordan.

I dialed his number and put the phone to my ear as I walked, keeping an eye out for trouble partly out of habit, partly if Owen decided to follow me.

Riordan picked up on the third ring. "Hello?"

His voice was deep and quiet, with a mild Texas twang, and I felt better at once for hearing it.

"Hey, it's Nadia," I said. "I'm not in trouble or anything, I just…you know, I just wanted to talk to you. This isn't a bad time, is it?"

"No, it's not," said Riordan. "In fact, we're all done here. I should be able to come back to Milwaukee tomorrow."

"Really?" I said. My voice went up an octave with excitement, but I was too happy to care.

"Yeah," said Riordan. "Our job here is finished," he wouldn't discuss the Shadow Hunters openly over the phone, just as I wouldn't talk about my jobs from Tarlia, "and I was just about to text you my flight information. If you don't mind picking me up from the airport."

"I do not," I said, stopping at a crosswalk. "I really, really do not."

"How are you?" said Riordan.

I hesitated.

"Well," I said, "I've got a job."

"I see," said Riordan.

"It's a bit like the one I had in New York, the one where we both wound up working on the same thing from opposite ends," I said. The light changed, and I crossed, the headlights of the cars waiting for the signal to change shining in my eyes. "I'm supposed to find something out."

"I see," said Riordan again. "I wish I could get an earlier flight."

"I'll be fine," I said, "though I wish you could, too." I glanced around and made sure no one was close enough to overhear. "Have you ever heard of a wraithwolf with two legs? Like, one that walks on two legs, like a human?"

"No," said Riordan. He paused. "Like a werewolf?"

"For God's sake," I said. "There's no such thing as werewolves."

"I know that," said Riordan, his voice dry, "but about a hundred thousand fantasy romance novels think otherwise."

I'd asked him once why there were so many novels about vampires and werewolves, creatures that didn't exist. He'd told me that back before the Conquest, people had written novels about Elves and orcs and dwarves. Except after the Conquest, people found out that Elves and orcs and dwarves actually existed and writing something negative about Elves would get the Inquisition or Homeland Security on your doorstep. So people wrote about vampires and werewolves instead.

I was glad Riordan didn't write novels about werewolves and vampires. I mean, I'd have still married him, but I was glad he didn't. Those novels annoyed me. The message always seemed to be that if the woman just loved the vampire or the werewolf hard enough, they'd stop being monsters.

Given that my first lover had been the man who had almost detonated a nuclear bomb in New York, I knew that wasn't true.

"Whatever the thing was, it was a wraithwolf, but it was walking on two legs," I said. "It had hands, and opposable thumbs, too. Have you ever seen anything like that?"

"No," said Riordan. "Never seen or heard of anything like that. I'll ask the others." He paused. "You've seen and fought this thing?"

"I saw it on some security camera footage at a pizza restaurant in downtown Milwaukee," I said. "You ever heard of a guy named Ronald Doyle?"

"No. No...wait. Isn't he getting sued about a collapsing building?"

"Not anymore, because he's dead," I said. "Check out the news reports from Milwaukee when you have time. It'll say that he and his family died in suspicious circumstances. I think the two-legged wraithwolf did it."

"I see," said Riordan. "If you get a chance, send me a picture. I'll show it to Nora and Alex and some of the others." He paused. "You might wind up getting help from my employer on this one."

I thought about that. Did I really want to pull the Shadow Hunters in on this? Heck yes. I didn't want to take off and fight an unknown threat by myself. And if Owen Quell tried to bully me, it would be useful to have backup.

"Okay," I said. "I'll send it right away."

"Thanks," said Riordan. "I'll text you before my flight leaves." He paused. "Be careful."

"I will," I said. "I'm sorry I made you worry."

He snorted. "I'm sure you've been worried while I was gone."

"Well," I said. "Yeah."

"I'll see you tomorrow," said Riordan. "I love you, Nadia."

"I love you, too," I said. "Have a good flight."

With that, the call ended.

I leaned against the wall outside of a restaurant for a moment, taking a screen capture of the best image of the two-legged wraithwolf and sending it to Riordan. I suppose I was technically sharing evidence of an ongoing Homeland Security investigation, but I didn't care. There was no one more qualified to deal with Shadowlands creatures than the Family of the Shadow Hunters, and if Owen was smart, he would see their help was a good idea.

Especially if there was more than one of those creatures.

Now there was a cheery thought.

A shiver went through me. I hadn't realized how cold I had gotten. With a muttered curse, I pushed off the wall and kept going, pulling my coat tighter around me. I knew Riordan would worry about me, but to be fair, we both worried about each other a lot. Only natural, I suppose, given that he was part of the Shadow Hunters and I was the High Queen's errand girl. Neither job was exactly safe.

I got back to the parking garage and started my car, intending to head home. I thought about stopping by the Marneys, but I wanted a quiet night to myself.

And if someone was summoning up two-legged wraithwolves to attack people, best not to draw attention to anyone near me. Especially since I had to work with Owen Quell. He seemed like the sort of asshole who would arrest someone because they annoyed him.

OWEN PULLED his car into the garage and shut off the engine, thinking.

He had a lot to think about. The case, certainly. He already had investigators digging through Doyle's life and financial records piece by piece. Someone had sent that two-legged wraithwolf to kill Doyle deliberately, and Owen needed to find out why.

But he also found himself thinking about Nadia MacCormac.

He didn't like her, and he couldn't tell if that was affecting his judgment or not.

She was obviously dangerous, and the aurasight had told him that she was not emotionally stable. That in itself was not worrisome. She had herself under control, as far as he could tell, and Owen had worked with a lot of damaged and dangerous people in his life.

But her contempt for Homeland Security caught his attention. He was used to seeing hatred and fear in the course of his duties. But that bone-deep contempt...he had only encountered a few times before. It was usually from people who had gotten away with their crimes and were convinced they would continue to do so.

The first time Owen had encountered that attitude had been as a teenager, with Peter Walsh, in the awful weeks after Christopher's death.

He hesitated, then pulled out his laptop, booted it up, and did a UNICORN search on Nadia MacCormac.

Preoccupied with reading Warren's case notes, he had only glanced at Nadia's information, but now he gave her records a more thorough look. Unfortunately, there wasn't much in her UNICORN file. Nadia Moran had been born on June 17th, Conquest Year 294, in Seattle. There were no records of schooling or employment. In July, she had received a royal pardon from the High Queen, retroactively granting her immunity from prosecution for everything she had done before that date. Probably that had been one of the things Tarlia had used to recruit her as a shadow agent. A few weeks after the pardon, Nadia had married a man named Riordan MacCormac, and they owned a house in Brookfield. Nadia and her brother Russell had also started a company called Moran Imports, of which they both owned half.

There wasn't much else in the record. Owen wondered Nadia had done that the royal pardon had covered up.

He did a search on Riordan MacCormac and came up with little else. Most of Riordan's records were protected. As a colonel, Owen had enough rank and access to see that Riordan's records existed, just not to read most of them. That probably meant Nadia's husband was a human Inquisition agent, a high-ranking employee for an Elven lord, a Shadow Hunter, or a senior officer of the Wizard's Legion.

Owen sighed, logged out of his UNICORN session, and shut down his computer. His earlier suspicions were likely true. On the balance of probability, Nadia MacCormac had been a high-ranking Rebel that Tarlia had coerced or convinced into becoming her shadow agent, probably because of some unique skill or ability she possessed. The fact that she had walked unnoticed and unannounced into a Homeland Security facility was proof of that.

He wondered how many crimes Nadia had committed, how many people she had hurt.

Well, Owen couldn't do anything about the past. Nadia had a royal pardon. That was that. But that only applied to everything that had happened before July. With her obvious contempt for Homeland Security and her emotional instability, Owen feared that Nadia MacCormac was a bomb ticking down to an explosion.

He would keep a very close eye on her, and make sure she didn't hurt someone and try to skate away from the consequences as Peter Walsh had thirty years ago.

With a sigh, Owen stowed his laptop in his bag, got out of his car, and locked the garage behind him.

To his complete lack of surprise, Cornelia Fischer was lurking by the fence. It was five or six degrees below freezing, but she was still outside, ready to hear gossip. He glimpsed a trash bag in her hand. No doubt she had waited to take the trash out until she had seen him pull into the driveway.

"Working late, Colonel?" said Cornelia.

"Crime never sleeps, Mrs. Fischer," said Owen. "And I told Anna I'd be home an hour ago," that was true enough, "so I'd better get inside, hadn't I?"

"Yes, you had better," said Cornelia. Owen got to the back door and let himself inside before Cornelia recovered her wits. The kitchen smelled of stir fry, and Anna was at the sink, washing a pan.

"Hi, Owen," she said, glancing up from the sink. "We had dinner an hour ago, figured you wouldn't want us to wait. There's a plate for you in the fridge. Do you mind keeping an eye on things? I need to get a couple of hours of work done before..."

Her voice trailed off, and she turned off the water.

"Bad day?" she said.

"Kids upstairs?" said Owen.

"Twins are downstairs, using the weights," said Anna. "Antonia and June are upstairs."

Owen let out a breath. "Yeah, it was a bad day. I met the other shadow agent today."

"What's she like?" said Anna.

Owen found himself lapsing into the clinical speech of a trained observer. "Caucasian female. Twenty-two years old. About five foot three inches in height, about a hundred and ten pounds. Brown hair, gray eyes."

"Twenty-two years old?" said Anna. "Is she pretty?"

She was teasing him, he knew, try to lighten his mood. "Quite."

Anna smiled. "Do I need to be worried?" Her tone was light, but not entirely. Owen knew he was at the proper age for a midlife crisis. He'd seen a few men his age launch themselves into doomed affairs with younger women, and while at times Owen could see the appeal, he thought that sounded exhausting. And then he would have to live with himself after.

"No," said Owen. "Not about that. She's bad news." He took off his coat and hung it up on the hook by the door. "I think she's a former Rebel. She probably turned on the Rebels, and the High Queen coerced her into becoming a shadow agent."

Anna's brow furrowed. "Isn't...that a good thing?"

"It would be. But Nadia MacCormac is emotionally unstable, and her UNICORN records are sealed or nonexistent," said Owen. "She probably got away with a lot."

"Like Peter Walsh," said Anna.

"I didn't say that," said Owen. He paused and sighed. "But yes."

"Walsh didn't get away with it in the end," said Anna. "You made sure of that." She hesitated. "How bad is it?"

"The case?" said Owen. "The murders were bad, and it's too early to tell. But Warren did a lot of good work in the beginning, and he left an excellent foundation. We've got a video of the killer entering the premises, and whoever did this would have gotten sloppy somewhere. We'll get them. It's just a matter of following the tracks back far enough."

He didn't have enough proof for that assertion, not yet, but he had a hunch, and after years doing this, his hunches were usually right. Someone had summoned up a two-legged wraithwolf and sent it after the Doyles. The sort of people who did that, usually Dark Ones cultists, tended to make mistakes. It was simply a matter of finding that mistake and following the thread.

"You'll only have to deal with the MacCormac woman until then," said Anna.

"Yeah," said Owen. "I can see why the High Queen sent her. She's smart."

"I thought you said you didn't like her," said Anna.

"I don't," said Owen. "If I had met her in any other context, I think I would be investigating her for something she had done. The sooner I can get this case wrapped up, the better."

But there would be complications, he knew. There always were.

"Well," said Anna, and she kissed him. "You'll handle it. You'll always do."

"I'll finish up in here," said Owen, "so you can get started on your work."

"No," said Anna. "Eat dinner first and go say hi to the girls. Then you can finish cleaning up in here."

"Yes, ma'am," said Owen, giving her a mock salute with two fingers. She grinned and walked out of the kitchen to get her laptop.

He opened the fridge, took out the leftover stir fry, and heated it up. His mind turned over what he had learned today. Someone had sent that two-legged wraithwolf to kill Doyle and his family, and Owen suspected the answer was somewhere in Doyle's financial records.

He sat down to eat and read over the case file one last time for the day.

7

CRONIES

The next morning, the morning of November 14th, I woke up in a foul mood.

I hadn't slept well, and I had a headache. A succession of bad dreams had plagued my sleep. Not quite the level of the nightmares that caused me to wake up in full-blown panic attacks, ready to start flinging blasts of lightning into the shadows, but still unpleasant. In the dreams, I had been stealing something for Lord Morvilind, and I had been fleeing for my life from Homeland Security officers, knowing that if they caught me, Russell would die of frostfever. I flung open a fire door, hoping to escape into the night, but instead, I found myself standing on the main street of the twisted simulacrum of a small town inside the Eternity Crucible.

I whirled to flee back through the door, but it had vanished. I was trapped, and I could hear the rasp of wraithwolf claws against the concrete as they stalked me.

That was how I knew it was only a bad dream. Real wraithwolves, when they creep up on you, are utterly silent. You don't know the wraithwolves are there until their fangs sink into your flesh.

Just one of the many things I had learned the hard way.

So I didn't wake up in the sort of panic attack where it took me ten minutes to stop shaking, but I had an absolutely foul mood. I wanted to exercise to utter exhaustion, but I had done a hard strength workout yesterday, and doing those two days in a row is a great way to hurt yourself. Instead, I settled on doing cardio. I swallowed some ibuprofen tablets with a mug of cold coffee, went to the basement, and pounded out a run on the treadmill.

I was at about seven and a half miles when my phone started ringing.

I blinked in surprise and paused the treadmill, my breath wheezing, sweat dripping from every inch of my body. The basement of our house was unfinished, with a poured concrete floor and cinder block walls. That suited us perfectly. Riordan and I had set up a gym down here soon after we had moved in, and in the corner was the gun safe and an area that was evolving into a workshop for the various kinds of specialized equipment we used. I'd left my phone on the treadmill console, in case someone tried to call, along with a bottle of water since I'd promised Riordan that I would make sure I stayed hydrated while I exercised.

Thomas Hawley was calling me.

Arnold Brauner's lawyer. Now why was Brauner's lawyer calling me at seven in the morning?

I accepted the call. "Hello?"

"Mrs. MacCormac?" said Hawley in his precise voice. "I hope that I'm not calling too early."

"No, I was up," I said. I moved the phone away from my mouth and took a long drink of water. That felt really good. "What do you want to talk about?"

"Governor Brauner wants to know if you were available for a conversation," said Hawley.

"Yeah, sure," I said. Was Brauner going to try and squeeze me for more money? "I'm going to be busy all day, but if he can call me before nine, that should..."

"Governor Brauner wanted to know if you were available for a conversation right now," said Hawley.

"Now?" I said. What the hell was so urgent that he wanted to talk about it right now? "Sure."

"One moment," said Hawley. "Governor?"

I heard him pass the cell phone to someone else, followed by a short, muffled conversation in the background.

"Mrs. MacCormac?" Brauner's bluff voice filled my ear.

"Governor Arnold," I said. "Everything all right with the contract?"

"What? Oh, yes, it's quite good. Very generous of Moran Imports to donate to the Brauner Foundation," said Brauner. "But I'm afraid I'm calling about something else. My friends in Homeland Security tell me that you're assisting Colonel Owen Quell with his investigation into the murder of Ronald Doyle and his family."

I paused. Brauner wanted to talk about that? A couple of different possibilities occurred to me. Maybe Brauner had arranged to have Doyle killed, and was worried we would catch him. It was possible, but it didn't seem likely. Murder really wasn't Brauner's style, and while he was a hard man, I didn't see him ordering the deaths of the wife and children of a man who had crossed him.

Or maybe he was worried. Maybe he was frightened that whoever had killed Doyle was going to come after him next. He and Doyle had been close.

"Yeah," I said at last.

"Might I ask why?" said Brauner.

I shrugged, and then remembered he couldn't see me over the phone. "Quell asked and I said yes." Which wasn't strictly true, but I wasn't going to walk around telling people that I was the High Queen's shadow agent.

"That seems…unlikely," said Brauner. "With all respect, Mrs. MacCormac, while you are a capable young woman, why would Homeland Security ask you to help with a murder investigation?"

"I did other stuff before my brother started a fruit company," I said. "Some of the skills are transferable."

"Yes, that video of you in New York," said Brauner.

I repressed the urge to sigh. That damn video. I wish that Tarlia hadn't allowed it to go out to the public. I wasn't exactly famous or a celebrity or anything like that, but anyone who did more than five minutes of research on me knew that I was the woman who had stopped New York from getting nuked. Which I suppose was why Tarlia had let it be released – it was occasionally useful when dealing with guys like Arnold Brauner.

"And if you saw me kill those guys on that video," I said, "then you know I might be useful when apprehending a murderer."

There was a silence on the line. I suppose Brauner could have interpreted that last statement as a threat.

"I don't doubt your capabilities, Mrs. MacCormac," said Brauner. A flicker of humor entered the voice. "As you proved with my toothbrush. But you have to concede the timing is curious. You and your brother agree to contribute to the Brauner Foundation…and then less than two weeks later you are brought on as a consultant for a murder case. An odd coincidence."

"But just a coincidence," I said.

Unless…

Maybe it wasn't a coincidence. Maybe Doyle had been killed because of his connection to Brauner.

And maybe Brauner was scared.

"Wait, let me rephrase that," I said. "I think it's a coincidence. As far as I know at the moment, it's a coincidence. But maybe you know better. Do you know why Doyle was killed, Governor?"

Brauner snorted. "Now you sound like a Homeland Security officer. Perhaps I should speak to you with my lawyer present."

"For God's sake," I said. "We're on your lawyer's phone. And I'm not a Homeland Security officer. If I have a problem with you, we're going to settle it face to face."

"As the toothbrush demonstrated," said Brauner. "All right. Let me ask you a question. You may or may not be allowed to answer it."

"Go ahead," I said.

"Were Ronald Doyle and his family killed by a Shadowlands creature?" said Brauner.

I remembered the two-legged wraithwolf on the video, the odd echo on my aetherometer.

"Yes," I said. "Beyond any possible doubt."

Brauner's breath hissed. "I see."

"Look," I said. "If you know something about why Doyle was killed, I think it's in your best interests to tell me. And not because of the investigation or the law or anything like that. Someone hated Doyle enough to send a Shadowlands creature after him, and that's not a trivial thing to do. And it's probably not something Homeland Security or your private security would be able to protect you against."

"Is that a threat, Mrs. MacCormac?" said Brauner.

"Nope," I said. "I'm just laying it out for you. Someone had a reason to send that creature after Doyle, and if you know what that reason is, or if it applies to you...then you had really better tell me." I felt the anger creeping into my tone. "Because the creature also killed Doyle's kids. I'm not going to forget or forgive that. When I find the summoner, and I'm going to find him, he's going to regret it. If that doesn't matter to you, then think about this. If whoever had a grudge against Doyle has it out for you, then you might be the next target."

Neither of us spoke for about ten seconds.

"You must be hell on wheels when you're angry, Mrs. MacCormac," said Brauner.

"I occasionally have anger management issues," I said. Among others.

"You've convinced me, so I'm going to be straight with you," said Brauner. I heard Hawley protest in the background. "No, Tom. If Shadowlands creatures are involved, this goes beyond Homeland Security. Sooner or later, the Inquisition or the Elven lords will take action."

"Yeah," I said.

"I don't know why Doyle was murdered," said Brauner, "but I can think of any number of reasons that he might have been."

I waited.

"As I'm sure you've realized, Doyle was in a lot of trouble," said

Brauner. "To save money, he had been cutting costs at his construction company, which included producing what turned out to be defective concrete. That led to a collapse of a building which killed several people and injured several more. Doyle was facing numerous civil lawsuits and the possibility of criminal charges."

"What about you?" I said. "Don't you own Doyle's company?"

"I own a substantial portion of it," said Brauner. "I personally stand to lose between five and six million dollars, depending on how and when Doyle's company enters bankruptcy. But to be honest, while a six million dollar loss would be painful, it wouldn't be more than an inconvenience. I suppose some of the families of the victims could sue me, but since I wasn't personally involved in directing Doyle's business, my liability would be minimal, and the lawsuits would likely not make it to court."

Yeah. I bet that Brauner had made sure that none of Doyle's business troubles would land on his doorstep.

"Okay," I said. "You're saying there are a lot of pissed-off people who might have summoned a Shadowlands creature and sent it after Doyle."

"Yes," said Brauner. "It is also possible that Doyle might have other enemies."

"What do you mean?"

"Ronald was having financial difficulties even before the collapse and the lawsuits," said Brauner. "I think he made several investments of questionable legality."

"You're worried about questionable legality?" I said.

"You know as well as I do that laws can be bent as easily as paperclips," said Brauner. "But there are degrees of illegality. Things that the Elven nobles would care about. I think that in hopes of a quick profit Doyle was investing in technologies that the High Queen has forbidden."

"Like what?" I said.

"I don't know," said Brauner. "As I've said, I don't completely know the extent of Doyle's businesses." A dry note entered his voice.

"People might think I know every damn thing about my associates, but I don't. Would be helpful if I did, but I don't."

"Who do you think summoned the Shadowlands creature and sent it after him?" I said.

"Probably one of the families of the victims of the collapse, or someone from one of his more questionable investments," said Brauner.

"Well," I said. "I suppose that narrows it down. Least it should give us a starting point."

Unless, of course, Brauner was the one who had summoned the wraithwolf, or he knew who had done it. But my gut feeling was to believe him. It didn't make sense for Brauner to talk to me about this if he had done it. Hell, he had sent Homeland Security officers to harass me, so if he had summoned the creature, he would have had the influence to shut down the investigation or push it in another direction.

"Mrs. MacCormac," said Brauner. "If you need any assistance with this matter, please give me a call. My resources will be at your disposable."

"That's very generous of you," I said.

"As you said, it may be a matter of survival," said Brauner, voice grim. "And you don't know how bad these matters can get." A reasonable assumption for him to make, but he was wrong about that. "It is surprisingly easy for people to summon Shadowlands creatures, and if they work a spell empowered by blood, they may not even need magical talent. But the bond with the summoned creature works both ways, and it can twist the mind of the summoner. These things can quickly escalate into a bloodbath."

"You're very well-informed about forbidden magic," I said.

Brauner snorted. "I was the governor of Wisconsin for twelve years. We had a few cases like this. Homeland Security and the Inquisition caught the summoners and suppressed the news, but I saw the details. I know you think I'm a thug and a racketeer, but Wisconsin is my state, and I don't want this kind of shit happening here. That a good enough reason for you?"

"As it happens," I said, "I agree with you. Thanks for the information. If we need your help, I'll give you a call."

"Good luck, Mrs. MacCormac," said Brauner, and he ended the call.

I blew out a breath and stepped off the treadmill. I had been standing still long enough to cool off, and the sweat soaking my tank top and shorts had chilled. Shivering, I stripped off my sodden clothes, dumped them into the hamper, and head back upstairs to take a shower. I thought about what Brauner had told me. That was a good starting point for further investigation. Of course, Brauner might have been trying to throw me off his trail, but I doubted it.

In another hour, I had my meeting with Owen Quell. He had more resources for investigation, and maybe I could get him to look in directions Brauner had suggested. I got dressed in black jeans, a blue sweater, and my black pea coat, and headed across Milwaukee to the Central Office. Traffic was unpleasant, but at least it was a cloudless day, though it was still cold. I parked in the same ramp as before and walked to the Central Office. I thought about using my consultant's badge to gain entry but decided I didn't want to deal with that, so once again I Cloaked and made my way up to the homicide department and settled into Owen Quell's guest chair.

It was three minutes before nine. I was on time.

Owen was on the phone, scowling and writing in a small notebook.

"Uh-huh," he said. "Okay, that's good. That many calls? Great. Thanks for taking care of that so fast, Barbara. I owe you one. I'll tell Anna hi."

He hung up, and I dropped my Cloak spell as he looked up from the notebook.

Owen didn't flinch, which was impressive, but his eye did twitch before I caught it.

"Morning, Colonel," I said.

"Mrs. MacCormac," said Owen. "You're very punctual."

"Yeah, I'm all kinds of punctual," I said. "Ready to get to it?"

"I am," said Owen. "Just had an interesting phone call from an officer in the cybercrime division. We got a warrant for Doyle's phone records and pulled them. We'd already been over his official office phone and his personal cell phone, but nothing stood out. But it turns out that Doyle had a burner phone that he paid for quietly on the side, and the day he was killed, he made seven calls to a guy named Pablo Leon. Know the name?"

"No," I said, my brow furrowing. "No, wait. He's in construction, isn't he?"

And, unless I missed my guess, he was another of Arnold Brauner's friends.

"His company's specialty is sewers and septic systems," said Owen. "He and Doyle had a cozy arrangement. Doyle built the buildings, and Leon laid the sewer pipe. I think we should start today by paying Mr. Leon a visit. Find out what they talked about over those seven phone calls."

"Agreed," I said. Owen started to stand up. "But before we go, I should tell you this." Owen sat back down. "This morning, I had a phone call from Arnold Brauner."

Owen frowned. "Did you now? I didn't know you knew a former governor."

"We met when he coerced me into paying one percent of my brother's company's profits to the Brauner Foundation," I said.

"Uh huh," said Owen. The look he gave me set my teeth on edge. It was the expression of a Homeland Security officer considering a suspect. "And what did you get from Governor Arnold in exchange for that one percent?"

"He leaves us alone," I said, irritated. "He wanted more, but I convinced him it was in his best interest not to make trouble for us."

"Sure," said Owen. "How did you manage that?"

I grinned my mirthless grin at him. "I'm very persuasive."

"If Brauner was trying to coerce you, why didn't you report him?" said Owen.

"To who? You people?" I said, making no effort to hide my derision. "Who do you think Brauner sent to bully us? Homeland Security officers on his payroll."

"Are you accusing Homeland Security officers of corruption?" said Owen.

"For God's sake, were you born yesterday?" I said. "Brauner is Duke Tamirlas's shadow councilor. If I accused him, what would happen? Evidence would disappear, his powerful friends would make trouble for the company, and God only knows what else. I'm sure he'd make a call to one of your superiors, and the investigation would disappear."

"You're part of Brauner's organization," said Owen.

"Nope," I said. "We donate to his damn foundation, and he leaves us alone. If he breaks the deal, we'll renegotiate."

"Bet we would find all sorts of interesting things in your company's tax records," said Owen.

"No, you wouldn't," I said. Not after what we paid for quarterly auditing. "But do you want to nitpick, or do you want to find whoever killed the Doyles? Which is what the High Queen told us to do."

Owen sighed. "What did Brauner tell you?"

"He said that Doyle was having financial trouble even before the lawsuits from the building collapse," I said. "Doyle was apparently trying to make up his losses by risky investment in illegal technology."

Owen's brows furrowed. "What kind of illegal technology?"

"Good question. Brauner claimed he didn't know," I said.

"Or he knows and was involved in it himself," said Owen. He fiddled with his pen a moment, thinking. "There's a couple different avenues here. Might be drug-related. That's pretty heavily restricted. Most illegal drugs are produced with protein printers in people's basements. Or automation technology."

"Automation?" I said.

"Yeah, anything that can replace a job," said Owen. "You've probably realized that the High Queen values social stability more than economic innovation. A couple years ago a chain of grocery stores tried to install self-checkout kiosks, and they almost got shut down, and the owners very nearly were prosecuted. That's been relaxed a little since the Day of Return, but maybe Doyle was working on something like that, something computer-related." He shrugged. "Or, hell, maybe he was straight-up involved in computer fraud. We're just speculating. We need more concrete evidence, and our best chance for finding it right now is to talk with Pablo Leon." He rose to his feet. "Ready to go?"

"You can drive," I said.

8

A SHAME IF ANYTHING HAPPENED

Pablo Leon's company, Modern Sewer Solutions, operated out of an industrial site in Menomonee Falls, northwest of Milwaukee proper. Owen got on Interstate 41, joining the flow of morning traffic.

Nadia sat in silence in the passenger seat, watching the scenery go by and ignoring him.

Owen decided that he had handled the conversation in his office badly. She had come with useful information from Arnold Brauner, and he had basically accused her of racketeering. That had been a knee-jerk reaction. She reminded him too much of Peter Walsh and Luke Corbisher, though she was nothing like them. But the idea that she was a powerful woman using her connections to escape punishment for her crimes set his teeth on edge and brought back memories of Christopher's death.

That didn't matter. Owen had to work with her.

"How did you wind up owning a fruit company?" said Owen.

"Why do you want to know?" said Nadia. "Going to make up some tax violations and report us?"

"No," said Owen. "Just curious. Not many twenty-two-year-old women own fruit import companies."

A ghost of a smile flickered over her face. "Don't believe what it says in UNICORN. I'm a lot older than I look. I just moisturize a lot."

She lapsed into silence. Owen had activated his aurasight, partly because he needed to work with Nadia and keeping from offending her was a good way to do that, and partly because it let him watch out for drivers in a state of rage or inebriation. Though even in Wisconsin, drunk drivers were not all that common on the interstate at half-past nine in the morning. From the corner of his eye, he saw the twisting in her emotional aura as irritation and dislike battled with reason. She, too, realized they had to work together.

Finally, she sighed. "It's not really my company. I own part of it, but it's my brother's idea. I'm just helping manage it until he finishes dealing with high school and can run it full time. Only another couple of months."

"He's, what, seventeen?" said Owen. Nadia nodded, the wariness in her aura increasing. "So how does a seventeen-year-old kid wind up with a fruit import company?"

"He asked nicely," said Nadia. "The High Queen came to my wedding. Apparently, it's traditional for an Elven noble to present her retainers with a gift on the day of their marriage." Owen hadn't known that, but he had already been married when Tarlia recruited him. "One of the High Queen's handmaidens brought a fruit basket. Russell ate half of it, and I don't know how he did it, but he convinced the High Queen to give him the exclusive right to import fruit from Kalvarion." She shrugged. "So, Moran Imports. If it makes you feel any better, it might not be profitable, so we wouldn't wind up paying the Brauner Foundation a cent."

Owen said nothing, his mind sifting through that. He had interrogated a lot of different people over the years and had a great deal of practice at reading people's motivations even without the benefit of the aurasight and mindtouch spells. Suddenly he realized why she had gotten so angry when he had implied her brother's company was part of Brauner's organization. Tarlia had somehow used Russell Moran to recruit Nadia as her shadow agent, just as she had used Owen's twin daughters to recruit him. Maybe Tarlia had healed

Russell or somehow gotten him out of trouble. If the data in UNICORN was accurate, Russell was Nadia's only family, not counting her husband.

She would be protective of him.

"Makes sense, I suppose," said Owen. "It's hard to have a large business in Wisconsin without at least kissing Arnold Brauner's ring. Sounds like you managed to get a good deal from him."

Her startled expression perfectly matched the emotion in her aura. "Wasn't expecting that from you."

"I don't like Brauner, and I know that he's a crook," said Owen, "but like you said, he's Duke Tamirlas's shadow councilor. And he's not as bad as someone like him could be. Some of the shadow councilors in South America and eastern Asia make Brauner look like a model citizen."

"Yeah," said Nadia.

"Seems like your brother started a good business," said Owen. "The High Queen is going to spend a mountain of money rebuilding Kalvarion, and a lot of people here are going to get rich. Some company in New York is building robotic tractors, and the Elves never allowed those here."

"Kalvarion's going to need them," said Nadia.

He gave her a surprised look. "You've been there?"

"I was, once, on the day of the Mage Fall," said Nadia, her expression distant. "Kalvarion was in bad shape. The Archons drove it into the ground. I think about nine billion Elves lived on Kalvarion when the Archons took over, something like that. When Morvilind killed all the Archons, there were less than a billion Elves still alive on Kalvarion. Archons killed them all." She smirked. "Suppose that puts dealing with a crook like Brauner in perspective, doesn't it?"

"Perspective is a healthy thing," said Owen.

"When we arrive, how are we going to play this?" said Nadia. It seemed she wanted to get down to business.

"I don't know," said Owen. "Depends on how well Leon cooperates. If he talks freely, that will be easy. If he makes trouble for us, we'll have to get a warrant."

"Or you could just look into his mind and find out what he knows," said Nadia, that annoyed edge to her voice and emotions once more.

"Maybe," said Owen. "It depends. You know the mindtouch spell?" She nodded. "Then you know it's not always the most pleasant experience. Looking into someone else's mind…you see things you'd rather not. And it doesn't always work, at least at my level of skill. The High Queen, she can use it to sift through your thoughts like a strainer. For me, I can find what I'm looking for most of the time, but if the mind is strong enough, it can resist."

"Well," said Nadia, "suppose we'll just have to play it by ear."

Owen laughed. "Welcome to Homeland Security."

She frowned. "Why is that funny?"

"Because we have procedures and policies for every damn thing, but we still have to play it by ear half the time," said Owen.

"Suppose that's true," said Nadia. "You can plan for everything, and it still all goes to hell most of the time."

Owen took an exit off the interstate and turned right. A half-mile later he drove up to Modern Sewer Solutions. It was a big building with cinder block walls and a corrugated steel roof. A chain link fence with barbed wire encircled the entire property. Parked in the yard were dump trucks and several bulldozers and excavators and stacked in one corner were several concrete segments of sewer pipe. A guy in a forklift was moving plastic-wrapped pallets in the other side of the yard. A row of pickup trucks and cars were lined up against one wall, and Owen parked the SUV in one of the empty spots. He and Nadia got out and looked around.

"Doesn't look like Leon's into forbidden technology," said Nadia.

"If he was, would he leave it lying around in the yard?" said Owen. Nadia inclined her head to concede the point.

The forklift shut off, and a paunchy middle-aged guy in a tan jacket, jeans, and work boots got out. He hurried over, a worried look on his face, but the sight of a Homeland Security officer intended to inspire that reaction.

"Hi," said the man. "There a problem?"

"Not right now," said Owen. "My name's Owen Quell, and I'm with Homeland Security. We're looking to talk with Pablo Leon. Do you know if he's around?"

"The boss?" said the man. "He doesn't come around too much. But we can check."

"Thanks," said Owen. "What's your name?"

"Dave Maddock," said the man. "I'm the yard supervisor." He gave Nadia a confused look. "Did…you bring your daughter?"

Owen repressed the urge to scowl as Nadia threw back her head and laughed.

"Sorry, no," said Nadia. "My name's Nadia, and I'm a consultant."

"Huh," said Maddock. "Well, let's check with Toni. This way."

Maddock led the way to the warehouse door. Owen had let his aurasight lapse during the drive, but he reactivated the spell. Maddock's aura was concerned, but held no trace of tension or worry. If Leon was involved in something illicit, Maddock didn't know about it.

Owen and Nadia followed Maddock into a shabby-looking office area. Worn gray carpet covered the floor, and several cubicle partitions had been set up. Some of them held desks, while others contained stacked boxes. Modern Sewer Systems did not look very organized. On the far side of the room was a small office, and a pretty middle-aged woman sat at a desk, typing on a computer. A little plaque on her desk said that her name was Tonette Caplan, office manager for Modern Sewer Systems.

"Hey, Toni?" said Maddock.

"Yeah?" said the woman, not looking up from her screen. She had dark hair arranged in a messy bun and wore a button-down shirt and jeans.

"Homeland Security's here, and they want to talk to the boss," said Maddock.

Toni looked up, her eyes widening behind her glasses. A flush of guilt and fear went through her emotional aura, and Owen realized they had found a lead. She knew something.

"Hello," said Owen. "I'm Owen Quell, and this is Nadia, a consultant working with the department. We were wondering if we could speak with Mr. Leon."

Toni frowned. "What about?"

"Questions concerning an ongoing investigation," said Owen. "Can we talk in here?"

Toni hesitated, looked around, the guilt and fear in her aura intensifying.

"Yeah," she said at last, wiping her hands on her jeans. "Yeah, we can talk in here. Can you close the door behind you, Dave?"

"Sure," said Maddock. Clearly, he had wanted to hang around and listen. He left the little office and closed the door behind him.

"So," said Toni. "What's this about?"

"All right," said Owen. "I'm going to have to read you your rights and responsibilities." He made the official statement as he had so many times before. "Do you understand them?"

"Yeah," said Toni. Her eyes were wide and frightened. "Am I under arrest?"

"No, we just want to ask some questions," said Owen.

"Okay," said Toni. She folded her arms across her chest, unfolded them. "Ask."

"We wanted to speak to Mr. Pablo Leon," said Owen. "We haven't been able to reach him. Do you know where he is?"

Toni shrugged. "No. Have you tried calling him at home? Or his cell phone?"

"We've tried," said Owen. "There's been no response."

"Oh," said Toni. "Well...maybe you should try again. He's really busy."

The guilt and fear in her aura flushed deeper.

"I'm sure that he is," said Owen. He decided to try a different tack. "When was the last time you saw Mr. Leon?"

"Um," said Toni. She wiped her hands on her jeans again. It was such a screamingly obvious tell that he would have known that she was lying even if he hadn't used the aurasight. "I'd say...three days ago? Yes, that sounds right. Three days ago."

That would have been the day after the Doyles were killed.

"Three days?" said Owen. "That's a long time to be out of touch."

Toni shrugged. "Mr. Leon is a busy man. He has a lot of responsibilities."

"Like running this company?" said Owen.

Toni nodded. "Yes, of course."

"Would you say that Mr. Leon is a very hands-on manager?" said Owen.

For some reason, Toni flushed at that. "Yes. He's always involved with the company's work. Sometimes he goes out to dig sites himself to supervise."

"Then isn't it a little strange that he hasn't shown up for work in the past three days?" said Owen. "Did he take a vacation?"

"No," said Toni. "Not...not that I know of. Sometimes Pablo isn't the best with paperwork, which is why he hired me."

"Do you happen to know a man named Ronald Doyle?" said Owen.

Toni stopped herself from flinching, but a quiver still went through her face.

"I do," said Toni. "He owns a construction company. I saw in the news that he died a few days ago."

"What kind of relationship did you have Ronald Doyle?" said Owen.

"I didn't," said Toni. "I mean, I knew him, and we sometimes chatted when he and Pablo were working together on contracts, but that was it. He seemed like a nice guy. I don't think he deserved what happened to him."

"What did happen to him?" said Owen.

Toni shifted in her chair. "Well...he died. That's what the news said, right? Some kind of accident or something."

Nadia's voice was quiet. "All the news said was that he died in suspicious circumstances." She was standing in the corner of the little office, arms folded, face grim. "Didn't say anything else."

"Accidents can be suspicious," said Toni.

"That's right," said Owen. "You said you last saw Mr. Leon three days ago. That would have been the day after Doyle was killed. Did Mr. Leon know about it?"

"Yes," said Toni. "It...he was very upset. He and Mr. Doyle were friends."

"Would you say that Mr. Leon was frightened?" said Owen. "Like he was worried that what happened to Mr. Doyle might happen to him?"

"What...what did happen to Mr. Doyle?" said Toni. "Pablo didn't say..."

Owen hadn't decided on how to answer that question, but Nadia spoke first.

"He and his entire family were killed by a creature from the Shadowlands," said Nadia.

"Oh, God," said Toni, eyes wide. "God. Even the kids?" Nadia nodded. "That's awful. Was it something left over from the Archon attack a few years ago? I remember that. One of the rift ways opened up on the street a few blocks away, and we all stayed inside the building with our guns until the battle was over."

"Ms. Caplan," said Owen. "We have reason to believe that Mr. Leon is in danger from the creature that killed Mr. Doyle and his family." That was only a hunch, but it seemed very likely. And it wasn't illegal for Homeland Security to lie to witnesses and suspects during an investigation. "If you have any information about his whereabouts, that would be helpful."

"I'm sorry," said Toni. "I just don't know where he is. He just...I haven't heard from him in a couple of days."

Even without the aurasight, he could tell that she was lying. With the aurasight, she all but glowed with guilt and fear.

"I see," said Owen. "I need to show you something. One moment."

He drew out his phone, went to the official website for Punishment Day videos, and selected a suitable one. The video started playing, and Owen turned the screen to face Toni. She flinched back in her chair as a scream came over the phone's speakers. The video was from California, and it showed a naked woman dragged to a post and tied to it, her arms bound over her head. An Elven noble wielded a whip with expert precision, lashing it across her back ten times while the woman screamed and sobbed. The spectacle turned Owen's stomach, as it always did, but he kept his face stony.

"What the hell?" said Toni. "Why are you showing me that?"

His aurasight detected a surge of fury, but not from her.

From the corner of his eye, he saw Nadia glaring at him, but he ignored her and pressed on.

"Ms. Caplan," said Owen. "This video is from a recent case. A woman was convicted of giving false statements to Homeland Security during an investigation. That typically carries a steep fine, but for a felony investigation, the penalty also includes ten lashes on a Punishment Day video. You have stated, during an interview with a Homeland Security officer, that you don't know of Mr. Pablo Leon's current whereabouts. I would like to give you a chance to reconsider that statement before it is entered into the official record of this investigation."

Tears filled Toni's eyes. "I don't...I don't..."

"I don't want to take you back to the Central Office for questioning," said Owen.

Toni let out a shuddering breath, tears sliding down her face. Owen paused the video.

"You don't understand," she said. "Nobody does. Pablo's been under so much strain, and he can't tell anyone. He..."

"You're having an affair with him, aren't you?" said Nadia. Her voice was quiet, sympathetic, but the hot rage in her aura hadn't abated.

"His wife doesn't understand him," said Toni. "She doesn't understand the business. I do. Pablo couldn't run it without me."

"Ms. Caplan, it is highly likely that someone sent a Shadowlands creature to kill Ronald Doyle and his family," said Owen. "If Mr. Doyle and Mr. Leon had some kind of business relationship that inspired the attack, it is possible that Mr. Leon is in extreme danger. Please, help us find him."

"It...you have to understand," said Toni. "The company had some tight years. Pablo was looking for a new way to make money, something to help the balance books. A few months ago, he and Doyle had a deal. Something with a new technology company. He didn't tell me the details." A flicker of resentment went through her aura, soon subsumed by the fear. "Then, three days ago, he came into the office. He was in a good mood. But he saw the news that Doyle had died in suspicious circumstances, and it was…it was like he panicked. I've never seen him so upset. He emptied out the safe in his office. He all but ran to his car, and I haven't seen him since. He hasn't responded to emails or texts or calls, nothing."

"Do you have any idea where he might have gone?" said Owen.

"No," said Toni. "He has a cabin in Minnesota, by the Boundary Waters, but no one is picking up the phone there. I don't know where he's gone, and I'm really worried."

"Did you consider filing a missing person report with Homeland Security?" said Owen.

Toni hesitated, some of the guilt in her aura intensifying. Likely Modern Sewer Systems had some business practices she didn't want examined too closely. "I didn't know what to do about it. I know what Homeland Security would have said. They'd just laugh at me or say he had gone on a trip."

"Or shove a Punishment Day video in your face," said Nadia.

"But can you help him?" said Toni.

"We're going to do our best to find him," said Owen. That was no lie. It seemed very likely that Doyle and Leon had been involved in something together, and whatever it was had gotten Doyle killed. If they found Leon, they would have their answers.

Unfortunately, it seemed probable that Leon had already been killed.

"Thank you," said Toni. "Thank you."

"Can we have a look around his office?" said Owen. "We might find something that will tell us where Mr. Leon went."

"Sure," said Toni, getting to her feet with a shaky breath, "but I don't know how much help that will be. He didn't leave much behind."

That was the truth. Leon's office was about the size of Toni's, but far emptier. The desk was bare of papers and documents. A safe in the wall stood open. There were cords for a laptop computer on the desk, but no sign of the laptop, which Toni said Leon had taken with him.

"Thank you for your cooperation, Ms. Caplan," said Owen once they had finished. "We'll contact you if we have any further questions."

"Please, please, let me know if you find Pablo," said Toni.

"We will," said Owen. He hoped he would not have to notify her of Pablo Leon's death, but that seemed probable. "We will pursue all avenues of investigation."

He walked back into the cold November day, Nadia following him.

The molten rage pulsed through her aura, unabated since the conversation.

9

BAD MEMORIES

Owen got behind the wheel of the SUV and opened the laptop mounted on the dashboard.

Nadia slid into the passenger seat, her face a hard mask.

"Give me a minute," said Owen, bringing up the UNICORN interface. "I need to update the case notes with Tonette Caplan's statement. That, combined with the fact that Pablo Leon seems to have disappeared, should be enough to get a warrant to go over his finances. If he's hiding somewhere, that might help us find him." He rubbed his jaw, his mind racing. "Do a UNICORN check on Leon quick, find out about his wife and kids. We need to check on his wife. If whoever sent the wraithwolf after the Doyles goes after Leon, they'll be in danger."

Nadia's expression was still hard, but she nodded and produced her phone.

"His wife's name is Carolina," she said after a moment. "Apparently she was a model in Portugal before she and Pablo emigrated here. Two kids, uh...boys both, ages 18 and 20, and they're both in service to Duke Tamirlas as men-at-arms right now. They're probably safer than Leon himself."

"Right," said Owen. "I'll get a call into Duke Tamirlas's office, have them check to make sure the kids are in the barracks. Then after I put in the request for the warrant, we'll stop by Pablo Leon's primary residence, see if we can meet his wife and get more information."

"Okay," said Nadia.

They sat in silence as Owen filled out the forms on the UNICORN interface.

"You might as well get it off your chest," said Owen.

"Get what off my chest?"

"Why you're so pissed."

"Suppose the aurasight told you that," said Nadia.

"Yup. Also, I've been married for eighteen years, and I have four daughters," said Owen. "I know when a woman's angry at me."

She did not smile at the joke. "You want to know? All right, fine. Why the hell did you shove that Punishment Day video into Caplan's face and threaten her with it?"

Owen blinked. "It worked, didn't it?"

"God," she spat, caught halfway between exasperation and disgust. "The end justifies the means, is that it? Doesn't matter who you hurt and what you break along the way, so long as you get results? Sounds like a Homeland Security officer for sure."

"Really?" said Owen, glancing up from the keyboard. "The end justifies the means? Sounds more like the method of a criminal who received a royal pardon."

"Looked that up, did you?" said Nadia. "I suppose deep down every Homeland Security officer is a bit of a voyeur."

That annoyed him. "Really? The High Queen orders me to work with you, and then you simply appear out of nowhere in my office while making no effort to hide your contempt for Homeland Security. If I didn't try to find out more about you, I'd be an idiot."

"And what did you find out?" said Nadia. "You've had all this practice as a voyeur, bet you found out something."

"I know you used to be a Rebel," said Owen. Her lips thinned further. "And I know you betrayed them and parleyed that into a pardon from the High Queen."

"Bullshit," said Nadia. "I was forced to work with the Rebels. An Elven noble held a gun to my head and told me that I had to do it. First chance I got, I screwed the Rebels over."

"I'm sure," said Owen. "No doubt that's the story you told yourself and the High Queen." He felt his own temper beginning to slip. "I've seen the results of Rebel attacks. I wonder how many kids you've killed over..."

This time she did snarl at him. "I have never killed a kid. Not now, not ever."

"I know exactly what you are," said Owen. He slammed the lid of the laptop shut and glared at her over it. "You're yet another rich and powerful person who used connections and money to escape punishment for your crimes. Someone like you deserves a Punishment Day video, but you'll never get it."

She jabbed a finger in his chest. "Fine. It's time for honesty, is it? You want to know what I think of you?"

"By all means," said Owen.

"You're a thug and a bully with a badge," said Nadia. "All that bullshit about protecting and serving the community? That's crap. Your job is to keep people in line for the Elven nobles. That's all you are, a thug and enforcer, and nothing else. Just another group of thugs, but with shiny badges that make them feel good about themselves. Like kindergartners with gold stars."

"Really," said Owen. "Someone like you would say that. You haven't had to clean up the messes that people like you make. You haven't had to notify the families that their loved ones are dead, you haven't had to stop killers after they've wrecked lives. You skate away from the consequences of your crimes, and..."

Nadia laughed in his face. "That's pretty rich. You had that video ready to go on your phone, didn't you? Is that what you do in your spare time, watch videos of women getting flogged on Punishment Day? Bet that's what you and the other officers do all day, sit around and jerk off while watching those. Or maybe you would have threated Caplan with arrest but changed your mind if she slept with you. Bet that's what you..."

Owen felt his temper snap. "I have never cheated on my wife."

"Oh, hit a sore point, did I?" said Nadia. They were both shouting now, and part of Owen's mind noted this would look bad if someone saw, but he was too angry to care. "That's the real reason you don't like me. Assholes with badges are used to pushing around anyone they like, but you can't push me around."

"I wonder how many crimes you got away with," said Owen, "and how the High Queen would react if she knew the truth about..."

"Gonna look into my mind?" said Nadia. "I know you want to." She leaned closer, glaring at him. "Go on. Do it. Use the mindtouch spell and break into my mind. Then I'll know that your precious daughters really do have a thug and a liar and a voyeur for a..."

That did it, the mention of his daughters. Owen knew it was a bad idea, but his anger had grown past his prudence. He summoned magic, cast the mindtouch spell, and sent his will plunging into Nadia's thoughts, determined to dig out evidence of her crimes. He caught a glimpse of her emotions – fury mixed with disgust and constant, wearying tension – and some of her memories flickered before his mind.

And then her will closed around his like an iron vice.

He had an instant to realize that he had made a serious mistake. Her magic was much, much stronger than his, and her mind was far older. She looked like a pretty woman in her twenties, but her mind was older than should have been possible for a human.

And the older a human mind became, the harder it was to control.

Then she sent some of her memories pouring into the link of the mindtouch spell, and Owen experienced them as if they were his own.

In one, Nadia lay pinned on her stomach, screaming and struggling. A dozen anthrophages swarmed over her, ripping open her clothes. Their fanged mouths plunged down, ripping chunks of meat from her back and buttocks and legs, and she screamed until she died from blood loss.

In another she stumbled through a darkened concrete tunnel,

bleeding from a dozen wounds. A mob of bloodrats poured after her, dozens of them, their crimson fur glistening in the dim light. Her left leg was a column of agony, and she collapsed and tried to push off the floor.

The tide of bloodrats rushed over her, their chisel-like teeth punching into her flesh as she screamed.

In another memory, Nadia was trapped in the wreckage of a burning house, her shattered right leg pinned beneath a beam. Flames burned through the house, and wraithwolves prowled outside, waiting for her to come out so they could kill her. But she was trapped, and she tried to free herself until the flames consumed her and she died in torment.

A dozen deaths ripped through his thoughts, and then a hundred, and more and more until it overwhelmed his mind, and Owen fell into merciful oblivion.

∽

I STARED AT OWEN, watching him twitch, my teeth bared in a snarl. My mind held his mindtouch spell in an iron grip, and my will ripped into his thoughts. His magic was stronger than I expected, but mine was stronger still, and I was really pissed off. When he had shown that video to Toni Caplan, it had been like a bomb going off in my head. I hadn't liked Owen from the beginning, and then he had shown himself to be a bullying thug, just as I had suspected.

I tore the knowledge of the aurasight spell from his memory. I had done this once before when Nicholas Connor's girlfriend Hailey Adams had tried to look into my mind. That hadn't ended well for her, and I had pulled the knowledge of the mindtouch spell from her, which was how I had learned it in the first place. I didn't need Owen Quell. I would track down Doyle's killer myself, and then...

I heard something rasping and realized it was Owen's shoes scraping against the floormats. He was jerking and twitching like he was having a seizure.

The anger evaporated, leaving a burst of sick dread in its wake.

Shit. Had I just murdered a Homeland Security officer?

What the hell was I doing?

I released my will, and the mindtouch spell faded, the mental contact evaporating. Owen collapsed into the driver's seat, his eyes closed. He was still breathing, which was good. I put two fingers on his neck and started counting his pulse.

Hundred and eighty beats a minute. Not good.

I waited, and his pulse and breathing slowed. Sweat dripped down his face, but his pulse dropped to a much less alarming rate. I sat back with a relieved sigh. What the hell had I been thinking? The Punishment Day video had pissed me off, but I shouldn't have picked at Owen.

But he shouldn't have implied that I had killed kids. That had really gotten under my skin. That was what had turned me against Nicholas Connor when I had discovered he planned to bomb that soccer stadium in Los Angeles to assassinate Duke Wraithmyr. I mean, I'm not the kind of woman who gets gooey over babies or thinks that kids are cute (I mostly find them annoying), but I don't want them hurt.

When Owen implied that, I had lost it. He shouldn't have said that.

But maybe I shouldn't have implied that he used his badge to coerce female suspects.

Damn it all, I was a hundred and eighty years old. I had to learn to control my temper.

I waited for Owen to wake up. It took about forty minutes. No doubt Toni and Dave were watching and wondering why the hell we hadn't left. I waited, and Owen's eyes blinked open. He saw me watching him and flinched back, one hand going towards his gun, the other coming up in the beginning of a spell.

"Give it a minute," I said. "Um. What just happened was that you looked at some of my memories, they were too horrible for your mind to process, so your brain sort of rebooted itself and you blacked out for the last forty-three minutes." I handed him a bottle of water I had found in the emergency kit under seat. "Drink this, it will make you feel better."

He blinked at me but took the water and opened the bottle.

"If it helps," I said, "you won't be able to remember it clearly. The mind sort of deletes the memories for self-protection."

Owen took a drink.

"I'm sorry," I said. "I shouldn't have provoked you into using the mindtouch spell. I knew what would happen, and I apologize for that."

He coughed out a laugh.

"Yeah, maybe," he said, "but I was the damn fool who did it."

"And I apologize for saying that you did...the things I said you did," I said.

Owen grunted. "I shouldn't have tried to look in your head. I'm a Homeland Security officer, for God's sake. I've been called every name and heard every threat in the English language." He shook his head. "And I lose my temper with you of all people."

"I'm just really that annoying," I said.

He snorted. "Not going to argue with that." He sighed. "Look, I don't know what you had in your past, but the High Queen pardoned you. That's that."

We sat in silence for a moment.

"Those memories," said Owen at last. "Did you project them? Or did they really happen?"

"They really happened," I said, staring at the dashboard. "All of them."

"Christ," said Owen. "How is that possible? You couldn't have lived through all that. You don't have to tell me what happened, but..."

"It...was something like a time loop," I said. "In a pocket domain in the Shadowlands. The same day repeated over and over again. Um...every time I died the whole thing reset."

"How many times did you die?" said Owen. "A couple hundred?"

"Just under fifty-eight thousand times," I said.

"Christ," said Owen again. It was the first time I had seen him shaken. "That's like…"

"A hundred and fifty-eight years, yeah," I said.

We sat in silence some more.

"How are you even still sane?" said Owen.

I let out a shaky laugh. "I'm not. Not really. Uh. I'm functional, which is almost as good as sane." I drummed my fingers on the armrest. "I had to keep it together. My brother would have died if I hadn't. And my husband…my husband is really helpful. He deserves better than me, but he still loves me, God knows why."

"I feel the same way about my wife," said Owen.

"Look," I said. "I flipped out when you showed Caplan that video because I was afraid of that for a long time. I had nightmares that looked like that. I was a shadow agent for an Elven noble…"

"Kaethran Morvilind?" said Owen.

I frowned. "How'd you know that?"

"I'm a detective," said Owen. I snorted. "You mentioned the Mage Fall, and you stopped the Sky Hammer. Not much of a logical leap."

"Guess not," I said. "Morvilind had me steal things for him. My brother was sick, frostfever. Morvilind cast one cure spell a year, and in exchange, I stole stuff for him. And he told me if I ever got caught, he would abandon me to Homeland Security or kill me remotely through magic, and my brother would die of his illness."

"That's messed up," said Owen.

I felt a weird surge of relief when he said that. I had grown up with that arrangement, so I had been used to it. For someone understand to see how screwed up my childhood had been was always…I don't know. Validating? Something like that. Anyway, I appreciated it.

"I did work with the Rebels," I said, "but I hated it. Morvilind ordered me to do it. A deal he had made to find some stuff he needed for the Mage Fall. The minute I was out from under the deal, I turned on the Rebels."

"The video of you shooting the Rebel leader and pushing the Sky Hammer into the Shadowlands," said Owen.

"That damn video," I muttered. "If it helps, the Rebel leader was an enormous asshole. He was the one who wanted to bomb New York. I regret some stuff, but I don't regret killing him. But...I've been running from Homeland Security most of my life, right up until I got that pardon. And all that protect and serve stuff just pisses me off. No one with authority ever protected me, not from anything. I was on my own. Shit." I sighed and rubbed my face. "I suppose I was taking out my issues with Homeland Security on you."

Owen nodded. "I'd appreciate it if you'd talk to a therapist instead. Hell, I'd even pay for it."

"Might be I should take you up on that," I said, half-seriously. Riordan had made a few tentative suggestions in that direction, but I hadn't listened. What sort of therapist can deal with someone who has my kind of mental problems?

"If it helps," said Owen, "you're not alone. I think I was doing the exact same thing with you."

I frowned. "What do you mean?"

"I became a Homeland Security officer," said Owen, "because of my brother Christopher."

"This isn't going to be a happy story, is it?" I said.

"No," said Owen. "I grew up in Minneapolis. One day Chris and I were walking home, and he was hit and killed by a man named Peter Walsh. Heard of him?"

I shook my head.

"He was a Minnesota state legislator," said Owen. "He was also seriously drunk at the time. It should have been a straightforward conviction, but Peter Walsh happened to be married to Luke Corbisher's niece...ah, I see you do recognize that name."

"Oh, yeah," I said. I'd never met Luke Corbisher, but I knew his son Martin much better than I would have wanted. "Go ahead."

"Walsh went to trial for it," said Owen, "and Luke Corbisher arranged for him to get off. My family was furious, but there was nothing they could do about it. But I started playing detective. I found a recording of Walsh drinking about ten minutes before the accident, and another recording of him actually running that stoplight and hitting Chris." His smile was hard and joyless. "That forced another trial. Corbisher washed his hands of it, and Walsh wound up getting convicted and executed for murder. The Corbisher family had it out for us, so we had to move to Milwaukee." Owen shrugged. "Ever since that, I was interested in law enforcement work. But then I manifested magic, and I wound up in the Wizard's Legion."

"So that's why you were so pissed at me," I said. "You thought I was someone like Peter Walsh."

"Seems I was wrong," said Owen.

"Well, I can't blame you for that," I said. "I am kind of a bitch even on my best days." I laughed.

"What?" said Owen.

"It's funny," I said. "Not what happened to you, that's not funny, but just...the coincidence. I know all about the Corbishers. Did you know that Luke Corbisher was the high priest of a Dark Ones cult?"

Owen looked taken aback. "What? Seriously?"

"Honest to God," I said. "The Corbishers were the head of a Dark Ones cult going back centuries. Luke wanted to keep it quiet. But his son Martin decided it was time to join the Rebels, so he murdered his dad, made it look like an accident, and allied with the Rebels. And then he tried to kill me...jeez, a bunch of times. I forget how many off the top of my head."

"What happened to Martin Corbisher?" said Owen. "I'd heard that he disappeared."

"I don't actually know," I said. "He's probably dead. I hope he's dead. If he was in the Shadowlands when the Sky Hammer blew up, it killed him with the rest of the Rebels. If he was in New York when the Sky Hammer went up...I don't know. He might be hiding someplace. Or he could have gotten killed in the battle. A lot of people got killed in New York, and not all the bodies have been found."

"Huh," said Owen. "Suppose that explains why Luke Corbisher cut off Walsh once I found that new evidence. He probably feared his cult getting exposed. I wonder how long the cult was going on. Do you know how the Corbishers originally made their money?"

"No," I said, curious. "I'd heard the family allied with the High Queen during the Conquest. Figured they got rich then."

"They were rich before the Conquest," said Owen. "Dug up some facts when I was playing junior detective. In the last couple of decades before the Conquest, the US government decided to resettle large numbers of African refugees in Minnesota. Luke Corbisher's ancestor took government contracts to build housing for them. He did it as cheaply as possible and pocketed the difference."

"That sounds like good old Marty Corbisher," I said. "Wonder how many of those refugees ended up as sacrifices to the Dark Ones."

"Probably more than we'll ever know," said Owen.

"Well, it's stopped now," I said. "All of Corbisher's followers died in the Sky Hammer, and the Corbisher Group in Minnesota is under new ownership. Wouldn't surprise me if the High Queen is the new majority shareholder of the company."

"That is one of her favorite strategies," said Owen. "Huh. You were on the bad side of the Corbishers, too. Never would have guessed."

"I don't think you'll be shocked to learn I have a gift for getting on people's bad sides," I said. Owen snorted. "I wound up working for the High Queen when she arranged to have my brother healed. How'd she recruit you?"

"Same thing, mostly," said Owen. "My wife was pregnant with twins. After they were born, we found out they had underdeveloped livers. They would live for a couple of days at most. The High Queen found me then. I had left the Wizard's Legion because I couldn't hide my talent for mind magic. She offered to have my kids healed in exchange for my service."

"So here you are," I said.

"Yeah," said Owen. "Seventeen years later."

"God," I said. "I've only been doing this since July."

"It's...not as bad as I thought it would be," said Owen. "I thought she'd have me kill people who crossed her. The High Queen's a hard woman." I remembered how Jeremy Shane had called her a cast-iron bitch. "But she's not corrupt, and she wants justice."

"Did she give you that speech about how justice is covered in blood and tears, but so are newborns, and they're just as important to the future?" I said.

"Several times," said Owen, and I laughed. "I get the hard cases. The ones that stump the other investigators, or that are politically sensitive. I can use the mindtouch spell to look into suspects' thoughts, and if I know they're guilty, I can gather the evidence I need to build a case against them in court."

"Suppose that makes it easier," I said.

"You would think so, but I've looked into a lot of depraved minds," said Owen. He sighed. "Look, I know you don't like Homeland Security. Thugs with badges, right?" I shifted in my seat. "There's some of that, I won't argue. But someone has to do this job. Someone's got to find justice for victims. Someone's got to help pick up the pieces after a crime. Sometimes we do a bad job, and sometimes you're right, there are officers who are thugs with badges. But we've got to do the job, even if it's done imperfectly."

"Why don't we start over?" I said. "I've said some things I shouldn't have, and you have, too. But we've got to work together. I don't want to explain to the High Queen that we screwed this up because we called each other mean names."

"She would not respond favorably," said Owen, which was probably the understatement of the year.

"So." I stuck out my right hand. "Nadia MacCormac."

He shook my hand. "Owen Quell."

"Want to go find who sent that wraithwolf after the Doyles?"

"Yep." Owen started the SUV and put it in reverse. "Besides, if we sit here too much longer, we're probably going to give Toni Caplan a heart attack."

~

Pablo Leon had a house in Wauwatosa, and a half-hour later Owen pulled the SUV to the curb in front of it. It was an impressive house, four or five bedrooms, three stories, and a two-and-a-half car garage.

"Nice place," said Nadia, squinting at the house. "Who knew there was so much money in sewage?"

"It's a good business model," said Owen, shutting off the engine. "The one thing we're not going to run out of is bullshit."

Nadia laughed at that.

He gave her a half-wary, half-amused glance. Owen didn't think he could ever be completely comfortable around her. Which was smart, given how dangerous she was. But he did think they could work together effectively, now that they had cleared the air. They had both served as reminders of past trauma to the other, and hopefully, they could put that behind them.

He thought they could manage it.

Because, in the end, she was just as pissed off about the murder of Ronald Doyle's children as he was.

"Let me do most of the talking," said Owen.

"Sure," said Nadia, hands in the pockets of her coat. "You're the Homeland Security officer. I'm just your daughter, seeing what Dad does for a living."

"For God's sake," said Owen, shaking his head.

Nadia grinned. It wasn't that ghastly rictus she displayed when pissed off, but a smile of genuine amusement. "I did warn you that I was kind of a bitch."

"And I know better than to respond to that statement in any way," said Owen, and she laughed.

They were halfway up the steps to the broad porch when the door flew open and Carolina Leon stalked out to confront them.

Owen blinked in surprise. He had seen Carolina's headshot when Nadia had looked up Pablo Leon's address in UNICORN, so he knew that she was a year younger than he was and reasonably attractive. But a picture didn't capture the beauty of the woman. If a film casting agency had put out a request for "attractive older Latin woman," then Pablo Leon's wife would have been the picture in their mind's eye. She was wearing stiletto heels, a snug purple skirt, a white blouse, and tasteful jewelry. She had a cloud of black hair around a face whose lines did not detract from its beauty. The blouse was just as snug as the skirt and Owen noted that Carolina was in excellent shape, both for her age and in general.

He made himself meet her black eyes, which were wide with fury.

"So!" she said. "He cannot even be bothered to come himself! Instead, he sends Homeland Security to do his dirty work!"

"Um," said Owen. "I'm sorry?"

"I know why you are here!" said Carolina, pointing at him. "My husband, he sends you to frighten me, yes? I know that he is sleeping with that skinny white bitch at his office." She glared at Nadia. "What, are you another of Pablo's lovers?"

"Nope," said Nadia. "Never even met the guy. I'm a consultant for Homeland Security." She jerked a thumb at Owen. "I just follow him around."

"I know he will lie," said Carolina. "What lies has he poured into your ears? What falsehoods?"

"Mrs. Leon," said Owen.

"I know how he thinks," said Carolina. "I looked at the other woman, this Toni Caplan, and she is not even that pretty! What, does he think to throw me out of my own home, the home in which I raised my sons? Does..."

"Mrs. Leon!" said Owen.

She blinked and looked at him, apparently shocked that he would interrupt her.

"We think your husband might be in danger," said Owen. "No one has seen him for three days. Do you know where he would be?"

"In danger?" said Carolina. The thought seemed to baffle her. "Why would anyone wish Pablo harm?"

Owen blinked. The incongruity of Carolina ranting at her husband and then claiming that no one wished him ill seemed to have escaped her.

"Recently Ronald Doyle was murdered," said Owen. Carolina nodded – she recognized the name. "The day after that, your husband disappeared, and no one has seen him since. Pablo had a business relationship with Doyle, but we're unclear on the details.

We're worried that Pablo might be in danger, and we want to talk with him."

"He probably went to his cabin," said Carolina. She waved a hand. "He has a cabin all the way up in Minnesota. God only knows why, it's so cold there. If he's upset, he probably went up there to sulk." She scowled. "Or he brought his strumpet with him."

"I don't think so," said Owen. "We just spoke with Ms. Caplan. She has no idea where Mr. Leon is."

Carolina sniffed. "She has no idea about a lot of things. You know she is forty and has never been married?" She looked incredulous. "If a woman has not been married by the time she is forty, then she is clueless about the world." Her glower turned in Nadia's direction. "You! Are you married?"

"For the third time," said Nadia, waggling the fingers of her left hand. "I'm really hoping this time is the charm. He's a printer repair specialist, and he plays guitar on the weekends."

Owen just stopped himself from giving her an incredulous look.

"Yes," said Carolina, nonplussed.

"Ma'am, I'm going to leave you with one of my cards," said Owen, handing it over. "My number's on there. If you see Mr. Leon, or if you know where he is, please give me a call. We need to find him."

"When you find him," said Carolina, "give him a piece of my mind. Tell him I know about his little whore!"

It was with some relief that Owen climbed back into the SUV and shut the door.

"Jesus," he said. "Maybe we're all wrong. Maybe Pablo ran to get away from her."

Nadia snorted. "Couldn't blame him."

He gave her a look. "A guitar-playing printer repairman?"

"What?" said Nadia. "If I had told her the truth, it's not like she would have believed me. Are you going to send someone to check on Leon's cabin in Minnesota?"

"I'll contact the Duluth branch office, they're closest," said Owen. "While I do that, break out your aetherometer, will you? Find out if there are any of those magical echoes in Leon's house."

Nadia nodded and dug her aetherometer out of her bag. Owen produced his phone, made a call, and spoke with the Homeland Security branch commander in Duluth.

"They're going to send someone out to check on Leon's cabin," said Owen. "We won't hear back for three hours. Apparently, it's a long drive. Anything?"

"Nope," said Nadia, staring at the dials on her aetherometer. "According to this, the only things nearby with magical auras are you and me."

"Makes sense," said Owen, starting the engine and putting the SUV into drive. "Our warrants for Leon's finances should come through soon, so let's start looking through his records. He's the closest thing to a lead we've found, so we're going to follow it."

10

BETTER HALF

The rest of the day was busy but unproductive.

Owen's warrants had indeed cleared, and we started sifting through Leon's financial data. It was a tangled maze, and about half of his business deals were on the legal side of sketchy. His finances were in bad shape – Modern Sewer Systems was carrying a debt load, and most of Leon's credit cards were maxed out. Carolina had expensive tastes, and so did Pablo Leon himself.

Halfway through the afternoon, Owen got a call from Minnesota. An officer had checked Leon's cabin, and it was empty and locked down for winter. No one had reported seeing Leon there since September. Wherever Leon was hiding, it wasn't in his cabin.

If he was still alive.

I decided to leave at about five. If Owen needed me, he had my number. Otherwise, I would check back in at 9 tomorrow morning. I had something I needed to do.

It was time to pick up my husband from the airport.

I drove home and got ready. I showered and did my hair and makeup, taking a lot more care than I did when going to the Moran Imports warehouse or walking into Homeland Security's Central Office. I donned a tight blue dress that dipped low in front, with a skirt that came just above my knees. Then I realized that it would be a pain to get out of it in a hurry, so I put the dress back in the closet and went with a snug black skirt and a white blouse with a few of the top buttons undone. I completed the outfit with a pair of boots with much higher heels than I usually wore, and then took a denim jacket in concession to the November weather. My clothes really weren't warm enough for the weather, but to be honest, I didn't plan to stay in them for very long once I got Riordan home.

Then I drove across Milwaukee to the airport.

Milwaukee's airport is named for a guy named Billy Mitchell. I'd never known or cared who he was, but Riordan had told me the story the last time I drove him to the airport. Evidently, Mitchell had been an old-time general, back before airplanes were in common use. He had claimed that airplanes would one day be the future of warfare, and he had gotten laughed out of the military for his trouble. Then World War II happened and he was proven right, so suddenly Mitchell was a farsighted genius.

See, someone like Owen Quell wondered why I lied to Homeland Security so often. I'm a shadow agent, so I suppose it makes sense that no one believes me when I tell the truth. But Mitchell was a freaking army general, and he told the truth, and still, no one believed him.

I suppose there's some sort of profound philosophical point there, but I didn't care. I was too excited to care.

I parked at the airport, waded through the tedium of security, and waited in the lounge for Riordan's flight. For once, the plane was on time, and a mob of tired-looking people disembarked from the plane. As the crowds thinned out, a man in a suit walked out. He was a big man, his coat and shirt tight against his chest and upper arms, and he wore a pair of wrap-around black sunglasses beneath a shock of brown hair. Underneath the glasses, I knew, his eyes would be the color of expensive bookcases, and underneath the suit, his body would be…

Let's not get ahead of myself. We were still at the airport.

He saw me and smiled, and I grinned and ran to him. I wrapped my arms around his neck and kissed him, and as I did, he hugged me, lifted me off my feet, and spun me around. I laughed in delight, ignoring the half-amused, half-annoyed glances of the nearby passengers at our obnoxious display of public affection, and he set me back on my feet.

"Hi," I said.

"Hello," said Riordan. "You seemed glad to see me."

"That's because I'm really glad to see you," I said. "If we weren't in public, I'd show you how glad."

He smiled. "Then let's go home."

"That's the best idea I've heard in weeks," I said. He took my hand, and we walked to the baggage claim. "How was the trip?"

He filled me in on the details as we claimed his suitcases and headed to the car, using various euphemisms in case anyone was listening. Riordan had gone to the UK on business for the Shadow Hunters. There had been a terrorist bombing in Edinburgh. Americans tended to think of Britain as one place, but it was divided between the English, the Scottish, the Welsh, the Irish, and the descendants of various African and Asian immigrants, all of whom had historical grievances against each other for reasons that went back thousands of years. The High Queen and the Elven nobles forbade open warfare between human nations, but sometimes dissatisfied people expressed themselves through bombings.

Except this time, it hadn't been a terrorist attack. A cult of Dark Ones worshippers had been murdering people in the city, and they had staged the bombing to cover up their sacrificial killings. Riordan and the UK Shadow Hunters had tracked down the cultists and killed them.

"It sounds like you could have used my help," I said. "Next time, I'm coming with you. I've finally got the paperwork cleared on my passport, so the next time you go to the UK for Shadow Hunters stuff, I'm coming."

"We definitely could have used your help," said Riordan. I opened the trunk, and he put his suitcases inside. "And I would have been glad to have you with us." He smiled. "For a variety of reasons."

"Yeah," I said. My throat was a little dry, and I forced moisture into it. "Let's go home and talk about those reasons."

We got into the car. I drove for home.

"The investigation the High Queen gave you," said Riordan. "Have you made any progress?"

"Not really," I said, some of my good mood fading. "I don't think I've handled it very well."

"What happened?" said Riordan.

I told him everything that had happened over the last two weeks, starting with Arnold Brauner's threats and ending with my little mutual snit fit with Owen this morning. I didn't leave anything out, even the stuff I wanted to keep to myself because it made me look bad. I had made myself a promise that I wouldn't keep any secrets from Riordan, and I wouldn't lie to him. It had to be difficult to be married to someone like me, and sometimes I wondered if he secretly regretted it. Or if he should have been with someone else, someone taller and curvier and more interested in books and intellectual crap than I was. That was just insecurity talking, I know. Riordan had gone to insane lengths to save my life.

But, still. I didn't want to make things harder. So, no lying, and no keeping secrets.

"I think you handled the problem with Brauner as best you could," said Riordan.

"Really?" I said, gratified.

Riordan shrugged. "If you had rolled over at his first demand, he would have ended up owning Moran Imports by the end of next year. If you give a man like him an inch, he'll take another ten miles. But he's smart enough not to push too hard once he realized that you can push back. It's just a fact of life that a large business must deal with the local shadow councilor, and Moran Imports is probably going to end up becoming very large. I suppose Brauner was clever enough to see that, and he wanted to get in on the ground floor. It could have been much worse."

"True," I said. "I don't think I handled things with Quell very well."

Riordan's voice hardened. "He attacked you with the mindtouch spell."

"I goaded him into it because I knew I could beat him," I said. "Please don't hurt him."

"I wasn't going to," said Riordan, "but I might have to join your investigation."

I frowned. "Why?"

"A Shadowlands creature of a type no one has ever seen before attacked and killed a family in Milwaukee," said Riordan. "That definitely falls under the interests of the Shadow Hunters. The creature, and whoever summoned it."

"Makes sense," I said. Truth be told, I would be glad to have Riordan's help. And not just as a counterweight to Owen. My husband was good at this kind of thing, had been doing it for decades. I had helped him a few times, but the Shadow Hunters hadn't really needed my help. My magic had just made things quicker in the end. Which was good, because when hunting Shadowlands creatures, the longer you delay, the more time they have to hurt and kill people. "I would like that. Thank you."

"And to make sure this colonel doesn't push you around," said Riordan.

"Please don't hurt him," I said again. "He's...well, he's all right. I mean, he's not my favorite person in the world, yeah, but he's not corrupt, and he's good at his job."

"A good Homeland Security officer?" said Riordan.

"I'm as surprised to hear myself say it as anyone," I admitted. "Hard for me to admit it. But...he seems like a decent man."

"Who used the mindtouch spell on you," said Riordan.

"Because I provoked him into it," I said. "And because he thought I was someone like Martin Corbisher."

"He must not be a very good detective, then," said Riordan. "You don't look anything like Corbisher."

I laughed at that. "But, seriously, I'll be glad for your help. If it doesn't interrupt your writing or your other work."

"The Shadow Hunters won't need more from me for a while," said Riordan, "and I'll be doing the Family's work by hunting down this two-legged wraithwolf. And it was a ten-hour flight from London to Milwaukee, with a two-hour stopover in New York. I finished four and a half chapters of my next book. Not much else to do on the plane."

"Then I'll be glad to have your help," I said. "Really, really glad."

The conversation turned to other topics – Moran Imports' potential growth, Russell's enthusiasm for the business, how Nora and Alex Matheson had bickered constantly in the UK – and then a short time later we were home. I pulled into the garage next to Riordan's truck, and the door slid shut behind us.

"Home," I said.

"Yeah," said Riordan, pulling off his sunglasses. His eyes seemed darker than usual.

"We're finally not in public," I said, my heart speeding up.

"No," said Riordan. "We are not."

He leaned over and kissed me, gently at first, and then harder. I wrapped my arms around him, and he pulled me closer, over the parking brake, so that I was half in his lap and half in the driver's seat. His arms coiled around me, and we kissed for a while, and then one hand started going up the back of my blouse and the other up my skirt.

"Um," I said when we broke apart for breath. My brain was not working at all. "We should go inside. Inside. Bed there."

Eloquent, I know.

While I had been talking, he had been undoing the buttons of my blouse, and then he tugged it open and pushed it down my arms in a single movement, the garment falling on the floor. "Why wait?"

"That so?" I said. I suddenly felt very impatient. "You're wearing too many clothes. Better rectify that."

I ended up completely undressed, and we only got Riordan halfway out his clothes, but that was enough. Had I been thinking clearly, I would have been skeptical about using the passenger seat of a car for a reunion with Riordan, but it turns out I was flexible enough to manage it, and I was short enough that my head wasn't bouncing off the roof of the car once we really got going.

It worked exceptionally well. That's all I'm going to say about that.

After, I slumped in Riordan's lap, facing him, my head resting on his shoulder as I caught my breath.

"God," I croaked. "I really missed you."

Riordan grunted out a laugh. "Noticed."

I straightened up, my arms braced on either side of him. "How am I both cold and sweating at the same time?"

"Because you're wearing nothing but a pair of boots in a car in November?" said Riordan.

"Huh," I said. Due to lack of space, I hadn't managed to get the boots off. "Look, we totally fogged up the windows. Just as well we're inside the garage. Else we'd have a Homeland Security officer knocking on the window. Um. Do you see where my skirt went?"

"I think it sort of got wrapped around your left ankle," said Riordan.

"Hell with it," I said. I wasn't getting dressed again in the car. I opened the door and climbed out, my clothes gathered in a bundle, and the chill air hit my body like a slap. We had been in the car an impressive amount of time. Riordan climbed out after me, pulling his suit trousers back into place.

"Go inside before you freeze to death," said Riordan. "I'll be right behind you."

"Good idea," I said, surprised at how quickly the warmth had drained out of me. I let myself into the kitchen and sighed in relief as I stepped into the heat. The kitchen, like the rest of the house, was in various states of assembly and unpacking, with boxes on both the island and most of the counters, but the security panel next to the door gave off a steady glow. I reset the alarm system and hurried upstairs to our bedroom. I caught a glimpse of myself in the bedroom mirror, naked but for my boots and disheveled makeup, and grinned at myself.

Yeah. Riordan had been glad to see me, too.

I got dressed in jeans and a hooded sweatshirt and went back downstairs to the kitchen. Riordan had opened the fridge and was making himself a smoothie.

"Travel food," said Riordan. "Haven't had a decent meal in days. And the Brits like to either deep fry everything or boil it."

"I haven't eaten, either," I said, and I grinned. "You'll want to get your strength up for round two."

"Round two?" said Riordan, smiling back. "You..."

Two things happened at once.

I heard a buzzing noise, like a phone notification, but louder. Riordan had brought in his own suitcases, but he had also left my laptop bag on the counter, and my aetherometer was buzzing. It had picked something up.

Second, the alarm panel by the garage door had started chiming and flashing.

"What the hell?" I said.

"The motion detector in the back yard," said Riordan.

When I said that I hadn't cheaped out on the security system, I hadn't been lying. I crossed to the panel and tapped in some commands, activating one of the night vision cameras installed outside. Most security systems trigger floodlights when something trips the motion detectors. Mine activates night vision cameras, so the intruders don't realize that they're being watched.

"Shit," I said. "Riordan."

He was at my side, and he let out a quiet curse.

A two-legged wraithwolf prowled through our backyard.

Our house has a big lot, and the backyard was about an acre. Behind that was a large patch of forest that had never been developed. I recalled vaguely that Brookfield had once extended in that direction, but it had been destroyed during an Archon attack some decades ago, and the forest had grown back up.

The two-legged wraithwolf was about halfway between the trees and the house. I tapped another command into the security panel, and the camera zoomed in. The pizza guy's cameras had been good, but mine were better. I got a good, clear look at the creature, albeit entirely in shades of night-vision green. The thing was about seven feet tall, and it walked on its hind legs with ease. It had hands and feet, though it looked like the hands could double as feet and vice versa and the thing could probably run on all fours without any trouble, kind of like a gorilla. The body was vaguely human-shaped, but heavily muscled, and covered with bristly black fur.

I checked to make sure the camera was recording. It was – all the cameras were wired to the server controlling the system, and it had enough capacity for three full weeks of video data before rolling over.

"Nadia," said Riordan, handing me something. "Your aetherometer."

"Yeah," I said, taking it. "Good idea. Okay, here's what I think's happening. Whoever summoned that wraithwolf knows me and Quell were investigating, so he's sent his pet monsters to spy on us." I wondered if there was a two-legged wraithwolf watching his house right now. I hoped not – he had kids, and while he had magic, it wasn't at the same level as mine. "But they don't know I have an aetherometer, so I'm gonna track the link back to the summoner, find him, and kick his ass halfway to…"

I frowned, my sentence trailing off as I glared at the aetherometer.

"What the hell?" I said.

"What?" said Riordan.

"This…doesn't make sense," I said. "It's like the wraithwolf summoned itself."

Shadowlands creatures all had their own magical signatures, for lack of a better word. But when those creatures ended up on Earth, those signatures changed depending on how they got here. Creatures that slipped through a rift way or found their way here on their own had a different signature, a different aura, than summoned ones. Summoned creatures always had the binding of a summoning spell on them, and with the aetherometer or the proper spell, I could trace that binding to back to the summoner.

Except this wraithwolf looked as if it had summoned itself.

"Itself?" said Riordan. "Then it came through a random rift way?"

"No, no," I said, watching the dials twitch. "That looks different. This thing definitely has a summoning spell on it…but the spell tracks back to itself."

"Look at that," said Riordan, pointing at the screen.

The wraithwolf had turned towards the forest. I could see the base of its spine, and there was a metal plate affixed there. It was a rounded rectangle, and I think it was about the size of my hand.

"You ever see a wraithwolf with a metal plate on it?" I said.

"No," said Riordan. "I've seen wraithwolves with enspelled collars, but never one with a plate on its back like that. Never seen one on two legs, either."

"Damn it," I said, shaking my head. "I was hoping we could end this right now. We'd better kill it."

"There might be more in the woods," said Riordan. "Out of range of the motion detectors."

That made my skin crawl. I had bad, bad memories of wraithwolves stalking me through the trees. The hellish little town inside Arvalaeon's Eternity Crucible had been surrounded by woods, and I had died there a few thousand times.

Not an experience I wanted to repeat.

"I'm not a veteran Shadow Hunter," I said, "but I think chasing wraithwolves into the woods at night is a bad idea."

"It's an exceptionally bad idea," said Riordan.

"But I think it's close enough to the house that I can hit it from the patio door," I said. There was a concrete patio behind the kitchen and the garage. Glass patio doors were a hideous security hole, but fortunately instead of glass doors, a single steel security door went to the patio. Delaxsicoria might have been vain and a little flighty, but she wasn't stupid. "Turn off the lights. I'll open the door and fry that damn wraithwolf with a volley of lightning globes. Then we can pry off the metal plate."

"Maybe it will have a serial number on it or something," said Riordan.

"Serial number?" I said.

Something scratched at my mind, some idea, but I lost it in the urgency of the situation.

"Get the lights," I said.

Riordan started to reach for the light switch and then froze.

"Nadia," he said.

The wraithwolf had gone motionless on the display.

It was staring right at the camera. Its eyes shone green on the screen. I had the uneasy feeling that the damn thing was looking right at me. The uneasy feeling turned to fury. If the creature wanted to take a swing at me, it was welcome. I would burn a hole right through its chest and out its back.

Then the creature whirled and raced away with terrific speed, vanishing into the woods behind the house.

We waited. Nothing moved on the screen, and nothing tripped the motion detectors.

"It saw the camera," I said. I looked up at Riordan. He was a lot taller than I was, so I had to crane my neck a bit. "You have more experience with wraithwolves than I do. Can they recognize cameras?"

"I don't have more experience with wraithwolves than you, Nadia," he said, voice quiet.

"What?" I said. "Oh, yeah, right, the Eternity Crucible. Let me put it another way. You have more experience not getting killed by wraithwolves than I do." He inclined his head to concede the point. "Are they smart enough to recognize cameras?"

"Probably not," said Riordan. "I've never heard of a wraithwolf smart enough to recognize a security camera, but I could be wrong." He ran a hand over his head. "But this isn't a normal wraithwolf. They don't usually walk on two legs. And you said the one that killed Doyle climbed up the side of his building?" I nodded. "Wraithwolves don't do that. A normal wraithwolf would have turned into mist, flowed up the side of the building, rematerialized in his living room, and then gone on the attack."

"Technology," I said. "Both Arnold Brauner and Pablo Leon's mistress said that Doyle was involved in some sort of technology deal. Maybe it was those metal plates on the wraithwolves' back."

"A technology that summons two-legged wraithwolves?" said Riordan. His frown deepened. "We saw those automated summoning circles in Last Judge Mountain."

"Hell," I said. "Now that's a bad thought."

"It is," said Riordan. "I think we'd better help Colonel Quell find Pablo Leon as soon as possible."

"Oh, yeah," I said. I crossed to the island and dug my phone out of my bag. "But first I had better call Quell. If someone sent a wraithwolf to watch me, they might have sent one to watch him."

"Good idea," said Riordan.

I dialed the number and lifted the phone to my ear.

11

BAD INVESTMENTS

Owen Quell spent a restless night on the couch in his living room, a shotgun with the safety on within easy reach.

Nadia MacCormac's call came at a little after ten PM, just as Owen was getting ready for bed.

"It was a two-legged wraithwolf," she said, her voice grim with concern. "Just like the one we saw on the pizza video."

"Was it the same one?" said Owen, scowling as he paced back and forth in the basement. He had gone downstairs to take the call, so he didn't wake his daughters, though Sabrina and Katrina were likely still awake in their room.

"I don't think so," said Nadia. "The one that killed the Doyles had those bony plates, and this one didn't. But it looked really close. It was definitely the same type of creature."

"Are you in any danger?" said Owen.

There was a pause.

"No, I don't think so," said Nadia. "The thing tripped the motion detectors around my house. We watched it on the night vision camera for a few minutes. I think it saw the camera following its movements, and it turned and ran into the woods."

Owen blinked. Her house had motion detectors and night vision cameras?

"Did you follow it?" said Owen.

"Hell no," said Nadia. "Our house is on the edge of Brookfield. A lot of woods nearby. Blundering through the forest at night to chase a wraithwolf? I might as well just cut my own throat and save everybody some time."

"Good point," said Owen. "Were you able to get a reading on your aetherometer?"

"Yeah," said Nadia. "And it was weird. The wraithwolf registered as a summoned creature, but the summoning spell twisted back onto itself."

"Then the wraithwolf...summoned itself?" said Owen.

"Looks that way," said Nadia. "It didn't get here through a random rift way, that would read differently on the aetherometer. It's definitely a summoned creature, and the spell reads like it summoned itself." She paused and said something to someone in the background. Probably her husband. Nadia had said very little about the man, but she had said she needed to pick him up from the airport. "I'm going to send you the video file from my security server. You remember how the wraithwolf we saw climbing Doyle's building had that metal plate at the base of its spine? This one has the same kind of plate."

Owen frowned. "You think it's some sort of summoning device?"

"Maybe," said Nadia. "I know it's possible to build a machine to summon Shadowlands creatures." Her voice darkened. "The US government was working on that kind of crap right before the Conquest. Maybe that was the 'technology' deal that Doyle and Leon were working on."

"It's possible," said Owen. His phone buzzed with a notification, and he glanced at the screen. Nadia had just sent him a message with a large video attachment. "But that's a reach. Doyle was the kind of guy to make his money by cheating his contractors and shorting his suppliers. Not by summoning Shadowlands creatures."

"He was also the kind of guy who didn't get all that upset when his building fell over and killed some people," said Nadia.

"Good point," said Owen. "Listen...are you safe? Do you want me to send some officers over?"

"What? No, no, I'm fine," said Nadia. "Those wraithwolves aren't getting past my security systems or my aetherometer, and if one tries to break into the house, I'll fry it." She hesitated. "Also, my husband is with me, and he has some...um, experience dealing with Shadowlands creatures. I'm probably safer than you are. Which is why I'm calling. The only reason the wraithwolf is following me is because I was investigating Doyle's murder. And if Doyle's killer saw us together..."

"Then he or she might have a wraithwolf following me, too," said Owen.

"Yeah," said Nadia. She hesitated. "Look, you want to bring your wife and kids and come to my house? It's pretty secure, and we've got the room."

Owen thought about the awful pictures of the Doyle crime scene. Then again, Owen was a veteran of the Wizard's Legion, and he had spells that could kill a wraithwolf. His house had doors with steel cores, and all the windows had wire mesh. And unlike Doyle's condo, all the windows were locked. Owen and his family were secure here.

Of course, Doyle had thought the same, right up until he died.

"I think we'll be fine for now," said Owen. "But we'll be careful. I'll see you at nine tomorrow."

"Okay," said Nadia. "You better be careful. I don't want to explain to the High Queen how you got killed."

"Same for you," said Owen, and he ended the call.

He opened the attachment Nadia had sent him and looked at the video file. The quality was excellent, especially for a night vision camera. Owen watched as the two-legged wraithwolf prowled over the lawn, froze, and then whirled and vanished into the nearby forest. It wasn't the same creature he had seen climbing up the side of Doyle's condo building, but it did look very similar.

Hopefully, there were just two of the things.

But wraithwolves liked to hunt in packs, and Owen saw no reason why the two-legged variant would act differently.

Anna waited for him at the top of the stairs. She knew that when he got calls at night, trouble followed.

"That was Nadia MacCormac," Owen said, closing the basement door behind him. "A creature liked the one that killed Ronald Doyle was prowling outside her house and ran off when she spotted it."

"Is she okay?" said Anna.

"She's fine," said Owen. "She's a stronger wizard than I am, and I think her husband is a veteran of the Wizard's Legion. If it tries to break into her house, she'll kill it. She was more worried about us."

"Are we in danger?" said Anna.

"I don't know," admitted Owen. "I don't think so, but I don't want to take any chances. I'll sleep on the couch tonight, and you'd better keep your gun nearby. If anything triggers the motion detectors in the yard, the floodlights will come on, and you and the girls can get to the panic room."

They'd done this a few times before. During some investigations, suspects had threatened both Owen and his family. He'd added a panic room to the basement, and during these times he'd slept on the couch, ready to greet any intruders with a shotgun.

Fortunately, the precautions proved unnecessary. Utter silence hung over the house all night, and nothing triggered the floodlights. Owen dozed on the couch and awoke tired and groggy, and showered and shaved while Anna and the girls got ready for school. He was reasonably confident the two-legged wraithwolf and its controller would not attempt anything during the day. Normal wraithwolves preferred to hunt at night, and so far, the two-legged creatures had not shown themselves during the day.

He drove to the Central Office and was at his desk by 8:30. Some of Giles' detectives had examined Leon's financial records and found a variety of potential leads, and Owen went over them while he uploaded Nadia's video file to the UNICORN records for the case. His spirits rose as he looked over the financial information. There were some definite leads there, and if luck was with them, they might find where Pablo Leon was hiding today...

At 8:54, his phone rang with a call from Nadia.

"Hey, do you mind meeting us on the front steps?" said Nadia. "My husband doesn't have a consultant ID, and it will take forever to get through security."

Owen paused. "You brought your husband?"

"Yes," said Nadia. "He was super jealous I'm spending so much time with you and came to beat you up."

A man sighed in the background of the call. Owen heard a male voice say something about threatening a Homeland Security officer via proxy, and Nadia laughed.

"No, seriously," said Nadia. "We'll be glad to have his help. He has more experience tracking down Shadowlands creatures than either of us. And if we want to wrap this up before anyone else gets killed, we need all the help we can get."

Owen was leery of the idea, but her logic was sound, and at the moment, he couldn't do anything about it. He just hoped Nadia's assessment of Mr. MacCormac's capabilities was correct. Love could skew a woman's judgment. Likely Carolina Leon had thought her husband would stay faithful when she married him.

Owen collected his phone and coat, locked his office behind him, and headed to the front steps of the Central Office. As an afterthought, he worked the aurasight spell as he took the elevator to the lobby. That would help him gauge whether or not Nadia's husband was the kind of man who could keep his head in a fight.

He stepped into the November air, the sky overcast with gray clouds. Nadia stood at the foot of the steps, hands thrust into the pockets of her black pea coat. She was wearing her usual combination of sweater, black jeans, and steel-toed boots. Her emotional aura swirled around her, and while the normal tension was there, she was more relaxed than usual, and Owen saw a distinct tinge of postcoital satisfaction in her emotions. Clearly, her reunion with her husband had gone well, at least until the wraithwolf had shown up.

She had accused him of being a voyeur. He didn't want to be one, but unfortunately, both law enforcement work and mind magic meant that Owen sometimes learned way more about people than he ever really wanted to know.

A man in jeans, a dark coat, and work boots stood next to her, his eyes hidden behind wraparound sunglasses. That seemed excessive since it was a cloudy day. He was a good foot taller than Nadia, and the chest and upper sleeves of his jacket were tight with muscle. Owen immediately pegged him as the sort of man who would do tremendous damage in a hand-to-hand fight, who would take five or six good jolts with a stungun to subdue.

His emotional aura...it looked cool, controlled. It was the aura of a veteran fighter keeping constant relaxed vigilance over his surroundings. But there was a dark core of hunger to his aura, something kept tightly constrained...

By the time Owen reached the bottom of the stairs, he had figured it out.

He was not in the least surprised that Mr. MacCormac was a Shadow Hunter. Owen hadn't been sure what kind of man someone like Nadia would fall for. He supposed she could have ensnared a rich man, but he didn't think Nadia could respect someone weaker than herself.

A Shadow Hunter, though...yes, that would definitely be her type.

"Colonel," said Nadia. "This is my husband Riordan."

"Colonel Quell," said Riordan. His deep voice was quiet and calm and carried a faint Texas twang. They shook hands, and Riordan squeezed just hard enough to let him know that he could have squeezed much harder.

Owen smiled and did the same.

"Nadia didn't mention that you were a Shadow Hunter," said Owen.

"Nadia's very discreet," said Riordan. "Is that going to be a problem?"

"I've been at a few crime scenes where we had to stop investigating because we found a writ of execution from the Family of the

Shadow Hunters," said Owen. "Of course, it always turned out the dead men were involved in something nasty and would have gotten executed in a Punishment Day video after a trial if we'd gotten our hands on them."

"It's the lack of a trial that bothers you, isn't it?" said Riordan. "There's a time and a place for that. But if we find whoever summoned the wraithwolves, there's not going to be a trial." He set it without boasting, without braggadocio or threats. He might have been asking Owen for a restaurant recommendation.

Owen let out a breath. "I know. Our mutual employer," he jerked his head at Nadia, "will want this stopped. She won't be too picky about how we stop it. But if it's at all possible to take the summoner alive, I want to do it."

"If it is possible," said Riordan with the same quiet calm.

"We've got to find the asshole first," said Nadia. "Riordan has some ideas on how to do that."

"From what Nadia has said, Pablo Leon sounds like a halfway clever rich man," said Riordan. Owen nodded. That matched his own assessment of Leon. "Smart enough to get rich, but not smart enough to hide his cheating from his wife, or smart enough to stay out of whatever trouble has caught him. He'll think he's hidden his money by moving it to shell corporations or some sort of false identity, but it won't be that hard to find. I would suggest looking for additional companies or maybe living trusts that Leon might have started."

Owen grinned. "Mr. MacCormac, I think you're a very smart man."

"Because you agree with me?" said Riordan.

"That, and because we're both right," said Owen. "Some of the homicide guys have been going over Leon's finances and turns out he does have a shell company. He's been quietly moving money and assets into it over the last two years, probably to protect them from his wife when she divorces him. The company owns three different buildings – a warehouse in Wauwatosa, a house in Waukesha, and a little farm out in Sussex. I'd bet that Leon is hiding at one of those buildings."

"Shall we find out?" said Nadia.

"I'll drive," said Owen.

~

I THOUGHT we would take a Homeland Security SUV, but instead, we took an unmarked sedan from the Central Office's parking ramp. If Leon was hiding from the summoner in one of his shell company's buildings, he might be watching the road, and the sight of a Homeland Security SUV could spook him into doing something stupid.

Owen drove, Riordan took the front passenger seat because he's a lot taller than I am, and I squeezed into the back of the old car. I was afraid that Riordan and Owen would not get along. Riordan had seemed very ill-disposed towards Owen Quell after I described the fight with the mindtouch spell, though that was at least half my fault. Yet Riordan and Owen got along without any difficulty. They both had the air of men going about an unpleasant but necessary job competently and professionally.

They had the same background experiences, I realized. They had both been men-at-arms and soldiers in the Wizard's Legion. I had never done either, but I suppose both my husband and my fellow shadow agent were used to working with people they didn't like under orders from higher authority.

As we drove, I practiced the aurasight spell I had taken from Owen's mind. I could see right away that it was going to be useful. When I cast it, I saw both Owen's and Riordan's emotional auras without any difficulty. Riordan's aura was calm but wary, with a dark core of leashed hunger that was his Shadowmorph. Owen's aura was likewise vigilant, but he was worried. Really worried. I wondered why, and then realized he was probably thinking about his family and the two-legged wraithwolf.

"You didn't have any two-legged wraithwolves show up last night, did you?" I said.

"No," said Owen. "I looked around this morning. No footprints in our yard, and no footprints nearby. We have a nosy neighbor, and if she had seen a wraithwolf in her yard, I would have heard about it at length." He shook his head. "Of course, the wraithwolf might have been clever enough to stay out of sight. Wonder why it was following us, though."

"Isn't it obvious?" I said. "The summoner knows we're investigating him and wants to see what we're up to."

"Probably," said Riordan. "Except if the summoner wants to kill Doyle, Leon, and everyone involved in the technology deal, killing a Homeland Security investigator isn't a good way to keep it quiet."

"Killing Doyle's wife and children isn't a good way to keep things quiet, either," said Owen.

"No," said Riordan. "But summoners...they tend to go homicidally insane. Especially the inexperienced ones. Working a summoning spell isn't hard, and you can cast it with blood if you don't have any magical ability. But calling a Shadowlands creature creates a link with it so the summoner can control it. And that door swings both ways. Without enough mental discipline, the Shadowlands creature starts influencing its summoner, and might even take control entirely. The summoner might have called up the creature just to kill one person, but the bloodlust takes over after a while."

"That matches what I've seen," said Owen. "You deal with summoners often?"

"More often than I would like," said Riordan. "The knowledge of the basic summoning spells keeps circulating, no matter how hard the Inquisition tries to suppress it. Which is why summoners must be stopped as soon as possible. Once they start murdering at random, the killings escalate until they draw enough attention to themselves to get killed, or they lose control of their creatures entirely."

"Well," said Owen. "If Leon's still alive, maybe we can get some answers out of him."

If he was alive. I kind of had my doubts about that.

We stopped at the warehouse first. That was a bust. It was a typical small warehouse, not all that different from Modern Sewer Systems, a small building with cinder block walls, a corrugated metal roof, and a chain-link fence. Except the gate stood open, as did the warehouse doors. We drove inside and around the building, and it was completely empty. The property was idle, and there was no hint it had been used for anything for years.

About forty minutes later, we pulled up outside of the house Leon's shell company owned in Waukesha. It was a three-bedroom house in a residential neighborhood, and it looked like it could have used some work. The paint was cracked and peeling, especially on the front porch, but the house was otherwise in good repair, and the grass looked as if it had been cut by a riding mower and there were no leaves on the lawn. Probably Leon paid someone to keep the place from becoming totally decrepit.

"Looks abandoned," said Owen. "There are a bunch of advertising circulars in plastic bags on the front porch, and all the curtains are open." Through the opened windows I could see empty rooms.

"If he was hiding there," said Riordan, "he might be smart enough to let the advertising circulars pile up."

Owen sighed. "I'll need to get a warrant before we can look around inside. We already got one for his financial information, so..."

"Or," I said, donning a watch cap, tucking my hair beneath it, and pulling on my gloves, "I can take a quick look around."

Owen paused. "I really can't condone that."

"I wouldn't ask you to condone it," I said. "But can you look the other way?"

He sighed. "Ten minutes." Then he made a point of staring at the street.

I cast the Occlusion spell and got out of the car. The Occlusion spell was a minor bit of illusion and mind magic, not as powerful as the Cloak or the Mask spell, but nonetheless useful. So long as I didn't do anything threatening or aggressive, anyone who saw me would forget I was there or fail to take notice of me. If I stood in the middle of a crowded sidewalk, people would walk around me without realizing that I was there.

Wrapped in the Occlusion spell, I jogged around the back of the house, peering into the windows. The interior of the house looked empty. The back door was locked, but a simple spell of focused telekinetic force opened it, and I stepped inside.

That proved a waste of time. I walked through the basement, both floors, and the attic, and I saw nothing but dust bunnies, some dead insects, and a few old mouse traps. There was no trace that anyone had been inside the building for years. On the main floor, I cast the aurasight spell and looked around. I could see the emotional aura of Riordan and Owen in the car, and the auras of a few of the nearby neighbors, but the house was deserted.

I walked to the car and let myself in the back. I was worried Riordan and Owen might have started arguing in my absence, but instead, they were discussing the pros and cons of various kinds of handguns.

"Nothing," I said. "I don't think anyone's been in that place for years. Leon isn't hiding there."

"Damn." Owen sighed and started the engine. "It seemed like such a good idea. Well, we've still got that farm to check."

A half-hour later we were driving through downtown Sussex, such as it was. Sussex was a little village northwest of Milwaukee proper, famous for a bunch of nearby stone quarries. It seemed to be mostly farmers and various quarry employees. Owen drove outside town, down a narrow country lane, and turned into a gravel driveway that led into a forest.

"A farm?" I said, looking around at the trees. "What does it grow, lumber?"

"It's zoned as a farm," said Owen. "I don't think it's actually been worked for a century or so. Forest must have grown up around...wait."

He tapped the brakes, and the car came to a halt.

The driveway ended in a small clearing, and in the center of the clearing was a somewhat dilapidated farmhouse. It had been painted red, but the paint was cracked and peeling, and the roof needed work. Parked in front of the house was a Royal Motors SUV adorned with the Modern Sewer Systems company logo.

I looked at the license plate. "That's Leon's car."

"Yup," said Owen. He backed out of the driveway, parked on the gravel shoulder of the road, and shut off the engine. "Looks like we found his hiding place. Better let me do the talking, at least at first."

We got out of the car and walked up the driveway.

The house's front door swung open, and Pablo Leon stalked out.

My first reaction was completely inappropriate confusion. Both Carolina Leon and Tonette Caplan had been striking women. Pablo Leon was short, fat, bald, sweating, and his mustache looked as if he had cut the bristles off a paintbrush and glued them to his face. How the hell had he seduced two pretty women? He wasn't that rich.

My second reaction was alarm because he was holding an M-99 carbine pointed at us.

"Stay back!" said Leon, waving the gun in our general direction. "Stay back! I know what you are!"

We raised our hands.

"Mr. Leon," said Owen in a loud but calm voice. "My name's Owen Quell. I'm with Homeland Security, and I…"

Leon yelped and pulled the trigger. I flinched, my reflexes starting to throw me to the ground, and a patch of dirt a dozen feet in front of us exploded.

"I'm not kidding!" said Leon. "I'll kill all three of you. I know that I can't hurt you after you transform, so I'm going to shoot you now. Turn around and walk away by the count of three, or I'll kill you!"

"Mr. Leon," said Owen. "We…"

"One!" shouted Leon.

"Oh, for God's sake," I said, my patience evaporating. "Follow me."

I gestured and cast the Shield spell, keying it to deflect kinetic force. A dome of hazy, rippling gray light appeared in front of me, and I stepped forward, putting myself in front of Riordan and Owen.

Leon started spraying bullets as we advanced. I caught them all on my spell, deflecting the rounds into the ground or the trees. Leon's weapon ran out of ammunition as we reached the porch, and he stammered out something terrified and started to fumble in his jacket for another magazine. Riordan was faster. He bounded up the stairs and snatched the weapon out of Leon's hands.

"That," said Riordan, "wasn't nice."

"No," said Leon, shaking with terror. "Oh, God! No, no, no, no."

"Mr. Leon," said Owen. "I'm not here to hurt you. I'm with Homeland Security. We're investigating the murder of Ronald Doyle..."

"No!" wailed Leon. He would have run back into the house, but Riordan caught his arm and held him without any particular effort. "No! I know you're part of it. Homeland Security's part of it! What... what do you want? I'll give you anything if you don't kill me. I didn't know. I didn't know it would be like this!"

He looked like he was on the verge of breaking down.

"Hey," I said. "Look at me."

Leon blinked and turned his gaze at me. I was half-annoyed, half-amused, to see his eyes flick down to my chest before settling back on my face. The man obviously thought himself moments from death, and still took the time for one last ogle. And I was wearing a sweater and a heavy coat, so it's not like there was even all that much to see.

"Watch this," I said, and I gestured. A sphere of fire whirled to life over my palm. "You know many Homeland Security officers who can do that?"

Leon gaped at me. "Who...who are you? How did you stop the bullets? That was a spell, wasn't it?"

"I'm not with Homeland Security," I said. "I work for someone else."

"The Inquisition?" said Leon.

"If you like," I said. No harm in letting Leon think I was a human Inquisition agent. After all, I worked for the High Queen, just like the Inquisition. "Ronald Doyle and his family were killed by a new variety of wraithwolf, and that caught our attention. I want to know what happened. And your life may be in danger, Mr. Leon." I closed my hand, the fire winking out. "Please, tell me what's going on. I might be able to help you."

"I didn't know," whispered Leon. "I didn't know it would end up like this. I thought…I thought it was legitimate. An Elf gave them to us!"

An Elf? Just what the hell was going on here?

"Why don't you start from the beginning?" I said.

Leon glanced at Owen. "He's not…one of them, is he?"

"Nope," I said. "He has absolutely no clue at all what's going on." Owen sighed. At least Leon hadn't thought that I was Owen's daughter. "Please, Mr. Leon. Let us help you. And help us keep anyone from getting killed the way Doyle's family was killed."

"Okay." Leon seemed to pull together the shattered wreckage of his nerves. "Okay. You have to understand. Business…hasn't been very good the last few years. And my wife has expensive tastes, and costs keep going up. But then the Mage Fall happened, and the Day of Return, and all these companies started getting contracts for reconstruction work on Kalvarion. Ron – ah, Ronald Doyle – Ron told me that we had to find a way to cash on in this. I mean, they're gonna need concrete and sewers on Kalvarion, right? Ron said he'd ask around. He has some contacts in Athyrvalis – um, that's a city of Elven commoners out in southwestern Minnesota. Humans aren't usually allowed in the Elven cities, but Ron had gotten a contract to do some building work there."

I hoped for Doyle's sake that none of the buildings he had raised in Athyrvalis had fallen over.

"What happened then?" I said.

"Ron came back with an Elf from Athyrvalis about a month ago," said Leon. "The Elf wouldn't tell us his name. He said we could refer to him as Mr. Hood."

"Mr. Hood," I said, unable to keep the incredulity from my tone.

"Well, yeah," said Leon. He waved his hands in front of his face. "He always wore a hood, you know? And he did some kind of magic thing so we could never see his face."

"And it didn't occur to you that making a business deal with an anonymous Elf who called himself Mr. Hood might be a bad idea?" I said. I remembered what Riordan had said about Leon being only halfway smart. Maybe greed had overridden the smart half of his brain.

"Well...you know, I didn't want him to think that I was elfophobic," said Leon, shifting. "Plus, he was offering us a lot of money, and he had friends in Homeland Security." He gave Owen an uneasy look. "Some of the same friends that Governor Arnold has, so I figured it was okay."

"What kind of deal did Mr. Hood want to make with you?" I said.

Leon sucked in a deep breath. "Well...he said that the world was changing, right? Everyone knows that. The Mage Fall happened, and the Archons were destroyed. The High Queen would rule both Earth and Kalvarion. And the Great Gate to Kalvarion is right here in Milwaukee." A little west of Milwaukee, technically, but now was not the time to quibble. "The High Queen was going to relax some restrictions on technology. I heard how a company out east got a big contract for making robotic tractors. Mr. Hood said the High Queen was going to let human use new kinds of weapons."

"Weapons?" said Owen. "What kind of weapons?"

"You don't know?" said Leon. "You're in Homeland Security. Don't you know all that top-secret classified shit?"

"It is entirely possible," said Owen, "that the Homeland Security officers Mr. Hood was in contact with did not have official authorization."

"Aw, hell," said Leon. "I should have known that it was too good to be true."

"What kind of weapons did Mr. Hood offer to sell Homeland Security?" I said.

"It wasn't so much as a weapon as it was a complete tactical system," said Leon. "Least that's what Mr. Hood said. It didn't look like much." He held out his hand, palm up. "Like this little metal plate thing, you know? Maybe about the size of a big deck of cards. Mr. Hood said it was part technology, part magic."

I shared a look with Riordan and Owen. We had seen the metal plates at the base of the wraithwolves' spines.

"So what does this 'complete tactical system' actually do?" I said.

"I dunno," said Leon. "I'm too old and fat to play with something like that. But if you use it, it's supposed to make you into some kind of freaking super soldier. Like, faster and stronger than a normal man, all that stuff." He shrugged. "Ron and I gave all the plates to Homeland Security for testing."

"Then you've never seen them used?" I said.

"Nah," said Leon.

"Can you tell us anything else about the weapons?" said Owen.

Leon shrugged. "There were a couple dozen of them. Um. Forty-eight in total. Mr. Hood paid us for taking them to Homeland Security, and he said we'd be paid even more if the government decided to start using them. A royalty on every sale, that kind of thing. He said he had gotten them from a company calling itself the Singularity, and…"

"What?" I said.

Leon flinched. My tone must have been harsher than I intended. "Sorry?"

"You said he got them from a group called the Singularity," I said.

"I think so, yeah, that's what he said." Leon hesitated. "A company called the Singularity. You've…heard of them?"

Oh, yeah, I had heard of them.

I didn't know who or what they were. I didn't know if the Singularity was an organization or a code name for an individual. But I did know they were up to no good. In New York, they had convinced the business manager of the dragon Malthraxivorn to dig up some old Catalyst Corporation technology. From what I had been able to gather, the High Queen had shut down Catalyst when they had started to do insane medical experiments, and one of their experiments had been a guy named Neil Freeman, a half-human, half-cyborg super assassin who had killed Malthraxivorn and had almost killed me and Riordan a couple of times. We'd freed Neil from his enslavement in the end, and now he worked for the High Queen, but it had been a close thing.

"Yup," I said. "I've heard of them. Mr. Hood didn't mention a group called Catalyst Corporation, did he?"

Leon blinked. "No. Never heard of them."

"Neither have I," said Owen.

"I'll tell you later," I said. "They're big bad news." I looked back at Leon. "And I think Mr. Leon here has figured that out. Else he wouldn't be hiding out here in the woods."

"I think the weapons drove the Homeland Security guys insane," said Leon. He cast a nervous look around the trees. "When I talked to them...it's like they were on drugs, you know? Like they confiscated a bunch of synthetic cocaine from a guy with a protein printer and snorted it all at once. It was like talking to crazy people. They'd say how the city of Milwaukee was corrupt, how the state of Wisconsin was corrupt, and it was up to them to clean things up." He took a deep breath. "When I heard what happened to Doyle and his wife and his kids...Jesus. I knew they'd gone off the deep end."

"Are you seriously accusing Homeland Security officers of mass murder?" said Owen.

"I'm not accusing anyone of anything," said Leon. "I know they did it. They kept talking about how Ron and I were corrupt, how Governor Arnold was the biggest crook in Wisconsin, and one day we'd get what was coming to us. Which was a load of crap, because I know Homeland Security does favors for Governor Arnold when he asks. But I didn't say anything because Mr. Hood was paying us a lot, but when I heard that Ron had been killed, I knew they'd done it." He shrugged. "I figured I'd hide out here. Eventually, the Homeland Security officers would screw up enough that they'd get caught and killed, and that would be that."

That was a pretty cowardly way to deal with the problem. Logical, though.

"You realize," said Owen, "that we're going to need the names of these officers. If they have been committing murders, they've betrayed everything their badge stands for." I bit back the sarcastic remark that came to mind. Wouldn't have been helpful just now.

"Am I going to be in trouble?" said Leon.

"You're not going to get murdered if you tell us the name of those officers," I said.

"That's a good argument," said Leon.

"I'm not going to lie, I think you're kind of a dumbass, but since you're hiding out in the woods because of a business deal, you've probably already figured that out," I said. Leon scowled, then shrugged to concede the point. "But if you cooperate with us, I think you should be fine. But the next time someone tries to sell you mysterious forbidden technology, call the Inquisition. Even if it makes you feel elfophobic."

"Okay," said Leon. "I just want it on the record that my cooperation is voluntary and freely given."

"Got it," I said. "So, the names of those officers?"

Leon took a deep breath. "You have to understand, I only talked to two of them. Lieutenant Kyle Warren and Sergeant Philip Hopkins."

There was silence for a moment. Owen's face had become a mask of stone. I remembered Lieutenant Kyle Warren standing outside of Doyle's condo, how I had disliked him on sight for some reason.

"Oh," I said. "Shit."

"Is...is that bad?" said Leon.

"Yeah, but not for you," I said.

"We need to get back to the Central Office right now," said Owen. "Warren is the second in command of the homicide division. Hopkins is one of the senior sergeants for the patrol and traffic officers." I remembered the older Homeland Security officer who had hassled Jacob Bowyer at the Moran Imports warehouse. "If those bronze plates are wraithwolf summoning devices and Warren and Hopkins have been giving them out...God, I don't want to..."

"Wraithwolves?" said Leon, his voice going up half an octave. "Wraithwolves? Mr. Hood didn't say anything about any damned wraithwolves!"

"Quiet," said Riordan. "All of you."

His voice was calm, but it cut through the talk like a knife. My husband had turned and was looking towards the woods. He had produced a handgun from beneath his coat.

"Someone's approaching on foot," said Riordan.

I didn't hear anything, but I didn't have Shadowmorph-enhanced senses.

"Oh, God," said Leon. "Oh, God. They're coming for me."

About a minute later, four men and one woman appeared on the gravel driveway leading to the county highway.

All five of them wore the blue uniforms of Homeland Security officers, and at their head walked a middle-aged man I recognized from the confrontation at my brother's warehouse.

The five officers walked towards the house and froze when they saw us.

There was a long silence.

"Ah, hell, Colonel," said Sergeant Hopkins at last, running a hand through his close-cut gray hair. "I always thought you were a good officer. I didn't want you mixed up in this."

12

MEN & WOLVES

Owen looked at the five officers, his heart turning to ice within his chest.

He knew them. He knew them all, had spoken with them, and worked with them on various cases. Sergeant Hopkins was a respected veteran of the force, trusted by both the officers and the rank-and-file. The other three men were younger, had only a few years under their belts. The woman was named Cecilia Sullivan and was in her thirties, in charge of prisoner handling, and had always done an exemplary job. Owen would have said that all of them were good officers.

But now…

Now there was something wrong with them, something off.

There was something wild and feral in their eyes. Owen felt like he was confronting a pack of rabid dogs, not speaking with fellow Homeland Security officers. For that matter, their movements were different. Cecilia Sullivan had been a quiet, mousy woman, though hard enough when the situation called for it. Now there was a strange grace in her movements, and that feral, hungry expression was out of place on her features.

His right hand drifted towards his sidearm, and his mind called magic for a spell. Nadia moved to the left, Riordan to the right, his gun pointed at the five officers. Leon shied behind them, trying not to whimper.

"Stay behind us," murmured Riordan. Leon was happy to comply.

"Phil," said Owen. "What the hell is going on?"

"Look, it's her," said Cecilia, pointing at Nadia. "The bitch with the fruit company." Nadia snorted, once. "Kirby said that she was corrupt, that she was one of that fat toad Brauner's flunkies. We're going to have to kill her too. Let me kill her, let me be the one to…"

"Quiet," snapped Hopkins. Cecilia stepped back and flinched, lowering her gaze. There was something peculiarly dog-like about the movement.

"Phil," said Owen again. "What the hell are you doing here?"

"Making an arrest," said Hopkins. "We have reason to believe that Pablo Leon murdered Ronald Doyle, and…"

"Don't bullshit me," said Owen. "I don't know what's going on, but I know it's not good, and I know that Pablo Leon didn't kill Ronald Doyle and his family." His hand moved closer to his gun. "I'm going to ask you for the last time. What are you doing here?"

Hopkins stared at him and then nodded. "All right. You're a good officer, sir, and I've always respected you. I'll tell you the truth." He pointed at the house. "We're going to kill him the way we killed Doyle."

Leon let out another whimper.

"Why?" said Owen, his heart sinking. God, five officers had gone bad. How many more? "What did he do?"

"What didn't he do!" snapped one of the younger men. "He's corrupt. They're all corrupt!"

"Quiet," said Hopkins. The younger man made that dog-like gesture of submission. "You know as well as I do that Pablo Leon's corrupt, Colonel. He's part of Brauner's organization, and Brauner is a blight on the state of Wisconsin. He's corrupt, all his associates are corrupt, and they need to be destroyed."

"Then bring charges," said Owen. "Build evidence. Gather a case against him. We are not animals…"

One of the younger officers let out a dark laugh.

"But you're just murdering people on suspicion," said Owen.

"The law," said Hopkins. "People like Leon and Doyle and Brauner twist the law and hide behind it to escape punishment for their crimes. Well, that day is over. I'm only going to ask you once, Colonel. Go back out to your car and go home. Forget all about this before it's too late."

"No," said Owen, "we…"

"Hey, Hopkins!" said Nadia. "I need to say something."

Hopkins looked at her. Cecilia glared.

"Yes?" said Hopkins.

"You are absolutely full of shit," said Nadia.

Hopkins' lip pulled back from his teeth in a snarl.

"You talk a big game about corruption, but you and your buddy Kirby were the ones Brauner sent to hassle my business, and I bet one of you slashed the tires on our trucks," said Nadia. "But, hey, that's just playing hardball. But if Doyle's all corrupt…why did one of you murder his kids?"

They didn't answer for a moment.

"They were corrupt, too," said Hopkins, but his voice was strained. "They benefited from their father's crimes…"

"The youngest kid was six," said Nadia. "Six years old, asshole. Bet whichever one of you killed him felt like a real big hero when you did it."

"I know what happened," said Riordan. The gun was steady as a rock in his hands. "You summoned the wraithwolves, but your link with the creatures is warping your mind. Their bloodlust is seeping into your thoughts. That's why you killed Doyle's wife and children. You couldn't stop yourselves…"

"Enough!" said Cecilia, her voice rising to a shriek. She glared at Hopkins. "Let us take them the way that Warren took Doyle."

Warren had killed the Doyle family? Christ. Owen felt the ice in his hart grow harder.

"Then you admit to summoning Shadowlands creatures for the purposes of murder?" said Riordan.

"Summoning?" sneered Cecilia. "You think that's what we're doing? Summoning wraithwolves? I suppose we are, in a way. Sergeant, let's kill them all. We have to rip out the corruption from the world. Let's start with them."

"That will be difficult," said Owen, drawing his pistol and leveling it at the five officers, "given that we have two guns already pointed at you."

"You don't understand, Colonel," said Hopkins. "Guns can't hurt us, not anymore."

He started forward.

"Take one more step," said Riordan, "and I will shoot you."

Hopkins grinned and took the step.

Riordan's weapon flashed, the crack of the discharge loud in the clearing. Hopkins grunted, cursed, and went to one knee. A crimson stain spread across the dark blue of his right uniform trouser leg.

"Ah, that hurt," said Hopkins.

He grunted and stood back up.

"What the hell?" said Owen.

"I'm sorry it has to be this way," said Hopkins, and he nodded to Cecilia. "Show them the truth."

Gray light flashed around them.

And as the light brightened, Hopkins, Cecilia, and the three younger officers changed.

Their bodies grew and swelled, each of them becoming taller. Fur sprouted from their limbs, their uniforms disappearing as they grew. Their heads crackled and lengthened, fangs sprouting from their jaws and claws erupting from their fingers. Fresh muscle rippled beneath their fur, and a sudden stench of rotting flesh and oily musk hit Owen's nostrils.

The transformation only took seconds, and when it was over, five two-legged wraithwolves stood before the farmhouse.

"Oh, God," said Leon. "Oh, God…"

"Bullets don't work on us anymore, Colonel," growled the thing that had been Hopkins.

"I'm going to rip you apart," said Cecilia, her voice now a horrid gurgling rasp. "I'm going to rip out your entrails and..."

She fell silent, blinking her harsh yellow eyes, and flinched in surprise.

Nadia was laughing a hard, bitter laugh that had no trace of humor, that mirthless rictus on her face.

"You idiots," she said. "You think that's scary? You want to see fear? I'll show it to you. I would kill you all, right here and now, but I think Colonel Quell wouldn't like it. So as a favor to him, I'll give you one chance to surrender. Do it right now, or I'll kill you all."

"Little girl," sneered Cecilia. "Little skinny bitch. You won't be so pretty when I rip your face off."

"Fine," said Nadia, and she stepped towards the horrors and gestured.

There was a flash of blue-white light, and suddenly lightning globes whirled and spun around her like small, angry planets orbiting a very pissed off sun. Owen could use the lightning globe spell himself, and he had seen Elven nobles cast it a few times.

But he had never seen anyone summon seven lightning globes at once.

Riordan stepped to Nadia's side, holstered his pistol, and rolled his right wrist. Suddenly he held a sword that looked as if it had been made from solid shadows.

"Last chance," said Nadia.

"Kill them," said the thing that had been Hopkins.

The five wraithwolves loosed chilling, tearing howls, and leaped forward, the claws of their feet ripping at the grass. Nadia gestured, and the lightning globes ripped forward and broke apart, striking each of the wraithwolves simultaneously. Lightning slashed up and down their bodies, the stink of burning fur filling Owen's nostrils.

Riordan moved in a dark blur, the black sword flickering in his hands, and suddenly Cecilia's head rolled away, her body falling to the ground. Likely Riordan had targeted her first because she had threatened Nadia. The surviving five wraithwolves recovered, and Owen cast his own spell. A lightning sphere leaped from his hands and struck the nearest wraithwolf, and the creature staggered back, roaring in pain. Riordan took off his head with a swift strike of his shadow sword.

The other three creatures lunged towards Nadia, and she gestured again. A sphere of fire burst from her hand and landed in the middle of the charging wraithwolves. Owen first thought that she had missed, but her spell exploded like an incendiary grenade. The bloom of fire engulfed the wraithwolves, and their howl of pain filled Owen's ears. One of the wraithwolves staggered out of the fire, and he cast the lightning sphere spell again. This time his strike hit the wraithwolf in the forehead and burned into its skull, and the creature went down.

The final two creatures emerged from the fading fireball only to meet Riordan. His dark sword flickered left and right. One of the wraithwolves fell, its head tumbling away in the opposite direction. Nadia shoved her right hand at the remaining creature, and there was a sharp crack of shattering bone as a burst of telekinetic force hit the wraithwolf in the chest. The creature flipped head over heels like a child's toy and landed hard with more broken bones.

Owen lowered his hand, breathing hard, but all the wraithwolves were down.

Nadia and her husband had mowed through them in less than a minute.

The smell of urine came to Owen's nostrils, and he glanced back and saw that Leon had wet himself, his body shaking with terror.

With a cold burst of clarity, Owen realized that he would have died here today. Suddenly he knew exactly why Tarlia had sent Nadia to work with him despite their diverging personalities and experiences. Owen would have tracked down Leon sooner or later, and when he did, the wraithwolves would have killed him. He had enough magic to maybe kill one or two of them, but the rest would have overwhelmed him and ripped him apart as Doyle and his family had been killed.

If Nadia and Riordan hadn't been here, he would have died.

He looked at Nadia. She was staring at the fallen wraithwolves, lightning crackling around her fingers, her teeth bared in a snarl. There was not the slightest trace of sanity or mercy in her expression. Probably she was reliving some of the horrible memories he had seen through the mindtouch spell.

"Nadia," said Riordan. "Are you okay?"

She blinked, looked at her husband, and something like lucidity came back into her eyes once more.

"Yeah," said Nadia. "Yeah, I'm swell." She scoffed. "Better than these idiots. I…"

There was a blur, and four of the wraithwolves blurred back into human form. Owen felt a misplaced burst of anger at the sight of four uniformed officers lying dead. One of the wraithwolves kept its form, and Owen saw that the creature was alive, though badly burned with broken bones jutting out of its legs.

"Sergeant Hopkins is still alive," said Riordan. "If we don't kill him, he's going to regenerate from his wounds in a few minutes."

"We should question him," said Owen.

"Good idea, but in a minute," said Nadia. "I want to have a look at the dead ones first. Hey! Puppy! Stay!"

She gestured again, and a spike of ice the size of Owen's arm shot from her hand. It stabbed through Hopkins' stomach and sank into the ground, and the wraithwolf let out a scream of pain.

With Hopkins pinned in place, Nadia turned and walked to the headless corpse of Cecilia Sullivan. Riordan followed her, putting himself between his wife and Hopkins as he kept an eye on the snarling, thrashing wraithwolf. Nadia knelt, grunted, and flipped Cecilia's corpse onto its stomach. She yanked up the back of Cecilia's uniform jacket and shirt, revealing an expanse of pale white skin.

And, at the base of her spine, a thin metal plate about the size of a mass market paperback book.

"I'll be damned," said Owen.

"Don't touch it," said Nadia. "Wish I hadn't left my aetherometer in the car. But I'm close enough that the sensing spell will work." She cast the spell to sense magic, holding her gloved palm an inch above the metal plate.

"What do you sense?" said Riordan, still watching Hopkins.

"Nothing good," said Nadia. "There's a summoning spell bound into this thing...that was the echo I picked up when we were in Doyle's building, Owen. Warren must have one of these plates on his back, too." Her brow furrowed. "I'm not sure...but I think this works by summoning a wraithwolf from the Shadowlands and binding it into the flesh of whoever bears the plate."

"That would influence their thoughts?" said Owen.

Nadia snorted. "They'd go bugshit crazy, that's what would happen."

"Direct summoning into a human body is rare, but it has happened," said Riordan. "It's rare because it's incredibly dangerous. The summoned creature would have massive influence over its host, and it might even take control. The host wouldn't even know that it's happening. That's probably why Warren killed Doyle's entire family. He likely only intended to kill Ronald Doyle, but with the wraithwolf influencing him, the bloodlust took him over."

Owen looked over the bodies. This was a catastrophe. Four dead Homeland Security officers, with a fifth likely about to die, officers who had violated the law and summoned Shadowlands creatures, earning an automatic death sentence.

And if Leon was right, there were still forty-three more plates out there.

He glanced at the porch, but Leon stood rooted there, still shaking. Owen really hoped he didn't have a heart attack.

"Okay," said Owen. "We've got to decide what to do next. Normally, if officers were involved in something illegal, I would notify our internal affairs division and have them open an investigation..."

"But you don't know how many officers have those wraithwolf plates," said Riordan.

Owen shook his head. "Warren was a superb officer. One of the best. If he was involved in this..."

"Wait a minute," said Nadia. "I've got an idea."

She patted Cecilia's leg, reached into the dead woman's pocket, and drew out a folding knife. Nadia opened the knife and worked the tip of the blade beneath the plate, blood welling around the tip. She pushed on the handle, and the bronze plate popped off Cecilia's back, exposing a rectangle of bloody, bruised flesh.

"Gross," said Nadia, ignoring the corpses around her. She flipped the plate onto its back, and on the side that had been touching Cecilia's skin, Owen saw dozens of rows of tiny sharp pins. "It kind of looks like a computer processor. Like, you know how a computer processor has hundreds of pins on the underside, and they have to line up perfectly to fit into the motherboard socket?" Owen didn't, but he assumed she knew what she was talking about, so he nodded. "I bet some of these pins reached her spine, like it was injecting the wraithwolf into her nervous system or something, and...shit. Shit, shit."

"What?" said Owen.

Nadia pointed with the bloody knife. The pins covered the back of the plate in neat rows, save for a square area in the center. Engraved in the square was a symbol that looked like a double helix of DNA in a circle.

"The logo of Catalyst Corporation," said Nadia, voice grim.

"You mentioned them before," said Owen. "What are they?"

"Don't know for sure," said Nadia, glancing at Leon. She lowered her voice. "They were an international corporation about a hundred and fifty years ago, did medical research and biotechnology, that kind of stuff. I don't know exactly what they did to piss her off, but the High Queen shut them down hard. Then a couple months ago someone dug up some of their technology in New York and used it to make trouble."

"And the Singularity is a terrorist group using that technology?" said Owen.

"It's starting to look that way," said Nadia. "The troublemaker in New York got his toys from something he called the Singularity. Let's see if Sergeant Hopkins knows."

She rose to her feet and walked towards Hopkins, Riordan at her side. Owen followed them, and Nadia stopped a few paces away, well out of reach of the wraithwolf's claws.

"Colonel," rasped Hopkins. The voice was deep and inhuman, and still recognizable as Hopkins, but it was disturbing to hear the words come from the fanged maw of a wraithwolf. "Are you going to arrest me? No cell will hold me. And the wounds you have given me will heal, and I shall find you and feast upon you..."

"Not if we get that gizmo off your back," said Nadia. Hopkins snarled in rage. "Riordan."

Riordan nodded, and Nadia cast a spell. She flung a single lightning globe into Hopkins, and the wraithwolf bellowed in fury, claws raking at the ground. In one smooth motion, Riordan kicked Hopkins onto his back, reached down, and ripped the plate away in a burst of dark blood. Hopkins screamed, his voice becoming normal again, and a second later, he returned to human form.

A dying, mortally wounded human, his shredded uniform red with blood.

"Oh, God," croaked Hopkins, and he flopped onto his back with a cry of pain. "It hurts, it hurts, it hurts..."

"Yeah," said Nadia with a total lack of sympathy. "It hurts when you get ripped up by a wraithwolf."

"Give it," moaned Hopkins, reaching for Riordan. He could barely lift his arms. "Give it...back to me, I need it..."

"Phil," said Owen. "This is crazy. You have to know this is crazy. Turning people into wraithwolves? It's going to end badly. What are you doing? You have to help me stop this."

The dying man looked at Owen, and something like regret came into his face.

"I'm sorry about your family," said Hopkins. "But Warren... Warren said that you'd be home, and..."

"My family?" said Owen, the cold feeling in his chest getting worse. "What about my family?"

But Philip Hopkins had stopped breathing, his unblinking eyes open to the sky.

13

NECESSARY CASUALTIES

For an awful, frozen moment, we didn't say anything. Then Owen cursed and yanked his cell phone from his belt.

"Calling your wife?" I said.

"Yeah," said Owen. "She's at home today. So are the kids. Day off from school, faculty meetings or something like that."

I heard the shrill beep from his phone. The number he had called was out of service. Or someone had cut the phone wires to his house.

"Shit," said Owen. "I'll call some officers, have them put a protective detail around the house...no, goddamn it, I can't. Those wraithwolves will go through any officers like paper."

"They need magic to hurt the wraithwolves," said Riordan. "You could try Duke Tamirlas's office, warn him the Shadowlands creatures are loose in the city."

"By the time they get there it will be too late," said Owen. I saw the fear eating him. "If we drive, it's at least forty-five minutes to get there."

"I have an idea," I said. "Do you have something connected to your house, like...um, a rock or a key or something?"

"Yeah," said Owen. "My front door key. Why?"

I took a deep breath. "Because we can take a gamble. If I open a rift way to the Shadowlands, that key will link back to Earth. If a nearby location within the Shadowlands corresponds to your house, we can get there in a couple of minutes."

It sounded good. But it was insanely dangerous. There was no telling what I would find on the other side of the rift way. Maybe nothing. Maybe a few wraithwolves. Maybe a thousand anthrophages, or a naelgoth, or something even worse. But if Warren had decided to kill Owen's family, we needed every minute.

But Owen knew that already.

"If you're willing to do it," said Owen, pulling a key from his pocket and handing it to me.

I nodded, took the key, shut off my phone so it wouldn't explode or catch fire when I entered the Shadowlands, and started gathering the power for the rift way spell.

"I'll go through first," said Riordan, his voice hard. He might not try to talk me out of this crazy plan, but if I tried to go through the rift way first, he would physically stop me.

"Fine," I said as he turned off his phone.

"What…what should I do?" called Leon from the porch.

"Get your ass in the basement and stay there until I come for you," said Owen. "Your life is still in danger. Don't call anyone, and don't call Homeland Security. If anyone figures out you're still alive, they're going to come for you."

Pablo Leon whirled and fled into the house. With my full attention on the spell, I barely noticed.

I gestured, and a curtain of gray mist and light rose up from the ground. The mist flickered and became translucent, and through it, I saw something that looked like a rocky forest. Except the boulders were all obsidian, and the trees were black with blue-glowing leaves.

Damn it. I did not want to go back to the Shadowlands.

"It's ready," I said.

Riordan went through the rift way, and I followed, holding the gate open as I summoned more power for a spell.

A flicker of nauseating disorientation and I was in the Shadowlands, the dark place that connected all worlds. The Shadowlands could look like anything – a forest, a plain, a mountain, a ruined city, whatever – and this part looked like a weird forest. My boots scraped against the rocky ground, and the trees with their blue-glowing leaves spread overhead. The sky was an empty black vault, devoid of sun, moon, stars, and weather, but despite that, I had no trouble seeing.

I could see the four anthrophages just fine.

Anthrophages were some of the more common creatures of Earth's umbra in the Shadowlands, a twisted reflection of humanity that preyed upon people. Much in the same way that some people preyed upon other people, I suppose. The anthrophages were human-shaped, but gaunt with gray skin, venomous yellow eyes, and black craters for noses. Fangs filled their mouths, and claws jutted from their fingers and toes.

We had caught them off guard. Even as I looked, Riordan killed one, and the remaining three circled around him.

I cast a spell, drawing more power even as I held the rift way open. The Shadowlands are the source of magic – I think technically magical force is actually "aetheric radiation" that seeps into our world, or at least that's what the Elves call it. That means magic is much stronger in the Shadowlands, and I could already draw in a lot of power for a human. I pulled in way more force than I intended, but I had a handy target close at hand, and I threw that power into a spell.

The fire sphere that I had intended to drill a neat hole through the nearest anthrophage's skull instead turned its head, shoulders, arms, chest, and most of its stomach to smoking ashes, and also set the tree behind it on fire.

Oh, well.

The remaining two anthrophages gaped at the unexpected explosion, and Riordan killed them without any fuss.

Strange, metallic hunting cries echoed in the still air.

"Hurry," said Riordan. His eyes had turned solid black as his Shadowmorph fed, and I felt an extremely ill-timed wave of physical desire for him, complete with a vivid mental image of him ripping off my clothes and throwing me to the ground beneath him. That was a function of his Shadowmorph, a way to draw life force to it, and I have to admit that in the proper time and place (alone in our bedroom with the door closed and the curtains drawn) that could be a lot of fun. Right now, it was just distracting. "I think these four were the outer scouts of a bigger hunting pack."

"Crap," I said, and I held up Quell's door key and cast the seeking spell.

It was one of the spells Morvilind had taught me a long, long time ago. Locations in the Shadowlands corresponded to various locations on Earth, but they weren't congruent. Like, I could enter the Shadowlands from Milwaukee, walk ten yards, open another rift way, and come back to Earth in Africa or Asia. Plus, the linkages constantly changed, so using the Shadowlands to travel to different locations on Earth was a bad idea.

Especially since the denizens of the Shadowlands liked to eat humans. A lot.

But there was one potential advantage. Locations tended to cluster together, and it was (theoretically) easier to travel within a city or a specific geographic area than from one side of the globe to another.

In theory.

I forced magical power through the key, seeking for a congruence nearby. I felt my will tugging at the key...

"There!" I said, looking to the left. I saw more obsidian boulders and glowing trees. "It's not far. We lucked out. About...um, three hundred yards."

"I'll get Quell," said Riordan. "Hold the spell."

I nodded, and he ran back into the rift way. About fifteen seconds later he returned with Owen.

"Damn it," said Owen as I closed the gate behind him. We were committed now. "Never wanted to come back here."

"You and me both, buddy," I said. "Now stop talking and run!"

I had to take the lead since I had the key. I sprinted over the uneven ground, running around the obsidian boulders and the glowing trees. The ground climbed in a shallow rise, and on the other side of the hill, the tugging of the key got stronger.

"All right, it's here," I said, gripping the key. "I'm going to get the rift way open."

"Hurry," said Owen

I wanted to snap back that I was moving as fast as I could, but he was frightened for his family, so I kept my mouth shut. Also, I needed my full concentration to cast the spell.

A gray curtain of mist rolled up from the ground, and the gate started to open.

"Nadia!" said Riordan.

I saw anthrophages running down the hill towards us.

A lot of anthrophages.

I said a very bad word and threw my full strength and power into the rift way.

It tore all the way open.

"Go!" I said.

Owen sprang through the rift way. Riordan grabbed my arm and all but pulled me off my feet after him. I looked over my shoulder and saw the anthrophages behind me.

Like, right behind me. I could have reached out and patted the nearest one on the head.

Then I was on a lawn in front of a row of houses. At once, I withdrew the power holding the rift way, and it snapped shut. An anthrophage tried to spring after me, but the creature timed it wrong. Its head, shoulders, and arms got through the rift way, and then the gate closed.

The head, shoulders, and arms landed on the grass at my feet, and the rest stayed in the Shadowlands.

Made a bit of mess, let me tell you.

"Did it work?" I said. "Are we here?"

We were standing on the grassy median between the street and the sidewalk. Good-sized houses rose over the street. We were in

Milwaukee somewhere, one of the upper-middle-class neighborhoods, but I didn't know exactly where.

But I did see the two Homeland Security SUVs pulled up to the curb, their lights flashing, their doors open and their interiors empty. They were in front of a house whose front door had been ripped open and lay in splinters on the porch...

"Goddamn it," said Owen.

To judge from his reaction, we had found the right place.

He started forward.

"Wait!" I grabbed his arm. "Aurasight. We can see if there are wraithwolves in your house."

"You know the spell?" he said.

"Yeah, sort of dug it out of your head during our little spat," I said, working the spell. He did the same.

I didn't add that we could use the aurasight spell to see if his family was still alive or not.

The aurasight flared to life before my eyes. I saw Riordan's grim, icy determination and the tight hunger of his Shadowmorph, saw the dread flooding through Owen beneath his stoic façade.

I also saw the twisted, warped aura of eight or nine wraithwolves in the house.

For a sickening moment, I thought we were too late, but then I saw another cluster of emotional auras. A woman, I thought, and four girls. Their auras were thick with naked terror, though I saw a growing resignation in the woman's aura.

She thought they were all going to die.

Well, to hell with that.

"Thank God, they're still alive," said Owen. "They're in the panic room in the basement."

"That going to keep the wraithwolves out?" said Riordan.

"Not for long," said Owen. "Doors and walls are concrete reinforced steel, but the ceiling's weaker. If the wraithwolves figure that out..." He looked at me. "Can you take nine wraithwolves at once?"

"Yeah, probably," I said, an idea coming to me, "but I think we need to take one alive so we can figure out where to find the rest of these assholes. You ever hear of the Seal of Shadows?"

Owen frowned. "It blocks summoning spells."

"More or less," I said. "But Shadowlands creatures can't enter the Seal of Shadows, and if you drop it on them, you can banish them back to the Shadowlands."

"What happens if you cast the Seal over Shadowlands creatures bound within human flesh?" said Owen.

"Don't know," I said. "Bet it's going to hurt, though."

"All right," said Owen. "But if it doesn't work, we have to kill them all."

"Yup," I said. "How many entrances to the basement?"

"Main stairs through the kitchen," said Owen. "Then storm doors in the back yard."

"They'll hear us coming through the house," said Riordan.

"Then let's go through the back," I said.

We ran up the driveway and around the house. I heard rasping noises coming from the basement windows, the sound of talons against concrete. I glimpsed an elderly woman watching us from behind the fence next door but ignored her as we came to the back yard. As Owen had said, there were a pair of storm doors on the ground at the base of the house.

"Sorry about your storm doors," I said, and I hit them with a push of telekinetic force. The doors ripped off their hinges and clattered down the concrete stairs, and I ran after them, Riordan on my right, Quell on my left. Power surged through me as I drew together magic for my next spell.

Owen had a nice basement. A polished concrete floor gleamed under harsh LED lights, and he had a gym set up in the corner and a laundry area on the far wall. The panic room had been built in the corner, and it looked like a walk-in freezer, albeit one built out of cinder blocks.

The steel door and the concrete walls were covered with scratch marks.

Nine two-legged wraithwolves crowded before the panic room

door, all of them glaring at us. I caught glimpses of the lights reflecting on the metal plates at the base of their spines.

"Hi guys!" I said. "Guess what? This is gonna suck!"

The wraithwolves started to spring forward, and I cast the Seal of Shadows.

The symbol covered the basement floor, a ring fashioned of blue-white light and filled with the Elven hieroglyph for banishment. I wasn't entirely sure what it would do to the weird hybrid creatures that the Homeland Security officers had become.

It worked better than I hoped.

The wraithwolves froze in place, pinned by the spell, and they started screaming and thrashing, their talons rasping against the floor. Their fur and flesh shriveled, as if they were on fire, albeit in invisible flames. Sparks burst from some of the metal plates affixed to the base of their spines, and some of the wraithwolves fell and stopped moving, shrinking back into human form as they died. Some of them kept moving forward.

Riordan and Owen killed them. Owen hurled bolts of magical lightning, sweat pouring down his face from the exertion, and Riordan flung lightning globes and slashed with his Shadowmorph blade. In less than a minute, eight of the nine wraithwolves were down, shrinking back into human form.

One of the wraithwolves staggered and leaped up the stairs to the kitchen.

"Don't let that one get away!" I said. "We need to take one alive!"

I ran up the stairs after the creature, holding magical power ready to strike. The wraithwolf staggered through the kitchen and slammed into the door, stumbling into the backyard. Riordan and I raced after it. We ran into the backyard as the wraithwolf loped into the driveway. The creature whirled to face us, its wounds healing, and it snarled.

I drew power for another spell, ignoring the growing fatigue in my mind, and prepared to strike.

There was a boom and a flash from the fence. The wraithwolf stumbled forward, starting to turn. Behind the fence, I saw the old woman, but she was holding a shotgun, and she raised the weapon and unloaded the second barrel into the wraithwolf. The weapon did nothing to the wraithwolf, but the kinetic energy of pellets staggered the creature.

My lightning globe struck the wraithwolf and stunned it. The creature fell, thrashing and snarling, and Riordan darted forward and ripped the plate off its back. The wraithwolf howled and shrank back into the shape of an athletic young man with close-cropped hair.

"Well," I said. "Officer Kirby. We meet again."

He snarled and started to reach for his sidearm.

I hit him with another lightning globe, and he went back down. Riordan stooped, relieved Kirby of his belt and gun, and used the belt to tie him up.

I let out a long breath and looked to see the old woman with the shotgun watching me.

"Hey," I said. "Thanks."

The old woman gave a cautious nod. "Who are you, young lady?"

"My name's Nadia," I said. "This is my husband Riordan. This asshole," the old lady's lips thinned at the profanity, "used illegal magic to turn himself into a wraithwolf and tried to kill Colonel Quell's family. We disagreed violently."

"Are Anna and the girls okay?" said the old woman.

"Yeah, they're fine, we got here in time," I said. "Who are you?"

"My name is Mrs. Cornelia Fischer," said the old woman. I glanced back and saw Owen jog up the storm door stairs. "The Quells are my neighbors. I've never seen a human woman use magic."

"I'm special," I said.

Cornelia frowned as Owen joined us. "What is your opinion of our sovereign the High Queen?"

That was her polite way of finding out if I was a Rebel or some sort of other subversive.

"Frankly, she scares the shit out of me," I said.

Cornelia frowned. "That seems...appropriately respectful. If uncouth."

"Your family?" said Riordan.

"Unhurt," said Owen. His voice was calm, but his eyes were flat and hard. "Scared to death, but unhurt. I told Anna to stay in the panic room for now." He rubbed his jaw. "Don't know if more of these wraithwolves are going to show up."

"Nine of them here, five more at Leon's farm," I said. "If Leon was telling the truth, there could be thirty-four more wraithwolves out there."

"Thirty-four," said Owen. "And if they've infiltrated Homeland Security...we can't trust anyone in the department." I could tell that the admission pained him. "Any one of them could be a wraithwolf."

"It's not as bad as that," I said. "Now that I know what to look for, I can spot the wraithwolves pretty quickly." I grimaced. "Of course, my aetherometer is still in your car back in Sussex."

"Yes," said Owen. He took a deep breath. "Thank you for my family's life, Nadia. If you hadn't been there, if you hadn't gotten us here in time...this would have ended differently."

I shifted, uncomfortable with the praise, and shrugged. "I did what I had to do. Just glad we got here before it was too late."

"What is going on?" said Cornelia, looking back and forth between us.

"Bad business," said Owen. "I think you'd better go back inside and stay out of sight."

Cornelia scowled. "I have a right to know."

"Okay, fine, you asked for it," I said. I didn't want to deal with an inquisitive neighbor. I sent an effort of will into my blood ring, and it projected a translucent image of the High Queen's seal, an elaborate thing with a lot of crowned lions and roses and Elven hieroglyphs. "I'm a royal herald, sent to help investigate these two-legged wraithwolves. In the name of the High Queen, I command you to never speak of what you have seen with anyone, and to follow my instructions until this crisis has passed."

I expected the old woman to get angry or to ask a lot of questions. Instead, to my mild surprise, she drew herself up with pride.

"How can I serve the High Queen?" said Cornelia.

"You got more shells for that shotgun?" I said, dismissing the seal. She patted the pockets of her gray cardigan. Which hung on her bony frame like there was something heavy in the pockets, come to think of it. "Super. Then reload and come with us. You can keep watch while we're questioning the survivor here."

Officer Kirby let out a groan, stirring.

"We're going to question him?" said Owen.

"Oh, yeah," I said. "One way or another, he's going to tell us what he knows."

14

QUESTIONS & ANSWERS

Kirby was still on his back from when Nadia had ripped off the Singularity device, so Owen used Kirby's own handcuffs to bind his wrists. Then he took the traitorous officer under the arms, and Riordan lifted his ankles. Together they carried Kirby to the cellar doors, Nadia following. Mrs. Fischer, obeying Nadia's orders, went to the front porch to keep watch for more wraithwolves, with strict instructions to return and warn them at once if more Homeland Security officers arrived. Owen was vaguely impressed that Mrs. Fischer jumped at Nadia's instructions. All it had taken to compel obedience from his nosy neighbor was the High Queen's seal.

But that was the least of Owen's concerns just now.

Thirteen Homeland Security officers were dead, and eight of them were in Owen's basement. There hadn't been that many casualties among the Milwaukee branch since the Archon attack several years ago. That had shaken up the Milwaukee branch badly.

This would be worse.

This would be much worse.

The treachery of the officers was bad enough. But using the illegal magic and forbidden technology to turn themselves into human/wraithwolf abominations was far more serious. The Inquisition was going to get involved. When it was over, the Milwaukee branch of Homeland Security would be gutted.

And Owen could not see that as a bad thing.

His family had almost been murdered today. If Nadia hadn't been with him, the wraithwolves would have killed Anna and the girls. If they hadn't been able to traverse the Shadowlands, it would have been too late. There had been threats against Owen's family before. Criminals he had investigated had threatened his wife and children, though nothing had come of it.

But never before had a pack of wraithwolves stormed into his house and tried to kill his wife and daughters.

God, if he hadn't built that panic room in the basement. Anna had always regarded it with bemusement, but now...

One way or another, Owen was getting to the bottom of whatever the hell was going on.

They descended to the basement. The smell of blood and burned flesh filled Owen's nostrils. The eight dead officers lay sprawled across the floor, some of them burned from the spells that had killed them. Owen and Riordan carried Kirby to one of the pillars, and Riordan unlocked the handcuffs and shackled Kirby's arms behind him, the officer's back resting against the pillar.

"Might want to take the kids upstairs," said Riordan. His voice was grim and flat. "This is going to get loud."

"Good idea," said Nadia. "I'll help if you want to keep an eye on Kirby." Riordan nodded. "Owen...after we talk to Kirby, I think we're going to have to contact the High Queen and ask for help. We can't trust anyone in the local branch of Homeland Security, and we're in over our heads. For that matter, even if we could trust anyone in the local branch, bullets wouldn't work on the wraithwolves. We need some serious backup."

"Agreed," said Owen. "Have you warned your brother? If the wraithwolves came after my family, they might go after your brother."

"I think they were after us," said Nadia. "They're not thinking clearly. The wraithwolves or the summoning spells are twisting their thoughts around. When we weren't here, they decided to kill your family." She tapped her phone, which she must have switched back on. "I texted my brother while you and Riordan were carrying Kirby. He's fine, and there hasn't been anything strange at the warehouse today." She took a deep breath. "But if there's any trouble, he'll give me a call."

"Okay," said Owen. "I'm going to get my family out now. I think I'll send them upstairs. If more wraithwolves show up, Cornelia should give us plenty of warning. God knows she's had enough practice peering out through the curtains."

He crossed to the panic room door and tapped the intercom button. "Anna?"

"Owen?" Her voice crackled over the speaker. "Owen, is that you?"

"It is," said Owen. "Everyone's safe out here. You can come out now. I think you and the girls should go upstairs until we've got everything cleaned up down here."

He glanced at the bodies on the floor. Maybe it just would be better to buy a new house.

"Where was our first date?" said Anna.

She was making sure that he was who he claimed to be. A sensible precaution.

"It was at a shooting club," said Owen. "When I was investigating your boss's murder, I had to interview you, and you said that shooting was one of your hobbies. So when I asked you out, we went to the shooting club for the first time."

"You met your wife at a murder investigation?" said Nadia. "Jeez."

Owen looked at her. "Where did you meet your husband?"

Riordan snorted, once.

Nadia opened her mouth, closed it again. "Never mind."

"Who's that with you?" said Anna.

"Nadia MacCormac," said Owen. "I told you about her."

"Okay," said Anna. "Okay. I'm going to open the door. Stand back."

The heavy locks in the panic room door buzzed, and Anna eased it open with her foot. Her face was tight with fatigue and fear, and she held a Royal Arms semiautomatic pistol in both hands. Behind her, Owen glimpsed Katrina, Sabrina, Antonia, and June, the girls tense with terror, and he all but sagged with relief.

"Dad!" shouted June. She darted past Anna and hugged him, and he picked her up.

"Owen?" said Anna, stepping out of the panic room. "What's going on? Is..."

"Oh my God," said Sabrina, looking at the dead officers.

"What happened?" said Owen.

"We got lucky," said Anna. "We were all in the living room after breakfast, watching TV and reading. I saw the SUVs pull up outside, and I thought...I thought you'd been hurt or killed. I started to open the door, and then I saw some of them...change. They changed, Owen. They turned into these two-legged wolf things."

"Like werewolves," said Antonia, arms folded tight across her stomach.

"I yelled for the girls to get into the panic room," said Anna. "We went downstairs and locked ourselves in. I didn't have time to get my cell phone, and I think they cut the phone line to the panic room." She let out a shuddering breath. "I could hear them clawing their way inside. How did you know to come?"

"They attacked me, too," said Owen. He gestured at Nadia and Riordan. "My new friends helped fight them off. One of them let slip they were coming here...and we got here in time, thanks to Nadia."

"What's going on?" said Anna. "Is this some kind of Rebel thing?"

"I don't entirely know yet," said Owen.

"The short answer?" said Nadia. "Some Homeland Security officers got their hands on spooky old technology that lets them become those two-legged wolf things. Unfortunately, it also made them go nuts, which is why we're all here."

"You're Nadia?" said Anna.

"Yep," said Nadia. She gestured to Riordan. "This is my husband Riordan. We've, uh...been helping Owen out."

"He said you saved his life," said Anna.

Nadia shifted. "Well..."

Anna stepped forward and hugged her. "Thank you. Thank you for looking out for him."

"Okay," said Nadia. "Okay. Um. You're a hugger. You're welcome."

By the pillar, Kirby let out a moan. He was starting to come around again.

Anna stepped to the side and leveled her pistol at him.

"Dad," said Antonia. "Are you...are you going to be on a Punishment Day video for all this?"

"No," said Owen. "These officers went bad."

"Don't worry about it, kid," said Nadia. "Once this is over, your dad's probably getting promoted."

God, he hoped not. He'd settle for getting out of it alive with his family.

"I think you had better go upstairs," said Owen. "Take the kids." Despite his fears, he was both a little amused and slightly alarmed to note that Sabrina and Katrina were staring at Riordan with nervous curiosity. Owen knew the effect a Shadow Hunter could have on women, and while he was certain Nadia would not have married the sort of man who would seduce a teenage girl, best not to put any ideas into his daughters' heads. "Mrs. Fischer is guarding the front porch. If she sees anything, she'll come running."

"Really?" said Anna. "How did you manage that?"

"I asked nicely," said Nadia.

"I'll get you when things calm down, and we know what we're doing next," said Owen.

"Come on, kids," said Anna. "We're going let your father work."

"Work?" said Sabrina, blinking. "This...this is work?"

"It's what your father does, Miss Quell," said Riordan, the LED lights of the ceiling glinting off his sunglasses. "He catches bad guys."

Nadia nodded. "What he said."

Owen felt oddly gratified by that.

"I'll help Mrs. Fischer keep an eye out," said Anna, and she escorted the girls upstairs.

"Your wife has a good head on her shoulders, Colonel," said Riordan. "Not everyone could keep their cool in a crisis."

"I know," said Owen. "And I still have her because of you and Nadia. Thank you both."

Nadia shrugged, and he felt a flicker of amusement. She clearly did not like getting compliments and wasn't sure how to respond. "That's what we do. Well, that's what Riordan does. I just do whatever our mutual employer tells me to do. Speaking of which," she turned towards Kirby, "it's time to see if Officer Kirby is going to do this the easy way or the hard way."

"Yes," agreed Owen.

Because one way or another, Kirby was going to tell them what he knew.

They crossed the basement, stepping over the dead men, and stopped before Kirby. His eyes fluttered open, and for a moment, he looked confused. Then rage flashed over his expression, and he lunged forward with a snarl, the chain of the handcuffs rasping against the pillar. It was disturbing to see the feral, wolf-like mannerisms in a human face.

"You took it!" said Kirby. "Give it back, give it back, it's mine! Give it to me!"

"What, this?" said Nadia. She tossed the metal plate in her gloved hand a few times. Kirby lunged forward, jaws snapping as if he wanted to bite her hand off. "That seems like a bad idea, so I'm gonna pass. But thanks for the offer, though. I appreciate it."

"It's mine!" snarled Kirby. "Mine! Stupid bitch, you don't understand. I'm more than human now. We're going to make a better world, and we're going to rip out the corruption." He turned his feverish eyes towards Riordan. "You understand. You're like us. I could smell the Shadowlands on you."

Riordan remained unmoved, his face like granite. "I know what it is to have power and strength, officer. But I don't know what it is like to kill innocent women and children to gratify myself."

"Why, Kirby?" said Owen. "Why did you come after my kids? You know me. We've worked together on cases, for God's sake. We caught bad guys and made sure their victims had justice. We did that, you and me. And now you're coming after my family? What did I ever to do you to make you do that? I mean, if you want to come after me, fine, I get that. But my kids?"

Kirby hesitated, something almost like guilt going over his face. "It...Hopkins was supposed to have killed you. He called us said he spotted your vehicle by that greasy little shit Leon's hiding place. You were supposed to have died there." He scowled. "Suppose that old bastard and that mouthy bitch Cecilia screwed it up."

"You could say that," said Nadia. "They're dead, and we killed them. That's kind of a screwup, I guess."

Kirby gave her a wary look. Someone like Nadia should have been terrified of him, not grinning that mirthless rictus of a smile. And Kirby had seen her fight the wraithwolves.

"Okay," said Owen. "I get that. I was in the way, I was looking too closely. Makes sense to come after me. But you knew I wasn't at my house, and you came after my kids anyway. Why?"

"You don't understand what it's like," whispered Kirby. "It's like fire in your blood, in your mind. You're so much faster and stronger. The senses are sharper. And the killing, it's like..." He shook his head, his eyes bright with something that reminded Quell of an addict thinking about his favorite drug. "It's better than booze, better than women, better than anything. Mr. Hood said we were the next stage of humanity." He tried to shrug in the handcuffs. "So why shouldn't we prey on the old humanity? You're just dumb animals who let the Elves rule over you."

"Aw, man, we're going to have to report you for elfophobia," said Nadia. Kirby sneered at her.

"You know Mr. Hood," said Owen. "Tell me about him."

Kirby laughed again. "I don't have to tell you anything. You're all going to die. We're going to get rid of everything wrong with the world, starting with people like you."

"And what kind of people are we?" said Nadia.

"You? You're part of Brauner's little gang," said Kirby. "You're probably banging him on the side so he'll let you keep your stupid little fruit company." Nadia rolled her eyes. "And you, Colonel? You're a toady. You're one of the idiots who lets the Elves rule over us.

They snap their fingers, and you jump." He looked at Riordan. "I don't know what the hell you are, but I don't like you, and I'll kill you, too."

"Eloquent," said Riordan.

"Sounds like you're a Rebel," said Owen.

"The Rebels were idiots," said Kirby. "Mr. Hood and the Singularity have a better way. We're going to evolve. We're going to become better than the Elves, better than the rest of humanity. Then we'll show you."

"Show us what?" said Owen.

Kirby hesitated, and then grinned and shook his head. "You're a good interrogator, I'll give you that, Quell. But I'm not talking. My pack brothers will come for me. And then you're going to regret all of this."

"Come on," said Nadia. "You saw me use magic. You know I can force you to tell me whatever I want."

"You can hurt me," said Kirby, "but you won't make me betray my brothers. And then when I get these cuffs off, when I am restored, I am going to rip you to pieces. Ever wonder what it feels like to have a wraithwolf rip your guts out foot by foot?"

"Not for a couple years now," said Nadia. She tossed the metal plate to herself again. "And I'm not going to hurt you."

"Then what are you going to do?" said Kirby, sneering.

"I'm going to give you exactly what you want," said Nadia.

She stepped next to him, slapped the plate into its previous place on his back, and then took several quick steps back. Kirby let out a shrill laugh, his eyes turning yellow, fur starting to sprout from his face, claws growing from his fingers.

His transformation was quick, but Nadia was faster.

Before he could finish, she cast the Seal of Shadows over him.

This time she made a small Seal, just large enough to encircle both Kirby and the pillar. The transformation froze halfway through, leaving Kirby a ghastly, misshapen mix of human and wraithwolf. Kirby began to scream and thrash, howling in pain, his twisted body bucking in agony. Something in Owen recoiled at the sight, but he remembered his daughters hiding in the panic room, and he said nothing.

Kirby shrank back into human form with a sobbing whimper, and Nadia released the Seal, its light winking out. There were harsh red burns on Kirby's neck and hands, and he was shuddering with pain.

"Aw, man," said Nadia. "That looked like it really hurt. Suppose having a wraithwolf halfway summoned into your body isn't at all comfortable. You should..."

"Bitch!" screamed Kirby, and he jerked again, his eyes turning yellow.

"Yes, I am," said Nadia, and she cast the Seal once more.

This time she let him scream and thrash for a full minute.

When she released the Seal, Kirby slumped against the pillar, sobbing. The burns had healed during his transformation, but new ones had appeared in different places. The half-finished transformation had torn his uniform to shreds, rather than making it disappear, and Owen saw more ugly burns on his chest and stomach.

Nadia waited until the burns healed, then she reached down and ripped away the plate. Kirby screamed again, still crying.

"All right," said Nadia, voice soft. "Want to try again?" Kirby shook his head. "Going to answer the Colonel's questions now?"

"Doesn't matter," spat Kirby, his voice full of fear and rage. "You're all going to die anyway."

"Then you should have no trouble answering my questions," said Owen. "Why did you try to kill me?"

"Because Lieutenant Warren said you were poking around, that we had to get you out of the way," said Kirby, sullen. There was still defiance in his tone, but more fear now. "We're going to do great things for Wisconsin, for this country, for all of mankind. We had to get people out of the way first. You, then probably Major Giles."

Owen nodded. He had hoped that his old friend Jacob Giles wasn't part of this mess.

"Tell me what happened," said Owen. "Start from the beginning. Make me understand."

"Some of us," said Kirby, "some of us were really frustrated. It started after that asshole Doyle's building collapsed. We all knew it was his fault. We all knew the law wouldn't touch him. Good old Governor Arnold was looking after his friends. Lieutenant Warren, he understood. So did Sergeant Hopkins. Then one day Warren talked to me, pulled me aside. The lieutenant said he understood my frustration. That he knew what it was like to catch the little bad guys while the big ones got away. He showed me the Fusion device…"

"Fusion?" said Owen. "It's nuclear?"

"What? No," said Kirby. "Do you think I'm stupid enough to walk around with a nuclear device strapped to my skin?" Owen refrained from comment, and Kirby kept talking. "No. He called it the Fusion device because it joins together the best of wraithwolf and human. The device summons a wraithwolf from the Shadowlands, but instead of giving it a physical form, the machine pushes it into a human body. The human gets all the strength and speed of a wraithwolf, but with a human intellect directing it."

"Which is why you decided to kill Ronald Doyle's wife and kids," said Owen.

Kirby looked to the side. "That was Warren. He did that one himself since he knew he'd get the murder investigation. But I know why he did it." That mad, addicted light came into his eyes again. "There's nothing like killing, nothing like it at all. It's like…we've become superior men, you know? Better than humans, better than Elves. The Elves are so smug because they're immune to bullets, but they're not immune to wraithwolf claws and fangs. The lieutenant's got big plans. We're going to kill Brauner and all his cronies, and then we're going to kill the Elves. That's why we killed Doyle, why we tried to kill Leon. We'll get rid of all the evidence, and then we'll clean up Wisconsin. And everyone will blame it on random wraithwolves from the Shadowlands, not us."

"All forty-eight of you?" said Owen.

"Not yet," said Kirby. "The lieutenant said he got forty-eight Fusion devices from Leon, Doyle, and Mr. Hood, but he didn't find enough people to take them." His mouth twisted with disgust.

"They'll understand. Everyone will understand. They'll know that killing is bliss."

"Including killing my kids?" said Owen.

Kirby smirked at him. "Yes."

Owen wanted to hit him, but he needed one more piece of information.

"Where is Warren's base?" said Owen. "He wouldn't be able to do this at the Central Office."

"Like I'm telling you..." started Kirby.

Before he finished the sentence, Owen stepped forward and cast the mindtouch spell.

It was a trick he had perfected over the years. Get the suspecting talking about something so the information was at the forefront of his mind, and then scoop it out of his thoughts. Entering another's mind was always a chaotic and risky business (as his quarrel with Nadia had proved), and this was the safest and the easiest method.

His mind touched Kirby's thoughts, and Owen's stomach roiled in disgust. Kirby was no longer sane. Truth be told, his mind was no longer entirely human. Images of bloodlust and hunger for flesh boiled in his mind. Yet the conversation had brought to mind Warren's base, the place where he tested the Fusion devices. Owen glimpsed an old church, its windows boarded up, the floor carpeted with leaves...

He knew it and stepped back.

"The Church of the Modern Apostles," said Owen, "out in Cedarburg."

Kirby flinched.

Nadia frowned. "Is that like a cult?"

"No, no, nothing like that," said Owen. "It was a little Baptist denomination, split off from one of the main ones. Thought the mainstream Baptists weren't strict enough. All the members died from old age, and the church dissolved. The building's still there, but no one has bought it. Someone dumped a body there a few years ago, so I was there for an investigation. It would be the perfect place for

Warren to test his Fusion devices. The church property is surrounded by trees, and you can't see it from the road."

"Great," said Nadia. "Trees and wraithwolves."

"How did you know that?" snarled Kirby.

Owen tapped his temple. "Detective work."

Kirby started to shout something, and Owen cast the mindtouch spell again. This time Owen's will hammered at the sleep centers of Kirby's brain. This wasn't always a reliable method, but the multiple transformations had exhausted Kirby, and the effort took hold. The traitorous officer collapsed into unconsciousness, and only the handcuffs kept him upright.

"Neat trick," said Nadia.

"It doesn't always work," said Owen.

"Important question," said Nadia. "What the hell are we going to do now?"

"You said you were going to contact the High Queen," said Owen. "We need help. Someone from the Inquisition or maybe the Wizard's Legion. I don't know how many of Warren's wraithwolves are left, but we've got to assume a minimum of twenty. Maybe even the full-thirty four."

"It's also possible," said Riordan, "that this 'Mr. Hood' obtained more Fusion devices for Lieutenant Warren, and neither Leon nor Kirby knew about it."

"And we should pick up Leon," said Nadia. "If we're going after Warren and his followers, I'm going to need my aetherometer."

"We also need official support," said Riordan. He faced Owen, and he felt the weight of the gaze behind those heavy sunglasses. "Is there anyone in Homeland Security you trust completely? Either in the Milwaukee branch or one of the others. Someone you're sure wouldn't have bought into Warren's plan."

Owen hesitated and then nodded. "A few, yes."

"All right," said Nadia. "You call your buddies. I'll use my ring to contact the High Queen. Then we'll figure out what we're doing next."

Or, possibly, Tarlia would tell them what they were doing next.

"Okay," said Owen, and he produced his cell phone and hit the contact for Major Jacob Giles, head of the homicide division.

Giles picked up on the second ring. "Owen?"

"Yeah, Jake," said Owen.

"What the hell is going on?" said Giles. "Two dozen officers are taking sick time today, and another dozen are absent without leave. Is there some kind of labor walkout going on? Or is flu season getting started early?"

"It's a lot worse," said Owen. "We've got serious trouble. Are you alone?"

There was a pause, and then the sound of a door closing.

"Yeah, I'm alone," said Giles.

"I'll give it to you straight," said Owen. "Lieutenant Kyle Warren somehow got his hands on machines that let people transform themselves into half-human, half-wraithwolf hybrids. They're going on murder rampages. Warren himself transformed into a wraithwolf and killed the Doyle family. Five officers tried to murder Pablo Leon an hour ago, and nine more tried to kill my family shortly thereafter."

There was a long, long pause.

"Please tell me this is a practical joke," said Giles.

"I really wish that it was," said Owen. "But Warren gave these devices to at least twenty officers, maybe thirty, and the wraithwolves are twisting their minds. They're going to start spree killing if we don't stop them."

"Christ," said Giles. "You said they went after your family? Are Anna and the kids okay?"

"They are," said Owen. "We got here just in time."

"We?" said Giles.

"Me and Nadia MacCormac," said Owen.

"The girl from the Sky Hammer video," said Giles. "I know you've been working together."

"We have," said Owen. "I don't know who I can trust inside the department." He took a deep breath. "I know the High Queen is sending either Inquisitors or soldiers from the Wizard's Legion, but I don't know how many and I don't know when they're getting here. If we're going to get a handle on this mess, we need help..."

"You have it," said Giles, and Owen felt a wave of relief. He had been prepared for suspicion and accusation. Thirteen Homeland Security officers had died in the last few hours, and another one was captive in Owen's basement. "I know you're solid, Owen. Tell me what you need."

"Find officers you can trust," said Owen. "If you're not sure about them, check their backs."

"Their backs?"

"The wraithwolf machine is called a Fusion device, and it looks like a thin bronze plate about the size of your hand," said Owen. "If they have one, it will be fixed to the base of their spines. Once you have some men you can trust, come to my house. We should be able to figure out our next move by then."

"Okay," said Giles. "We'll be there soon. Keep your eyes open, Owen."

"You, too," said Owen. "If Warren and his followers figure out that you're helping me, they might come after you."

"Well, you're the veteran of the Wizard's Legion," said Giles. "If we've got wraithwolves running around, we need magic. See you soon."

Giles ended the call, and Owen returned his phone to his belt.

"Any luck?" said Riordan.

"The head of homicide is a friend of mine, and he's on his way," said Owen. He looked at the dead and sighed. "Might want to arrest me after all this, but..."

The blood ring shivered against his right hand, and the message filled his thoughts.

When Owen had sent telepathic messages to the High Queen in the past, sometimes she had responded at once, and sometimes it had taken days for her to answer.

Evidently, she agreed that this was a serious situation.

"Nadia, Owen," came Tarlia's voice inside of Owen's head. "You are to act at once to destroy the hybrid wraithwolves. Take some of them alive for questioning if you can, but only if it is practical. I am sending ten soldiers of the Wizard's Legion to you, commanded by my handmaiden Tythrilandria. Once they arrive, the three of you will take command and destroy the wraithwolves. Make sure all the Fusion devices are secured. Tythrilandria's helicopter will land in Owen's backyard in another five hours at the most. Be ready to act at once."

The mental contact ended.

Owen blinked and looked at Nadia.

"You got that, too?" said Nadia.

Owen nodded.

"For the benefit of those of us who do not have magic rings?" said Riordan.

"The High Queen's sending Tyth and some soldiers of the Wizard's Legion to help us," said Nadia. "Looks like we're going wraithwolf hunting."

15

WOLVES' DEN

The next five hours were busy.

Major Jacob Giles arrived about thirty minutes after Owen summoned him. I was skeptical about calling in anyone from Homeland Security, but Riordan had a point. We needed the help of Homeland Security officers who hadn't been corrupted. Thirteen dead Homeland Security officers were impossible to hide.

Well, maybe not impossible. Had it been up to me, I might have opened a rift way, pushed their bodies through it, and let the anthrophages and wraithwolves of the Shadowlands scavenge on the dead. No one would ever know what happened. But Owen was a Homeland Security officer, and I could tell he was upset by what we had learned. I mean, yeah, Warren's followers had tried to murder his entire family. But they were Homeland Security officers, men and women who had sworn the same oath that Owen took very seriously, and so their betrayal stung.

I supposed we were doing this as officially as possible.

I just hoped it didn't come back to bite us.

Two more Homeland Security SUVs joined the first pair, and Giles and five other officers emerged. I stood next to Owen on the porch and watched them, ready to start raining destruction if they transformed into wraithwolves. But they stayed in human form. Giles was a thin, dark-skinned man with lined features. Probably a lot stronger than he looked.

"Jake," said Owen. "Thanks for coming."

"This is a mess, Owen," said Giles. "But we're not having a bunch of wraithwolves run around Milwaukee, not on my watch." He glanced at me. "Don't you own a fruit company?"

"It's my brother's company," I said. "I do consulting gigs on the side."

Giles grunted, and then looked at Owen. "Better show me the bodies."

We went downstairs. I half-expected Giles and his men to erupt with anger at the sight of dead Homeland Security officers, but they regarded the scene with sober eyes. It helped that some of the dead officers had been halfway between human and wolf form when I had killed them. It helped even more that Kirby was awake and threatening to eat us all alive once he got his Fusion device back.

"Christ, Owen," said Giles, shaking his head. "I hoped you were wrong about all this, I'll admit that, but…"

"I know what you mean," said Owen.

They settled on a plan. Some of Giles's men started documenting the dead, taking pictures and gathering identification. Giles had friends in the county coroner's office, and he made some calls to collect the dead. His men began bagging up the corpses in the basement. Giles and Riordan went to Sussex to pick up Leon and take care of the dead there, and to retrieve my aetherometer.

If the High Queen wanted us to go after Warren and the Fusion wraithwolves, I was going to need the instrument.

I gathered up all the Fusion devices and stuffed them into a paper shopping bag. I wasn't sure what I was going to do with them, but I didn't think it was a good idea for them to go to the coroner's office. I wasn't entirely sure what would happen if someone touched one without a glove, but I didn't want some poor mortuary worker to find out the hard way.

Anna and her two oldest daughters emerged from upstairs, saw the large number of guests, and then decided to make an enormous pot of chili to feed everyone. I suppose everyone deals with stress in their own way, and cooking seemed to be Anna Quell's. Come to think of it, I was pretty hungry. I hadn't eaten breakfast or lunch, and I had used a lot of magic today, and using magical force was at least as taxing as intense exercise. I took a bowl of chili, thanked Anna, and went out to stand guard on the porch with Owen.

I wondered what the neighbors thought of four Homeland Security SUVs parked on along the curb.

"That's really good chili," I said around a mouthful. I liked spicy food. The textures of certain foods reminded me of some of my more unpleasant experiences in the Eternity Crucible, but spice was a good way to overcome that. Riordan, Russell, and the Marneys were all bemused at how I had started putting hot sauce on almost anything.

"Anna's a good cook," said Owen. "She wasn't when we got married. She ate smoothies and stir fry and nothing else. But once the twins came along, she decided to teach herself and got good at it."

"Question," I said. "Your first three daughters are named Katrina, Sabrina, and Antonia, right?" Owen nodded. "The names all end with the letter A. So why'd you break pattern with June?"

"Well," said Owen, "we thought we'd stop with three kids. Then we took a vacation in June, and Anna got pregnant again, and..."

"You named her after the month she was conceived in?" I said.

"Yup."

"Ew."

Owen shrugged. "It's a good name. And we didn't have any female relatives named June. Where were you from originally? Milwaukee?"

"No, Seattle."

Owen nodded. "Well, maybe there's a Nadia Park somewhere in Seattle, or a Nadia Street or a Nadia Avenue, and your parents..."

"Nope," I said. "Not thinking about that."

Though I had a sudden urge to pull out my phone and see if there really was a Nadia Street or something in Seattle, but I decided that I really didn't want to know.

Riordan and Giles returned an hour later, and Riordan handed over my bag. I retrieved my aetherometer, and we walked the basement, making sure that we hadn't missed any of the Fusion devices. We hadn't, and for lack of a better place to store them, we stashed the things in the Quells' panic room.

Tyth and the Wizard's Legion arrived at about three in the afternoon.

We heard the roar of the chopper's rotor before it came into sight. I walked into the backyard with Riordan, Owen, and Giles, and a minute later, a big black helicopter appeared over the trees. It circled a few times, and then began to descend, the wind blowing over the Quells' yard. Just as well that the trees had already lost their leaves, or else the gale from the rotor would have knocked them down. The helicopter blocked the driveway when it landed, but between the yard and the driveway, there was just enough room for the big craft to set down.

The engines powered down with a whine, the rotors spinning to a stop.

"Okay," said Owen. "I've never had a helicopter land in my back yard before."

A door on the side of the helicopter opened, and an Elven woman got out.

She was wearing a strange costume – combat boots, cargo pants, a T-shirt, and a weapon harness and tactical vest. Which wasn't the strange part. No, what was strange was that she wore a knee-length leather coat colored an eye-watering shade of pink over her combat clothing. It looked extremely out of place. But I knew that she had a good reason for it. Lord Morvilind had enspelled the coat so that its pockets could hold much, much more than their interior volume would otherwise allow. Tythrilandria, handmaiden to the High Queen (and shadow agent) could fit enough weapons and ammo to equip a battalion in her pockets. You know how some women cart around giant purses that hold everything they could potentially need? Tyth's coat was like that, just times a thousand.

Behind Tyth human men in black uniforms emerged from the helicopter. They had stylized silver lightning bolts on their collars, the symbol of the Wizard's Legion, and wore tactical equipment similar to Tyth's, albeit with no pink coats. I walked forward with Riordan, Owen, and Giles, and Tyth jogged forward, her dark hair streaming behind her.

She grinned when she saw us, silver eyes glinting. She was glad to see Riordan and me. And why not? We had done some crazy stuff together and survived. I mean, we had gone to Mars and back.

"Lady Elf," said Owen. "Thank you for coming."

"We all go where the High Queen commands, Colonel," said Tyth. Whoever had taught her English had managed to give her a pronounced California accent. She talked very fast, except for the vowels, which she tended to draw out. Her eyes shifted to me, and she grinned. "And it's good to see you and Riordan again, Nadia."

Before I could react, she caught me in a hug. Giles and Owen looked nonplussed. I am not a hugger, as I have mentioned before. Tyth, however, definitely was.

"Hey," I said when we broke apart. "It's good to see you, too. This is Colonel Owen Quell, head of the local branch of Homeland Security's special investigations. Major Jacob Giles, head of homicide. Guys, this is Tythrilandria, handmaiden to the High Queen."

"Lady Elf," said Giles with a polite bow.

Some Elven nobles were rigid to the point of pedantry about ceremony. Tyth wasn't one of them. She wasn't even a noble since her family had essentially been survivalists hiding from the Archons in the wilderness of Kalvarion. But the Archons had murdered her entire family and kept Tyth as a "comfort woman" until Morvilind killed that particular group of Archons.

Yeah. I don't feel bad that I helped Morvilind kill all the Archons on the day of the Mage Fall. But if I ever start to feel bad, I think about Tyth's family. Or all the other Elven families the Archons murdered in the three centuries they ruled Kalvarion.

"Just call me Tyth," said Tyth with a sunny smile. "Tythrilandria is way too long to say in a fight." Her smile faded. "And we're about to be in a fight. Captain?"

One of the soldiers came up to join us. He was a leathery-faced man of about forty, which graying black hair and hard black eyes. I couldn't tell his nationality at a glance, but I thought he looked Mediterranean. Maybe Italian or Greek. I felt his arcane aura as well. Quite a bit weaker than mine, but still stronger than most human wizards.

"Lady Tythrilandria," said the man in English with a heavy Spanish accent.

"This is Captain Alcazar of the Wizard's Legion," said Tyth. "He's brought a squad with him. All veteran wizards."

"I have been ordered to obey the commands of Lady Tythrilandria on this excursion," said Alcazar.

"But you guys have more experience with this kind of thing than I do," said Tyth. She gestured at Riordan and me, and the ring of a shadow agent glinted on her hand, invisible to everyone but me and Owen. "So I want you to plan it, and we'll do whatever you decide."

"Sir," said Alcazar to Riordan. "I am given to understand that you are a Shadow Hunter?"

"That's right," said Riordan.

"That is good," said Alcazar. "You have experience with this kind of thing. I understand we are clearing out a nest of wraithwolves?"

"Not quite, Captain," I said. "If it was just wraithwolves, we could get the local Elven nobles or the Shadow Hunters to take them down. But traitorous Homeland Security officers have obtained devices that allow them to summon wraithwolves into their flesh." Alcazar raised one dark eyebrow. "It turns them into hybrids of human and wraithwolf. They're fast, strong, deadly, and absolutely crazy. We need to kill them or force them to surrender and take back the devices that allow them to transform." I took a deep breath. "But the wraithwolves have twisted their minds, so we're probably going to have to kill them all."

"Well," said Alcazar. "Just another day in the Legion."

To his mild surprise, Owen wound up running the briefing.

Captain Alcazar's squad filled the living room. Some of the men sat on the couches, others on the floor. Two of the wizards stood near the front door, watching for any sign of the enemy. It brought back memories of Owen's own time in the Legion, of attending briefings like this. The Wizard's Legion tended to act as Tarlia's personal force during Shadowlands campaigns, but the soldiers of the Legion also did special operations like this.

Anna moved through the soldiers, serving coffee, which they seemed to appreciate.

"Our targets," said Owen, tapping a key on his laptop, "are here." A picture of the abandoned Church the Modern Apostles appeared on the TV screen. It looked like a traditional white church with tall windows, though the white paint was peeling, and several shingles were missing from the roof.

"Where did you obtain that photograph?" said Alcazar, frowning over his coffee.

"Commercial realtor's website," said Owen. "The property has been for sale for the last five years, but no one wants to buy the church or tear it down and develop the land. And the commercial realtor's website," he tapped another key, and the image changed, "also has this handy floor plan of the building."

Alcazar grunted in approval.

"Based on intelligence gathered from our prisoner," said Owen, "our targets use the church's basement for their base and for practice and training with their transformation devices."

"What kind of numbers are we looking at here?" said one of the other soldiers.

"Between twenty and thirty," said Owen. "Our intelligence indicates that Lieutenant Warren has access to only forty-eight of the transformation devices." Nadia had told him not to share any details about the Singularity or Catalyst Corporation with the soldiers, and Owen agreed with her caution. In this instance, what the men of the

Wizard's Legion didn't know wouldn't hurt them. "It's possible that there are more. Warren may have been able to obtain new devices. However, there are indications that Warren wasn't able to find enough recruits to use all his machines, so we don't know exactly what kind of numbers we will face."

"If they're all in that abandoned church," said another lieutenant, "why not just dump a bunch of firebombs on it and blast them all to hell?"

"Won't work," said Nadia, leaning against the wall next to Riordan. "They'll regenerate. If we do bomb the place, we'll have to wait until they come out to get away from the fire, and then we'll have to kill them anyway."

"And we need to capture all the transformation devices," said Tyth. "The High Queen was very clear on that. She doesn't want any of the things loose in Wisconsin. Or anywhere."

"What's our tactical plan?" said Alcazar.

"Lady Tythrilandria and Nadia have exceptional scouting capabilities," said Owen. Despite what she had said, Owen could not quite bring himself to call her Tyth. "They will go ahead and scout the church and report back to us. The four Homeland Security SUVs sitting out front? We'll take them to the church and park out of sight on the county highway. Lady Tythrilandria and Nadia will scout and return to us. If the targets are in the basement, we will drive onto the church property, encircle the building, and attack. Remember, the targets are no longer sane and will be irrationally aggressive. Unless they immediately surrender by removing their transformation devices, you will have no choice but to use lethal force." He nodded to Giles. "Major Giles is the only one who doesn't have access to magic, so he'll coordinate from the vehicles. Any questions?"

There were several. The soldiers of the Legion were all veterans, and they knew that proper planning and preparation could mean the difference between life and death. Most of the questions dealt with the capabilities of the hybrid wraithwolves, and since Nadia had killed most of the hybrids, she answered the questions. Owen watched the growing respect among the wizards as they spoke with

Nadia. The men of the Legion were probably the best-trained and most capable human soldiers in the world, and they were unfailingly professional. It was obvious they had thought Nadia the Shadow Hunter's pretty girlfriend and nothing more, and watching their wary respect would have been amusing under other circumstances.

Then it was time for a comms check, and they piled into the SUVs and set off for Cedarburg and the Church of the Modern Apostles.

I RODE in the backseat of Owen's car, with Giles sitting up front. Riordan and Tyth sat in the back, and since I was shorter and smaller than both of them, guess who got to ride squeezed in the middle seat?

Yeah. Being short is sometimes really annoying.

"So," I said to Tyth, who was fiddling with her radio earpiece. "How do you like being the High Queen's…well, secretary?"

"Personal assistant?" said Riordan.

"The title of handmaiden, like, includes all those duties," said Tyth. "I do whatever her Majesty asks of me."

"That must be a great honor," said Giles. The poor man seemed a little starstruck by a handmaiden of the High Queen and the soldiers of the Wizard's Legion. But he'd had a rough day. Not as bad as ours, of course, but learning that dozens of Homeland Security officers had become ravening insane monsters had come as a shock.

"Oh, it totally is," said Tyth with complete sincerity. "Her Majesty is always traveling all over Earth and Kalvarion. I think I've seen more of Kalvarion than I ever did when I actually lived there, and definitely more of Earth. It's not like the old days when we both worked for…"

I coughed. Tyth was a friend, but she liked to talk, and I didn't think she 100% grasped the "shadow" part of a shadow agent. Then again, she was a handmaiden of the High Queen, and that carried a lot of authority among both Elves and humans.

"For our old boss," said Tyth without missing a beat. "I hardly ever left the Elven free cities in the old days." She paused. "I think our old boss would be proud of what we're doing now. He knew that humans and Elves had to stand together, or else our enemies would destroy us separately. I just wish that he was here to help her Majesty now."

I sure didn't. Tyth had actually loved Morvilind. I mean, he wasn't a lovable man by any stretch of the imagination, but Tyth had regarded him with a good deal of awe. In her eyes, he had been a lone hero, the man who had single-handedly defeated the Archons, opened the Great Gate, and heralded a new and hopefully better age for both Elves and humans. I suppose all that was true from a certain angle, but that overlooked Morvilind's cruelty, his callousness, his utter ruthlessness, and the fact that he had gone through shadow agents like paper towels.

Tyth and I were just the ones who had happened to outlive him.

But she was a friend, and I didn't want get into a fight with her.

"Sure," I said.

"How's that fruit company?" said Tyth. "I was there when your brother talked her Majesty into giving him the license. I think it's going to do a lot of good for the farmers of Kalvarion. In the old days, the farmers had to give a big part of their produce to their lords, and then the Archons just enslaved everybody. If they can sell to the humans of Earth, that will be, like, a really big deal."

"So far, so good," I said, which was mostly true. "We haven't turned a profit yet, but we should be able to do it next year when the harvest comes in." I talked about distribution and grocery stores and refrigeration costs for a while. Either Tyth really was interested in the topic, or she was good at faking it.

"We're here," said Riordan.

The SUVs pulled off to the side of the county road. We were in a wooded area, forests rising on either side. I bet drivers hit a lot of deer here during the winter months. A few feet ahead, a gravel driveway turned to the right into the trees. It looked old and half-overgrown with weeds.

But. Some of the weeds had been pressed down by recent tire tracks.

"Okay," I said, pulling out my aetherometer. "Give me a second, and I'll see if there are any two-legged wolves hiding in the trees."

I scowled at the aetherometer. The device took a moment, and then the dials settled into a reading. It detected the auras of Tyth and Owen and the soldiers of the Wizard's Legion. I didn't see any of the peculiar auras of the Fusion devices nearby. But there was a big concentration of them not all that far away, maybe a couple hundred yards into the trees.

"Okay," I said again, putting the aetherometer away. "It doesn't look like they've seen us. But there's a big group of those summoning devices nearby. Probably in the church basement like Kirby said."

"I think we had better scout ahead," said Tyth.

"Yeah," I said.

"That's your rally point," said Riordan, pointing at the end of the driveway. "If you're both not back there in ten minutes, we're going in after you."

I nodded. "We'll be back."

"Be careful," said Riordan.

I started to make a joke, but I stopped myself. Riordan looked so serious. But that man had put himself through hell to keep me safe, often with no help from me whatsoever.

"I will," I said.

I took a deep breath and got out of the car, and Tyth followed suit.

We walked along the shoulder of the road to the driveway, our boots crunching against the gravel. Just as well there hadn't been any snow yet. We reached the end of the driveway, and I started up its length. I thought the driveway was about a hundred and fifty yards long, and the barren forest around it created sort of a tunnel effect. At the end of that tunnel, I saw a clearing with a dilapidated white church and a crumbling parking lot.

There were a half-dozen cars in the lot. Guess Warren's followers had used their own vehicles to drive to their weird little murder club.

"Ready?" said Tyth.

"Yep," I said. "On the count of three. One, two, three!"

At three, we both cast the Cloak spell and vanished from sight. I could hold the Cloak spell in place for about twelve or thirteen minutes while moving around. Tyth could do it for three-quarters of an hour. I was a more powerful wizard overall than Tyth and could unleash far more destructive power than she could, but she simply had a better natural ability for illusion magic. She had offered to scout alone, but I had nixed that idea. If something happened to her, she would need help.

Better to send in two.

I jogged up the driveway, wrapped in the Cloak spell, and came to the parking lot and the church. I took a loop around the church, looking for guards, but I didn't see anyone. Evidently, Warren and his goons thought themselves safe.

Like wolves in their den.

The church's doors stood open, and I climbed up the concrete steps and into the lobby. Or the narthex – I think the lobby of a church is called a narthex, but don't hold me to that. It was a wreck, the carpet moldering, the paint peeling, the air stinking of mildew and rot. I walked into the church proper. Rotting pews faced the altar, and shafts of dim gray light leaked through holes in the ceiling and the broken windows.

There was no sign of the wraithwolves.

But the smell of blood was very strong.

I stepped into the corner, dropped the Cloak spell, and took a moment to catch my breath, keeping track of the count in my head. After I got my breathing under control, I cast the spell to detect magic, focusing it on the floor. At once, I felt the strange, twisted power of the Fusion devices beneath my feet – they were in the basement. I cast the aurasight spell and focused it. I saw numerous auras below the floor, all of them tainted with the bloodlust and rage I had seen in Kirby's emotions.

I counted twenty-two of them.

I wondered if that was all the wraithwolves.

Well, we were about to find out.

I looked at one of the broken windows, and an idea came to me. I cast the Cloak spell again, and hurried outside, circling around the church's foundation. As I expected, the basement had window wells, and most of the windows were broken. Through one of the windows, I saw the harsh glare of LED work lights, and I crouched by the window well, peering through it.

I saw several men wearing Homeland Security uniforms, and the smell of blood rose to my nostrils. A man's voice rose to my ears, pleasant and commanding, and I recognized Kyle Warren.

It sounded like he was giving a pep talk.

"We'll do it tonight," said Warren. "That's our best opportunity. Brauner and all his cronies will be there, and some of the Elven nobles. We can rid humanity of them both with one stroke – both the corrupt human politicians and the leeches of the nobles."

He definitely wasn't worried about a charge of elfophobia.

"The Elven nobles can use magic," said another voice.

"We'll eliminate them first," said Warren. "Then we can take care of Brauner and his friends."

I'd heard enough, and I had used six of my ten minutes. I jogged back to the mouth of the driveway, dropped my Cloak spell so Riordan could see me, and waited. About halfway through minute nine, Tyth reappeared. She wasn't nearly as winded as I had been, but she was better with the Cloak spell.

"Cutting it close," I said.

"I wanted to get really good information for the soldiers," said Tyth. "I watched the enemy through a broken window well." I nodded. "There's twenty-two of them, and they're listening to the leader. I think it's that Warren guy you mentioned."

"He is," I said. "Let's check in with Owen and Alcazar...and then it will be time to move."

The familiar pre-fight tension settled over me. But I was used to it. I had spent over a century and a half fighting to the death every single day, so I knew how to handle myself. And my magic was probably the single biggest advantage that we had in this coming fight.

We got back into the car.

"Well?" said Owen.

"Twenty-two of them," I said. "They're gathered in the basement.

Looks like Warren is giving them a pep talk. I think they're getting ready to go after Arnold Brauner tonight." I suppose Brauner would make an easy target. I'd broken into his house without much trouble, and while his security would stop a normal thief, it wouldn't do anything against the Fusion wraithwolves.

"The charity dinner," said Giles.

"Has to be," said Owen.

"What charity dinner?" said Riordan.

"Every year," said Owen, "Governor Arnold has a charity dinner on the main floor of the sports arena in downtown Milwaukee. It's tonight. Arnold Brauner will be there, along with his sons, his friends, and a lot of the business and political leaders of Wisconsin. Duke Tamirlas himself sometimes makes an appearance."

"They were talking about Elven nobles," said Tyth. "How that might slow them down."

"Well, we're going to slow them down first," said Owen. He tapped his earpiece. "Captain Alcazar?"

My earpiece crackled with voices as Alcazar gave orders. The soldiers of the Wizard's Legion settled on a simple plan. We would drive at speed into the clearing and surround the church, and the soldiers would throw flashbang grenades into the basement. That would stun the humans, who would promptly transform into wraithwolves, and the killing would begin.

Hopefully, we would kill them before they killed us.

"Stay close to me," said Riordan. "I'll keep them off you."

I nodded. When we wound up in fights, that was our usual approach. Riordan, with his Shadowmorph blade, could kill nearly anything, and that weapon had already proven effective against the Fusion wraithwolves. While he did that, I unleashed volleys of destructive magic.

"Time to move, people," said Alcazar. "Go!"

The SUVs roared to life, turned, and shot down the driveway. Owen went last, his unmarked car rolling along the gravel. We skidded to a halt in our assigned position, just outside the church's front doors, and I saw the SUVs moving around the church, Wizard's

Legion soldiers storming out of them in full tactical kit. Several of them advanced a few steps and flung flashbang grenades. The grenades clattered into the window wells and smashed through the glass, and a half-second later I heard the thumps as the grenades went off.

Riordan settled himself in front of me, his Shadowmorph blade ready. Tyth and Owen stood on either side, already summoning magic. I saw a few wisps of smoke drift through the church lobby (narthex?) and I heard the roar of wraithwolves through the doors.

"Here they come," said Riordan, and five Fusion wraithwolves burst through the ruined doors and rushed down the stairs towards us. I heard glass shatter throughout the church as other wraithwolves erupted out of the windows and charged. Fire and lightning and ice exploded through the cold afternoon air as the Wizard's Legion unleashed their spells.

My own power surged through me, and I hurled a volley of lightning globes. There were five wraithwolves, so I summoned five globes, and each one struck the chest of a wraithwolf. The creatures howled in agony as my lightning ripped through them, the power crackling up and down their furred limbs, but I hadn't hit them hard enough to kill.

Riordan did, though, when he attacked. His sword of force took off the head of the nearest wraithwolf, and the next creature lunged at him. He dodged out of the way, and the wraithwolf caught its balance and turned to attack again, only for Owen's blast of magical fire to burn into its skull. The other two wraithwolves, recognizing me as the greater threat, bounded towards me, but Tyth struck first. She hurled a lightning globe that shocked the first wraithwolf, and the creatures tangled into each other.

It didn't slow them down for long, but more than long enough for me to pull together power for another spell. I flicked my wrist, and a thumb-sized sphere of fire leaped from my hand. It had all the force of a large explosion but bound together in a small space. The sphere drilled a tunnel through the head of the first wraithwolf, and then I sent it burning through the skulls of the next two. When I did that to anthrophages, I could kill eight or nine of them before the spell ran out of power. The skulls of the hybrid wraithwolves were far thicker, and the dense bone soaked up the fire more quickly.

But it was still enough to kill them.

The five wraithwolves lay dead at our feet, and even as I looked, they shrank back into human form.

"That is weird," said Tyth.

"And it's not over yet," I said. The boom and rumble of spells echoed over the clearing, and I heard Giles giving orders over my earpiece, sending one group of soldiers to reinforce the other. "Let's move!"

Riordan, Owen, Tyth, and I ran around the church. We helped three struggling men overcome wraithwolves, and by the time we completed our circuit of the church, the battle was over. None of our men had died, though four of them had taken wounds, one of them severe enough that he might lose the leg. Sixteen wraithwolves had gone down.

Six of them had gotten away, racing into the woods to the south.

"I'm sorry, sir," said one of the soldiers over the radio. "They hit us too fast. We were fully engaged. If they had attacked us from the back, we'd have been dead. Instead, they ran for it."

"That doesn't matter right now," I said into my microphone. "Captain Alcazar, what we need right now is a count of the devices. Your men all know the spell to sense magic?"

"They do, ma'am," said Alcazar.

"Then have anyone who's not hurt search the church and collect the devices from the dead officers," I said. "We need to know how many hybrid wraithwolves are left."

Even with four of their number wounded and two more soldiers attending to them, the remaining six wizards went about their work with efficiency. Five minutes later, sixteen Fusion devices sat in a heap on the church steps.

A thorough search of the church with both spells and my aetherometer had found no more.

So. Mr. Hood had given Warren and Hopkins forty-eight Fusion devices. Fourteen of them were currently sitting in the Quells' panic room. Sixteen more were sitting on the steps of the abandoned church. Six more had escaped, and Giles hadn't found Warren's body as he identified the dead officers. Which meant the remaining wraithwolves still had their leader.

Fourteen in the Quells' basement, sixteen on the church steps, and six more with Warren.

Then where the hell were the other twelve?

I thought it over while Owen and Giles identified the dead and Alcazar tended to his wounded. An ambulance was on its way. Tyth was making a report to the High Queen of our progress. Riordan stood next to me, a wary eye on the woods as the sun went down and the sky darkened.

And all at once I figured it out.

"Oh," I said. "Shit."

I said it over the open channel, so the clearing suddenly went quiet.

"Mrs. MacCormac?" said Alcazar.

"Owen, Major Giles," I said. "Brauner's charity dinner is a big deal, right? A lot of fancy rich people." I suppose I was technically a rich person, but I definitely wasn't fancy.

"Yeah," said Owen. "What does…"

I saw him get it.

"Will the dinner have a guard of Homeland Security officers?" I said.

"It will," said Owen, voice grim.

"I'm calling them," said Giles. "Right now."

He tried. There was no answer.

"Okay," I said. "I know where Warren and the other wraithwolves are. Or where they're going to be."

"We'd better move," said Owen.

16

SPEED LIMITS ARE FOR OTHER PEOPLE

I didn't like working with Homeland Security, but I had made my peace with it, or at least for working with Owen Quell.

That said, there was one big advantage to working with law enforcement.

When you're in a hurry, you can blast the sirens and ignore the speed limits.

Alcazar, seven of his men, and Major Giles took two of the SUVs, and Riordan, Tyth, Owen, and I piled into the unmarked car, which fortunately had concealed sirens. Under other circumstances, I wouldn't like leaving the wounded men behind, but three of them could still walk, and someone needed to guard the Fusion devices we had taken from the dead officers.

Besides, Warren wasn't coming back for them.

I knew exactly where he was going.

"I repeat!" shouted Owen into his radio as the car roared at ninety miles an hour down the county highway, its lights flashing and siren wailing. "Terrorists have infiltrated the security detail for Arnold Brauner's dinner and are planning an imminent attack! We need to warn them now!"

Riordan was driving, thankfully, which let Owen shout warnings into his radio, which weren't doing any good.

Milwaukee's basketball venue was named the Ducal Arena, and neither Owen nor Giles had been able to get a message to anyone there. Attempting to contact the Central Office or any of the other Homeland Security facilities in Milwaukee had gotten mixed results. I suspected that Warren might have sabotaged the Central Office's radio dispatch system. Neither Giles nor Owen could use their radios to get through to any other officers, at least not consistently.

I suspected that it wouldn't matter. No one in Homeland Security had weapons that could fight the Fusion wraithwolves.

It was up to us to keep Governor Arnold's charity dinner from becoming a slaughterhouse.

Given that a few weeks ago Brauner had tried to pressure me into giving up a piece of my brother's business to him, I suppose it was funny (in a dark sort of way) that I was racing to save his life. But Brauner wasn't the only person there. Owen had said that something like five hundred people attended this thing, maybe seven hundred and fifty, and most of them weren't guilty of anything. Hell, a lot of people brought their kids, and like I had told Owen, people attacking kids just pissed me off.

And I was going to take out that anger on Warren and his followers.

"Did you try calling the Ducal Arena directly?" said Riordan. We turned a corner, and Riordan skidded around it, slowing just enough to keep from rolling the car. I was wearing my seat belt, and I was still thrown to the side, almost landing in Tyth's lap.

"Yeah," said Owen, glaring at his phone. "I can't get through. Number's out of service, and I can't get any of the guests. Probably a cell phone jammer. Warren put some thought into this. He wants to make sure no one can warn Brauner or the guests. If we don't get there in time, this is going to be bad."

The problem was that we might not make it in time. Cedarburg wasn't all that far from downtown Milwaukee (I think it was about twenty miles), but it was still a half-hour drive under perfect conditions. And these were far from perfect traffic conditions. It was 5:30 PM, and we were in the middle of rush hour. The sirens and lights on the SUVs and Owen's car helped, but there were just too many damned cars.

"I don't suppose you could open a rift way?" said Owen.

Tyth frowned. "To the Shadowlands? Why would that help?"

"We crossed the Shadowlands to get from Pablo Leon's hiding place to my house in time to stop the wraithwolves from killing my family," said Owen.

Tyth's silver eyes widened. "You did that? That was, like, really dangerous!"

"It was," I said. "We got lucky, and we almost got eaten by anthrophages in the process. I wouldn't have done it if there had been any other choice." I shook my head. "But it won't work now. I've never been to the Ducal Arena. We don't have any physical objects linked to the Ducal Arena, so I can't follow the path in the Shadowlands. If we try to get there via rift way, we're just going to get eaten by other Shadowlands creatures."

Owen nodded. "I'll keep trying to contact someone who can help."

"Did the High Queen respond?" I asked Tyth.

She shook her head. "Not yet. If she's busy with something or her attention is elsewhere, she might not notice the message. Her Majesty told me how the blood ring works. One of her own rings stores the messages from her shadow agents in sort of...telepathic voice mail, I guess. She checks it regularly, but if something is holding her attention, she won't notice."

"Freeway's coming up," said Riordan as we followed the two SUVs onto the ramp for I-43 South. "Hold on."

The SUVs roared onto the interstate, and we followed.

There were a lot of damned cars.

"Oh, I don't like this," said Tyth.

We had one advantage. There were more cars in the northbound lanes than the southbound, as commuters drove home from work in Milwaukee. But not all that many. The SUVs veered across the freeway to drive on the left shoulder, and Riordan followed them.

"Don't worry about it," I said to Tyth. The concrete divider between the lanes was maybe two inches outside the left window, shooting by in a gray blur. "We went to Mars together. What's driving at ninety miles an hour on the interstate during rush hour compared to that?"

Tyth swallowed. I got the impression she did not like cars all that much. "Well, we walked to Mars."

"There isn't a single naelgoth on the freeway," I said.

"True," said Tyth. "That's very true."

"You went to Mars?" said Owen, glancing up from his phone. He scowled at it and punched in another number.

"We walked to Mars," said Tyth. "Through the Shadowlands."

"Wouldn't really recommend it," I said. "Mars is cold and full of magical traps. These nasty things called azatothi used to live there, and…"

"I got through to someone!" said Owen, and he lifted his phone to his ear. "Yes, hello?" A short conversation followed. Owen's tone changed halfway through, going from urgent to respectful. "Yes, thank you, my lord. Thank you. The situation is urgent. I will explain more at the Ducal Arena."

"Who was that?" said Riordan.

"Lord Tyrdamar, the Baron of Wauwatosa," said Owen. "A friend of mine is his chief of security. I got through to him, and he let me talk to the Baron. Lord Tyrdamar believed me, and he's bringing some of his knights to the Ducal Arena."

"Surprised the Baron isn't there," said Riordan.

"He doesn't like Brauner," said Owen, and I snorted. "But Duke Tamirlas and some of his knights will be at the dinner. They might be able to put up a fight if we get there in time to warn them."

That was something, at least. Tamirlas and his knights could all use magic, so hopefully, they could stop the Fusion wraithwolves. Then again, they wouldn't be expecting trouble, and Warren and his followers might be able to surprise and kill the Elves. In fact, Warren had planned to target the Elves first to eliminate any threats.

"Jake?" said Owen, and he spoke into his earpiece for a minute. "Uh huh. Okay, that makes sense."

"What is it?" I said.

"A couple of reports came in from Cedarburg," said Owen. "Carjackings. Warren and the survivors from the church stole vehicles. Didn't kill anyone, at least. We could be right behind them."

"Okay," I said, rubbing a hand through my hair. There were too many variables moving. Would we get to the Ducal Arena before Warren? Would Lord Tyrdamar arrive? At this time of day, it would take too long to get from Wauwatosa to downtown Milwaukee. And some of Warren's followers were already at the Arena. They might decide to start killing before their leader arrived. Warren had cut off communications to the Arena, but he might still be able to contact his followers.

Too many different pieces were in motion.

I should have known. Solve a murder, the High Queen's message had said. Simple, right? Solve a murder...and a few days later I was racing to stop insane hybrid wraithwolves from slaughtering hundreds of innocent people. How the hell did I keep getting into these situations?

The High Queen hadn't been kidding when she said that she wouldn't give me the easy jobs.

Then I saw the flashing yellow lights ahead.

"Riordan!" I shouted.

We were driving on the left shoulder, and ahead of us was a semi, its hazard lights flashing. It must have had engine trouble or blown a tire. The two Homeland Security SUVs had dodged it, but we were coming up fast.

Riordan jerked the wheel hard to the right. We skidded off the shoulder and onto the left lane with a screech of overstressed rubber. I caught a brief glimpse of the truck driver, illuminated by his cab's headlights, his mouth hanging open in surprise. We missed him by like three inches, and then we veered back onto the shoulder, still following the SUVs.

"Holy shit," I said. "That was a good recovery."

"Thanks," grunted Riordan, watching the road. "Too bad Nora isn't here. She loves breaking the speed limit."

"I really don't like cars," said Tyth.

I blinked at her. "Didn't you crash a municipal bus into a tree in front of my house?"

"Why do you think I don't like cars?"

We reached downtown Milwaukee a short time later, but it felt like an eternity. It was another gray November night, with a tinge of icy mist in the air. The tall buildings of downtown glimmered like candles in the gloom, casting city glow against the cloud cover overhead. I spotted the building that held the Doyles' condo, and I remembered the odor of blood and chemicals. Ronald Doyle had been an idiot to make a deal like that with the mysterious Mr. Hood – but he hadn't deserved to die for it, and his family sure as hell hadn't.

And a lot more people might suffer those horrible deaths if we didn't get to the Ducal Arena in time.

I gritted my teeth and held on.

About eight minutes later, through a combination of reckless driving, ignoring stoplights, and flagrant abuse of every traffic law in existence, we skidded to a stop in front of the Ducal Arena. It was a big building with a curved roof and walls of glass and steel and giant green banners for Milwaukee's professional basketball team. I couldn't remember their name off the top of my head – the Deer? The Antelopes? The Caribou? I don't know, something with hooves, I don't really care.

There was valet parking in front of the building, but there were only a few cars in sight. I checked the time – 5:48 PM. Brauner's dinner was going to start officially at 6, though this kind of event always ran a little late.

Warren and the Fusion wraithwolves might be killing the guests even now.

We clambered out of the vehicles. Two security guards and a uniformed valet approached.

"Sir," said one of the guards. "You can't park..." His eyes widened as he saw soldiers in full tactical kit getting out of the SUVs.

"Homeland Security," said Owen. "This is an emergency. We need to talk to Governor Arnold and Duke Tamirlas right away."

"They're in the main arena," said the guard, eyes wide. "What's going on?"

"Stay here and if anyone else shows up tell them to go home," said Owen. "We..."

His voice trailed off, and I saw two uniformed Homeland Security officers hurrying from the main doors towards us.

"Can you tell if they're wraithwolves?" said Giles.

"Quick and dirty way to do it," I said, pulling together power for a spell.

I cast the Seal of Shadows over the two officers, the symbol of blue light appearing beneath their feet. I could have produced my aetherometer from my bag or cast the spell to detect magic, but that would take too long. This was faster, and as an added bonus, if the two officers were wraithwolves, the Seal would stun them.

And as it happened, the officers did have Fusion devices.

The two men froze in place and began screaming in agony. One of them, quicker on the uptake than the other, threw himself clear of the Seal and started to transform, claws sprouting from his fingers. Fortunately, Alcazar and his wizards were ready. A volley of fire and lightning ripped across the two Homeland Security officers and dropped them dead to the sidewalk.

"Jesus Christ!" said one of the security guards.

Owen jabbed a finger at him. "Shadowlands creatures disguised as officers are about to attack the dinner. The Wizard's Legion is here to take care of it." Technically true, if an oversimplification.

"Man," said the valet as Alcazar relieved the dead men of their Fusion devices. "This was supposed to be my night off. I knew I shouldn't have traded shifts!"

"The three of you stay here and keep any other guests from

coming in," said Owen. "Also, Lord Tyrdamar of Wauwatosa is arriving with reinforcements soon. When he does, send them in. Got it?"

The three men bobbed their heads. I gave it a fifty-fifty chance that they were going to run like hell the minute we went inside. Not that I could blame them. I really wanted to run right after them.

"All right, people, let's move," said Owen.

We hurried into the lobby of the Ducal Arena. It was a big place, all polished concrete and steel, with ticket stations and a long concessions counter, currently closed. Though the neon beer signs still glowed behind the counter. Maybe basketball games were more enjoyable when you watched them while drunk. Beyond the concession counters were doors leading into the arena proper, and we jogged into it.

The arena was a huge space, with rows of tiered seats descending to the basketball court. I remembered hearing that the arena could hold twenty thousand spectators. Brilliant lights glowed overhead, and over the center of the court hung an enormous four-sided display for showing the score and game highlights and probably beer commercials. Right now, the screens showed CONQUEST YEAR 316 THANKSGIVING CHARITY DINNER – GOVERNOR ARNOLD BRAUNER WELCOMES YOU! The screen changed to show an image of Brauner in a hard hat and an orange fluorescent vest, standing alongside a bunch of construction workers with optimistic expressions. BUILDING AFFORDABLE HOUSING FOR OUR VETERANS, the caption read. Probably a slideshow of all the various charitable things the Brauner Foundation did.

Instead of tall men in jerseys and shorts, the basketball court currently held rows of tables covered in white cloths, fancy plates, and silverware. Hundreds of guests were seated below, men and women in black evening clothes. Under the basketball hoop on the right of the court, a small stage had been set up, and a long table faced the others. Duke Tamirlas was sitting there, along with Arnold Brauner and Martin Brauner, who was the current Governor of Wisconsin, though everyone knew that Dad really ran the show.

There were no screams, no blood, no dead bodies, and no two-legged wraithwolves killing at random.

We'd arrived in time.

But how long did we have until Warren showed up and started killing?

17

GOVERNOR ARNOLD BRAUNER WELCOMES YOU

Owen looked around, trying to spot the blue uniforms of Homeland Security officers.

He could see six of them, standing guard at the various aisles descending to the court. The Wizard's Legion soldiers had killed two of the Fusion wraithwolves on the way in. That meant if their count was accurate, there were potentially as many as sixteen hybrid wraithwolves somewhere in the Ducal Arena.

"Nadia," he said. "Those six?"

"On it," said Nadia. She produced the bronze disk of her aetherometer from her bag, which was slung crosswise over her chest, and scowled at the dials. "Hang on...yeah. All six of them have Fusion devices. I can't find any other ones nearby." She shook her head. "But that doesn't mean they're not there. Sometimes the aetherometer doesn't always detect things that I can't physically see. The High Queen called it..."

"Quantum uncertainty," said Tyth. "The act of observing an object changes the object being observed. It's sometimes a difficulty in creating powerful magical artifacts."

Owen had an instant to consider that hearing someone discuss quantum physics in a thick California accent was somehow surreal, and he thrust the thought of out his head.

"Should I use the Seal of Shadows on them?" said Nadia.

"No, not yet," said Owen, thinking fast. "They're spaced around the arena, see? Covering all the entry aisles. You can't hit them all at once, and if you expose one, the others will transform and start killing. We need to get these people out of here, now, before Warren shows up." He nodded. "I've got an idea. Follow me."

He strode down the aisle, hurrying down the broad concrete steps and past the rows of seats. Memories flashed through his mind. Owen had been here numerous times – he and Anna had gone to see basketball games while they were dating, and sometimes the department had family nights where officers could bring their spouses and kids to watch games or to shoot hoops on the court. Those were good memories.

Owen hoped a bloody slaughter wouldn't drown those out. There were only a half-dozen Elves on the stage, Duke Tamirlas and some of his knights. If Warren and his remaining wraithwolf pack struck hard and fast enough, they could overwhelm the Elves and kill the rest of the guests with ease.

The basketball court would become a slaughter pen.

The officer guarding the aisle looked at them, eyes narrowed, hands straying to his weapon.

"He's one of them," murmured Nadia.

"Get ready if he puts up a fight," said Riordan.

The officer stepped into their path, hand raised.

"You can't be here," said the officer. His mouth tightened with repressed rage. No doubt the wraithwolf had twisted his mind and was screaming for him to transform and attack. "You can't be here without an invitation."

God, he was so young. Late twenties at the most. What had Warren told him? Likely the officer had been a decent man before the Fusion device had warped him into a monster.

Warren was going to pay for that.

A few of the guests turned to look, frowning at the sight of soldiers in full tactical dress.

"Son," said Owen, using what his daughters called his Scary Dad voice. "I'm Colonel Owen Quell, head of Milwaukee special investigations, and this is Major Jacob Giles, head of homicide investigations. We are here with an urgent message for Duke Tamirlas that his lordship must hear immediately. Step aside."

"I can't let you through without an invitation," said the young officer. His teeth were bared in a snarl, and the fingers of his free hand had curled like he was preparing to slash invisible claws.

"Either you get out of my way," said Owen, "or I'm going to arrest you for obstructing a superior officer."

And if the kid refused, he would lose his temper and transform. Either Nadia or one of the other wizards would blast him, and the fight would begin right here.

At last, the officer gave a curt nod and stepped to the side. Owen strode past him without looking back, though that made his back itch.

But the officer didn't attack, and Owen and the others walked down the basketball court to the stage. The guests stared as they walked past. Owen's eyes flicked over the tables, noting details. No plates had been set out yet, though he did see small trays of bread and appetizers. Probably the main course would be served while Brauner was giving his remarks.

They reached the stage, and Owen felt the gaze of the Elves and the human political leaders.

"I know you," said Arnold Brauner in his bluff, hearty voice. He wore a black suit that was just slightly rumpled, like a farmer who had put on his best clothes. The cold, shrewd eyes belied the image of the simple farmer than Brauner liked to cultivate. Next to him, his wife Tansy looked remarkably attractive for her age in a sleek black dress. "You're Colonel Quell."

"Sir," said Owen. He offered a bow to the Duke, and the others followed suit. "My lord Tamirlas."

"Colonel Quell," said Tamirlas, Duke of Milwaukee, in his quiet, deep voice. The Duke had thick black hair with silver wings at the temples. His alien, aloof features put Owen in mind of a fierce hawk. The Duke wore a knee-length blue coat with golden trim, and Owen glimpsed an ornate sword at his waist. Around him, his knights wore similar blue coats, though less elaborate. "I remember you. You fought well under my command during the Archon attack a few years ago."

"Thank you, my lord," said Owen. "I have an urgent message for you."

He risked a glance around. None of the wraithwolf officers were within earshot. Of course, the wraithwolves might have given their hosts improved hearing, much the way the Shadow Hunters seemed to possess enhanced senses.

And all six of the officers were staring at Owen.

"Well, what is it?" said Tamirlas. The stern Duke seemed caught between amusement and annoyance.

"I ask your lordship not to react with alarm," said Owen, "but your life is in danger, right now. Assassins are watching you as we speak."

Tamirlas's golden eyes narrowed, and his knights shifted, hands moving towards weapons. "Indeed? Explain, Colonel."

"A group of Homeland Security officers have been subverted," said Owen. "An enemy of the High Queen gave them magical devices that allow the officers to transform into hybrids of human and wraithwolves. The wraithwolves have twisted them into spree killers. My lord, the Wizard's Legion and Lady Tythrilandria, handmaiden of the High Queen, have dealt with several of the creatures so far. But between sixteen and twenty of the corrupted officers are still alive, and they are going to attack you at any moment."

"Bullshit," said Martin Brauner, Governor Arnold's eldest son and the current governor of Wisconsin. Arnold Brauner looked like an honest farmer, even if he wasn't. Martin looked like the evil lawyer in a TV drama who foreclosed on the family farm. He lacked his father's charisma, and Owen frankly doubted he would have gotten elected without Arnold's influence.

"My lord, you can put this to the test yourself," said Owen. "I'm afraid the six officers guarding the aisles are part of the conspiracy. If you cast the spell to detect magic on them, you will sense the presence of their transformation devices."

Tamirlas said nothing, and then his gaze swung to Nadia.

"I know you, woman," he said. "Or I know of you. The Worldburner. The one who helped the Magebreaker destroy the Archons and reclaim our homeland at last."

Nadia offered a hasty bow. "Yes, my lord. My lord, I think you should listen to Colonel Quell right now."

"I owe you my life," said Tamirlas. "I was in New York to greet the High Queen. I would have burned with all the others had you not thrown the Sky Hammer weapon into Venomhold." A cold smile went over his hawkish features. "And the Knight of Venomhold was long our foe. It pleases me to think that she was overthrown in her hour of triumph."

"Thank you, my lord," said Nadia. "And I would very, very much like to save your lordship's life again, but we need to act now."

"Very well," said Tamirlas. His voice rose slightly to address everyone at the table. "Remain calm, but we must evacuate the building. The wraithwolves can only be harmed by magic, and there are too many without magical skill here. Arnold, what do you suggest?"

Governor Arnold had been staring hard at Nadia, but he shook himself and gave a sharp nod. "A gas leak, I think. I'll announce that there has been a gas leak and everyone needs to vacate the building immediately."

Tamirlas half-smiled. "Cunning as ever, Arnold."

"I very strongly suggest we hurry," said Nadia. "When the wraithwolves attack, they will target any Elves first."

Tamirlas frowned. "You have soldiers of the Wizard's Legion with you. Will that not deter them?"

"It didn't when we fought them in Cedarburg an hour ago," said Owen.

"So be it," said Tamirlas. "Arnold, make the announcement. See to it that the guests are evacuated in an orderly fashion. My knights, prepare for battle." His intense golden eyes swung back to Owen. "You, the Worldburner, and the soldiers of the Wizard's Legion are with us?"

"Yes, my lord," said Owen. "Those officers have betrayed everything that Homeland Security is supposed to stand for, and they have innocent blood on their hands." He felt Nadia's gaze on him. "I want to see them stopped before they add to that blood."

"Then let us proceed," said Tamirlas, and Governor Arnold stepped to the podium.

"Everyone?" said Brauner, his voice crackling over the sound system. "Everyone, if I could have your attention please?" All eyes turned towards him, including those of the Fusion wraithwolves. Owen kept watching the arena. This would be a perfect time for Warren to attack. "It seems there is a gas leak on the lower levels of the arena." A murmur went through the guests. "I would like everyone to calmly and in an orderly fashion to head for the lobby. Hopefully, this will get taken care of soon, and we can come back to dinner. Meanwhile, let's show Duke Tamirlas how the people of Wisconsin keep their cool in a crisis. Please head out by table. Table one?"

Owen watched the arena as Brauner directed traffic. He did a good job of it – Owen could see how Governor Arnold had ridden herd over the state legislature for twelve years. In short order, all the guests were on their feet and moving up the aisles to the lobby. Owen kept a close eye on the Fusion wraithwolves, fearing that they would attack while the guests were packed together in the aisles. Yet the six officers remained where they were. They looked confused. Perhaps they hadn't expected this.

More likely they were awaiting orders. In the Shadowlands, wraithwolves always hunted in packs commanded by an alpha. Perhaps Warren and Hopkins were the alpha wraithwolves, and they would not deviate from instructions until Warren said otherwise.

Tamirlas rose to his feet, and he made a small gesture with his left hand.

"Yes, I see what you mean, Worldburner," he murmured. "I can sense the aura of corrupted power around them. The poor fools. They were lost the minute they summoned the wraithwolves. Only the most accomplished and skilled magi and archmagi can summon Shadowlands creatures without suffering corruption effects. I would not want to attempt it myself save for a grave emergency."

"Yeah...I mean, yes, my lord," Nadia said.

"Men of the Wizard's Legion," said Tamirlas. "Once the guests are clear, prepare to strike, we…"

One of the locker room doors opened.

Owen turned in that direction, flexing his fingers as he pulled together power for a spell. He remembered all the times he had seen basketball teams emerge from those doors.

As he looked, all six of the Fusion officers turned in that direction as well.

Six more Homeland Security officers walked onto the court, their expressions angry, almost feral.

Lieutenant Kyle Warren walked at their head.

18

OF MEN & MONSTERS

Warren and his goons stopped halfway between the stage and the locker room doors, and I tensed. My aetherometer was buzzing in my hand, and I shoved it back into my bag, preparing my mind to summon magic for spells. I was tired – I had cast a lot of spells and used a lot of magic today, but I ignored the fatigue.

The thought of facing a mob of hybrid wraithwolves made it easy to ignore the weariness.

I shot a look at the aisles to the lobby. The guests filed out in an orderly fashion, and most of them had made it out. Another minute or so, and the guests would be out of the arena. Would Warren attack them while they were packed together in the lobby or the sidewalk? I doubted it. He needed to take out the Elves first, else they could use their magic against his wraithwolves one by one.

Riordan took one step forward, putting himself between Warren's men and me.

"Colonel Quell," said Warren at last. The five men with him looked enraged, but Warren himself seemed at ease, almost relaxed.

"Lieutenant," said Owen. "Seems that you've been busy."

"My lord Duke," said Warren to Tamirlas. "We have received word of a threat against your life. I urge your lordship to come with us at once so we can take you to a place of safety."

Tamirlas only raised a single eyebrow.

"You know better than that, Lieutenant," said Owen. "We know everything now. We know about Leon's and Doyle's deal. We know about the summoning devices. We know that you killed Ronald Doyle and his family." His voice hardened. "And we know that you sent officers to murder my family."

"Goddamn it, Kyle," said Giles, a mixture of weariness and anger in his voice. "You were the best detective I had in the department, the best officer. You could have been the branch commander someday. Instead, you did…this."

Warren smiled. He looked charming and gallant, like the sort of Homeland Security officer you see on posters urging the public to stay safe and contact the authorities if you see anything suspicious. "I just took the next step, Major. We're supposed to protect and serve, right?" Owen's lips thinned at that. "But how can we protect and serve if scum like Ronald Doyle and Pablo Leon and Arnold Brauner," his calm wavered for an instant as he looked at Brauner, "can escape justice with their money?"

"So that's why you killed Doyle's wife and kids, is that it?" said Owen.

Again, Warren's calm flickered.

"I mean, I get why you killed Doyle," said Owen. "Doyle hadn't been punished for the people who died when that building fell over. So you decided to go vigilante. Except you also killed his wife and children. What, did a six-year-old child mix the bad concrete? Did…"

"His wife and children benefited from his corruption," said Warren. "They were just as guilty."

"Uh huh, sure," said Owen. "And when your men tried to kill my family?"

"They were there to kill you and the MacCormac bitch," said Warren, glancing at me. I smirked and gave him a cheery little wave, my magic ready to strike. "Except you weren't there. You were defending that toad Pablo Leon from justice."

"Leon's greedy and stupid," said Owen, "but that doesn't merit getting torn apart by wraithwolves. And Doyle's kids didn't deserve what you did to them. And my kids? What is it, Lieutenant? What did I do that deserved to have my children attacked? I'm not on anyone's payroll except Homeland Security. Explain that."

"The corruption in the department..." began Warren.

"And you're getting paid by Homeland Security, buddy," I said. Warren glared at me, his calm fading further. He was keeping control of himself, but only just. I wondered why he hadn't attacked yet. "If you're on a crusade against corruption, kill yourself first and save us all a lot of trouble."

"They were all corrupt, and they deserved to be executed, to have their flesh torn apart by claws and their hot blood spilled on the earth!" said Warren.

"That's the wraithwolf talking," said Owen, and he let pity and disgust fill his voice. "That's the danger of summoning spells. The bond with the summoned creature goes both ways. Maybe you can control it, but it can also influence you, and it's twisting your thinking around..."

"The Fusion device is not a summoning spell!" said Warren. "It's science, not magic. It's something new. It's the next step for humanity, the next phase of evolution. It will make us better and stronger than the Elves, and we can use it to purge the corruption from among ourselves."

"It's nothing like that," said Owen. "You've let a monster into your head, and it's warped you into one."

"I will kill the corrupt and free mankind of them!" said Warren.

"You can't," I said, remembering one of the books Riordan had mentioned.

"I can do what I wish, and you cannot stop me," said Warren.

"No, you can't, and yes, I can," I said. "Because your entire idea is stupid. You can't kill all the corrupt people because everyone's got good and bad both inside them. You'd have to kill everyone. And you can't change what people are. Trying to do that just makes people into monsters. Like you've become."

"Trite," spat Warren, his eyes starting to turn yellow. "Useless clichés. You ought to be a Sunday school teacher." He swept a furious glare over the stage and the Wizard's Legion soldiers. "You are all corrupt, you are all cancers to be cut from the world. You, Major Giles and Colonel Quell, protect the corrupt like that leech Brauner and his cronies." Brauner gazed back at Warren with a stony expression. "And you, my lord Duke!" Tamirlas seemed only contemptuously amused. "You are the author of all this corruption. I know that Brauner is your shadow councilor. I know you turn a blind eye to his crimes in exchange for money. You and all the Elves are rotten, and I shall rid the world of you."

"Young man," said Tamirlas, "I have been the Duke of Milwaukee for a long time, and I came to the same realization as the Worldburner centuries ago. There will always be corruption, no matter what I do. It can be managed and controlled, but the world cannot be made clean with the edge of the sword. That was the error of both the Archons and the Rebels, and it is the same error that has now ensnared you."

"You are a..." growled Warren.

"Enough!" said Tamirlas. "I command you to surrender immediately and face justice for your crimes. Else my knights and the soldiers of the Wizard's Legion will take you by force."

Warren laughed, high and wild, his calm mask gone entirely.

"I know why you are talking to me," said Warren. "You're hoping to delay, letting all your stupid guests get out of the building."

"And it worked," said Owen. The arena was empty but for the Elves, the Wizard's Legion soldiers, and Arnold, Tansy, and Martin Brauner. I have to give the Brauners credit for not running. Though that would have been the smart thing to do.

"Do you think I'm stupid?" said Warren.

"Well, yeah," I said.

But maybe that wasn't the right way to put it. The wraithwolf had corrupted his intellect and driven him insane. But he still had the cunning of a hunting predator. Things had been going well for him until I had gotten involved, and he couldn't have seen something like me coming. I mean, if I hadn't been there, he would have gotten rid of Owen and Pablo Leon at the same time, and he probably would have been able to surprise and kill Duke Tamirlas and his knights and wipe out Brauner's guests.

Surprise...

Maybe he was stalling for a surprise, an ambush. I didn't see how, though. We were in the center of a basketball arena, for God's sake, and there was no way the hybrid wraithwolves could sneak up on us, not when we could see in every direction at once. The creatures were so big it wasn't as if they could hide behind the rows of seats, and the Fusion wraithwolves didn't seem able to transform themselves into mist the way normal wraithwolves did.

Wait. Every direction?

I looked up. The ceiling was far overhead, buttressed with massive steel girders. Heavy lights were mounted on the girders, bathing the arena with their glow, and I saw thick ducts for the HVAC equipment and speakers for the sound system.

And catwalks so technicians could repair the speakers.

Hybrid wraithwolves moved along the catwalks.

Of course. Warren's little speech was just a distraction. It must have taken all his remaining self-control to stand there and rant instead of attacking, but he had been able to do it because he knew the sucker punch was coming.

"Guys!" I shouted, pointing. "They're above us!"

Some of the human wizards and the Elves looked up.

And everything exploded into chaos.

"Kill them!" roared Warren, his voice dropping an octave as he began to transform. The six officers guarding the aisles transformed as well. With tearing metallic cries, the wraithwolves on the catwalks leaped over the railing, plummeting towards the basketball court like missiles of claws and fangs. One was headed right towards me, and I shoved power into a spell. The fireball soared from my hand and struck the falling wraithwolf in the chest. It exploded in a bloom of fire fifty feet overhead, and the detonation threw the burning wraithwolf into the seats.

Another wraithwolf crashed into the stage. The creature landed atop one of Tamirlas's Elven knights and ripped out the Elf's throat before the others could react. Tamirlas bellowed and flung a spell, and a blast of magical flame burned through the wraithwolf's head. The creature stumbled and fell, shrinking back into human form.

The other wraithwolves rushed from all directions, and the soldiers and the Elves fought back, hurling blasts of magical fire and lightning and ice. A wraithwolf lunged at Tyth, and she hit it with a lightning globe. As the creature stumbled back, I flung a sphere of fire that drilled through the dense bone of its head, zipped to the left, and killed a second creature. A third bounded at Tyth, and Riordan killed it with a swift slash of his blade of dark force.

I caught a glimpse of Warren. He was bigger than the other wraithwolves, substantially, and unlike the others, he had a scorpion tail. Armored plates of bone covered his body. He was the alpha wraithwolf, and the others obeyed him. Alcazar and two of his soldiers flung a constant barrage of spells at Warren, but he growled and advanced step by step, his claws ripping up the wood of the basketball court.

I gathered my will to strike at him, and a metallic crash caught my attention. One of the wraithwolves hit the stage, and Tansy Brauner fell off it with a shriek. She landed hard on her back, and the creature raised its claws to rip out her throat. I began pulling my power together to strike, but I knew I wasn't going to hit in time.

Arnold Brauner yelled, jumped off the stage, and swung a folding chair like a club. The chair smacked across the wraithwolf's muzzle, and the creature stumbled. It roared and swung its hand, and its talons tore through both the metal of the chair and Brauner's left arm. He yelped but kept his feet, keeping himself between Tansy and the creature, and the wraithwolf tensed to spring on him.

And I almost let the creature do it.

It would have been easy. A half-second of hesitation, the wraithwolf would kill Arnold Brauner, and then I would kill the wraithwolf. That would make sure Brauner didn't go after Moran Imports ever again. Hell, Brauner would be remembered as a hero – former governor dies in defense of his wife and Duke Tamirlas. He'd probably get a statue or something at the State Capitol, maybe a park named after him.

But like I told Russell, I didn't want to be the kind of woman who used her power to kill everyone who got in her way.

I didn't want to be a thing like Kyle Warren.

Even by proxy, as it happens.

I hit the wraithwolf with a sphere of fire and burned through its skull. Tansy screamed, and the creature staggered back, hit the ruined stage, and fell over, its body shrinking into human form. Martin Brauner scrambled to his mother's side, helping her up, and Arnold stayed with them, clutching his wounded arm. His eyes met mine across the court, and I saw him realize that I had saved his life.

I didn't have time to spare to chat, because the fight was still on.

But we were winning.

One of Tamirlas's knights had fallen, and I think one of Alcazar's men was down, dead or wounded. But we had killed most of the wraithwolves, and the rest were falling.

Only Kyle Warren was still on his feet, his bone armor scorched, his claws ripping furrows in the wood of the floor. He looked back and forth with a furious cry, and then whirled and bounded back towards the locker room.

His pack was slain, and he was running for his life.

"Stop him!" thundered Duke Tamirlas.

I ran after Warren, Riordan and Owen keeping pace with me.

19

LET US CLEAN THE WORLD

Owen burst through the doors to the locker room.

Except the locker room wasn't on the other side. Owen found himself in a wide utility corridor, and memories from televised basketball games flashed through his head. During the games, he had seen shots of teams running down this wide corridor, flanked by their trainers and coaches and various media people. The locker rooms were likely another forty or fifty yards down the corridor. For that matter, there were half a dozen doors on either side of the hall. Owen didn't have any idea where those might go – offices, maybe, or utility rooms.

"Shit," said Owen, looking around.

"Don't worry," said Nadia. Owen glanced back at saw that she had followed him. So had Riordan and Tythrilandria. Nadia lifted the bronze dial of her aetherometer. "I've got a fix on the bastard. He's not getting away. He went...um, that way." She pointed, and Owen saw that a door about fifty yards down the corridor was ajar, its lock smashed open.

"This place is a maze," said Owen. "There are a hundred places he could hide. If we bring the Elves and the soldiers, it might be a slaughter."

"You want to take him alone?" said Riordan.

"The four of us?" said Owen. He took a deep breath. "I think that's best." He tapped his earpiece. "Giles? Alcazar? You there?"

"Where are you, Owen?" said Giles. His voice was tense. "All the wraithwolves are down. There was a panic among the guests, but Lord Tyrdamar's knights and men-at-arms have arrived and are keeping things under control. EMTs are on their way to the Arena, and they've picked up the men we left at the church."

"Warren's still alive," said Owen. "He's hiding somewhere. I'm going after him. Nadia's leading us to him, and then she, Riordan, and Lady Tythrilandria are going to take him."

"You want some help, Lady Tythrilandria?" said Alcazar.

"Negative," said Tyth. "We're afraid of an ambush, captain. You saw that Nadia and I have...um, scouting abilities. We're going to use that to turn the tables on Warren and surprise him."

"As you command," said Alcazar. "Should you need us, we will come at once."

"Thank you, captain," said Tyth. She looked at Owen. "You want us to surprise him?"

"Yeah," said Owen. "He hates my guts, you saw that. If I go ahead alone, that will draw him out. Except I won't be alone, and you guys can turn invisible, follow me, and then hit him when he attacks."

"You realize that will put you at considerable danger," said Riordan.

"This has to end tonight," said Owen. "We can't let Warren escape. There are two million people in the Milwaukee area, and every one of them is at risk. Warren won't stop killing until he's brought down."

"You're right," said Nadia, her voice dark. One of the memories that Owen had absorbed from Nadia flickered through his mind. He couldn't remember it clearly, thank God for that, but he did remember the image of blood and fangs and wraithwolves. The thing that Kyle Warren had become wouldn't stop killing, not for any reason. "All right. Let's catch up to it. This way."

"I'll take point," said Riordan, stepping to the front, that strange sword of darkness in his hands. Owen was not inclined to argue.

They moved down the corridor and to the damaged door. Riordan eased it open and behind were the harsh LED lights of a concrete utility corridor, bundles of cables and pipes running along the wall. They moved down the corridor, following both Nadia's aetherometer readings, Owen's aurasight, and the claw marks Warren had left on the polished concrete, and came to another half-open door. Beyond was a large room filled with enormous humming air handlers.

"An HVAC room," muttered Nadia. "Why do these things always happen in HVAC rooms? He's in there somewhere. Can't pinpoint exactly where. But it's within twenty yards." She tucked the aetherometer into her bag. "You're sure about this?"

Owen nodded and flexed his fingers, ready to pull together power for a spell.

"All right," said Nadia. "Tyth and I will be right behind you. Get Warren to show himself, and we'll take him. Ready?" Tyth nodded, and both she and Nadia cast the Cloak spell, vanishing from sight.

"I'll be here," said Riordan. "Warren knows I can hurt him, so he might not attack if he sees me. When I hear the fight start, I will join you."

Owen took a deep breath, nodded, and stepped into the room.

It was an enormous concrete vault, with a row of six garage-sized air handlers, narrow aisles between them. Beyond the door was a metal landing, a flight of a dozen stairs descending to the floor. Owen noted the scratches on the steps and the concrete beyond as he came to the floor. The scratches vanished – Owen suspected that Warren had taken a running leap and landed atop one of the air handlers.

He remembered how the wraithwolves in the arena had attacked from above.

"Warren!" shouted Owen at the top of his lungs, wondering if the Fusion wraithwolf could hear him over the hum of the air handlers. "Lieutenant Kyle Warren! It's just me. Come out and talk!"

There was no response, and then a rumbling voice came from no particular direction.

"Talk?" said Warren. "You slaughtered my pack!" Something clanged. Owen looked around, sweat dripping down his back. "You chose your side, Colonel. You picked the side of corruption and injustice."

"Injustice?" said Owen, taking slow, cautious steps down the aisle between the wall and the row of air handlers. "Why don't you tell me about that?"

Warren let out a snarling laugh. "Getting me to talk, is that it? I took the hostage negotiation training too, you know. I bet you've got the Elves and that wizard bitch waiting outside to kill me."

He was only half wrong.

"I want you to surrender without any bloodshed," said Owen. "Officer to officer. You were a Homeland Security officer, you deserve that much from me. Christ, Kyle, you were sworn to serve and protect. A lot of people are dead. Can you help me keep more people from getting killed?"

"Those people deserved to be killed," said Warren.

"What about your other officers?" said Owen. "Your packmates? Did they deserve to get killed?"

There were no words, but a deep, rumbling growl.

"See," said Owen, an idea coming to him, "I think you got screwed. You got sold a defective product."

"I am more than human!"

"Yeah, you might be stronger and faster, but you have less self-control," said Owen. He was about halfway down the vault, and he still couldn't spot Warren. His aurasight showed the wraithwolf's malevolent emotions, but he couldn't get an exact fix on Warren's position. "Because otherwise you wouldn't have gotten all your pack killed, and you wouldn't have killed Doyle's family just for the fun of it. I think Mr. Hood screwed you over."

"You don't understand anything," said Warren.

"I think your buddy Mr. Hood built those Fusion devices, but he wasn't sure if they would work," said Owen. "He needed test subjects.

He found Doyle and Leon, who were greedy and stupid enough to distribute them, and they found some Homeland Security officers gullible enough to use the devices."

"You're wrong!" roared Warren.

"And the Fusion devices were defective, you know?" said Owen. "I bet Mr. Hood was taking notes. He figured out that this first batch didn't work all that great. For the next round, he'll fix some of the bugs. Maybe not let the wraithwolf have so much influence over the host. But you, Warren? You were just a guinea pig. A lab rat. Mr. Hood tried his little experiment on you, and it didn't work. You got a bunch of Homeland Security officers killed for nothing, and…"

That did it.

Warren moved so fast that Owen had no time to react, no time to dodge. There was a dark blur, and something hammered into Owen with terrific force. He overbalanced and fell hard to the floor, his head bouncing off the concrete, and the armored nightmare form of Warren loomed over him, jaws yawning wide, talons stabbing for his throat.

~

THE HYBRID WRAITHWOLF MOVED QUICK, so quick I barely had time to respond.

Warren leaped from the top of one of the air handlers and fell into Owen, driving him to the floor, and I dropped my Cloak spell and attacked.

Magic surged through me, and I cast the ice spike spell. I wanted to use lightning or fire, but Warren was in physical contact with Owen, and I didn't know if the lightning would conduct through the wraithwolf and into Owen's body. Fortunately, the ice spike proved effective. It punched through Warren's chest and erupted out his back in a spray of dark blood, and the wraithwolf reared back with a scream.

And as he screamed, Tyth dropped her Cloak, seized the bronze plate of the Fusion device, and ripped it from Warren's back.

Again, he screamed, and his armored form shrank down to a human body. Kyle Warren stumbled and fell to one knee, the front of his uniform jacket soaked with blood, his face gray.

He collapsed onto his side, breathing hard.

"You okay?" I said, helping Owen to sit back up. Riordan joined us, and Tyth took several quick steps back from Warren, who was reaching for the Fusion device. Not that it would do Warren much good. He didn't seem to have the strength to stand.

"Yeah," said Owen, getting to his feet. "Going to have a nasty headache, but could be worse." He looked at Warren. "Could be worse."

"Idiot," wheezed Warren, blood dripping from his lips. "You don't...you don't understand..."

"I understand just fine," said Owen. "You got a lot of people killed for nothing."

"You don't understand," hissed Warren. "The Singularity...the Singularity is coming, and..."

He let out a sigh, and stopped breathing, his eyes frozen open in hate forever.

We stared in silence at his corpse for a moment.

"Suppose we solved the murder," I said at last.

"Suppose we did," said Owen. He sighed. "Who wants to let the High Queen know the good news?"

Because we had fulfilled the High Queen's mission. We had found and caught Ronald Doyle's killer.

But it had turned into a hell of a mess.

20

THANKSGIVING

To my complete lack of surprise, the entire thing got hushed up.

The Inquisition and the Department of Education couldn't completely shut down the story. There had been too many witnesses and too many dead Homeland Security officers. But they did spin the story. A rogue rift way had opened in the Ducal Arena, and a mob of wraithwolves had attacked. Duke Tamirlas and his knights, ably assisted by soldiers of the Wizard's Legion and Homeland Security, drove back the wraithwolves with minimal loss of life to the public. Forty-eight Homeland Security officers fell in the line of duty.

That news report left a foul taste in my mouth. Kyle Warren and his followers hadn't died in the line of duty. They had died while planning mass murder on a widespread scale.

Still, you can't believe anything you see on the news. Why should this be any different?

A team of Knights of the Inquisition arrived, and I cheerfully handed over all forty-eight Fusion devices to them. I hoped they destroyed the damned things.

The High Queen was pleased with what Owen and I had done.

I found that out in person the Monday before Thanksgiving.

~

Owen walked into his office and stifled a yawn.

It was a bad sign. It was only 8 AM, and already the prospect of the paperwork that awaited him was exhausting.

Because there was an enormous amount of work to do.

The Milwaukee branch of Homeland Security employed about twenty-five hundred people, give or take, and the loss of forty-eight of them was just under two percent of the entire force. The department branch had taken heavier losses during the Archon attack, but battle against open enemies was one thing. The official story was that wraithwolves had attacked Governor Brauner's dinner, that those forty-eight officers had fallen in the attack, and the general public had accepted that account. But inside the department, it was different. Too many people knew too many details, and they could work out that something had gone very wrong.

It was easy to figure out that those officers had turned traitor.

Morale, as expected, was low in the wake of the revelations. Nobody liked to know that their fellow officers had gone bad, though it had happened all too many times before in Homeland Security's history. And there was an enormous amount of paperwork to process. The families of the killed officers had to be notified and given an edited version of the truth. Owen had spoken with the parents and spouses of the Fusion officers, and he had found it galling to tell them that their loved ones had fallen in the line of duty.

But would it be better to tell them that their loved ones had become insane hybrid wraithwolves, that they might have been murdered by their husbands and sons and brothers?

Owen didn't know. He remembered Nadia's cold anger during their argument. But in the end, she had conceded that law enforcement had a difficult, messy job that didn't lend itself to quick, easy solutions. Some days were messier than others. Some days offered no good outcomes, only choices of evils.

Today promised to be one such day.

Then Owen sat down, and the day got messier.

The blood ring on his right hand shivered.

"Colonel Quell," said Tarlia's voice inside his head. "Please come immediately to the branch commander's office. Bring Major Giles with you if he is available."

Owen remembered the day in the hospital years ago when the Royal Guard had brought him to the chief of medicine's office. He remembered the pact he had made with the High Queen, how he would do anything she asked if she healed his daughters. She had kept her word – the twins were alive and healthy and at school right now.

He kept paying the price for that bargain.

Still...it wasn't such a steep price, was it? Someone had needed to stop Warren before more people got hurt. And even if Owen had not made his pact with the High Queen, he still would have tried to stop Warren. He just wouldn't have had the help of someone like Nadia MacCormac, which was the only reason they were successful.

In the end, the High Queen's price had not been so high. She simply asked him to follow his own nature in her service.

Owen took a deep breath, got to his feet, and walked into the homicide department. Owen circled around the wall and came to Giles's office. The head of homicide sat scowling at his computer, his face weary. The last week had been exhausting for him as well.

"Jake," said Owen. "Got a minute?"

"Yeah, what's up?" said Giles.

"We've been summoned to the branch commander's office," said Owen.

"Shit," said Giles, but he locked his computer and stood. "The old man probably wants to chew us out about the amount of overtime we've been burning up."

"Probably," said Owen. Despite his grim mood, he nonetheless felt a flicker of amusement. Giles was about to get a big surprise.

They took the elevator to the top floor of the building and came to the branch commander's office. The outer office had a desk for his receptionist, but it was empty. Instead, two Elves in the silver armor and red cloaks of the Royal Guard stood by the walls, motionless as statues, swords and submachine guns on their belts.

Giles faltered for a half-step. "What..."

"We've been summoned," said Owen.

One of the Elves nodded. "Proceed, Colonel. She awaits you."

Owen crossed the outer office, knocked briskly on the door, and opened it.

The branch commander's office was a large space with a thick carpet and an enormous polished desk. Framed certificates and awards lined the walls, along with various pictures of the commander shaking hands with politicians. Arnold Brauner and his sons featured heavily among them. Behind the desk was a wide window with a good view of downtown Milwaukee. It had started snowing, heavy white flakes falling from the gray sky.

Two more Royal Guards stood by the walls, watching Owen.

Nadia MacCormac waited next to the desk, wearing her usual combination of work boots, black jeans, and pea coat over a heavy sweater. Owen vaguely wondered if she had ever worn a dress in her life and decided he would rather not know.

Tarlia, the High Queen of Kalvarion and Earth, sat behind the desk. She wore the silver armor of a Royal Guard, her red hair bound back with a golden circlet. Her eerie blue eyes considered both Owen and Giles. In her right hand was one of the Fusion devices, and she was making it jump from finger to finger, like a card shark about to perform a trick.

Giles sucked in a startled breath and then offered a deep bow. Owen followed suit. "Your Majesty. It is an honor."

"Close the door, Colonel," said Tarlia, her musical voice quiet. Owen obeyed. "Such an overdramatic way to meet, is it not? But that has its purposes. It is when people are startled that you can often see who they really are."

Owen didn't say anything.

"Do you know that this really is defective?" said Tarlia, lifting the Fusion device. "Nadia tells me you taunted Lieutenant Warren with that, and you were more correct than you knew. It is a very clever design, I admit. Typical of Catalyst Corporation technology. But it lacks a vital feature. Properly designed, this should have a…buffer, for lack of a better word, to shield the mind of the user from the malign influence of the wraithwolf. Nothing of the sort was included, and I conclude it was left out deliberately."

"An experiment, then?" said Owen.

"Perhaps," said Tarlion. "Or?"

Owen blinked. "Or?"

"Or what else could it have been?" said Tarlia. "Do hypothesize, Colonel."

"A suicide bomber," said Owen. "Like when terrorists strap on explosive vests and walk into cafes and schools. Whoever gave the Fusion devices to Warren wanted to cause chaos."

"Most probably," said Tarlia. "I have looked through the memories of Pablo Leon. A terrified little rabbit of a man whose greed overrode his limited good sense. But, alas, Leon could tell me nothing useful about our mysterious 'Mr. Hood' or the Singularity. No matter. Leon will go back to his sewer business, and I will find the answers. But that is not your problem, Colonel and Major. This is. Homeland Security has disappointed me."

Giles swallowed. "Your Majesty, I take responsibility for failing to see that Kyle Warren was…"

"What?" said Tarlia, irritated. "Do you have a sword? No? Then stop trying to fall upon it. Even with all my magic, I cannot always read people's hearts, cannot predict what people will do. The whole point of treachery is that it is unforeseen. No. You and Colonel Quell have performed admirably. Homeland Security has lost my confidence. You might have heard that several branches of the department sided with the Rebels during the battle at New York?" Owen nodded. "Before the end of the year, the American Congress will pass a bill, and the President will sign it. The bill will reduce Homeland Security's powers and give responsibility for law enforcement to local municipal police departments. The Milwaukee branch of Homeland Security will become the Milwaukee Security & Police Department.

For the first time since the Conquest, Milwaukee will have a police department."

"Can I ask why?" said Owen.

"You may," said Tarlia. "The truth of the matter is that I have two worlds to rule. In the past, I favored large, centralized organizations because they were easier to control from the top. But large organizations are too easily subverted and corrupted. The Mage Fall means that we live in times of great upheaval and change. And that means I need capable local leaders who can face the challenges of their areas." Her eerie blue eyes fixed on Owen. "I would like you to be one of them."

"Your Majesty?" said Owen.

"If you accept, starting January 1st, you will be the first chief of the new Milwaukee Security & Police Department," said Tarlia. "Major Giles will be your first deputy chief, and you can appoint others as you see fit. This will be a challenging task, Colonel. With the Great Gate and the growth of some import businesses," she turned a dry look in Nadia's direction, "Milwaukee will become the crossroads of two different worlds. What do you say?"

Owen said nothing for a moment. All that responsibility...

"It's a rough job, Owen," said Nadia. "But someone's got to do it. Might as well be you."

Owen laughed as he remembered their argument. "High praise."

"And I would, of course, expect my agents to call upon each other for help should the need arise," said Tarlia.

"But only if you really need it," said Nadia.

"Well, Colonel?" said Tarlia, leaning back in the chair. "The current branch commander is going to retire at the end of the year. I'm afraid he doesn't have the flexibility of mind necessary for the changes, and it's time for him to enjoy his RV and his golf club membership. You, however, do have that flexibility. Earth and Kalvarion both are going to have to change, and you can be part of that change."

Owen hesitated. Part of him wanted to refuse. The thought of taking on such a large job was daunting. Yet he remembered Christopher's death and how Peter Walsh had almost gotten away with it, how the wraithwolves had stormed into his basement. Perhaps Owen could do what he could to keep such things from happening again. The world wasn't fixable – that had been Kyle Warren's mistake. But Owen could do what was within his power to keep evil men from preying upon the innocent. The world wasn't fixable – but refusing to act at all was cowardly.

"Anything you want," Owen said in his memory.

"That's right," the High Queen had said. "You will."

Seventeen years after that conversation, Owen took a deep breath and looked at Tarlia.

"I accept," said Owen.

"Very good, Chief," said Tarlia. She closed her fist. Purple fire flashed around her armored fingers, and the Fusion device crumbled into dust. "I suggest that you and Deputy Chief Giles began at once. You have a great deal of work to do."

~

I WATCHED as the stunned Owen and Giles left the office, leaving me alone with Tarlia and the two Royal Guards.

"What do you think?" murmured Tarlia.

"Um," I said. I wondered why she had invited me here to see this. "About what?"

"About Milwaukee's newest police chief," said Tarlia.

"I don't think he really wanted the job, but he's going to do his damnedest to do it right," I said.

"The reward for work well done is more work, or so one of your philosophers claimed," said Tarlia. "Owen Quell is a creature of duty. He will do that duty." Her voice grew distant. "Of course, he is a creature of duty because I made him that way."

I frowned. "Like...personally?"

Tarlia smiled briefly. "On a...societal level, let us say. The schools, the culture, popular entertainment, all of it is shaped towards making humans into creatures of duty. And sometimes it works as it should.

Not for you and me, darling girl. No, we're what Kaethran Morvilind made us to be."

"What's that, your Majesty?" I said, a little uneasy. When there was no immediate problem at hand, Tarlia tended to indulge herself in philosophical monologues. Maybe it was to blow off stress. Or maybe she enjoyed unsettling those around her. Or perhaps she was planting ideas in her retainers' minds that she would use later.

Knowing her, it was probably all three.

"Creatures of loyalty, are we not?" said Tarlia. "You spent a century and a half trying to save your brother. I assumed responsibility for Earth after the Conquest, and here I still am three centuries later, even though there are nobles who would like us to abandon Earth entirely and return to Kalvarion."

I thought about that, and couldn't find a way that she was wrong.

"As you say, your Majesty," I said.

She smiled. "Tell me, how badly did you and Quell fight when you started working together?"

I hesitated. Lying to the High Queen was a bad idea, but I didn't want to paint Owen in a bad light. "I...um, well, we did quarrel, loudly, and I wound up learning the aurasight spell when he used the mindtouch on me. But we worked it out."

"Good," said Tarlia. "I thought you might argue. Your personalities are somewhat divergent. But you will have to work together, and it is better that you learned to do so in a somewhat less fraught situation."

"Less fraught?" I said before my brain could halt my mouth. "We almost got killed by a mob of hybrid wraithwolves."

"I told you that great changes are coming," said Tarlia. "And change is a coin. Upon one side is growth, and the other is ruin. And we're going to make sure that the coin lands in a way favorable to Elves and humans. I suspect you will need a friend in a high place... and Chief Quell will need someone with your flexibility of mind. Until then, Nadia Moran MacCormac, you have my thanks. You and Quell safeguarded my subjects and destroyed those who would have done them harm." She smiled again. "You will be paid the standard rate paid to Shadow Hunters for destroying wraithwolves. You'll have to split it with Quell, of course. He does need to send four daughters to college."

"I...thank you, your Majesty," I said with a bow. I had spent so long living on the edge of penury that I never turned down money.

"You have my leave to go," she said.

I bowed again and turned towards the door.

"Oh, and darling girl?"

I paused. "Your Majesty?"

"Do try to avoid killing Arnold Brauner if at all possible," said Tarlia. "You have displayed admirable self-control thus far. I'm afraid he really does an excellent job as Duke Tamirlas's shadow councilor. And the Duke has been a loyal supporter of mine, so it would be poor form if one of my shadow agents killed Brauner."

I swallowed. "Yes, your Majesty."

I bowed again and closed the door behind me.

That was the unsettling thing about Tarlia. She wasn't nearly as harsh of a master as Lord Morvilind had been. For that matter, Morvilind had been all stick and no carrot, and Tarlia was much more generous. But she expected her shadow agents to think for themselves in a way that Morvilind had discouraged. And I suspected that Tarlia did not care how I got results, so long as I did… but I was the one who would have to live with the consequences after.

I was the one who would have to live with myself.

But, hell. I knew that already, didn't I?

I took a deep breath and left the Central Office for the Moran Imports warehouse.

∽

EVEN THOUGH I had a late start, I got a lot of work done at the warehouse. I helped get three trucks loaded and then retreated to the office to finish paperwork. Russell had somehow gotten the day off from class, and me and Robert Ross went over the account books with him. It was Russell's company, and once he finished his last exams, he would work full-time on the business.

There was a knock at the door, and I looked up and saw Riordan standing there.

"Hey," I said, grinning.

"Riordan, man," said Robert, and he and Riordan shared a vigorous handshake. "How was the UK?"

"Cold and rainy," said Riordan.

Robert laughed. "Cold and snowy, here. Not that much difference, I suppose. But our food's better."

"Speaking of food," said Riordan, "I'm going to kidnap Nadia for lunch."

"Great," I said, standing and stretching. "Something spicy. I..."

Two of the warehouse workers knocked on the door.

"Yeah, guys?" said Robert.

"Um." They looked nervous. "The governor's here."

"Governor?" I said.

"Arnold Brauner," said the second man. "You know, the Governor of Wisconsin."

"Former governor," I said.

"Yeah, well, he's here," said the first worker.

"Send him in," I said.

A few minutes later, Arnold Brauner walked into the office, flanked by two burly guys in suits. His left arm was in a sling, and his color was a little pale, but he looked healthy otherwise.

"Governor," I said. "How's the arm?"

"Uncomfortable," he said. "It'll get better eventually." He reached into his pocket and produced a little rubber ball. "The nurses have got me squeezing this damn thing every hour. Says it will help with muscle recovery." He grunted and stuffed the ball back into his pocket. "I spent my childhood pitching hay and cleaning up after the cows, and now they want me to squeeze a little ball."

"It's a good idea to listen to your doctors," said Riordan.

Brauner blinked at Riordan. "You must be the redoubtable Mr. MacCormac." He held out his hand, and Brauner shook it. "Saw you at that very memorable charity dinner. Not every day you meet a man who can cut a wraithwolf in half. I don't suppose you're looking for a job?"

Riordan offered a brief smile. "You couldn't afford me, Governor."

"Suppose not," said Brauner. He looked at his men. "Do you mind if I have a word with Mr. Moran and his sister alone? Should just take a minute."

The goons in suits left the office. Robert hesitated, and I nodded to him. If this was going to get ugly, we wanted as few witnesses as possible. Riordan remained leaning against the wall, giving the impression that it would take a bulldozer to move him. Brauner didn't try to ask him to leave, no doubt because he had seen Riordan cut a wraithwolf in half. I sat on one side of the table next to Russell, and Brauner sat on the other, grunting a little as he adjusted his weight.

"Well, Governor," said Russell, "what can we do for you?"

"There's no beating around the bush," said Brauner. "Your sister and her husband saved my life. Saved Duke Tamirlas and his knights, too." His bombastic voice became quiet. "And you saved my wife and my boy Martin."

"I saw you," I said. "During the fight. The wraithwolf was about to rip Tansy in half, but you shoved yourself in front of her. You're lucky you kept the arm. And your life."

"There's nothing more important than family, Mrs. MacCormac," said Brauner. "Nothing. I know you think me a hard man…"

"Reaping where thou hast not sown, and gathering where thou hast not strawed," murmured Riordan.

Brauner blinked and then smiled. "Yes, just so. The Bible, isn't it? But you saved my life. I want to show my appreciation."

"By canceling our one percent donation to the Brauner Foundation?" I said.

Brauner feigned shock. "I wouldn't dream of it. By contributing to the Foundation, you're showing you care about our communities here in Wisconsin. And think of the tax benefits. No, I had something else in mind." He reached into his briefcase and drew out a sheaf of papers. "I had Thomas Hawley draw this up. Basically, it's a shipping contract for one of my trucking companies. We're willing to carry Moran Imports produce at cost for a year."

"At cost?" said Russell. "What's the catch?"

"No catch, Mr. Moran," said Brauner. "Just a simple gesture of goodwill."

I smiled. "And then at the end of the year, your rates will go up a little. And then next year they'll go up a little more. And then some more."

Brauner shrugged. "Business is business, my dear."

"Governor, this is very generous, but I think Moran Imports had better pass," said Russell.

"That's disappointing, Mr. Moran," said Brauner.

"But if you really want to show gratitude for, you know, me saving your life and your wife and oldest son and all, I have an idea," I said.

A crafty look came over Brauner's face. "And what would that be, Mrs. MacCormac?"

"Pizza," I said.

Brauner blinked. I had the distinct pleasure of seeing the old devil taken off guard. "Pizza?"

"And maybe subs, too, and some bags of chips," I said. "Some soda and plastic cups. It's lunchtime, and my workers are about to go on their break. I would like you to buy all of them lunch. And I would like you to stay for lunch, chat a little. You're really charming when you set your mind to it, and so I bet a lot of my workers would vote for Martin or Luke or whoever the next time an election rolls around. And, you know, if we get a picture of you shaking hands with Russell or something, that would go down well."

I saw him get it, and Brauner smiled and raised two fingers to his brow in a little salute.

"You know, Mr. Moran," said Brauner, "your sister really is a formidable adversary."

"Glad I'm on her side, then," said Russell.

I didn't get to go to lunch with Riordan that day. Instead, we had lunch with Arnold Brauner and the entire warehouse staff once the pizzas and subs arrived. Brauner, true to his word, stayed for the entire meal and two hours after, and he had the workers roaring with laughter to his various stories. (The man also ate five large slices of triple-meat pizza and an entire meatball sub, which was a terrible idea at his age.) Halfway through lunch, some reporters arrived and took pictures of Russell shaking Brauner's hand in front of a pallet of wrapped Elven fruit.

Since the week of Thanksgiving was a slow news time, and the announcement of the new Milwaukee Security & Police Department would not drop until December, the news clip of Brauner shaking hands with Russell played a bunch of times.

Naturally, we had a big spike in orders from grocery chains, some even in surrounding states.

FORMER GOVERNOR MEETS WITH YOUNG ENTREPENEUR, said the headline.

I read one of those articles on my phone while sitting in the passenger seat of Riordan's truck, killing time as we drove across town to have Thanksgiving dinner at the Marneys. Riordan had wanted to go to church in the morning, so I had put on a nice dress that didn't show an inappropriate amount of skin and sucked it up and gone with him. It wasn't too boring.

"I think you handled that well," said Riordan.

"Yeah, well," I said, putting my phone into my purse. "The High Queen told me not to kill him."

"Even if she hadn't, would you have?" said Riordan.

"Nah," I said, leaning back in the seat and watching the barren trees go by. "See, that was where Kyle Warren was wrong. Nicholas Connor, for that matter. They thought if you kill or hurt enough people, you can fix the world. Doesn't work that way." I shrugged. "The best you can do, I guess…is to try and do the best you can."

"Be ye therefore wise as serpents, and harmless as doves," said Riordan.

"Argh," I said. "You're quoting something at me again, aren't you?" He did that a lot. All those damned books he had read.

"It means," said Riordan, "to keep your nose clean, but don't be an idiot."

"Yeah," I said at last. "Yeah, that makes sense. I can do that." I grinned at him. "Mostly." I paused. "I'm pretty lucky, you know?"

He pulled into the Marneys' driveway, shut off the engine, and put his hand on mine. "I think that of myself. I'd say I'm thankful."

"Thankful," I said. "Yeah."

We got out, and I took care not to slip on the icy sidewalk in my heels. Lucy insisted on doing all the cooking, but Riordan had bought a bottle of fancy wine, and me and Russell would insist on doing the cleaning up. We went inside and greeted James and Lucy and Russell for Thanksgiving dinner.

Thankful. A good word. Yes, despite everything I had survived in my life, or maybe because of it, I was indeed thankful.

THE END

Thank you for reading CLOAK OF WOLVES.
Nadia's next adventure will be CLOAK OF ASHES, coming in 2020.
If you liked the book, please consider leaving a review at your ebook site of choice. To receive immediate notification of new releases, sign up for my newsletter, or watch for news on my Facebook page.

ABOUT THE AUTHOR

Standing over six feet tall, *USA Today* bestselling author Jonathan Moeller has the piercing blue eyes of a Conan of Cimmeria, the bronze-colored hair of a Visigothic warrior-king, and the stern visage of a captain of men, none of which are useful in his career as a computer repairman, alas.

He has written the DEMONSOULED series of sword-and-sorcery novels, and continues to write THE GHOSTS sequence about assassin and spy Caina Amalas, the COMPUTER BEGINNER'S GUIDE series of computer books, and numerous other works. His books have sold over a million copies worldwide.

Visit his website at:

http://www.jonathanmoeller.com

Visit his technology blog at:

http://www.computerbeginnersguides.com

Contact him at:

jmcontact@jonathanmoeller.com

You can sign up for his email newsletter here, or watch for news on his Facebook page or Twitter feed.